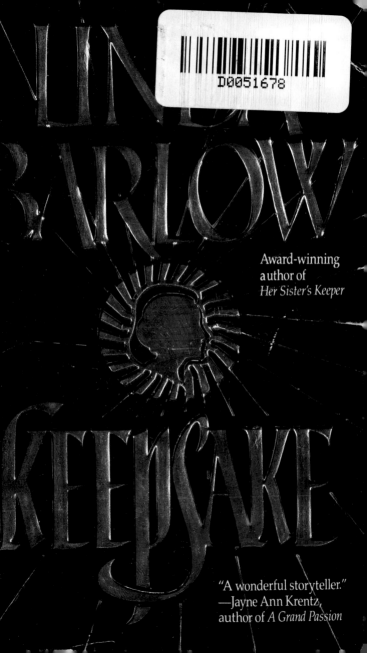

LINDA BARLOW

Award-winning
author of
Her Sister's Keeper

KEEPSAKE

"A wonderful storyteller."
—Jayne Ann Krentz,
author of *A Grand Passion*

D0051678

ALSO BY LINDA BARLOW

HER SISTER'S KEEPER

Published by
WARNER BOOKS

LINDA BARLOW

KEEPSAKE

WARNER BOOKS

A Time Warner Company

Enjoy lively book discussions online with CompuServe. To become a member of CompuServe call 1-800-848-8199 and ask for the Time Warner Trade Publishing forum. (Current members GO: TWEP.)

WARNER BOOKS EDITION

Copyright © 1994 by Linda Barlow
All rights reserved.

Cover design by Dan Bond

Warner Books, Inc.
1271 Avenue of the Americas
New York, NY 10020

W A Time Warner Company

Printed in the United States of America

First Printing: December, 1994

10 9 8 7 6 5 4 3 2 1

For Shirley, my sister
With love

Author's Note

A sincere thank-you for information, assistance, and support during the writing of this novel goes to Steve Axelrod, Jeanne Tiedge, Susan Elizabeth Phillips, Charles Clifford, and all the folks on the Prodigy Alternative Lifestyles bulletin board.

And my very special thanks to Curt Monash, whose ideas, enthusiasm, and encouragement throughout this project have been invaluable to me.

Prologue

Cape Cod, 1963

Well, hot damn, thought April, not again.

She hockey-stopped her bike just outside the range of the cloud that was billowing out from the back door of the cottage. The dust danced and glinted in the light from the setting sun as Rina wielded an industrial-strength broom. A glance at the full garbage cans and the clean laundry blowing on the line confirmed what April had already guessed: her mother had a new lover.

Other women celebrated such occasions by fussing with their nails and makeup and hair, but Rina ignored her appearance—which didn't need much maintenance—to perform a face lift on the cottage. She washed the road-grimed windows and vacuumed the sorry excuse for a carpet that was glued to the floor. Bright new curtains, whipped up on Rina's portable sewing machine, replaced the sun-faded ones of the cottage's narrow windows.

April figured the new curtains went up on the average of three times a year. The windows they went up on changed almost as often as the curtains. Rina believed in moving around a lot.

But this was already the second set here at Sea Breeze Housekeeping Villas in Brewster, MA, the summer place where they'd been living for a little over a month. This year her mother must be going for some kind of record.

Grabbing her worn baseball glove from the basket, April mounted the steps and entered, one hand covering her nose and mouth.

"I had a game," she said, taking the most direct, belligerent approach. "You said you'd come."

Rina Flaherty, clad in a man's shirt with the tails drawn up and knotted around her slender waist and only panties, a garter belt and hose underneath it, gave her broom one final sweep. April leapt out of the way. Rina tucked a long strand of pure gold hair that had escaped its high ponytail back behind her ear. Her hair was natural blonde and, loose, fell to the end of her spine. Combined with her bachelor-button blue eyes, her delicate nose, her pink, up-curved mouth, and the overall gracefulness of her petite body, Rina looked like an angel.

April was convinced she was going straight to hell.

"I said I'd try to come," Rina said. Her voice, unlike the rest of her, was not delicate at all. It was low, almost like a man's, and devoid of inflection. A voice to which commanding came more easily than submission. "As it turned out, I couldn't. I'm sorry you're disappointed."

"You always disappoint me." April knew her own voice sounded weak and mushy but she couldn't seem to help it.

"People who expect too much are frequently disappointed," her mother said. "You should learn to rely more on yourself."

"It was a good game. We won. Alice St. Claire's father was there. Remember him? The divorced guy you said

looks like Little Joe Cartwright? He asked about you."
April could hear the pleading note in her voice and hated
that even more.

If there has to be a man, she thought, can't he ever be a
nice man? A single man? Someone who'll love you and
marry you and maybe even love me a little as well?
Someone who'll stick around for a while and buy us a real
house and real furniture and make enough money so we
won't have to pack up the cottage again in the dark and hit
the interstate before the bill collectors catch us? Someone
who'll live with us and make us into a real family?

"I'm not interested in Alice St. Claire's father," Rina
said. "Nor am I interested in your attempts to matchmake
for me. I'm quite capable of managing such matters on
my own."

April glared at the sparkling inside of the cottage.
"Who is he this time? The chief of police? The mayor,
maybe?" Did Brewster, Massachusetts have a mayor? Her
mother had a saying, "Always mate with the top dog."
She stuck to it religiously. Trouble was, the top dog was
usually married.

"You've been doing real well this year," she added.
"Last year in Texas the highest you could snag was county
dog-catcher."

One of Rina's delicate hands flashed toward April's
face, stopping just an inch away. She flinched anyway,
then flushed red as her old Radio Flyer. This was a new
trick of her mother's—pretending to slap her and pulling
it back at the last second. The sudden movement invariably left April feeling like a mealy mouthed coward for
flinching when no blow was struck.

Rina smiled. "I've told you before, you can say whatever you like around other people, but you'll damn well

control your mouth with me. I won't tolerate your insolence. Now sit down and eat your supper."

April eyed the peanut butter and banana sandwich, canned potato sticks, and a bottle of Coke that her mother had laid out in the tiny kitchenette area of the cottage. Rina cleaned and sewed, but she didn't cook. "I hope you're not going to make me sleep out in the tent tonight," she said. "I hate it. There are bugs."

"You collect bugs."

"Once I saw a snake trying to get into the tent. I'm not too crazy about snakes, even if I did have one as a pet that summer we were in Georgia. One could crawl into my sleeping bag and slither up my leg and bite me like Cleopatra's asp. Then I'd scream and sweat and my tongue would stick out and I'd thrash all over the place and turn blue and die. Just imagine how sorry you'd be in the morning when you found my poor dead body."

"There are no poisonous snakes in Massachusetts," Rina said.

"Well, there are wild animals."

"On Cape Cod? The only animals around here are cats and dogs."

"Vicious cats. Haven't you seen their sharp teeth and claws? And the dogs that hang around the cottage park are lean and mean and—and violent. I'll bet some of them even have rabies. Just suppose I was laying under there—"

"Lying under there."

"Lying under there and patting one and suddenly he turns on me, all fierce and foaming like Old Yeller after the rabid wolf got him?"

Rina sighed. "Where'd I ever get such a melodramatic kid?" She pushed her own sandwich aside and lighted a cigarette. April noticed that she had repainted her nails from crimson to a more sedate shade of pink. "You read too many books. They're rotting your common sense."

April bit her lip. She was proud of all the books she read. Her teachers said she was a great reader—way above fifth grade level. Books took her away into a better world. She loved books.

"How many times have I told you that a woman's got to control her imagination?" her mother went on. "Particularly when it makes her afraid. You can't be afraid, April. The minute you show any fear, they get you."

April knew better than to ask who "they" were. There was never a clear answer. Her mother had been drumming this into her head for as long as she could remember.

"Anyway, you don't have to sleep in the tent. Fact is, despite your speculations, I'm not seeing anybody new, so stop that self-righteous sulking you do so well. God only knows how I ended up with such a morally upright child. Wait until your tits sprout, then you'll change your tune."

April kicked at the table leg. Her mother was immoral and she didn't even care. It was disgusting.

Anyway, Rina was lying. There was a new man. There had to be. The broom-and-curtain test had never failed before.

She had a new lover and she refused to admit it.

He must be married. Or important. Or both.

For the next few days April watched her mother's every move, even following her to her waitress job at the Captain Chapin's Cape Cuisine, and hiding out in the bushes to make sure she wasn't meeting some swank summer vacationer, but she turned up nothing. She was just beginning to think she'd been wrong about the new boyfriend when, early one morning, the limousine pulled into the gravel driveway of Sea Breeze Housekeeping Villas.

It was sleek and black and the windows were tinted so you couldn't see inside. Two men in suits and hats—one big and broad and the other shorter and trimmer—got out and climbed the rickety steps to the front door of the cottage. April was pumping up her bicycle tires in the shade of the cottage. If the men saw her, they paid no attention.

As he knocked, the tails of his jacket pulled tight over the larger man's back, and April saw the outline of a concealed weapon. Holy Halloween. Gangsters.

"No!" she cried, knocking over her bike as she erupted from her shady corner. She ran straight at the men, yelling at her mother not to open the door. "He has a gun, Rina! He's here to kill you!"

The leaner of the men caught her. He turned his face aside from her flailing fingernails. "Calm down, son," he said.

She scored big with her teeth on the wrist. He let her go, yelping. "I'm a girl, you creep!" she shouted. "Rina!"

Her mother opened the door. She was dressed conservatively for once, in a light-weight gray suit with a knee-length skirt and a pale blue blouse. Her hair was subdued into a French braid, and her makeup was light. "Stop your noise," she ordered her daughter. "Did you bite that man? Really, April, your behavior is disgraceful."

"Mom! They're gangsters! The big one has a gun."

"We work for the United States government, Miss," the big one said politely, adjusting the rear of his jacket. "There's nothing to be afraid of. We're here to protect you."

Oh, sure, thought April. U.S. . . . government agents didn't drive around in flashy limousines. Everybody knew they used unmarked Chevys or Fords.

The man with the gun turned to Rina. "Are you about ready, Mrs. Flaherty?"

"I'll be with you in a moment, gentlemen." Rina's voice was calm but her eyes were very bright. "I just wish you'd given me more notice."

"We didn't expect him, ma'am."

"Not on his schedule, you see, ma'am," the slim man said. He was rubbing his hand and glaring at April.

"Well, I'd hardly be listed on his official appointment calendar, would I?" Rina said with a laugh.

"No, ma'am. Sorry, ma'am. I just meant—"

"We don't like it any better than you do, Mrs. Flaherty. The security arrangements are problematic when the notice is so short."

"Rina," April interrupted. "Who are these guys?"

"Come inside, April."

April squeezed past the Mob enforcers, or whatever they were. "You look funny in that suit," she said to her mother. "You look like you're going to Mass."

Rina laughed. She closed the door and led her daughter into the kitchenette area. "I'm going out for a few hours. Stay in and do your homework."

"It's summer. I don't have homework."

"Then clean up this cottage. It's a pigsty."

"You've been scrubbing it all week!"

"April—"

"I know you're going to meet your lover. He must be rich and important. But I still say those men are gangsters. They've got guns, Mom, huge ones. And that limo—that's disgusting. What is he, a Mafia chieftain?"

"Yes, as a matter of fact," Rina said. "He's the regional capo and a very powerful man. He hates ill-natured children and has methods of disciplining them that would make your blood run cold, so he'd better not receive any bad reports about you from his men. Understand?" Casting a quick look in the mirror that was pasted onto the front of the refrigerator, she adjusted a strand of golden hair and pursed her lips to check the line of her lipstick. Then she nodded. "Well, I'm off. Behave yourself."

April watched through the new curtains as Rina walked serenely between the two gunmen to the black limousine. God! Her mother had really done it this time.

She ran out the back door and swung herself onto her bike. She knew a shortcut to the main road. She couldn't hope to keep up, but maybe she'd be able to see which direction they were headed.

But the limo never reached the main road. Doubling back, April found its tire tracks in the sandy dirt leading down to the private drive that wound along the ocean. The fresh trail was easy to follow. It ran for just over a mile to an isolated house set on a low bluff overlooking Cape Cod Bay.

April abandoned her bike and crept closer on foot. She hadn't really believed what Rina had said about the gangster's methods of discipline, but she didn't want to take any chances.

Not one, but three black limousines were parked outside the house. Around the perimeter were several guards wearing suits and cradling high-powered rifles. "Mary, Joseph, and Baby J," April whispered. "It's an armed camp."

Also present was a Hyannis patrol car. Crouched in the tall dune grasses, April clearly saw the big man in the suit who had come for her mother—now equipped with a walkie-talkie—shaking hands with a smiling local policeman.

God! This must be a super-powerful criminal. He'd corrupted the Hyannis police.

"Mommy, they're going to kill you," she whispered. "They'll have to. You know too much."

The door to the cottage opened and out came her mother with a pitcher of lemonade and a tray of glasses. There was no sign of her crime-boss lover. Rina was still dressed exactly as she had been before.

What was she doing here? Waitressing?

The men gathered around, drinking the lemonade and glancing at their watches. Then they all looked skyward as they heard the familiar whop-whop-whop of a helicopter. April craned her neck. Over a curve in the coastline came a small military chopper. Military?

It set down on the dry shingled beach to the right of the cottage. Three hard-jawed suits emerged first and fanned out, securing the location with swift, professional movements.

April's heart was thundering. It was all coming together in her head. She'd seen men like these before. They weren't gangsters. She knew them from TV. They all looked the same, tough, professional, nondescript. She'd even seen this helicopter, or one very like it, over on the other side of the Cape at Hyannisport late one Friday afternoon.

"Holy Mother," she muttered. "I don't believe this."

Escorted by two of the security men, Rina walked toward the chopper. She looked sensational. She had shed the jacket of her suit, and April could see that in the bright sunlight, the pale blue blouse was almost transparent. Her skirt was demure, but fit her small waist and rounded hips snugly. Her slender legs gleamed in her silken hose, and the wind had loosened her blonde hair just slightly from its French braid.

A tall man with a full head of hair and a blindingly familiar face stepped down from the helicopter. When he saw Rina, his face lit up with his famous smile. He opened his arms, and she ran into them, raising her angelic face for his kiss.

April toppled to her knees in the dirt. Always mate with the top dog. Her mother's lover was the president of the United States.

Part One

Chapter One

Anaheim, California

"You're kidding me," Maggie said. "Your mother had an affair with JFK?"

"That's right," said April. She stood, flushed, and unlatched her stall in the ladies room of the Anaheim convention center bathroom. She collected her sack of pamphlets, flyers, advance-reading copies, and one thick-bound galley and moved to the mirror to brush her shoulder-length auburn hair. It was still thick, and mercifully, no gray had yet appeared, but she should have had the ragged ends trimmed before coming out to California. She pulled it taut and knotted it atop her head.

Rina's blonde hair had always been perfect.

"Wow," said Maggie from one of the other stalls. At least two others were occupied and a tense-looking woman with a severe chignon was washing her hands at one of the sinks, but Maggie made no attempt to lower her voice. "How'd she meet him? Was this when he was president? Did you meet him, too?"

"I met him, sure," April said. She adjusted her skirt, tucking her blouse in more smoothly, and straightened the name tag that was pinned to the lapel of her suit jacket. April Harrington, it read. Bookseller, *Poison Pen Bookshop,* Boston, MA. "I was never very nice to him, though. One day I told him that both he and my mother were going to hell." She smiled. "I was a judgmental kid."

Maggie came out of her stall, smoothing her red dress down around her generous hips. "What was he like?" she asked, joining April at the mirror. The name tag on Maggie McKay's chest identified her as a bookseller from Somerville, MA, where she specialized in romance novels. She and April had met at a New England Booksellers Association conference four years before and become close friends. "Was he as sexy as everyone says?"

"God, Maggie, I was only nine years old. Besides, I was very angry with him. He had been my hero—as he was to so many of us in those days. I'd looked up to him, respected him, adored him. I watched the Kennedys on television and yearned for a family just like theirs. Then I found out he was sleeping with my mother, and I hated him for that. It wasn't common knowledge in those days that he was a philanderer. I'd believed, like everybody else, in the Camelot myth of the perfect marriage to Jackie, the darling children, the American dream. When that was shattered, well . . . I just didn't understand."

"So it was a relationship? Your mother saw him more than once or twice?"

"Oh, yes. My mother was quite a woman and this was quite a coup. She wasn't one to let go of such a golden opportunity."

"This is an incredible story, April!" Maggie said. "I can't believe you never told me this before."

With a flick of her wrist April replaced her lipstick. She

pursed her lips to even the color, trying to concentrate on the mundane task she was performing. But her stomach was churning and her palms were sweaty. There were a lot of things she had never told Maggie, not only about her mother, but also about herself.

"We moved to Washington." She took a tube of mascara from her purse to touch up her lashes. She opened it, then changed her mind and put the tube away. She always made a mess with mascara. "She saw him off and on for the next several months. She was good. 'Always sleep with the top dog' was my mother's motto. Once she got him, a man didn't want out on Rina, even if he was president of the United States."

"Wow," Maggie said again. "In all the time I've known you, you've never even mentioned your mother."

April caught her eye in the mirror. "I haven't mentioned her because she abandoned me when I was twelve years old to follow her newest lover—a Frenchman whom she met through her association with Kennedy—back home to Paris. She promised to send for me. She never did."

Maggie nodded, her dark eyes sympathetic. The woman with the severe chignon nodded, too. She had been taking an inordinately long time to wash and dry her perfectly manicured hands. Now, picking up her own pile of convention material, which was topped by the latest celebrity biography, she turned to April and said, "Pardon me, but I couldn't help overhearing." She considered the name tag on April's lapel, then said, "You're the mystery expert, aren't you? April Harrington? I saw the piece about you in *Publishers Weekly* a couple of months ago."

"Well, it's our readers who are the real experts," April said. "All we do is try to cater to their tastes with a broad selection of new and classic mystery novels."

"Is your mother still alive?" the woman asked. She obviously wasn't interested in the mystery bookselling business. "If so, she should do a book." She reached into her purse and pulled out a card, which she extended to April. Sandra Lestring, Literary Agent, the engraving read, followed by an address and telephone number in New York.

April nodded as she recognized the name. Sandra Lestring represented several well-known clients, including a couple of movie stars, politicians, and even a novelist or two.

"A lot of people are still interested in anything to do with JFK," the agent added.

April smiled. "Thanks, but you're too late. She's already got an agent."

Sandra Lestring shrugged. "Nevertheless, I'd appreciate it if you'd keep me in mind. You never know. Sometimes these things don't work out."

"I'll do that," April said politely as the woman turned to leave the ladies room.

Maggie was watching April in the mirror. Her huge brown eyes were round with speculation. "April? What do you mean, your mother's got an agent? Who exactly is your mother? Is she in publishing? Jeez, April, is she here at the convention?"

April met her eyes and nodded. This, after all, was why she had come all the way out to California for this year's American Booksellers Association convention, leaving Brian, her business partner, to run the bookstore and deal with the customers, which was his special talent, anyhow. Brian could spend hours discussing the plot, characters, and every red herring of a fictional murder case with a happy group of middle-aged women who gathered around to listen to him lecture. He remembered whodunit in every Agatha Christie novel. He could recite Adam Dalgleish's poetry. He seemed to possess intimate knowledge of James Lee Burke's New Orleans, and he loved to tell the customers that he'd once ridden in a taxi driven by Carlotta Carlyle.

Brian knew the genre, and the customers adored him. It was good to know that she could leave the business in the capable hands of somebody she trusted.

She glanced at her watch. In fifteen minutes, Rina, her mother, whom April hadn't seen in nearly thirty years, would be making one of her rare public appearances.

She was planning to confront her.

Rob Blackthorn was staring at Jessie's photograph again.

Shouldn't do this, he told himself.

Pointless.

Waste of time.

Unhealthy.

He should be beyond this now. Everybody said so. It had been nearly two years.

He glanced over at the minibar, which was tastefully disguised as a cabinet in the luxurious Four Seasons Hotel in Newport Beach. It had been tempting him ever since he'd checked in the previous evening. The minibar key was on top of the chest of drawers, right next to the ice bucket and the wine glasses.

Blackthorn glanced at his watch, which read 12:39 P.M. It was not 12:39. It was twenty to ten. He'd forgotten to set his watch to California time when he'd arrived last night.

Only 9:30 in the morning, and he wanted a drink.

Not that he had a drinking problem. That is, not anymore.

Nah, man, you're addicted to something else. Someone

else. You're a Jessie junkie. Hung up on a woman who's dead and gone. And there's no damn Betty Ford Center to treat that.

Blackthorn's eyes flicked back to the minibar. Bound to be some Chivas in there. Chivas was just the thing to help him escape the fact that he was back in California, where Jessie had died.

Jessie. Oh, Jesus. Jessie, Jess, Jess.

The hell with it. He picked up the key, jammed it into the lock, opened the small refrigerator, and removed a tiny bottle of Scotch. He placed it on top of the TV, where he could admire its sensuous, dark golden color as the sun from the plate glass window struck it.

You can look, but you'd better not touch, darlin'. You ever start drinking like those other idiots in your family and I swear I'll come back and haunt you.

That a promise?

You won't like my haunting. I won't be one of those sad, wispy little ghosts. I'll be a demon, clawing at you, destroying your sleep. So no booze. No sinking into the great Blackthorn Escape. Promise me.

He'd promised, of course. And kept it, too. So far. In all the months since he'd buried Jessie he'd managed to avoid cracking open that top. Today, though. . . .

The name *Rina de Sevigny* assaulted him. That's who he was supposed to be concentrating on. Focus on Rina. That oughtta cure you, sucker, he thought.

Come on, then, Jessie, haunt me. That's what you've been doing anyway for all this time. I'm no good without you, sober or drunk.

He reached for the bottle of Scotch. The phone by the king-sized bed interrupted him before he could break the seal. Blackthorn smiled and shook his head. The same thing had happened once or twice before. Maybe she *was* still around. Not his demon, but his guardian angel.

He walked over and picked up the receiver. "Yeah?"

"Blackthorn," said a sharp female voice that he recognized instantly—Carla Murphy, who worked for him at World Systems Security. "I'm calling from the convention center in Anaheim."

"Hey, Carla. What's up?"

"I think you'd better get on over here."

"Why? I'm not due on the scene until the glitzy party this evening."

"Well, it turns out the client is not happy about that arrangement," Carla said. "Actually it's her husband who'd like to have you here. Says he'd feel safer that way."

"Yeah, right," Blackthorn said. He didn't much like Armand de Sevigny.

"Listen, I sympathize," said Carla. "The whole case is a waste of our time, in my opinion. She's not even a particularly famous author, as far as I can tell."

"Actually, she *is* pretty famous," said Blackthorn. "A little more so in Europe than here, perhaps, but she's had a large following here, too, ever since the release of that TV video piece that runs on cable at odd hours of the night with all the senators, astronauts, and movie stars lauding Power Perspectives, her personal transformation program."

"Yeah, so who wants to kill her? Somebody whose personality didn't get transformed? Jeez. I could be at a Mafia stakeout and here I am stuck at a goddamn booksellers' convention."

Blackthorn grinned. Then he sighed, eyeing the whiskey again. At his direction, Carla had done most of the work for this case so far. She'd been the one to analyze Rina's needs and lay out a plan to protect her. This had been fine with Blackthorn. Perfect.

"So why do you think somebody wants to kill you?" he'd asked Rina when she'd insisted, in her imperious way, that he take the case.

"Perhaps because I know too many secrets about too many people," Rina had said, which had reminded Blackthorn that she knew a few of his own secrets, as well.

"Blackthorn?" Carla said. "You still there?"

"Yeah, I'm here. You want to run it by me again? What exactly is the problem this morning?"

"It's not just the husband who's complaining," Carla said. "Rina's friend Daisy Tulane is concerned as well."

"The feminist who would be senator."

"Exactly. Apparently Rina helped Ms. Tulane get her head together a couple of years ago and now Daisy's turned protective. She insists they contracted with us for four bodyguards and we've only given her three."

"The contract says, 'multiple bodyguards' and 'sufficient protection,' for chrissake. Two would have been more than sufficient."

"Well, not really. It's a tricky situation, Blackthorn. Rina insists on meeting her 'friends,' as she calls them— the strangers who have bought her books and tapes and tried out her empowerment program. She's signing autographs as I speak, in this cavernous hall with hundreds of people crowded about."

"We didn't authorize that. How does she expect us to protect her if she won't follow orders?"

"How do I know? All I can tell you is there's a lot about this situation that's making me crazy. This place is impossible to secure. It's huge, for one thing, and there are people milling all over, with arms full of books and assorted publisher giveaways. It'd be easy as hell to slip in a piece. You could hide an Uzi in one of those book-bags. We can't cover her adequately with only three of us. Shit, it'd be difficult with ten."

Terrific, Blackthorn thought. It looked like he'd have to show up, after all.

"Blackthorn?" Carla paused, then said slowly, "I'm not interrupting anything, am I? You don't have a date, do you? I could, uh, call back in a little while."

He grimaced at the eagerness in her voice. Along with all his friends, Carla was always watching for some sign that he was ready to resume the life of a normal, red-blooded, single male. Everybody seemed to think there was something wrong with him because he hadn't been able to let go of his dead wife.

Well, maybe there *was* something wrong. Maybe there was a lot wrong. And maybe he was taking care of it in his own way.

"Look," he said. "Cut off the autograph session right now. Then stow Rina in her hotel room until I get there. I'll have a little talk with her ladyship about what she can and cannot do."

"I can't stow her anywhere until after her talk. She's conducting a session on Power Perspectives at 10:30. The seminar room's secure, but we can't screen every single person who crowds in to hear her."

"Do your best, then. I'll be there soon."

"Thanks, Blackthorn."

"You bet."

He hung up the phone and put the little bottle of Chivas back into its rack in the minibar. "Good for you, Jessie," he said.

God, how he missed her! Out there in the real world you knew who your enemies were—the guys with the guns. You could do something about them. But there wasn't a single damn thing you could do about the silent, cellular-level killer that had taken Jessie. Not even the best bodyguarding in the world could protect you against cancer.

Still, she didn't have to *die* of it, dammit. She might have lived, if she'd only been willing to accept the proper medical care.

Stop it, he ordered himself. Focus on Rina de Sevigny, whose life you've been hired to protect.

"We'd better get moving if we want to make this seminar," April said to Maggie. She consulted the floor plan one more time, then led the way through the crowd in one of the more congested aisles of the main display section of the convention center.

Publishers, both major and minor, had booths lining the aisles. These areas were crammed with displays of the fall lines. The most renowned American and international publishers had the largest allotments of floor space for their displays, some of which were outlandishly extravagant. There were huge posters of book covers and blowup photographs of famous authors.

Celebrities—including novelists, sports figures, politicians, film and TV stars—were making appearances all over the hall, many of them promoting their latest books. At one booth, advance-reading copies of a new work by a well-known black female novelist had just been laid out by her publicist. The crowd buzzed as the rumor flew that the author herself was about to make an appearance. She was hot, her books were wildly successful, and everybody wanted to meet her.

April barely glanced at the celebrities. Instead, she steered Maggie toward the large room that had been reserved by Crestwood-Locke-Mars Publishing, Inc., better known as CLM. The room was filled with rows of folding chairs facing a dais that was graced with life-size posters, a podium, and a large video screen. Taped music with an upbeat, energizing tempo was playing loudly as eager conventioneers pushed into the room and settled into the rows of chairs.

Maggie hung back. "Jeez, April, you're not going to subject me to one of those crazy human potential, seize-your-power sort of things? I've heard that under all that jazzy music are a bunch of subliminal messages saying stuff like 'pay your money, join our team' to sucker you into signing up for their week-long seminars in Hawaii or the Cayman Islands."

April grinned. "Don't worry, I'll hold you down if you start to stumble mindlessly toward the dais to testify."

They found two seats together toward the back and sat down. April took an aisle seat, just in case she felt the need to get out in a hurry.

A crimson banner hung over the dais. It read, Power Perspectives—the Key to Inner Strength and Outward Success. Suspended from the ceiling just in back of the podium was a bright yellow poster with a blowup of a book jacket, a portrait of the female author's animated face, and several quotes in large blue letters extolling the book's "incredible, life-transforming inspiration."

"I know business hasn't been so hot this year, but this is ridiculous," said Maggie.

April barely heard her. Her gaze was fixed on the author's photograph. Her mother was still attractive, even after thirty years. The lines of her face were softer, somehow. But of course it was a glamour shot. There was nothing soft about Rina. Nothing at all.

The noise of the crowd around her faded. She was in

the Port of New York in early 1965, in the cavernous hall of the steamship docks, clinging tight to her mother's hand. She remembered all sorts of small details—the gray-black color of the sea, the ear-splitting hoot of the steamship's whistle, the way the cold air fogged in front of her face when she breathed. Most of all she remembered Rina, all trim and stylish in a red fur coat that sported a little fox head and tail around the collar. She was wearing maroon gloves and a matching hat was coyly angled atop her spun-gold hair.

At her side was the trim, suave Frenchman who was taking her away. Armand. He was a widower with two young children. He needed a new wife, a mother for them.

April hated him. She hated his two motherless children. Most of all, she hated Rina, who was going away.

The ship was waiting. It was huge. It was smashed right up against the dock, its black hull looming tall as a mountain. A gangway poked out from its side and people were boarding, waving good-bye to their friends and family on shore.

"It's only for a little while," her mother was saying. "I'll send for you as soon as we are married and all our papers are in order. We'll need to get you a visa, you see. There are certain conditions to fulfill."

April knew she was lying. She knew she would never see her mother again.

She was trying very hard to pretend it didn't matter.

"Come, *cherie*, make your farewells," Armand ordered in that falsely solicitous manner of his. "We must board or we shall be left behind."

"Sister will take good care of you until I'm able to send for you," Rina said, nodding to the stern, bulky nun of the Convent of the Sacred Heart Boarding School for Young Ladies where April had been enrolled. But she wasn't going to stay in that smelly old convent. She'd run away. She'd stow away aboard another steamer and go to Paris all on her own. But she wouldn't even visit her mother when she got there, oh, no. She'd find a better mother to live with. She'd find someone who really loved her. She'd have a family, a real family.

"Come and kiss me," Rina said, leaning down. The pointed little head of the dead fox poked April's cheek and she slapped it away. "Be good," Rina whispered. "I love you. We'll see each other soon."

Liar, liar, liar, April was screaming inside. *Don't leave me, Mommy. Oh, Mommy, please don't go.*

Sister held her unresisting hand while Rina and Armand mounted the gangway together. Rina turned back at the last moment and waved gaily. The tail of the red fox collar fluttered in the wind.

Then the huge ship swallowed her up.

She had never been sent for, not even when Rina and her new family had returned to New York.

She hadn't seen her mother since 1965. She'd been abandoned, and horrible things had happened to her— things that she could barely bring to consciousness. Violent, secret things that were all her mother's fault . . .

"You okay?" Maggie asked, gently touching her arm.

April nodded. Her stomach was churning and the palms of her hands were slick. Get a grip, she ordered herself.

There was a stir at the entrance to the room. Along with everyone else, April craned her neck to see the group of people who entered together. As they moved up the center aisle toward the podium, the public address system boomed out a crescendo of music.

She saw the others first. Armand, who had aged well: an imposing, compact figure of medium height with a more youthful appearance than one would expect of a seventy-year-old man. His hair was silver, his skin tan and smooth, except for slight crinkles around the eyes, and his somewhat stocky build was disguised by the expert tailoring of his thousand-dollar suit.

In the years since Rina had sailed away with him, April had learned all about him. A French industrialist from a distinguished family that alternated between residences in Paris and Manhattan, Armand had been flirting with politics and diplomacy at the time when he and Rina had met, testing the waters by serving as a consular officer in the French embassy in Washington. After their marriage and return to Paris, he had devoted himself to his family's extensive industrial and financial concerns, the largest of which was an international shipping business, based in New York.

In addition to Armand, April recognized the two other members of her mother's entourage—a woman and a man. She had studied the voluminous brochures put out by the Foundation carefully enough to know who they were. The slim, black-haired woman was Isobelle de Sevigny, one of the two children of his first marriage whom Armand consigned to Rina's care. At her side was Charles Ripley, Rina's personal assistant, a sandy-haired young man with a ruddy complexion and a broad, quick smile that rivaled Magic Johnson's in sincerity and charm. As they mounted the steps, he briefly touched Isobelle's hand. Lovers? April wondered.

Isobelle's brother Christian was not in attendance. He was his father's heir, although rumor had it that they had never had a smooth relationship.

To the upbeat sounds of the music, Armand, Isobelle, and Charles joined hands and stood in a line, smiling and bowing to the audience. April noted that they made an exceptionally attractive group. All were fit and slender, all were beautifully dressed and exquisitely coiffed. All had obviously been successful at finding their Inner Strength.

An upsurge of music. The star of the show entered through an inconspicuous doorway just to the left of the stage. A tall, solidly built young woman whom April did not recognize hovered at her side, following the elegant blonde up the steps to the podium.

"There she is," April said to Maggie. She was shocked at the dry sound of her own voice. "She's done pretty well for herself, huh?"

"Uh, who?" said Maggie.

"Sabrina de Sevigny, empowerment expert, inspirational speaker, and three-time *New York Times* bestselling author," said April, reading the phrases off the front of the glossy brochure she'd been handed at the door. "She looks well-preserved, doesn't she? Even after thirty years, it's not hard to glimpse the remnants of the beauty that attracted JFK."

"Jesus, April. Rina de Sevigny is your mother?"

"Yes. And do I have a surprise for her."

He moved easily through the crowds, finding a seat in the back, attracting no particular attention. Getting inside the convention center had been easy. As arranged, his registration had been made in advance in the name of Gerald Morrow, a small independent bookseller from Indianapolis. All fees had been paid; he had simply to sign in. Security was lax. Nobody frisked him and nobody discovered the gun.

It was a .22 Colt Woodsman. Semiautomatic. The clip had eight rounds; he had another clip in his pocket. Not that he expected to use more than one or two. A relatively quiet, efficient pistol—accurate, easy to use. He would hide it under a folded newspaper when the moment came to fire. The security people here would never even notice.

Bunch of amateurs. This job was almost too easy. No challenge. He liked a challenge. He liked to use all his faculties—clever mind as well as clever body—while performing the duties of his chosen profession.

He'd wandered the hall, collecting giveaways, nodding, smiling. Killing time until killing time.

He had found the target without difficulty, consulting the schedule and making his way here to the seminar room. She was punctual. He admired that. He, too, made a point of sticking to his schedule, doing everything precisely on time.

His client had described her very well. Blonde. Elegant. Obviously wealthy. Aging, but well-preserved.

He could have taken her earlier—after the autographing—but she had a seminar to give and he'd decided to let her give it. Who knows, maybe he could learn something from her. He liked to read, liked to learn. He believed in improving his mind. He, presumably, had a long life ahead of him. Unlike the woman. His target.

She had less than an hour to live.

He decided to take her as she left the seminar room. The moment would be perfect. The crowds would be at their heaviest, the aisles clogged with bustling bodies. He'd blend in well. He was accustomed to cultivating a nondescript appearance—medium height, medium weight, medium brown hair. No distinguishing marks or features. A pleasant face, or so the women told him. He had the sort of face people trusted.

He stretched, making himself comfortable in the cheap folding chair. Preparing himself to listen, and to learn.

Killing time until killing time.

Chapter Two

Due to nasty traffic on the freeway, it took Blackthorn longer to reach the convention center than he'd anticipated. Although it was mid-morning, it looked like rush hour in New York. He hated southern California—in his opinion it was dry, artificial, and culturally barren. And driving was hell.

But as soon as he did arrive he saw Carla's problem. The convention center was a nightmare. Too many people crammed into too small an area. Too diverse a group.

Everyone needed a participant's badge to get through the barrier, but they could be easily faked. People were wandering in and out past bored, inattentive credentials checkers and no one really seemed to care. Blackthorn had credentials but didn't bother using them. He flashed a fake press card, and they waved him through.

Terrific. Anybody could get in. A professional would yawn over the lack of challenge.

Blackthorn glanced at the program, then at his watch.

Rina was giving her presentation right now. If I were the killer, he thought, I'd wait for her to finish, then walk up to her in one of these crowded aisles as she was making her way out, shoot her quickly at close range with a silenced gun, let it slip out of my hand onto the floor, and melt away into the crowd.

Blackthorn consulted the map for directions to the seminar room. All his instincts urged him to hurry.

When the music and the applause finally died down, Rina took a mike from the podium and stepped forward to the edge of the stage. She extended her arms briefly to the sides, as if to embrace everyone in the room. Then she raised the mike to her mouth and spoke:

"Welcome, my friends, and thank you." She flashed her famous smile. "I'm delighted to see so many of you here today. Perhaps this will be the beginning of the transformation of your lives."

April was sitting, literally, on the edge of her seat. Her mother was almost as beautiful as she remembered her. She had kept her figure—with the help, no doubt, of a trainer and a plastic surgeon. There were very few lines on her face. Her chin was firm, her throat still slender and graceful, her hair expertly cut and colored. She still had the liveliness and energy that had allowed her to bustle through the trailer, scrubbing and cleaning furiously.

"There are few among us who have not been hurt by the global recession," Rina said. "Many of you, I know, have suffered, as have the people who shop in your bookstores. Yet even now, even in a time of economic upheaval, I'm here to tell you that abundance can be yours. Anything, my friends, can be yours if you have the will and the courage not only to desire and dream, but also to dedicate yourself to the active pursuit of your goals."

Anything? April thought. All she had ever wanted was a family. Her mother had never given her that.

Briefly, she thought of Jonathan Harrington. They'd been married for three years. But in the end, like so many of her other relationships, it hadn't worked out.

Which was, she reminded herself, one of the reasons she was here. Professionally, her life was successful. But personally, she remained unfulfilled. She had friends, lots of them. But she'd devoted herself to her work—and her beloved books—and she couldn't seem to trust the men in her life deeply enough to make a commitment to anyone.

Time was passing. Middle age was looming, and if she was ever going to have a family of her own, it would have to be soon.

"We all have a limitless source of power within us," Rina went on. "Deep inside we are all creative, dynamic, electric individuals. The trick is learning to tap into our own power. To channel it outward until it lights us up with an irresistible inner glow!"

She spoke in exclamations. Quickly, energetically, with a little lift at the end of each sentence. Always that warm and charming smile.

But April suspected it was all carefully programmed. She remembered the days when Rina would stand in front of a mirror in the cottage, practicing her various expressions, gestures, tones of voice. Sometimes she would even ask her daughter what she thought of one or another pose. "Do I look sincere?" she would ask. "Do I sound well-educated? Do you think I'm pretty?"

No longer a mirror in a grimy old cottage, oh, no. These days she could use videotapes, coaches, computer-generated audience response curves. Her act had been more than thirty years in the making, and it was no wonder that she'd perfected it. From the rapt way her husband and her assistants were hanging on her every word, April decided that even they were deceived.

It was unnerving. She felt like a ten-year-old again. She was the only one who recognized her mother's true face, and the only one who knew it was all a clever game.

And she felt sad. She'd listened to Rina's self-help tapes, and she'd actually found them moving. She wanted to believe that Rina was a different person than the selfish woman who'd abandoned her so many years ago. She'd longed to discover that her mother was truly transformed.

There was a quick burst of applause which Rina acknowledged with an even broader smile.

"What are some of our most pressing issues?" she was saying. "Let's talk about them. I want to hear from you— yes, all of you. What are some of the areas of blockage in your lives?"

"Trust," said a middle-aged woman in the third row. She had two of the Foundation's books under her arms as well as a stack of tapes. "I was abused by my stepfather, and now I'm incapable of trusting anybody. All my relationships seem to be doomed."

April felt a quiver. Trust had always been a big issue for her, as well.

"Your relationships are doomed," said Rina, "if that is what you sincerely believe." Looking directly into the woman's eyes, she added, "I know exactly how you feel."

Oh, please, thought April.

"For many years my relationships suffered too, but I am free of that now. For I don't believe for one minute that you—or any other human being—is incapable of trusting others. In fact, we all trust others constantly, every day.

That is part of what it means to live in a modern, civilized society."

"I don't see how—"

Rina stopped her with a quick, impatient gesture. But her voice was earnest and strong: "For example, would you ever trust your life to a stranger?"

"No, of course not," the woman said.

"Or get into a strange car with a man you didn't know?"

"Never."

"Tell me, did you come to this convention from out of town?"

The woman nodded.

"How did you get from the airport to the convention center?"

Silence. Then, "I took a taxi."

"Had you ever met the driver of the taxi before? Or was he a stranger to you?"

"Well, I hardly think—"

"Do you have any idea how long the taxi driver had been driving his cab? Whether he has ever had any accidents? Whether he's in the habit of having a beer before he goes to work? Or perhaps a few sniffs of cocaine? Do you know when was the last time the car he was driving had a routine maintenance check?"

"No," said the woman. "I don't know any of those things."

"Yet you trusted the taxi driver to get you safely from the airport to the convention center."

The woman was silent.

"You trusted him, just as you trusted the good judgment of the people who hired him and the mechanical expertise of the people who service his taxi. And the driving ability of all the other drivers who were on the road at the same time you were. Not to mention the pilot of the plane you took. And the air traffic controllers. And the engineers who designed the plane. You trusted them all."

Around the room, people were nodding, obviously relating the example to their own lives.

"The truth is," Rina went on, leaning forward earnestly, "we all trust dozens of people with our very lives each day. No matter what happened to you as a child, do not ever make the mistake of believing that you are incapable of putting your faith in others. For if you believe that, it will be true. All of us are at the mercy of our beliefs."

"I never thought of it that way," the woman admitted.

"You have convinced yourself that you are deficient in an important human quality. I submit to you that you are not deficient. That none of us is. In order to improve your relationships, you must take control of your own power. You must acknowledge your own unique strengths. And most of all, you must change your negative beliefs about yourself. They serve no purpose other than to hold you back. Do you understand?"

The woman looked as if she had been shot with a bolt of sunshine. "Yes. Yes, I do. Thank you."

Rina extended her hands down toward the woman as if to embrace her. "Bless you," she said. She paused dramatically, and looked around the room, making eye contact with one person after another. "Believe me, all of you," she continued. "I know how it feels to be unable to trust." Her voice was low but intense. "To feel worthless. To lose heart. To know that no matter how hard I try, nothing will ever come right for me again. Oh, yes, my dear friends. I know what it is to be entirely without power or self-esteem.

"When you look at me now you see an energetic successful woman who loves life and wakes up every morning feeling excitement and joy. Would you believe that ten years ago I was fifty pounds overweight? That I'd frittered away all my financial resources and was deeply in debt? It's all true, my friends. I was in a state of despair. I spent all my waking hours contemplating the quickest and least painful manner of ending my miserable life."

The audience was hanging on every word, and April wanted to stand up and laugh at all of them. How could they believe this garbage?

"But I chose not to die," Rina was saying. "I chose instead to seize the dynamic potential of my own inner power and seek change. Change, my friends. It's a word many of us fear. But it is only through our ability to change—to adapt to changing conditions in the world around us—that we humans have been able to survive.

"I survived. So can you." She paused. "But, unlike myself, you don't have to do it alone. You don't have to wander in that lonely wilderness. All you have to do is reach out—" she stretched her right arm out toward her rapt audience "—and take my hand."

April stood. It happened suddenly. It wasn't what she'd planned at all.

It was as if she were suddenly possessed.

"You are a fake and a fraud, Rina Flaherty," she said in a ringing voice. "You are a self-absorbed, self-congratulating, self-obsessed monster who would not even trouble yourself to extend your hand to your own child."

Heads turned. Beside her, April heard Maggie gasp. Onstage, Rina went still. Even from twenty feet away, April could see her skin pale.

"Do you even remember that you have a daughter? Easy to forget, isn't it, after almost thirty years? But I remember very well, Mother. I remember all too well that when I reached for your hand, all you gave me was your back."

"April?" All the dynamism had leaked from Rina's

voice. It sounded thin and reedy, and she looked every year of her age.

"I'm astonished that you remember my name. You betrayed me. You ruined my life." April pushed out of her row and into the aisle, where it was standing room only. She was trembling. She felt as if she were about to burst into a spectacular display of tears. She had to get out of here.

"April, wait!" Rina cried, and started forward. Her movement broke the spell that had descended on the crowd. Everybody began moving at once. People were exclaiming, shouting questions.

The place devolved into chaos. People surrounded April, asking who she was, shouting questions. She was pressed toward, rather than away from, the stage.

Even more people surrounded Rina, who was trying to push through them. Dimly, April heard a frustrated female voice say, "Grab her, for chrissake, get her out of here, we can't allow this."

As she fought the crowd, April was ashamed to feel tears overflow her eyes and slide down her cheeks. Desperately, she reached into her purse for a tissue. She came up with a lipstick as well, which she clutched, as if for reassurance.

There was a sound like a champagne cork popping.

Somebody screamed.

"Shit," muttered Blackthorn. He launched himself toward the slender auburn-haired woman. She was stunning—auburn hair and huge eyes and fantastic legs—and she was deadly.

"She's been shot. My God, someone shot her!" a voice was crying in disbelief. "Help her! She's been shot!"

"Goddamn," said Blackthorn. A big man, he forced his way through the milling crowd. Panic was setting in. Not a pretty sight.

He couldn't see Rina. He assumed she was down.

But he could see the so-called abandoned daughter. She was a mental patient, more likely. This was the first he'd ever heard of any long-lost daughter.

She was making for the door. No way, lady. With a savage lunge, he threw his arm around her throat and jerked her off balance. She fell backwards against him. He caught the subtle scent of fine perfume as he jammed her against his body and twisted her left arm up behind her until she cried out.

"Drop it," he whispered in her ear. His free hand found and wrenched her right wrist.

For an instant she went limp against him, then her entire body stiffened in response to his assault. She moaned softly in the back of her throat. It was a faintly sensual sound. She writhed against him, but he held her fast. She was soft, yet lithe and strong at the same time.

"Blackthorn?" somebody screamed. It sounded like Carla. "Blackthorn, dammit, we're losing her. We're not getting a pulse . . ."

There was a chorus of agitated voices: "Somebody call the EMTs! Get an ambulance! We need an ambulance, quickly!"

"Sweet Jesus, she's been shot!"

"Get down everyone, get down! There's a killer in this room!"

"Let me through, I beg of you. *Mon dieu,* please, she's my wife."

The adrenaline was singing in Blackthorn's ears. He wrenched his captive's arm again and felt her flinch. "You know where assassins end up in California?" he whispered to the woman who was jammed so tightly against his body. "In a snug little room called the gas chamber. Drop it, I said."

The hand he was twisting relaxed as she loosed her death grip on the gun. There was a light metallic click as it slipped from her fingers and struck the floor at their feet.

Both Blackthorn and the woman stared down at the silver-colored lipstick tube.

Blackthorn pried open the fingers of her other hand. It was empty.

She shuddered. Her voice was muffled, but clear. "Get your hands off me."

He eased up some. But he kept her firmly locked in his professional embrace. All around, people were watching them. "Where's the gun?" he said.

She was breathing hard. He could feel her body vibrating against him. "What gun?" she whispered.

"The shot came from this direction, damn you. I saw you reach into your purse and come up with something metallic. A split second later the shot was fired and she went down."

The woman struggled, or tried to. He was holding her so close he could feel the warmth of her breasts, her thighs. "Is it Rina?" she asked. "I don't understand. I was reaching into my purse for a tissue. What—what happened? Who are you? Is Rina dead?"

Blackthorn's instincts were screaming that he'd made a mistake. She didn't look like a coldblooded killer, and people were muttering and nervously scanning the room for other suspects.

It had happened so damn fast. The acoustics in the room had distorted the sound of the gunfire, confusing everybody about the angle of the shot.

Still, he was loath to release her. Without letting go, he turned her around to face him. With one hand in her hair, he tipped back her head. God, she was pretty. Big blue eyes, wide with confusion, fright, and—hmm—a distinct flash of anger. "What's your relationship to Sabrina de Sevigny?" he demanded.

"I'm her daughter." Her chin came up. "I didn't shoot her. She's my mother."

"You're a liar," he said. "I know the family, and you're not one of them."

She seemed to recoil. Her face flushed and she looked away.

Freeing her, Blackthorn stepped back a pace. The woman shook her head, and some of her reddish hair escaped from its chignon. She convulsively hugged herself. She looked around wildly. "Where is she? I have to see her. Take me to her, please."

He hesitated only for a moment. This could be revealing, depending on her response. "Okay. Let's go." He reached out and gripped her hand, ready to pull her along. To his surprise, she did not resist his touch. Her fingers pressed back, and he realized she was scared . . . and quite probably in a state of shock.

"Security," he said, pushing through the gathering crowd. "Stand back. Security. Let us through."

A hushed little group was clustered around the body on the floor. Blackthorn saw Armand, who was gesticulating in a Gallic manner, tears running down his jowls. And Isobelle, the lovely Isobelle, her face white as paper, kneeling and holding her stepmother's head between her palms while Carla, straddling the client, frantically administered CPR.

The gunshot wound was to the head. Either a .22- or a .25-caliber bullet, he'd bet, considering the diameter of the small bluish-black hole. The entrance wound was directly through the center of the forehead, just above the bridge of the nose. He doubted they'd find an exit wound. A bullet that size would have spent its momentum within the skull, doing plenty of deadly damage to the soft tissue of the brain.

The slack mouth and dilated eyes confirmed the obvious—Rina de Sevigny was dead.

Beside him, the fraudulent daughter moaned and stumbled. Blackthorn caught her around the waist before she could go down. She clung to him, apparently forgetting the brutality to which he'd just subjected her. She turned her face into the front of his neck and burrowed against him, shivering. She mumbled something.

It sounded like: "Don't leave me, Mommy. Oh, Mommy, please, don't go."

Chapter Three

April leaned over the receiver of the pay phone in the corner of the lobby of the police department, speaking softly and wondering if the line was tapped. This, she remembered, was how it felt to be afraid of the very authorities who were supposed to protect you . . .

"Don't delay on any new shipments that arrive," she was saying to Brian, her partner back in Boston. "I'm expecting several cartons of new paperback releases from three major publishing houses. I want them unpacked and shelved as soon as possible. The regulars are all asking for the new Kinsey Milhone."

"Wait a minute," said Brian. "You're under arrest and you're worrying about getting new books to our customers? I know you're a bookseller who cares, but—"

"I'm not under arrest," April said. Gotta keep it together, she said to herself. She cast a quick glance around at the bustle of people going in and out. "They were questioning me, but they're finally finished and they said I could leave. But we're three hours behind out there, and I wanted to catch you before you closed up the store."

"April, are you okay? You sound awful. How close were you to this shooting? You mean it happened right there at the ABA?"

"I really can't talk now." She twisted the phone cord around her hand. She should tell him more details, she knew, but right now it was beyond her. She was hot and tired. And she felt numb.

This had not helped her with the police, she suspected. Although nobody had come right out and said so, the underlying question seemed to be, "If she's your mother, why ain't you cryin', lady?"

But they hadn't arrested her. They'd grilled her for hours, but they'd let her go. Thank God they hadn't arrested her! She couldn't have borne that . . . not again.

Had they learned anything about her past? Was it computerized somewhere? Did they have police computers back in 1969? There must be some way to check. What would happen when they found out?

"What I want to do is leave immediately and come home," she said, "and I will as soon as the police allow me to leave California." She pressed her palm to her forehead, which was pounding.

"You're surely not suggesting that they consider you a suspect?"

"God, it's so ironic." She pictured Brian sitting at her desk surrounded by stacks of crime novels in *The Poison Pen*. "I trade in fictional murders and here I am in the middle of a real one."

"But, Boss, I don't get it. Who was she—a rival bookseller?" He laughed awkwardly.

"She was my mother."

Silence on the other end of the line.

Out of the corner of her eye, April saw several people approaching her. Several of them held TV cameras slung on their shoulders. "Brian, I've got to go. I'll call again tomorrow."

"Look, wait a minute—"

"Good-bye," she said, and hung up.

The press would of course have heard about the murder. Rina de Sevigny was famous—this was big news. Her long-lost daughter was being questioned regarding her murder—what a story. The reporters—some of *them* would undoubtedly dig into her past. If the police didn't get her, the press would.

Shakily, she gathered up her things—her handbag and the armful of books and papers from the convention that she'd been carrying around with her all day—and walked quickly in the other direction from the reporters. She found an exit on the side of the building and descended down a flight of concrete stairs into the sultry heat of a blast from the Santa Anas.

She felt dazed and battered. Maggie had stayed with her for most of the afternoon, but she'd had to rush off to a special cocktail party that she and several other romance booksellers were hosting that evening for Sandra Brown and Jayne Ann Krentz, both *New York Times* bestselling authors. She'd apologized profusely and promised to return as soon as her official duties were over.

The reporters were following her. April hurried out to the sidewalk and looked around for a taxi. But this wasn't New York or even Boston. Everybody in California owned cars. There were no taxis in sight.

Damn. She'd have to go back inside and call.

Despite the heat, April shivered. She hugged herself. Rina was dead. She was actually dead.

"Ms., uh, Harrington?" somebody with a camera said. "That's you, right?"

"Got any comment about the murder of Sabrina de Sevigny?"

"Hey, April, is it true that you knew the deceased?"

"Are you Rina de Sevigny's daughter?"

"I have no comment," she murmured, turning her face away from the still and video cameras.

"Did you see who shot her?"

"What do you think of the way the police are handling this case?"

"Did you kill her, April?"

April. They already knew her name and felt free to use it. She imagined the headline in the tabloid: APRIL SHOWERS BULLETS ON LONG-LOST MOTHER.

She started as she felt a touch on her shoulder. "Let me take you away from all this," someone said.

She turned to see a tall, dark-haired man. The policeman—or, no, the security agent. The same one who had assaulted her and wrestled her to the floor in the convention center. The first of several people who believed that she had murdered her mother.

He was handsome in a rough-cut manner, she noted—with his rugged features, powerfully built torso, and long limbs. His eyes were brown and graced with thick dark lashes. He must be about her age, she guessed—pushing forty.

"I have a car," he said. "Are you going back to your hotel? I'll drive you."

"No, thanks."

"The car's parked right across the street. You'll never find a cab around here. California's not like New York or even Boston. You're staying at one of the convention center hotels, right?"

"Yes, but I really don't want—"

"I insist." He took her arm in a firm grip.

"Hey, buddy, who're you? Her husband or what?" one of the reporters demanded.

"No comment," he said. To April he whispered, "C'mon."

Her will seemed to melt under the force of his. This was unusual, she thought, not like her at all. But the idea of being able to escape the reporters and sink into the seat of an available car and be driven back to her refuge was irresistible.

What the hell, she thought as she allowed him to urge her in the direction of his car. He was strong and she felt protected. Even this guy was better than the police. *Anybody* was better than the police.

"I don't even know your name," she said.

"It's Blackthorn. Rob Blackthorn."

Blackthorn. An ominous sort of name, she thought.

"Why did you tackle me? Did you think I was the one with the gun? I didn't shoot her, Mr. Blackthorn."

"I know."

She felt absurdly grateful to hear him say so.

He unlocked the door on the passenger's side, and she climbed in. The reporters had followed them to the car, but he ignored them and she did the same. By the time he had come around and seated himself in the driver's seat, she was leaning back with her head against the headrest.

"The police gave you a rough time?" he asked as he started the engine.

"Rough enough," she said. It could have been worse, she knew. The cops weren't very friendly when they suspected you of a crime.

The memory was like a knife in her gut. How long would it take them to find out what she'd done all those years ago in Washington? And when they did . . . what impact would it have on the current investigation?

"When a prominent person like Rina de Sevigny is

murdered, the police take their job somewhat more seriously than when some poor bastard from the projects gets offed," Blackthorn said.

She didn't comment. Through half-closed eyes she watched the palm trees slide by out the top of the passenger's side window.

"I take my job more seriously, too, when I lose a client."

"Too bad you didn't take it a little more seriously beforehand."

He did not reply, and April regretted the comment. She sneaked a glance at him from under her lowered lashes. His face in profile was rigid, but she noticed a slight twitch of emotion around his jaw. She glanced down at his hands—one on the wheel and the other on the gearshift. They were big hands, powerful. They moved with authority as he drove through the busy traffic.

"I made a mistake," he said after a few moments. "I intend to rectify it as best I can. I intend to find Rina's killer and bring him—" he cast a glance in her direction "—or her to justice." He paused, then added, "You didn't shoot her, but you could have hired it done."

Her eyes popped all the way open. "What do you mean?"

"I mean it was a professional job. An assassination. Rina was hit by a hired gun who picked his moment then disappeared into the crowd. It was skillfully handled."

"Well, the police didn't mention that theory to me."

"The scene was confusing for the first few seconds." April thought she saw a trace of color wash his cheekbones. "I imagine that even Anaheim's finest have sorted out what really happened by now, though. At this point their investigation will be centered on establishing a motive. If they know why, it will lead them to who."

"Not necessarily," April said. "There might be several people who had a reason to want her dead."

"In fiction, perhaps," he said with a sidelong smile. "In real life, all it takes is one."

"I see. You're saying that there's a world of difference between art and life."

"Art and death," he corrected gently.

"Look, Mr. Blackthorn—"

"So you're really Rina's daughter?"

"Stop this car, please, and let me out. I'll find my own way back to the convention center."

"Relax. We're almost there." The wheels of the rental car squealed as he took a sharp corner. But he retained complete control of the car. Probably trained to do all sorts of maneuvers to avoid terrorist attacks, April thought.

"I'm personally acquainted with the family," he said. "But until today, I've never heard of you before."

"My mother abandoned me when I was twelve years old. Today was the first time I'd been in the same room with her in twenty-eight years."

"She abandoned you? Why?"

"Why?" April gave a short laugh. "For the usual reason that women neglect or abandon their children. There was a man. She wanted him. He was going to change her life. And I was in the way."

"You sound bitter. Twenty-eight years is a long time. You're an adult now, a successful woman."

"Some emotions are untouched by time."

Something altered in his face, as if a cloud had passed over his features. He dropped eye contact. After a moment he cleared his throat. "You'll be investigated, you know. Both by the local authorities and by the FBI."

"The FBI?"

"When somebody conspires to hire a killer in one state to kill somebody in another, the feds get interested. Given the fact that the de Sevignys are based in New York, there's every indication that that is indeed what happened. It'll be an FBI matter, all right." His voice was clipped and there was a distant expression in his eyes. "We'll see whether or not your story checks out."

April clenched her fists. "I have nothing to hide." *Liar, liar,* her conscience screamed at her.

With a jerk he pulled to a stop in front of the Hyatt. "It's a pretty basic understanding in my business that everybody has something to hide." He leaned across her and popped the handle on her door before the liveried doorman could attend to it. For an instant, his arm was warm and hard across her middle. "Whatever your secrets are, I will unearth them," he said softly. "I'm making it both my personal and my professional business to know everything there is to know about Ms. April Harrington."

She believed him. He would dig into her past, and God only knew what he would do when he found out.

She was shaking as she stepped from his car.

He watched her as she walked away from him, toward the entrance to her hotel. She was beautiful—an isolated figure, quiet, pale. Her long reddish hair was pulled cruelly back from her face and restrained in a chignon which might have looked sophisticated if a few strands had not persisted in escaping and forming a lazy curve against the side of her cheeks and throat. Every now and then during the drive she had pushed the errant lock behind her ear, but within minutes, it would fall forward again.

Was she capable of rage, hatred, revenge? It seemed hard to believe. But his years in law enforcement had made him cynical. A woman was no less deadly for being beautiful.

In the hours since the shooting, he'd been dissecting every move he'd made in Anaheim—the packed conference room, the angry confrontation between Rina and the strange woman, the confusion, the surge of the crowd, the flash of metal, the shot, the screams.

He replayed it like a videotape, stopping the action, lingering over this detail or that. All too frequently his mind lingered on what had happened after the shot rather than before it. His move on the red-haired woman. Seizing her. Holding her hard against his body. Inhaling her scent.

Dammit, it shouldn't have gone so wrong. He had been in control. At least, he should have been.

Amazingly, he felt no desire for a drink. And yet, he thirsted. He stared at April Harrington. She was the key, he was sure. Whoever she was.

"I don't believe her claim," Christian de Sevigny had said when they'd spoken on the phone. "She's clearly an imposter. With your background in intelligence and other forms of skull-duggery, you must be good for something, Blackthorn." He spoke with his usual contempt. "Investigate her. Expose her for the fraud she is."

"But who is she?" Isobelle had asked him on their way to the police station. "I can't bear to see her. If she hadn't caused that confusion in the conference room, the killer would never have dared . . . and Rina would still be alive."

"I'm afraid she may be telling the truth," Armand had told him. "Sabrina did have an illegitimate child. In fact, I met the girl, many years ago. My memory of her is not very clear, but this could be the same woman. We were told she had died. Perhaps I was too quick to believe it."

Of course, one of *them* could have done it.

It wouldn't take long to find out who benefited from Rina's death.

Not me, that's for sure.

Shit, he needed a drink.

Help me, Jessie, he thought.

Chapter Four

April sat in a high-back chair, her eyes fixed on the face of the Manhattan attorney who was preparing to read Rina de Sevigny's last will and testament. She was trying to resist the temptation to study the faces of the others in the room. A few years ago she would have done it, staring insolently at each one and pretending not to care that they hated her and resented her presence here. As a child, she remembered, she had been indefatigably insolent and brave.

Spirited, one of the more tolerant of her teachers had said.

She wished she could dredge up some of that cocky old spirit now.

But the police and a rabid group of print and television journalists had given her no peace. All week long she had been stalked, followed, interviewed, harassed. But at least she hadn't been arrested, and no one had questioned her about those awful days when she'd been a teenage run-away . . .

She had come to New York on her way home from California because she'd felt the need to attend her mother's funeral. She'd told herself that her desire to do so made no sense at all, but she couldn't seem to help wanting one last chance to resolve her feelings toward Rina, and to say good-bye.

Besides, she couldn't help feeling curious about the murder. After all, murder was her business. Fictional murders might be neater and tidier than real ones, but her desire to find the answers and solve the mysteries was very strong.

An associate from the law firm of Stanley, Rorschach and McGregor had notified her yesterday that her presence was required at the reading of the will. Incredibly, she was one of the beneficiaries. To what extent, she had no idea. From the way they'd been looking at her, she concluded that this was a matter of much speculation among the rest of the family.

It was evident that the family took no joy in seeing her here. Armand de Sevigny had been the only one of them to greet her. His wife's death, although clearly upsetting to him, had not interfered with his impeccable manners. Nor with his undeniable charm.

"I am so sorry we must meet under such unhappy circumstances," he'd said to her at the funeral. "My wife spoke often of you."

"She did?" April had been unable to hide her surprise.

Armand had embraced her warmly. "She had come to regret her actions toward you. As do I. If there's a way to make it up to you, I intend to try."

Admirable sentiments, she had thought. But a little late.

Rina's stepchildren, Christian and Isobelle, had both

avoided her, remaining distant and silent. Charles Ripley, Rina's handsome assistant at Power Perspectives, had approached her and shaken her hand. "Thank you for coming," he had said, and April had noticed that he had tears in his eyes.

She wondered what they were all thinking this morning as they took note of her presence among them. She glanced at Isobelle, who seemed distinctly hostile. Her color was high and as she waited, she aggressively chewed on her bottom lip. One of her high-heeled pumps tapped persistently against the floor as she fidgeted, her scarlet-tipped fingers clenched into fists.

Her gaze moved to Christian, Isobelle's brother, who was leaning impassively against the far wall, his elegant body loose and languid, his eyes closed in evident boredom.

He was an attractive man with classical features that must have been almost too pretty when he was young. Maturity had chiseled a few lines and creases into his visage, giving him an air of sophistication that April had no doubt he deserved.

She'd done enough research on the family before going to the ABA to know something about the people whom she might reasonably consider her stepbrother and stepsister. Christian was said to treasure the finer things in life, from the finest wines to the most expensive women. He worked for his father, whose many commercial interests included De Sevigny Ltd., an international shipping company that made both oil tankers and cruise ships. It was based in New York, still one of the premier ports in the world.

Isobelle did not work directly for her father, and rumor had it that there was some kind of tension between them. Instead, she had worked with her stepmother at Power

Perspectives, helping her to run an enterprise that had grown far more rapidly than anybody had expected.

She had never been married. April knew nothing else about her personal life.

Also present were Charles and several other people who April could not identify, although they looked familiar from the funeral. But she did know Rob Blackthorn, who stood in one corner of the room and settled himself, leaning his powerful shoulders against the richly paneled wall and folding his arms across his chest.

For a bodyguard, April was thinking, this guy was pretty damn persistent. Whom was he protecting now?

He caught her eye and smiled. He didn't appear to be actively hostile. Implacable, yes. Relentless, undoubtedly. She remembered his vow to learn everything there was to know about her. By now he must know that she was truly Rina's daughter.

What else had he found out?

Arthur Stanley, Esq., loudly cleared his throat. "I hope to get on with this as quickly as possible, but I've been asked to wait until the authorities arrive."

"What authorities?" Isobelle asked.

"Well, a representative of the local bureau of the FBI, I believe."

There was a stir in the room. Isobelle laughed, Christian frowned, and Armand gave a classic Gallic shrug. Only Blackthorn, April noted, did not seem surprised.

"Is that really necessary?" Armand asked. "Surely, considering all we've been through during the past few days, they will grant us some privacy?"

"I know this is a difficult occasion for all of you," the lawyer said. "Believe me, it is difficult for us as well. Madame de Sevigny was not only a valued client, but a personal friend."

She had had a lot of personal friends, thought April, if the impressive turnout at the funeral was a reliable indication. But so far no one had stepped forward admitting to be her deadly enemy.

"But her death is a police matter," the attorney continued, "and I'm afraid the authorities do indeed have the right to the information contained in the will . . ."

He was interrupted by a sharp rap on the door. A tall, lanky, middle-aged man entered the room. He held up a wallet and a shield. "Agent Martin Clemente, FBI. I hope you'll all excuse the intrusion, but our Manhattan division has taken charge of this investigation."

"Well," said Stanley, "let me say that this is most unusual, at what would normally be a private reading of the decedent's will, but I do understand that when a death is a police matter—"

"Just so," Agent Clemente said.

"I'm sure the FBI have every right to be here," Christian de Sevigny said. "Why don't we get on with it?"

Stanley nodded and began.

The will was the usual instrument, filled with legalistic phrases and long passages that were of no particular interest. He finally began reading the bequests, which apparently began with the small ones, to friends and distant relations, which seemed to April an unreasonable method of heightening everyone's suspense. Charles Ripley received a legacy of $20,000 which was earmarked for him to "return to college, should he desire to do so." Blackthorn also received a bequest (so that's why he was here) of a landscape painting, "in memory of his wife and life partner, Jessica."

He'd had a wife who had died? April watched his face and noted that his face appeared drawn and weary. She felt a brief rush of sympathy.

"As you know," Stanley said, looking up from the document, "many of Madame de Sevigny's financial interests were jointly held with her husband. This includes real estate and securities. However, she maintained separate ownership of her business, Power Perspectives, Inc., and, as the sole proprietor, she was entitled to determine the deposition of that property."

He paused. There was a collective shifting in the room as everybody waited. April glanced again at Isobelle. She was leaning forward eagerly. April had heard that during the last couple of years Isobelle had been a creative partner with Rina in building Power Perspectives into a successful business. Would she be as charismatic a leader as Rina had proved to be?

"Mme. de Sevigny made an alteration in her will just a few weeks ago," said Stanley. "There is no evidence that she was under any stress or coercion at the time. I personally handled the matter myself."

He sounded slightly defensive, April thought.

"I will read you the relevant portion of the will, which says, in essence, that Madame de Sevigny has left Power Perspectives—both its controlling interests and all its assets—which are considerable, to her daughter, April Harrington."

What?

April heard a gasp from somewhere on the "family" side of the room. She tried to control her own response, although she was sure everyone must have heard the sound of her convulsive swallow.

"The will further provides that if said April Harrington is unable to be located, if she refuses the legacy, or if she dies without issue, Isobelle de Sevigny will inherit in her stead."

Isobelle stood, her dark eyes flashing. "So suddenly I

am second in line to the throne?" she spat out. "This is impossible. Who is this woman? She turns up out of nowhere and lays claim to my stepmother's estate? It's unbelievable. I object to this. There's something very suspicious going on."

Armand touched his daughter's arm. "Isobelle. Please. This is not the place for an outburst. Sit down."

"No, Papa, I won't sit down. Rina has been murdered in front of our eyes and now this woman . . . this woman who may have been her murderer . . . she is the one to inherit control of Power Perspectives? I've been working very closely with Rina. I had understood that I was her heir. What is this nonsense about an alteration in her will?"

"Isobelle." Armand's voice was low but the air of command in it was powerful. He gave a quick glance at Agent Clemente, who was watching the proceedings impassively. "That will do."

April sat still with her hands clasped in her lap. This is crazy, she was thinking. It made no sense at all. She couldn't really blame Isobelle for protesting. If she'd been in her shoes, she'd have squawked about it, too.

She rose unsteadily. I've got to get out of here, she thought. To the group at large she murmured, "You'll have to excuse me for a few minutes, please."

April found the nearest ladies room and locked herself into a stall. She felt queasy, excited, and scared—all at the same time. All she could see was the expression on her mother's face during the last few moments of her life, when she'd suddenly realized that she was looking once again at the face of her only child. "You ruined my life!" she had cried out to her mother, and Rina had reached out toward her. "April, wait," had been her last words. Whatever she'd meant to say after that, whatever explanation she might have tried to give had been blasted into silence by the murderer's bullet.

Now her mother, who had left her standing on a cold pier mourning the departing hulk of an ocean liner, had acknowledged her at last.

In her mind's eye she saw Blackthorn's cold, unfriendly gaze. Great, she thought. Now he must be convinced she was guilty.

Chapter Five

"I'm going to challenge the will."

"You'll do no such thing," Armand de Sevigny said to his daughter.

"Don't interfere with me, Papa," Isobelle cried.

The scene in the conference room after the will reading had devolved into exactly the sort of chaos, thought Rob Blackthorn, that murder investigators love. The family was upset, and the terms of the will had been a surprise. He couldn't have picked a better time to observe them all.

He exchanged a quick glance with Marty Clemente, whom he knew well from his former days with the FBI. Marty raised his eyebrows slightly in acknowledgment. Blackthorn was glad Marty was on this case, and not some young, overly idealistic, wet-behind-the-ears type. He might even be able to trade some information with Marty.

"Isobelle, I strongly suggest you control your emotions before you say something you regret," Armand said.

His tone was scathing, and Blackthorn noted that Armand seemed to have lost much of his usual geniality. He had aged in the few days since his wife's death. His eyes were duller, his step heavier. Blackthorn had wondered if their marriage was a happy one, but there was no denying that Armand was grieving.

Was the new will a revelation to him or had he known his wife's wishes in advance?

Clearly it had been a revelation to Isobelle. Her face was crimson and her eyes were blazing. This was very much in character, for she was the sort of woman who never missed an opportunity to be dramatic. With her raven hair and her striking figure, she usually had everyone's attention, anyway, but everyone's attention was never enough. Blackthorn knew that the one person whose love and respect she had always yearned for was her father's, and that, for some reason, she'd never been able to secure.

Christian, as usual, was inscrutable.

How different the siblings were, Blackthorn thought. Both in looks and in temperament. Isobelle was passionate, nakedly so. Christian, on the other hand, was cold.

He didn't like Christian much. He didn't like the way he masked his feelings with that cold chiseled expression; he didn't like what he suspected was going on behind those Arctic blue eyes.

Isobelle, though . . . She was an interesting woman. Full of energy, always on edge. Isobelle, he knew, had a great hunger for life and all its adventures. Most of all, she needed to prove to her father and her brother that they had sadly underestimated her talents.

Gaining control of Power Perspectives would have been a way for her to do it. No wonder she was upset.

The conference room slowly emptied of everybody except the family, Ripley, Clemente, and Blackthorn. Now that the initial outburst was over, nobody was saying much. Blackthorn knew that this was because his presence and that of Marty Clemente placed inhibitions on the family that they otherwise wouldn't have felt.

Well, to hell with their inhibitions.

"So what are you all going to do about her?" he asked.

Several pairs of eyes shifted in his direction.

"April Harrington. I take it from the reactions that the terms of Rina's will were something of a surprise?" He paused. "Or had she shared her intentions with any of you?" He looked at Armand.

"Is this some sort of official inquiry?" Christian bestirred himself to ask. "Didn't you used to be associated with the FBI?"

Marty said, "Mr. Blackthorn is no longer associated with the FBI. I am in charge of this investigation." He removed a small tape recorder from his jacket pocket and laid it in the middle of the conference table. "I will be speaking with each of you individually, but yes, this is an official inquiry, beginning now." He switched it on, identified himself, the date and time, and the others in the room.

"Don't you have to read us our rights, or something?" Christian said sarcastically.

"Not at this time, no. None of you is being charged with a crime."

"Well, I'm not afraid to speak on the record," Isobelle said. "I have nothing to hide. And I'm convinced that the will that was just read is fraudulent. Somehow or other the Harrington woman got to Rina, pressured her, maybe even blackmailed her. She convinced her to change the will, and then she had her killed. She ought to be in prison, not inheriting Power Perspectives."

"Sounds rather far-fetched to me," Christian said.

Isobelle ignored him. "I'm going to have our attorneys get to work immediately on challenging the will."

"No," Armand said. "That would be most inappropriate."

"Papa, please—"

"It is clear enough that everyone is upset by the developments this morning," Armand said. "And I suspect that the more we brood about it, the more upset we will be. Therefore, now, without delay, I will tell you that I have made up my mind about this situation." He paused. "Your stepmother's will must be allowed to stand unchallenged."

"Excuse me, Papa, but there's no way I can agree," Isobelle said.

"I haven't asked for your opinion," Armand said.

"No, you never do."

Blackthorn could hear the resentment in her voice. For years, he knew, Isobelle had hoped to be her father's successor. But congenial though he was, Armand was an old-fashioned sexist. He had insisted upon grooming his languid son to succeed him, even though, as far as anybody could tell, Christian could have cared less.

"Kindly do me the courtesy of hearing me out," Armand said. He was either ignoring the tape recorder, Blackthorn thought, or posturing for it. He wasn't certain which.

"The truth is, an injustice has been done. For this I blame myself. I knew that Rina had a daughter. I even met her, many years ago. As I recall, she was a difficult child. Uncouth and wild—quite unlike the woman we have seen today. If I had ever dreamed that she would turn out so well—so dignified. But it did not occur to me.

"I'm afraid I encouraged Rina to send the child to boarding school in the States rather than bringing her to Paris. As you know, Rina was at the time quite a different class of woman than I was accustomed to associating with. Although she was never ashamed of her beginnings, I confess that I was."

Armand shook his head sadly. "I take no pride in admitting that I felt a need to mold her into the woman I wanted her to be. The prospect of molding the child as well seemed an impossible task. Rina had never disciplined her. She was out of control. My concern was for you. I thought April would be a bad influence . . ." His voice trailed off.

Blackthorn was intrigued by the description of April Harrington as uncouth and wild. But how she could have been a bad influence on Christian and Isobelle was more than he could imagine.

"I now believe that out of snobbery and fear I made the wrong decision," Armand went on. "I am ashamed of myself for this. I separated a mother from her child. It was inexcusable."

Too bad April Harrington had left the room. Blackthorn wondered what she would think of this admission.

"The child grew up, naturally, to resent us. As for her mother—" he shrugged "—it is clear from the dispositions made in her will that she wished to rectify the wrong done to the only child born of her body. Power Perspectives was Rina's inspiration, her own personal adventure. She, not I, created it and built it into what it is today. I wish everyone to know that I support my wife's right to decide what to do with the company. And I believe that she has made a just choice.

"Therefore, it is my decision that her will will not be contested. I trust that is clear to all of you?"

"I haven't the slightest interest in contesting Rina's will," Christian said. "The entire subject is a matter of supreme indifference to me."

Armand turned to Isobelle. Her arms were crossed over her chest, and her dark eyes were burning. "A just choice?" she repeated. "Even if there is some justice in trying to make up for past wrongs, there were other ways she could have done it. Certainly her choice was not a wise or a sensible one. This is business, Father. How can you sit there and assert that some woman we don't even know—some—some shopkeeper—is the right person to run a multi-million-dollar company? For all we know, she'll destroy it! Or is that what you secretly hope?"

"That is enough, Isobelle," Armand said.

"You're mistaken if you think I won't fight for what is rightfully mine."

"Why don't you just kill April Harrington," Christian suggested with a sudden flash of emotion. "Then you'll inherit, after all."

Isobelle glared at her brother, whose cold eyes glared right back at her.

Armand shook his head sadly.

Blackthorn and Clemente exchanged another glance.

Something rotten here, Blackthorn thought.

He cleared his throat. "Personally, I don't give a damn who ends up running Power Perspectives. What I want to know—and intend to find out—is who murdered Rina."

"The brilliant detective at work?" Christian's tone just missed being snide—a great talent of his—to be offensive in a manner that no one could proclaim as offensive.

"Brilliance is rarely required in a murder case," Blackthorn said. "We simply don't get that many brilliant murderers." And we certainly won't find one in this family, was the message that he hoped his words implied. "Dogged determination usually works better than clever deductions. Killers leave tracks. Sometimes these tracks are difficult to find. Sometimes we go in circles trying to separate a false lead from a true one. But eventually we find the real tracks, and they lead us where we want to go."

"Seems to me you were hired to prevent this from happening, not to clean up the mess afterwards," Christian said.

"Yeah, and I blew it," Blackthorn said levelly. "Now it's a matter of professional pride to clear up that impression."

He paused, looking at each of them in turn. As in any suspicious death, the closest relatives were the most obvious suspects. The motivations that drive people to murder were often mundane, even trivial. Real and imagined slights, conscious and unconscious cruelties. Despite the popularity of the murder mysteries that April Harrington sold so successfully in her shop, there often were no grand, intelligent plans behind a real killing. For every sophisticated life insurance scam there were thousands of pointless, profitless murders—lives ended and people consigned to the earth over passions that would have faded by morning had they not been precipitously acted upon.

Rina's death was different, of course. A contract had been made, a shooter had been hired. The means were sophisticated, and the motive would have to have been sufficiently complex to justify all the trouble.

Most of the people with complex motives were right here in this room.

"It's more than professional pride, though," he said. "Rina helped a lot of people, including my wife during her illness. And when I needed someone, she was there." Blackthorn had to take a slow careful breath to hide his emotions from them. "I owe her. And since there's no longer any way to settle up with her directly, I'm making it my business to settle up with her memory. I intend to see justice done. I'm going to unearth her murderer and put him—or her—away."

For several seconds, nobody said anything. Then Armand leaned over and put one of his hands on Blackthorn's arm. "Thank you for your dedication. If there's anything I can do to help you, you have only to ask. I will hope and pray that you succeed."

Christian and Isobelle said nothing, although Isobelle looked agitated, as if she wanted to speak. Christian's expression was as cold and unreadable as carved marble.

Blackthorn exchanged a quick glance with Martin Clemente. His former colleague's expression was grim. He probably knew as well as Blackthorn did that at this point the tracks led exactly nowhere.

Isobelle de Sevigny slammed the door behind her as she entered her Chelsea apartment. She stomped through the huge living room area of the converted factory to the master bedroom and sat down at the antique dressing table. She stared at her face in the mirror. She was not beautiful, or at least, she had never considered herself to be so. Her features were a little too sharp, especially her nose. She thought they looked sharper than ever now because she had not been eating properly since Rina's death.

Actually, she reminded herself, she hadn't been eating properly for quite some time. Her weight was down. Charlie had been fussing. He was quick to tell her that he liked some covering of flesh on her bones.

But Isobelle preferred herself thinner. When she exhibited herself, she wanted no one to see and smile over extra flesh, extra fat.

She felt a surge in her belly as it occurred to her that she could exhibit herself tonight.

She glanced at the diamond watch on her wrist. Just after eleven. Things at the Chateau would be heating up.

It was Friday night, and straights were welcome. During the week the rooms and apparatus in the Chateau were reserved for homosexuals—lesbians on Tuesday and Thursday and gays on Monday, Wednesday, and Friday. But on the weekend, the heterosexual players took over the place.

Isobelle hadn't planned on checking out the scene this weekend, but she also hadn't planned on April Harrington. Her anger and frustration were unexpected; she had to work them out.

She picked up the phone and dialed Charlie's number. "Are you alone?" she asked.

"Of course I'm alone," he said, sounding surprised that she might think otherwise.

"I'm going to the Chateau. Would you like to come?"

"Are you all right?" he asked.

"I'm fine."

"I can't stop thinking about what happened today, Isobelle. I'm so sorry. I can't believe it. I hope you're going to challenge that new will."

"Look, I'm trying to get the whole unpleasant situation out of my head. Do you want to meet me tonight or not?"

"Okay. Sure. I'm concerned about you, that's all."

"Thanks," she said, "but there's no way you can fix this particular situation."

"I can try. You know I want only the best for you, always."

Her voice turned husky. "Yes, because you're my slave, pet."

Silence. Then he said, "Shall I meet you there?"

"Mmm. I'll arrive by midnight."

"I'll be there," Charlie murmured as she rang off.

She sat for a few moments staring at the phone. Charlie was loyal and loving, and she could relax when she was with him. But being involved with somebody from work was never smart. Perhaps it was time to start looking for someone to replace him.

She stripped off her clothes and, naked, poked around in the back of her closet until she found some of the things she needed. She donned a black corset made of soft leather. It laced up in front, and barely covered her breasts. She stepped into a pair of matching leather bikini panties that covered her crotch in front but was high cut on the sides and back. She added a short leather skirt, black fishnet stockings with leather garters, and four-inch patent leather heels. No blouse. It would come off, anyway . . . as would the skirt.

As would she.

Charlie was waiting for her inside when she arrived at the Chateau at a few minutes past midnight. He wore a black leather vest over a dark turtleneck shirt. Tight leather pants encased his long legs. With his blond hair, gray eyes, and pleasant features, he was a good-looking man. Isobelle could sense several women giving him the eye from various dark corners of the club. If she did break up with him, he wouldn't have any problem hooking up with someone new. Assuming he wanted to do so. More and more lately, he had been declaring his love for her.

She walked over to him and arched her neck to receive his kiss.

"You look gorgeous, Mistress," he said.

"Thank you, slave."

"I've missed you. I'd really like to see you someplace other than here and in the office."

"This is all I can handle right now."

They moved into a large central area of the club where other couples wandered, most dressed in fetish costumes with a heavy emphasis on leather and shiny black vinyl. Some were barely dressed at all.

At one end of the room was a shadowy group gathered around some dimly illuminated apparatus. There was the sound of a paddle striking bare flesh, accompanied by cries that spoke far more eloquently of pleasure than of pain. This was indeed the case. The whips were real, but they were made of soft leather, bluntly cut and unlikely to injure or mark even the most tender skin.

"Are you okay?" Charlie's gray eyes studied her. "Are you worried about something?"

"I'm fine. Let's play."

He shrugged. He was only an average submissive, she thought. Giving up power was something that didn't come naturally to him.

Perhaps she had been too indulgent with Charlie. The best dominants were control freaks. Type A personalities. They wanted—indeed they needed—to control every detail of the scene. The power this gave them was the turn-on.

Isobelle liked having control, yes, but she was not interested in the fine level of detail that some dommes obsessed about. No, for her it was more a matter of power. She loved the rush of having a man—or even better, several men—kneeling at her feet.

Removing a pair of fur-lined leather cuffs from her toybag, she indicated to Charlie to hold out his hands. She felt the familiar surge go through her as she buckled the cuffs around his wrists.

As she led Charlie toward the back room—toward the pillory and the whipping post—Isobelle closed her eyes against the image of Rina, lying broken and silent on the convention center floor.

Chapter Six

"Okay, we fucked up," said Blackthorn to Carla Murphy.

He had his feet up on his desk in his suite of fancy offices on Seventh Avenue just a couple of blocks away from Central Park. "There's no way to undo it, but we're going to have to engage in a little damage control. Hell. A lot of damage control."

"You have a personal stake in this, I know," Carla said.

"True. But right now I'm thinking more about the business than about my personal relationship to the de Sevigny family." That had better be true, he told himself. Besides Carla, he had three other people working for him. He was responsible for putting food on their tables every night at suppertime. If he went under, so would they.

"It doesn't look good, does it, a celebrity like Rina de Sevigny being assassinated right under our noses. This kind of thing is not likely to bring new clients pounding on our doors."

"Yeah," Carla said morosely.

"We've already lost a couple possible contracts, and both the Saudi gentlemen Jonas is supposed to be baby-sitting in Washington during next week's oil trade negotiations have telephoned to ask for our assurances regarding their safety."

"You reassured them, I hope?"

"I bowed and scraped, yeah. We've guarded them before and they've been happy. Jonas speaks Arabic and knows where to take them to get them laid, so I don't think they'll cancel." Jonas was a good man, and Blackthorn trusted him. He was young and sometimes a little over-eager, but he was smart and good with foreign languages. Jonas was also Blackthorn's computer expert. He could electronically hack his way into any system.

"Even so, we could sure use a little positive public relations," he went on. "Best way I can see to achieve that is to outrun the police and the FBI and figure out who killed Rina ourselves."

"Look," said Carla. "I know you used to be an FBI agent. And that World Systems Security started out as a detective agency. But it's been a long time since we've been so much as peripherally involved in a murder investigation. And besides, it happened in California, and this is New York."

"I have friends," Blackthorn said. "A few of them have already filled me in." He dropped a folder on the desk between them. "Here's what we know so far. The killer was a professional shooter. He didn't get close enough to Rina to transfer any physical evidence to her body. He escaped with his weapon, a .22-caliber pistol. Anaheim PD interviewed lots of witnesses who claimed to have seen the guy, but no two descriptions are the same. We know he was in the room with her, but so were over a hundred other people. It was a nightmare for the crime scene folks, who got enough irrelevant hairs, fibers, fingerprints, and other crap to fill an entire evidence room with little glass jars and paper bags. At the end of it, we got zip. This is one case that won't be solved by physical evidence."

"And the gun hasn't turned up, right?"

"No. He probably used it then broke it down, took the pieces up to LA, and dumped 'em into the ocean. We won't find it. In these cases they either leave it on the scene—the untraceable ones of course—or they hide them. I suspect they go into the same black hole with odd socks that vanish in the dryer."

"You figure he picked up the piece in California?"

"Couldn't fly in with it, that's for sure."

"On the other hand, maybe the doer is from California—they got hit men in LA."

"You're absolutely right. He could be from anywhere, that's the trouble."

"Maybe this case isn't going to be solved at all."

"Yeah, it will. Somebody wanted Rina de Sevigny dead. And when I find out why, I'll know who. The long-lost daughter's the obvious suspect, of course. Especially now that she's turned out to be Rina's heiress."

"That reminds me," said Carla, "is it true that you were a beneficiary, too?"

"Yeah, she left me a painting. That was a surprise."

"I didn't know you knew her that well."

"Jessie and I both knew her, during Jessie's illness."

"Jeez, Boss, next the cops'll be investigating you."

"Yeah, right." Blackthorn brushed this aside. "Okay, I want to know everything there is to know about the Harrington woman—her business, her sex life, her friends, her life with her mother, assuming they ever had a life together. I've ordered Jonas to do one of his infamous computer searches on her. I want to know which side of the bed she sleeps on, her astrological sign, her blood type, her grades in high school, her first boyfriend, her last boyfriend, and what she had for lunch last Tuesday. Think you can handle that?"

"Think you're obsessing a bit?" Carla said dryly. "So we fucked up. It happens."

"Just do it, Murphy," Blackthorn growled.

Was he obsessing? he wondered as she left his office. Maybe, but it was important to get the details right.

Briefly, he thought back over his years with the FBI. His father had been a New York City cop, and law enforcement had been what he'd always wanted to do—ever since childhood.

Vietnam had almost changed that—he'd seen too much violence, too many horrors, and lost his clarity about the difference between the good guys and the bad. After Nam, he'd sometimes thought that the only thing he could do well was kill . . .

That was when the drinking had started. It had only been bad for a few months before he'd realized that he could either sober up or watch his life go down the toilet. He'd chosen the former, graduated NYU with honors, joined the FBI.

They'd been good years, and he'd been good at his job. But you had to be an organization man to advance far up the chain of command, and he was forever being called on the carpet for being too damn independent.

It had been Jessie who'd convinced him to start World Systems Security.

It had been a good move. But losing Jessie had been bad for business. He'd been unable to focus. He'd been overwrought, and he'd made some bad decisions, taken some unfortunate actions . . .

Now he figured he only had one chance to put things right.

Rina de Sevigny was dead.

And anybody could have done it. A relative. A friend. A business associate. A religious fanatic. Someone who'd been helped by her program. Someone who'd been harmed by her program. Someone who believed Power Perspectives was essentially full of shit.

Or Rina's long-lost daughter.

"I still can't understand it," April said. "It's been twenty-eight years since I last saw my mother. Why would she leave her business to me?"

Arthur Stanley shrugged. "She did not take me into her confidence," he said.

Stanley had urged her to come back to his office for a Saturday morning meeting so he could explain to her the terms of Rina's will. He'd just informed her of the extent of her inheritance. It staggered her imagination. Power Perspectives was a multi-million-dollar operation. During the past few years when Rina had become guru to movie stars, politicians, and ordinary people with a yearning for peace in their hearts, the Foundation had been inundated with cash. Stanley told her, with obvious pride, that it was one of the fastest growing private companies in the country.

"The intent of her wishes is clear," he said. "Not only has she left you the company, but she also expects you to run it. Indeed, it was her fondest hope that you would decide to carry on in her place."

"That is out of the question," April said. "I have my own business to run."

"Madame was apparently aware of that," Stanley said.

"In fact, her instructions state that it was your obvious competence at running your own business that convinced her of your talents. She did not make this change because of a sentimental whim. She was convinced that you—and only you—were a fit successor to her."

April shook her head. "She didn't even know me. I'm a different person from the child she left on a dock in New York Harbor."

"It seems that she has followed your progress, particularly in recent years. Of course, she was still a young woman. I'm sure she didn't expect to die so soon. I am reasonably certain that she expected to be in touch soon, and to begin grooming you for the job. It is unfortunate that things have worked out so tragically. It will be difficult for you with the family, I am sure. One or more of them might decide to contest the will. But it was carefully drawn up, and Madame de Sevigny's wishes were clear."

"Her wishes, perhaps. But not mine. I never asked to be my mother's successor."

"I understand." He handed her a slick folder with a glamour shot of Rina smiling on the cover. Inside was a thick sheaf of papers about Power Perspectives. "But I hope when you have read this material that you will change your mind."

April took the material. In truth, she wasn't sure how sincere her protests were. The more she thought about inheriting Rina's business, the more tempting and exciting it was beginning to seem.

"This is all so impersonal," she said to the lawyer. "Besides the business interests, did she leave anything of a personal nature to me?"

"There is a co-op apartment that she owned—or, I should say, that is owned by Power Perspectives. I believe it may have some personal items in it. Otherwise, only this," he said, handing her a large manila envelope. "My instructions were to turn this over personally to you, should anything happen to Madame. I gather from what she told me that it is of sentimental value only. A keepsake, was the term she employed."

April unclipped the envelope and removed a 4-by-6-inch framed photograph of herself and her mother leaning against their cottage that summer on Cape Cod. Rina was clad in short shorts and an oversized man's short-sleeved shirt with the tails knotted about her middle. April was wearing ragged shorts and a Boston Celtics T-shirt. They were both barefoot and April was clutching her baseball glove.

The photograph was faded and the frame was tin. That had been her last carefree summer. Her life until then had been restless and peripatetic, yet she had been happy with her mother.

Stanley cleared his throat. "It is a modest remembrance, but I am sure it was left to you with love."

April shook her head. "Neither the word nor the concept were part of my mother's vocabulary."

The lawyer shrugged.

April rose and paced the office, trying to calm down, to focus. She stopped in front of the window and looked out over the city. To her, New York was a new place. To her mother, it had been the place where she had achieved her highest and most dramatic success. Power Perspectives. Rina de Sevigny's personal empire.

Bequeathed to her only daughter. Whom she had abandoned at the age of twelve.

Why?

She turned. "Mr. Stanley, you seem to know a good deal about the de Sevigny family. Surely you can tell me—at least give me some idea—why Rina would leave this legacy to me instead of to one of them?"

"I have already told you everything I know."

"She apparently believed her life to be in danger, isn't that right? Why else would she have hired a bodyguard?"

The lawyer shrugged.

"Is it possible that she trusted no one in the family? That it's because she didn't trust them that she left her fortune to me—the one person in her life who has had nothing to do with the de Sevigny family?"

"Anything is possible," Stanley said slowly. "But I repeat that Mrs. de Sevigny did not confide her concerns to me."

"Is there anything you can say that will help me? Isobelle seemed quite shocked when she heard the will. I take it she had expected to inherit instead?"

"I don't think it's any secret that she was the chief beneficiary under Madame de Sevigny's prior will. For some reason Rina replaced Isobelle with you."

"And you have no idea why?"

The lawyer shook his head. "I'm sorry, Ms. Harrington."

"Dammit, Mr. Stanley, my mother was murdered. Now I am being asked to step into her place. Before I even consider doing so, I'd like to know something about how to navigate my way through what appears to be a viper's nest!"

He pursed his lips. "You could, I suppose, refuse the legacy. Isobelle would inherit in that case."

"That would certainly be the easy way out for everyone involved." Easy, yes, but nothing worth having had ever come easily to April. "If you'll excuse me, I have some decisions to make."

"Of course."

April returned the photograph to its oversized envelope and hugged it to her chest as she hurried from his office.

"It's worth six thousand pounds, but I doubt if they realize that," Christian de Sevigny said over the phone to his agent in London. "I suggest we offer four and be prepared to go as high as five. If their responses indicate a more sophisticated assessment of the value than I've seen them display in the past, we'll pay them the full six, but no more." He paused. "I'm expecting a bargain here, Giles. That's what I employ you for."

"Of course, sir, and I'm most appreciative of your patronage," Giles replied quickly. "You may rest assured that this matter will be concluded completely to your satisfaction."

Obsequious flunky, Christian thought. "I trust so, Giles," he said, and broke the connection.

Christian leaned back in his leather-padded desk chair in the library of his townhouse on Fifth Avenue and flicked a gold-plated lighter at the end of a cigarette. As he inhaled the mentholated smoke he felt calm descend over him. He wanted the piece—wanted it badly, in fact, since it was a rare example of a particular style of Chinese export porcelain that would make an excellent addition to his collection—but it wasn't worth wasting so much energy over. He had more important things to think about, dammit.

Like the mess his father had gotten them into.

Blowing out smoke, he swiveled his chair around so he was facing his computer screen and called up the relevant financial information. Using his mouse, he flicked through a rapid series of screens. He shook his head. He ground out his cigarette. Shit, he said to himself.

The numbers hadn't changed since this morning.

Not that he'd expected them to.

For the past three months, Christian had been treasurer and chief financial officer of what he had at one time thought of as the de Sevigny empire. Ten years ago when he'd reluctantly begun working for the corporation in a trivial job at his father's insistence, the corporation had been astonishingly successful. What had been started in Marseilles by Christian's great-grandfather at the turn of the century as a small shipping and hauling business had grown over the years into pan-European trucking and international shipping.

The Second World War had paralyzed De Sevigny Ltd., whose headquarters had moved to Paris shortly before the Occupation. The family, several of whose forbears had been Jewish, had fled west to the U.S. and set up shop again in New York. They'd been able to reestablish the Marseilles connection, where the company's largest shipping factories were located, and the business became multinational—and prosperous.

During the fifties and sixties, the de Sevigny corporation, which had resisted all temptation to turn public and had always remained in private, family hands, had expanded into constructing cargo ships, luxury liners, and military transports. Their oil tankers had been ready to transport Middle Eastern oil during the energy crisis of the seventies, and the market for new luxury cruise ships had boomed so mightily during the crazy-spending days of the eighties that they'd expanded the New York subsidiary and essentially moved their base of operations from Paris to here.

Now, though, after several years in a row of tight money, military cutbacks, and global recession, the shipbuilding business was in shambles.

Times had been tough for everyone, but the de Sevignys had suffered more than most because Armand, in his son's considered opinion, had been very foolish about his investments of the corporation's once-impressive profits. Hanging on during recessionary times was something the de Sevignys had done more than once in this century, and there should have been plenty of cushion to accomplish this without struggle. Indeed, there would have been if Armand hadn't poured the company's resources into a series of bizarre ventures, almost all of which had lost horrifying amounts of money.

His father couldn't have had a more devastating effect on de Sevigny Enterprises if he'd planned it.

Dammit, he thought, in spite of everything he missed Rina. She'd been the one levelheaded person around here. On business matters, her advice had always been remarkably sound.

The phone rang again. "Hi, hon," said a familiar feminine voice when he put the receiver to his ear.

"Daisy," Christian said.

"You still got your ass in the saddle, boy? It's late and it's Saturday night. You should get out more, enjoy your youth."

He smiled. Daisy Tulane, widow of a Texas millionaire, had a lovely Southern twang to her voice—it had been one of the attributes that had attracted him to her. Newly fledged as a politician, Daisy had been a close friend of Rina's. As a result of "seizing her power," she was now running for the Senate.

"Speaking of asses," he said, "when are you planning to get yours back to New York? We hardly saw each other at all during the funeral. I was hoping you'd stay for the weekend."

"My schedule's tough, but it's on my mind, believe me. I'm hoping I can slip in next weekend. Maybe not till

Sunday morning. I'm doing one of those charity benefit things in Dallas next Saturday night."

"Need an escort?" he asked, regretting the question as soon as it was out of his mouth. He didn't have the time to fly to Dallas next weekend.

"Well, I'd love one, hon. I was thinking of going in on the arm of the local police commissioner, but I'd can him in a second for the chance to go with you."

Yeah, right, Christian thought cynically. Being tight with the local police would pick her up some votes, which, to Daisy, was probably a lot more important than romance.

"Never mind, I can't do it," he said coldly. "I'm looking at the mountain of work here."

"Poor baby," she said. "I miss you, hon. It's been awhile since we've had any privacy, hasn't it?"

In fact, he thought, they'd never had much privacy. Daisy had whisked in and out of town for Rina's funeral, and they'd only started seeing each other a few weeks before her death. The relationship was still in the early stages, and he'd really like to be with her more often. Daisy was a fascinating woman—strong in so many ways, and yet vulnerable, almost shy, in others. Sexually, in particular. Her husband couldn't have been much of a lover.

There was so much he'd like to introduce her to . . . if only she'd make a little more time available for him.

On the other hand, what he really ought to do was find himself a woman in New York. Maybe even a woman his own age. Or younger.

At forty-nine, Daisy was considerably older than he was. Oh, sure, she didn't look it. She took care of her body and she was graced with lovely, ageless skin. But the fact was, there were bound to be younger, more attractive women available if he only had time to seek them out. No doubt they'd be more compliant as well—and less independent than a rich Texas widow who'd set her sights on a career in national politics.

"How y'all coping, hon?" Daisy asked.

"It's been difficult," Christian said. He could hear that his words were clipped. Christian was aware that people thought of him as cold and overly controlled, which suited him just fine. He'd spent many years learning to contain his emotions, and he was pleased that he'd finally succeeded. "The police and the FBI are hanging around constantly, that asshole bodyguard is asking questions, and the latest is that the long-lost daughter is taking over Power Perspectives—a task she's ill-suited for as far as I can tell."

"Taking it over? What d'you mean?"

"Seems Rina changed her will and April Harrington has inherited the business. Isobelle's bouncing off walls with frustration. It's something to see."

"Darlin', I wish you'd be a little more charitable toward your own sister." Daisy's voice was gently chiding.

"Isobelle and I haven't been charitable towards each other in years."

"Why did the daughter inherit?"

Christian laughed shortly. "Who knows. Rina was unpredictable to the last."

"Have the police made any progress towards finding the killer?"

"None that I can see."

"Well, I sure hope they get him. Your stepmother was the closest friend I ever had. In fact, she—" her voice broke for a second. Christian heard her take a steadying breath. "If it weren't for her, I wouldn't be headed for the Senate. She changed my life, and the thought that her murderer is running around free turns my stomach something fierce."

"Yeah, well, maybe the Dallas police commissioner can

do something about it. They've got a history there of trying to solve mysterious assassinations."

A beat. Then, "You're not jealous, are you, hon? The man is happily married." Her smoky voice devolved into a laugh. "He's also about five-six and two hundred fifty pounds. Not my type, I promise you."

"No," he said impatiently, "I'm not jealous. But if you can fit New York into your busy schedule sometime soon, I'd like to see you. Now I've got to go. I've got another call."

"I'll be there next Sunday morning, hon, I promise. Miss you!"

"Bye," Christian said and dropped the phone back into its cradle.

There was of course no other call.

He lit another cigarette and turned back to his computer screen.

Concentration proved to be impossible, though.

Christian stared into space for several minutes, then pulled out his wallet and searched for the card he and everyone else had received from Agent Martin Clemente, FBI. He noted the number and dialed.

He got an answering machine. He waited for the beep, identified himself, then said, "You asked us to contact you with even the most trivial information, so here's one for your list. It's been a badly kept secret in our family that my stepmother had a brief affair with President Kennedy just before his death. I've never been a conspiracy buff, personally, but what if there was some kind of plot? And what if Rina knew something about it?

"I know it's far-fetched. You'd be better off investigating Rina's clients, not to mention the strange and unpleasant people my sister hangs out with. But I'm sure you don't want to leave any stone unturned."

Christian hung up the phone.

Then he leaned back in his desk chair and smiled.

Chapter Seven

As April entered the building on Park Avenue whose address she had been given over the phone, she was aware of venturing into a world that was very different from what she had seen so far in New York.

There were doormen at many buildings, but this one was as prim and correct as a British butler. She'd expected to have to explain who she was, but he knew her.

"The elevator will take you right up, Madame," he told her and ushered her into a large, dark-wood paneled elevator with a plush oriental carpet on the floor.

"Which apartment?" she asked.

He smiled gravely. "It's the penthouse, Madame," he said.

There were no controls that she could see on the inside of the elevator. It must have been controlled by the doorman, however, since it sped her directly up to the penthouse on the twenty-second floor.

She stepped off the elevator into a small room papered in a Chinese design. A large blue-and-white porcelain vase stood on a pedestal beside a tall double door. There was a brass knocker on the door that was as large as an andiron. April was about to see if she could lift it when the door opened and she was greeted by a middle-aged uniformed maid.

"Ms. Harrington? Welcome. Do come in." She had a British accent and April had to repress the thought that she looked very similar to Jean Marsh from *Upstairs Downstairs*.

This was an apartment on the twenty-second floor? It looked more like the ground floor of a mansion. The front door opened directly into a large gallery, complete with Roman pillars on either side, and several yards ahead of her a wide grand staircase swept upward to another floor. The floor underfoot was black marble, and there were faded, yet beautiful tapestries hanging on the walls. One showed a hunting scene, complete with sylvan woods and horsemen; the other was an exquisite representation of the Judgment of Paris.

The maid took April's cardigan and hung it out of sight behind a massive oak door that April assumed must hide a closet. "Monsieur awaits you upstairs," she announced. "Please follow me."

"Would you do me the honor of joining me for dinner this evening?" Armand de Sevigny had said on the telephone this morning after the reading of her mother's will. He had been very courtly, and it had been impossible to refuse.

Besides, she was curious.

They were partway up the staircase when Armand appeared at the top and began descending to meet her. "Miss Harrington, welcome!" He nodded to the maid and said, "That'll do, Anna. We really needn't stand on ceremony so much around here."

Anna climbed on past him while Armand held out his

hand to April. "The servants take themselves much too seriously," he whispered with a smile. "They have me terrorized!"

"I doubt that very much," April said, also smiling.

"Sabrina knew how to manage them, but I don't." His expression grew somber. "I can't believe she's gone."

April squeezed his hand. "I'm sorry."

"This must be an exceedingly strange situation for you, April. May I call you April instead of Miss Harrington?"

"Of course."

"I hope you were not too upset by what happened yesterday at the lawyer's office. My daughter behaved regrettably."

"It was a shock to everyone," April said.

The hallway at the top of the stairs opened into a huge living room. The colors were muted, the furnishings elegant, and the lighting low. Armand ushered her to the sofa; he remained standing until she was comfortably seated, then took the easy chair opposite her.

"Thank you for coming," he said.

"Thank you for asking me."

"Anyway, as I was saying, this is an awkward situation for you. I have my children to offer their support. You are in this alone."

From what April had seen of his children, she couldn't imagine that too much support would be forthcoming, but she kept this thought to herself. "I'm used to it," she said without rancor. "I've been fending for myself for a good many years." She shrugged. "It's been good for me."

"Yes. You strike me as strong, self-assured, and independent. Sabrina, I'm sure, would have admired those qualities in you."

April drew a quick breath. "She chose her own path."

He nodded. "But not entirely without regret. I would like you to be able to understand that, someday."

April saw little hope of that.

He turned the conversation to other matters, and after a few minutes she found herself relaxing and enjoying his company. He proved to be an adept conversationalist— witty and knowledgeable—and his courtliness shone through in his every word, his every gesture. His twinkle-eyed charm reminded April of an old Maurice Chevalier movie. His French accent was clear, but not thick; in many ways Armand seemed very Americanized.

He bore little in common with the man whom she vaguely remembered as the suave and dashing lover who had sailed off with her mother, leaving her standing alone on a New York City dock. It was as if he had softened with age instead of hardening the way most people did.

"And now, if you will permit me—" Armand led the way into a dining room that was large enough for a diplomatic banquet "—I suggest we eat. I find it difficult to concentrate on business when my stomach is empty. Plus, I would like to get to know you better."

As it turned out, it wasn't until the entree had been cleared away and the coffee served that Armand shifted the discussion to what April suspected was the real reason they were together this evening.

"Have you given any consideration yet to coming to work for us at Power Perspectives?" he asked.

"I haven't had much chance to think about it."

"I suspect that when all is said and done, your impulse will be to decline." He paused. "But, if I may, I would like to urge you to accept."

April put down the cup she had just raised to her lips. "Forgive my surprise, but I would have wagered a month's income that you'd invited me here tonight to try to talk me into declining."

He tipped his head slightly to one side and smiled gravely. "If you will permit me, I would like to try to explain. You see, I loved your mother very much. Her business meant everything to her—indeed, it was far more than a business. It was a vocation. She has helped so many people—both individually and in groups. But none of it could have been accomplished if it were not for her inspired leadership."

He stopped, sipped his coffee, then continued more slowly, as if somewhat reluctant to go on, "As you know, I have two children, Christian and Isobelle. They are both exceptional in their own way, but neither of them, I fear, well—" He shrugged, looking pained. "What I mean to say is that neither my son nor my daughter strikes me as a suitable replacement for your mother at the helm of Power Perspectives."

"Why not?"

"You will hear of these things anyway, so I might as well be entirely forthright. My son and I have had some conflict between us over the years." He shook his head sadly. "I have never understood him. He keeps such a tight hold on his emotions, you see. But recently he has been doing an excellent job working for De Sevigny Ltd. One day I hope to make him my successor. He had never been interested in Power Perspectives and therefore there would have been no point whatsoever in Sabrina's naming him."

"But what about your daughter?"

Again, Armand shook his head. "Isobelle has a good head for business. But she lacks discipline. She has always run with the wrong crowd, as I believe you say. Her choice of friends leaves much to be desired. In truth," he added with a sigh, "she has caused me much heartache and worry over the years. You have read, of course, your great English playwright, Shakespeare?"

April nodded.

"Sadly, I have felt in recent years much empathy for the great King Lear. 'How sharper than a serpent's tooth it is to have a thankless child!' "

"I see." Armand, she sensed, was a dramatic man, who would not hesitate to grandstand emotionally if it were to bring the desired response. Courteously, she said, "But what has any of that to do with your daughter's business acumen? Unlike your son, Isobelle seems quite an emotional woman. If passion is necessary to lead the Foundation, surely this is something your daughter possesses in full measure."

"Passion must always be balanced." He was speaking with more ease and fluency now. "In my son and daughter I have two opposite sides of the spectrum. One is ice, the other fire. I seek some element that is between the two, blending passion with good judgment." He steepled his fingers and rested his chin upon them. "That is why I am so impressed with you."

"Excuse me, but what do you know of me, monsieur?"

"I have done some checking, my dear. I know that you have successfully started and run your own business, and that you are highly respected for what you do. You are considered an expert by your colleagues, and you are very well-liked by your employees and friends."

April twisted her cup on the table. Everyone, it seemed, was checking into her past—the police, the FBI, Blackthorn, the de Sevignys. How far back, she wondered, were they checking? How much would they find out?

"I wish I knew as much about you as you apparently know about me," she said a bit testily.

"I would like to give you that opportunity. That is part of the purpose of this meeting." He opened his hands in a gesture of willingness. "Please. Ask me anything you like."

"Well," she took a deep breath and looked him directly

in the eye. "Maybe you could begin by explaining how you justified separating a mother from her only child?"

He returned her gaze. "There is no way to justify it," he said. "I was young and selfish. The same could probably be said for Sabrina. She led me to believe that you and she were not—" he stopped and shrugged. "Well. Let's just say she seized an opportunity to escape from a life of hardship, a life she was never suited for. We both thought that in sending you to an exclusive boarding school we were giving you an advantage that she had never had." He paused. "But what you really needed, of course, was our love, a sense of family, a feeling of belonging. It is much easier to see that now, in retrospect."

He paused again, gazing at her with sympathy etched on his aristocratic features. "If it's not too late, I want to offer you now some of what you were deprived of as a child. I say this with complete sincerity. I know that the past cannot be erased, but I would like to try to make amends in whatever way I can. And I know that this is what Sabrina would have wanted me to do."

He reached across the table and took one of her cold hands gently into his. "Come and work for us, April. Please. Life is offering you an exciting new adventure. And I am asking for a chance to make up for some of my past follies before I, too, slip into the silence of the grave."

April felt herself wavering. He sounded very much in earnest in his regrets about the past. His eyes looked directly into hers, and she began to have a sense of what must have so attracted her mother.

"I'll need more time to think about it. Until yesterday such a possibility had never occurred to me. I have a business back in Boston. What would happen to that?"

"And you have a partner, no? Surely he could run the

bookstore for a few months while you see how you like working with us."

"It does seem unfair to Isobelle. If she expected—"

"Isobelle had always expected far too much."

April had nothing to say to that. The family dynamics were not yet clear to her.

"Take a few days, by all means," he said. "You have many unanswered questions, I'm sure, both about Power Perspectives and about your mother. You didn't know your mother well, did you?" he added in a neutral tone.

"Obviously not."

"She was a complex woman. I loved her dearly, make no mistake about that. But she could be—" he paused as if seeking the right word "—difficult."

April waited. She hoped he would elaborate as he eventually had about his children, but instead of continuing, he gave another shrug. "Perhaps the best way for you to get to know her is to have a look at the place where she lived. I will give you the key to Sabrina's apartment. It was her private sanctuary, and has been left entirely as it was when she was using it."

April raised her eyebrows. "I thought—you mean she didn't live with you?"

Armand smiled and shook his head. "No, I see I have not made myself clear. Sabrina lived with me, of course, but she also maintained a place of her own. A small apartment on the Upper West Side. It was initially the headquarters of Power Perspectives, until the Foundation grew so large that she had to acquire professional office space. Sabrina kept the apartment to use as her office space, where she could be alone to think, to plan, to meditate." He opened his hands. "She used to describe it as a room of her own."

"Important to every woman," April said with a smile.

"Yes, so every woman tells me. I could show you

around, but perhaps a better idea might be simply to give you the key. You see, it was her private place. It is alien to me, in a way. I've been over there of course to go through her papers and sort out her affairs, but otherwise I've left everything the way she kept it."

She presumed he was referring to the co-op apartment that the attorney had mentioned—the one which was actually owned by Power Perspectives and part of Rina's legacy to her. Had it been ethical of Armand to go through the papers and other personal items contained in the apartment? she wondered. As her husband, he may have felt that he had the right to do so. Given what had happened, the police had probably been through the place, too.

"I'd very much like to see it," she said.

"Would you like to go now? Tonight? Do you think it might help you make up your mind about Power Perspectives?"

She told him yes. Anything that would give her more insight into her mother would help her make up her mind.

"I'll have my driver drop you off there as soon as we finish our coffee." Armand reached into his pocket and removed a set of keys. "This, I believe, will open both the inside and the outside doors. There is a doorman. I'll phone over to him so he will be expecting you."

"Thanks," she said as he put the brass keys into her hand.

"Please spend as long a time there as you desire. After all, technically, the apartment is yours now. And remember, if you come to work for us, you'll need a place to live."

How odd, thought April. It was as if she were taking over her mother's life—first her job and now her apartment.

Just as long as you don't die the way she did.

Chapter Eight

"I hate my father," Kate de Sevigny muttered to herself as she rode up in the elevator of the apartment building where Gran used to live. She'd been repeating the words like a litany ever since fleeing her own home where she lived with her father and catching a cab. The driver had looked at her funny until she'd pulled a fistful of cash out of the pocket of her jeans, then he'd hopped to it fast enough.

"He's such a fuck-up," she added as she got off the elevator on the tenth floor and hurried down the corridor to Gran's door. Well. What used to be Gran's door.

I miss you, Gran! she thought.

It was almost 10:00 at night, and Dad would take a hissy when he got home and found her gone. Good. She hoped he got really worried. She hoped he called all the hospitals and funeral homes. She hoped every cop in the city started looking for a skinny seventh-grader with yucky brown hair who hated her dad.

'Cause they weren't gonna find her.

Once inside the apartment, Kate headed for the spare room that Gran had always let her use when she visited. She dumped her backpack there, then went next door to Gran's room to see what they'd done to it.

They'd been through it—that was much evident as soon as she looked around. Gran had been very particular about where she kept her things. Looked like they had all been moved.

What losers, she thought. Couldn't they just leave her stuff alone?

During the last couple of years since Gran had been spending so much time in New York, this place had been Kate's refuge. She'd even skip school sometimes to come and visit Gran. And the best part of it was that nobody knew. Dad didn't like Gran much. He always said nasty things about her behind her back. She suspected that Gran wasn't too wild about Dad, either, although she was careful not to say so. But she listened sympathetically whenever Kate poured out her misery and unhappiness.

Gran had been such a good listener.

It wasn't fair that she was dead!

Not that things were ever fair. She'd learned that two years ago when Mom had been killed in that car wreck. Before that she'd never even known that people you knew and loved could die. And now it was pretty clear when you looked around at all the lousy things that happened in the world that fairness had not been too high on God's great list of benefits to humankind. Assuming there was a God, which Kate wasn't so sure about.

But Gran's death hadn't been some awful random accident. She'd been murdered. Shot, just like on TV. Dad had said that a professional hit man had shot her, probably somebody who'd been paid to do it, although nobody knew by whom or why and so far the cops hadn't done much to solve it. They probably never would. Someone had killed Gran, and it looked like they were going to get away with it.

Well, not if I have anything to do with it, Kate thought.

Kate returned to the guest room and curled up on the bed. She pulled the familiar comforter around her. From her backpack she pulled out the laptop computer that had belonged to Gran and switched it on. Maybe if she wrote for a while, she'd be able to see things more clearly.

"The Mystery of the Murdered Grandmother," she typed at the top of a brand-new file. She looked at it then shook her head. Made you think of an old white-haired lady clubbed by a teenage gang while she was doing her knitting. Gran was a grandmother, but she hadn't looked like one.

She deleted the line. "Murder at the Podium," she typed instead. Now that sounded much better. Kate had learned the details of the shooting by questioning Delores, Gran's secretary, who had tearfully spit them out after much prodding. While they had seemed to disgust Delores, Kate had been insistent about knowing such things as the kind of gun that had been used (Delores had had no idea) and the appearance of the wound in Gran's head (Delores had scolded Kate for asking—apparently twelve-year-old girls weren't supposed to want information about such things).

Kate wanted information about everything. She wanted the entire world to be open to her. Most of what she wanted to learn was the good stuff, like all the wonderful art at the Metropolitan Museum of Art and all the great literature in the New York City Public Library—both of which she haunted on a regular basis. But she also wanted to know that bad stuff as well. She wanted to understand human nature. You couldn't be a great writer if you didn't know what would make your characters tick.

And more than anything, Kate wanted to be a writer. She didn't know if she could be a great one, but she certainly intended to try.

All writers should keep a journal, Gran had said. A few days later she had solemnly presented Kate with a leather-bound book inscribed on the front with her full name—Katerine Marie-Claudine de Sevigny. The book was beautiful, but she hated the name almost as much as she hated the father who had stuck her with it. The other kids made fun of her. "You gotta be some kinda weirdo or lesbo with a name like that," Barney Chassen had taunted her last year.

Kate had attacked Barney Chassen and made him pay for this insult with her fists. Last year she could have beaten up most of the boys in the sixth grade. Only a couple of them had been as tall as she was and none was as scrappy. This year, though, well, secondary school was more dignified. You didn't go around beating up boys the way you had in grammar school, no matter how much you wanted to. You had to try to be a little more mature.

She hated being mature, though. She'd started getting her period six months ago and it was awful. All that blood and you never knew when it would hit. It was disgusting, really. God must have made a big mistake when he'd invented women's reproductive systems.

Which proved God—if he existed—was a male. If She were a female, She'd have come up with a system that didn't require one week per month of those disgusting sanitary pads.

Yawning hugely, Kate focused once again on the small screen of the laptop. She'd been trying to keep a journal, but she'd been writing it here instead of in the book Gran had given her. It was so much faster to write on a computer, and she'd always thought the laptop was a pretty neat one. She didn't think Gran would mind that she wasn't using the official journal, but had instead appropriated her computer.

Kate was going to be a writer when she grew up, but in order to be one she'd better get cracking. No one ever got to be a writer by staring at a blank page and daydreaming about other things.

She was going to write a novel about what had happened to Gran. Of course she'd change the names and everything. But the big difference would be that in her novel, the crime would get solved. She'd make the police smarter and more dedicated than they were in real life. The chief investigator on the case would be a woman, of course. She'd have the usual trouble getting respect from the male chauvinists she worked with, but eventually her brains and her courage and her determination would impress them and they'd give her their respect and affection. Together she and her men would examine all the clues and unmask the killer. Justice would prevail.

"Murder at the Podium." Good title. She set aside the laptop and curled up on the bed to think about what would happen in the first chapter. It would be similar to what had happened in real life.

As she drifted into sleep, Kate thought of how she was going to solve the murder and capture the killer, all by herself.

Daddy would be proud of her then.

Having seen the de Sevigny residence on Park Avenue, April was somewhat surprised when Armand's driver dropped her off at the high-rise on West Sixty-Second Street opposite Lincoln Center shortly before eleven o'clock. Several yuppie residents who appeared to be her own age and younger were congregated in the downstairs lobby, suggesting not Old World wealth and manners, but the high energy of a fast-paced contemporary lifestyle.

She identified herself to the doorman and was waved unceremoniously towards the elevators. "Tenth floor," he told her, and she noticed as she entered the elevator that there were twenty-eight floors. Rina's apartment was clearly not the penthouse.

She found the right door at the end of a hallway and used the key Armand had given her to unlock it. She entered a modern apartment, spacious and airy. To the left was a large L-shaped living room, furnished with two modern, low-slung but cozy-looking sofas covered in soft green. The oriental rug was ivory with vines and tendrils that were subtly picked up in the wall paper. There were several large plants that gave the room a refined jungle atmosphere.

Through a large picture window in the living room, April could see the lights of the Metropolitan Opera House and, in the distance beyond them, the shore of New Jersey across the black waters of the Hudson River.

April glanced at the curtains, wondering how often Rina changed them. She remembered the various tiny "housekeeping cottages" and one-room apartments where they'd lived together, the dancing new curtains revealing each change in Rina's love life. Had she stopped taking new lovers when she'd married Armand? He was a charming, dynamic man. Thirty years ago he must have been an extremely handsome and sexy man as well. Had he been enough for her or had she never abandoned her freewheeling ways?

If she had been unfaithful, could this have been a motive for her murder? She'd taken her own separate apartment, a room of her own. Did that suggest that she'd needed a place to meet a lover?

Were the police examining this possibility? Armand had mentioned during their dinner that he had spent several hours answering questions from the authorities this morning. Was he a suspect?

They were all suspects.

Particularly in a case like this one, where large sums of money were at stake, everyone close to the deceased was bound to be considered a suspect.

She began to explore.

Kate woke up suddenly. The room was dark, and for a moment she had no idea where she was. Everything seemed alien and strange.

She reached for her favorite stuffed dog to cuddle but her hands came up empty. She pushed herself up, confused. She could see that she was in a bedroom and that the furniture was looming all around her as if it had a life of its own.

Then she remembered. Gran's house. She'd run away— again. Another fight with Daddy. Seemed like all she did these days was get into arguments with Daddy.

So here she was at Gran's, just like a million times before, except Gran was dead, and—

If she's dead, how come there are noises coming from her bedroom?

Her heart started slogging as Kate realized that it must have been the noises that had awakened her so suddenly. Someone was in the apartment. They were moving around in there.

The killer, she thought. He'd come here to go through Gran's stuff. Maybe he wasn't a hired professional. Maybe he was someone she'd known, someone who could be linked to him. Maybe he was searching for crucial evidence that needed to be destroyed.

If so, he'd search this room as well.

And if he was searching, there would be no place to hide.

Kate crept from the bed, straightening the comforter as well as she could in the dark. She did not dare turn on a light.

She peered around. Not the closet—he'd look in there for sure. Behind the curtains? No, they were too thin; she'd show. Sneaking out of the apartment somehow was probably the wisest course, but what if he came out into the hall just as she entered it?

She padded over to the door, which she had left open halfway, and touched it. Her fingers were slick with sweat. To her surprise, she saw that the lights down the hall in the living room were on. Whoever the killer was, he wasn't being very discreet.

What if it was somebody from the family? Wasn't that what the cops always said on TV—that most murderers were known to their victims? Jeez, maybe one of her own relatives was a coldblooded killer. Maybe Daddy had done it.

Great, she thought. It was one thing to hate your father because you were confused and unhappy and full of what the adults loftily called hormones, but it was something else to wonder if he might actually be a murderer. Daddy and Gran were always arguing about something. Well, as always, Daddy didn't have much to say that wasn't sarcastic and cold. Gran had done most of the arguing. It had been one of the things Kate had always liked about Gran— she actually talked. You might not always agree with everything she had to say, but at least you knew what she felt about everything. With Daddy it was harder to tell.

A door closed and Kate heard the sounds of footsteps coming toward her. Too late to escape! There was nothing to do but hide behind the door and hope for a chance to slip out while the killer was right here in the room . . .

She pressed herself flat against the wall, trying to fight an illogical desire to step forward and give herself up to whatever fate awaited her. It would be less humiliating than to be caught cowering here. I wish I were braver, she thought. If I were the heroine of a novel, I'd be doing something clever instead of hiding behind the door!

The door to her bedroom swung inward, sheltering her behind it. Heels clicked on the hardwood floor. High heels, she realized. The killer was a woman!

She must have touched the switch because the room was flooded by light from the fixture overhead. And then she did what they never did on TV—she turned around and closed the door.

The woman gasped and Kate yelped as she propelled herself away from the wall like a swimmer pushing off from the end of the pool. She lowered her head and butted the woman smack in the middle of her body, knocking her backwards. Kate ended up sprawled on top of her, scrambling to get back up and run away.

But before she could do so, the woman grabbed her.

"Let me go!" Kate screamed, and started digging in with her claws. She must have bitten them down, though, because they didn't seem to be doing any good at all. This lady was strong. Kate was astonished at the power of her grip as she rolled her over, stuck her knee into Kate's crotch, and jammed her down on her back just like one of those bullies in a gang or something.

Looking up from where she was pinned to the floor, Kate blinked in disbelief. Her captor was soft-looking and pretty. She had auburn hair, and it was that thick blunt texture that Kate had always longed for. Blue eyes. Fat lips like the models in those putrid lipstick ads. She was wearing this frilly lace blouse and a short skirt and jewelry and stockings. She didn't look like a coldblooded killer.

"You're just a kid," the woman said.

"Fuck you," said Kate.

"A foul-mouthed kid," the woman amended. "Who are you?"

"I belong here," Kate cried. "Who are you?"

The woman considered. Kate thought she could detect some curiosity in those soft blue eyes. "Are you a member of the family?"

"This is my grandmother's place so I guess I've got every right to be here." Kate seized on a possibility: "I suppose you're here to try to sell it or something. Like, before she's even cold in her grave."

"Your grandmother?"

There was a pause while the woman looked her over. She seemed doubtful now, and Kate took advantage of the moment by beginning to squirm again. The woman tightened her grip. Not a real estate agent, then, thought Kate. Real estate agents were wimps.

Coldly, the woman said, "Rina de Sevigny has no grandchildren."

"Uh, stepgrandmother, actually," Kate amended. "We weren't actually related."

The weird look in those blue eyes cleared. "In that case, you must be Christian de Sevigny's daughter? I'd heard that he had one. But—" she paused "—you weren't at the funeral, were you?"

Deep inside her, something clenched as all the tension Kate had been suffering threatened to give way and burst out of her. "I wanted to be there," she said in a shaky voice. "More than anything. But he wouldn't let me go. He's like, 'It'll be better if you don't go.' And I'm, like, 'But I want to go.' And he doesn't care because he's, like, 'You'll have to trust me because I'm your father and I know more about these things than you do.' Which is total bullshit. He doesn't know anything. He doesn't know me."

Kate couldn't believe she was actually spouting this garbage, and to some stranger, as well, some stranger who was sitting on her, but she couldn't seem to stop herself.

"He tells me he went to his mother's funeral when he was a kid and that it was horrible and he got scared because they made him kiss her dead body or something and that he'd never gotten over it. But I don't see what that has to do with anything. I'm not him. I had a right to go to my own grandmother's funeral! He's an asshole. I hate him."

Somewhere in the course of this narrative, the woman had taken most of her weight off Kate. She realized she could sit up if she wanted to. She wasn't sure if she did want to. She was so tired, and she felt like she was going to cry any second. That would be so humiliating!

But the strange woman's eyes were kind now, and her face alert and sympathetic, and Kate couldn't seem to stem the tide of words that were flowing out of her. "We always fight," she went on. "We had a fight tonight and I ran away. I always used to come here if things got too bad and Gran used to listen to me. She was good that way. She didn't treat me like a stupid kid. He always treats me like some kind of retard or something. He's, like, 'You can't do that because you're too young,' and I'm like, 'Stop treating me like a child,' and he's like, 'As long as you're under eighteen and under my roof you'll do as I say,' and I'm like, 'Fuck you, Daddy, I hate you' only I don't say that out loud because he'd probably beat me or something and then I'd get mad and call the cops and have him arrested for child abuse."

"Whew," the woman said. She was kneeling on the floor beside Kate. She was holding both of Kate's hands in hers. "This may sound crazy," she said, "but I understand exactly how you feel."

"I don't even know why I'm telling you this," Kate said miserably. "I don't even know who you are or what you're doing in my grandmother's apartment in the middle of the night."

"I'm here because I was having dinner with your grandfather this evening and he gave me the key. My name is April Harrington."

This didn't help much.

"Hasn't anybody told you about me?" April Harrington asked.

"Nobody ever tells me anything."

"Me neither," the woman said with a sigh. She rolled over and got up slowly from the floor. She was graceful in the way that Kate hated. Once again she was tempted to bolt, but once again her curiosity was too strong.

"Rina de Sevigny was my mother. She sent me to boarding school when I was about your age so she could marry Armand. They went to live in Paris. I stayed in this country, in Connecticut, in a school run by nuns. I hated it. Used to run away all the time. When they found me, they'd thrash me. That ever happen to you?"

Kate shook her head, her eyes wide. "People are always threatening to thrash me but nobody ever does. I didn't mean that about Daddy. He yells but he never hits. First he yells and then he makes me go to the therapist."

"How do you like your therapist?"

"He sucks."

April Harrington nodded as if hearing that a therapist sucked was routine. Kate decided she liked her. "I sorta did hear about you," she admitted. "If you're the one who claims to be Gran's daughter. They didn't tell me your name. But the whole family's talking about you, that's for sure." ·

"I can imagine."

"What I heard was, you murdered Gran," Kate said. "Like you didn't actually shoot her, but you hired the guy who did."

"Yes, I've heard that one, too." She smiled and pushed one long lock of hair behind her left ear. "I run a mystery bookstore so people seem to think that makes me an expert on murder."

"What's a mystery bookstore?" said Kate. "You mean it's all full of mystery novels?"

April Harrington nodded.

"I love mystery novels," Kate said.

"Me, too, but a book's a book. This is real. There are people who really think I'm a murderer." She shook her head. "It's horrible."

"Why would you kill your own mother?" Kate asked.

The pretty woman shook her head. She looked away, focusing on something across the room. Shit, thought Kate. She knew that look. It was the never-mind-I've-already-said-too-much look. She hated that look.

"I don't mean you did," said Kate. "I was just wondering why anybody would."

"Well, I suppose one reason might be that when I was your age, she never had time for me. I hated her for that. Just like you say you hate your father. More, probably."

Kate nodded, wondering if she'd hated her mother enough to want revenge after all these years. Enough to kill. She couldn't imagine hating anybody that much.

"Also, I've inherited her business," April Harrington went on. "I didn't want it; it's not even something I've ever been interested in——this New Agey self-help sort of stuff—but it's apparently worth millions and any time an inheritance is worth millions, you have a motive for murder."

"Only if you know you're going to get the millions," said Kate. "Did you know?"

April smiled and shook her head. "You're a smart kid," she said. "No, I didn't know. I'd had no contact with her—or with anybody who knew her or her business affairs—for many years. But so far I haven't managed to convince the police of that. I think your grandfather believes me, but so far he's the only one."

Kate studied her face. There was something about her . . . she didn't know exactly what it was, but it was a strong feeling. She liked her. It was probably a stupid way to feel. It was the murderers you liked that were the truly dangerous ones. They were the ones who slipped under your defenses and slit your throat when you least expected it. It was dangerous to like somebody before you even knew them.

"I believe you," she heard herself say.

April Harrington smiled and gave her a warm, tight hug.

It was late before April left the apartment that had been used by her mother. Kate had shown her around, telling her anecdotes about Rina's life, and her own, as they moved from room to room. April had learned that Kate loved to write, and dreamed of being a novelist. And that she also loved drawing and painting, and that one of her favorite things to do on a rainy day was hang out in the Metropolitan Museum of Art and study—"really get into the pictures, you know?"

Somewhere in the course of all this April had realized

that she was beginning to care about the twelve-year-old girl who reminded her very much of herself at the same age.

Kate, like April, was an only child. She had lost one of her parents, and she clearly had a conflict-ridden relationship with the parent who was left. She was bright and imaginative and poised on the brink of life. So full of potential that could so easily be squandered.

Rina had apparently tried to give to Kate what she had failed to give to her own daughter.

Now she was gone, failing, as usual, to be there when she was needed.

But this girl, April decided, was not going to be abandoned. Nothing horrible was going to happen to her.

Maybe it wasn't the best reason in the world for making a complete change in her life.

Maybe it wasn't even the real reason.

But something had changed in her even before Rina's death . . . something that had enabled her to journey to Anaheim in the first place, to enter that seminar room, and to stand up and confront her mother.

Her life was nothing to be proud of so far, anyway. Yes, she had a small, successful business. She had friends. But she had no decent relationships with members of the opposite sex, and she remained haunted by a past that she couldn't change and that she must come to terms with.

No more waffling. Time to act.

In the morning she would call Armand de Sevigny and inform him that she intended to accept the position of head of Power Perspectives.

Part Two

Part Two

Chapter Nine

The Madison Avenue office of Power Perspectives was modern, bright, and thoroughly upbeat, despite the tragic death of its founder.

On the morning that April arrived there for the first time, she was greeted with an enthusiasm from the staff that she couldn't believe was sincere. She was a stranger. They must have heard the rumors that she had been a suspect in Rina's death. She had expected to be met with hostility and suspicion.

Instead, everyone from Charles Ripley to all the clerical workers gave her a warm welcome. There were smiles, handshakes, even hugs.

Ripley, she quickly realized, was the orchestrator of her welcome. He had been her mother's right-hand man. He was a handsome young man of about thirty with a winsome smile.

He accompanied her into the large, sunny office that had been Rina's and was to be hers now. "We want you to feel entirely at home," he said. "Please feel free to order anything you'd like for this office in order to make it your own. You can toss out all the furniture, replace it with something new if that would suit you. I can give you the names of several decorators."

"That won't be necessary," April said, looking around her in amazement and pleasure. The office was fresh and simple, with softly muted pinks and greens accenting the basic ivory of the walls and curtains. "The room is lovely the way it is."

"Rina did all her own decorating," Ripley said. "She had a marvelous visual sense."

April thought of her mother decorating their cottage with tacky photos of Hollywood stars clipped from movie magazines.

"She was an extraordinary woman in every respect," he added.

This, she noted, was what everybody seemed to think. Rina was talented. Rina was charismatic. Rina was generous. Rina was the Most Wonderful Woman in the World.

"You must miss her very much," said April.

"Yes. I do."

Am I the only one, she wondered, who knows Rina was a fraud?

"You'll want to get acclimated as quickly as possible, I'm sure," Ripley said. "I've left some of the company's material here for you." He pointed to a colored brochure that sat prominently displayed on the desk. Power Perspectives—the Key to Inner Strength and Outward Success, it read.

"And of course, there's this." Ripley touched the button of a small tape recorder that was on April's desk. Upbeat music flooded the room. It blasted out for several energizing seconds, then dropped to a softer register.

"We all have a limitless source of power within us," said Rina's voice on the videotape. "Deep inside we are all creative, dynamic, electric individuals. The trick is learning to tap into our own power. To channel it outward until it lights us up with an irresistible inner glow!"

It sounded familiar. April remembered that Rina had said something very similar during her presentation at the American Booksellers Association convention just before she'd been shot.

"In order to improve your relationships, you must take control of your own power. You must acknowledge your own unique strengths. And most of all, you must change your negative beliefs about yourself."

The same spiel. It was upon these platitudes that the Foundation had been built. Pep-talking had made Rina and her associates rich, admired, and respected.

April reached over and pressed the off switch. You must take control of your own power. She looked up at Charles Ripley and smiled. "Thank you, Charles," she said. "This is all a little new to me, and I appreciate your help."

"Please call me Charlie. Everyone does."

"Okay. Now if you could leave me alone here for a few minutes. There's so much for me to get accustomed to."

"Okay, take your time," he said genially, and left.

April studied her surroundings—the comfortable yet utilitarian furniture, the abstract art on the walls, the luxurious pale-green carpet. Quite a difference from the cramped storeroom in the rear of her bookstore where books were stacked to the ceiling. She had squeezed an old roll-top desk into one corner, using it to do her accounts . . .

She sighed. There was no going back. She had taken this opportunity to turn the Poison Pen Bookshop over, temporarily at least, to Brian. He'd been so enthusiastic about it that she'd had to laugh.

The intercom on her desk buzzed. "Call for you, Ms. Harrington," someone said.

She picked up the receiver from the console. "So," said a familiar male voice. "I see that you are indeed benefiting from your mother's death."

Blackthorn.

"I decided to accept the position, yes," April said slowly.

"How sad for the Boston mystery novel business. It doesn't matter to you, apparently, that Isobelle has worked hard for this, that she wants it, that it's vitally important to her?"

"Perhaps it seems unfair," she said carefully. "But my mother—" she put the faintest of stress on the words "—must have had some reason why she left the controlling interest in Power Perspectives to me. Besides, I was asked to take the position by Armand de Sevigny himself." She paused then added, "By the way, Mr. Blackthorn, you failed to mention to me that you were more than just a professional associate of the de Sevigny family. It certainly makes your hostility a little clearer to me."

"I wouldn't exactly characterize myself as close to the family—" he paused "—any more than you would."

"You were apparently close to Rina. You were named in her will. In fact, for all I know, you're angry because Power Perspectives wasn't left to you."

Silence on the line. Then Blackthorn chuckled and said, "I'm trying to picture it. Me, running an inspirational self-help organization for troubled folks all over the world. Hell, I have trouble enough getting myself through the day without advising others on how to do it." His tone grew more serious as he added, "No, Ms. Harrington, I'm not interested in what happens to Rina's company. But I am interested in seeing her murderer brought to justice."

"I hope you succeed," she said tightly.

"I intend to." He paused, then added, "And I warn you, Ms. Harrington. I'm going to be there, watching you, dogging your steps. I am far from satisfied with your account of your role in this entire thing. There is something about you that just doesn't add up, and I intend to find out what it is."

April slammed down the phone.

From deep inside her, dark memories erupted. Washington, D.C., the summer of 1969. She'd been a homeless runaway . . . sixteen years old . . .

I shouldn't be here, she thought.

This is madness.

They'll find out.

April spent the rest of her first day at Power Perspectives familiarizing herself with the staff, the office environment, and the Foundation's general operating procedures. Both Charlie Ripley and Delores Delgrecco, who had been Rina's secretary, went out of their way to be helpful and informative. Delores was an attractive, if tough-looking young woman with a thick Noo Yawk accent who managed to make it clear from the moment they met that she'd taken no shit from Rina and would take no shit from April either.

"I'm good ad my job, so whad'dya wand from me?" she'd said when they were introduced. Somehow she managed to sound cocky but not obnoxious. "Just ask and y'ill geddid, no sweat, no problem."

"Thanks," April had said.

"Hey, doncha even mention nid."

April listened to tapes and viewed videos. She attended a brainstorming session on the next two-week Power Perspectives Advanced Seminar that was now being put together for next February. A convention hotel on Maui had already been secured, but it was unclear whether the block of rooms that had been contracted for would be sufficient. Business was booming, and there was a new book and video due out in the fall that might propel reservations for the seminars over the top.

"It's sad and ironic," said Charlie during the meeting, "but the publicity that surrounded Rina's mysterious death has brought us even more into the public eye. We're going to have to take it into consideration as we plan next year's events."

It was incredible what people would pay for advice and methods on getting their lives in order, April thought. A phenomenal number of people needed to know how to develop their potential for wealth, success, and happiness. And for this they were willing to pay handsomely.

"We'll teach you the secret of taking control of your own power," April muttered. "Pull out your checkbooks and sign on the dotted line."

In the middle of the afternoon she received a call from Marjory "Daisy" Tulane, the former lieutenant governor of Texas, who was running for the Senate. April had met her briefly at the funeral and been struck by the woman's great personal warmth and charm. Daisy had participated in the most famous of Rina's thirty-minute infomercials, speaking passionately about the way Power Perspectives had changed her life and urging viewers to give the program a try.

"Just wanted to tell you that me and a lot of other folks got faith in you, honey," the candidate told April. "Your mama was a smart woman. I reckon she knew what she was doing when she named you in her will."

"I'm not so sure about that, Mrs. Tulane," April said dryly.

"You call me Daisy, honey, and you be sure. Your mama never did anything without thinking it through. She taught me a lot. I wouldn't be where I am today without Rina. She was the best friend I ever had, and I loved her."

April wasn't sure how to respond to that.

"You ever need anything from me, you don't hesitate, okay?" Daisy continued. "Rina would have watched over my kids if I'd been the first one to be called to the Lord, so I'm gonna be your guardian angel, April, hon, y'hear me talkin'?"

"I hear you," April said with a smile.

"Next time I'm in the Big Apple we'll hook up for some good gossip and some hard shopping. I can't do this campaigning shit all the time. I need a little retail therapy."

April laughed. "Sounds like fun."

"Some flunky's poking me in the ribs with the latest polls or something. Gotta go, honey. Seize your power, and give 'em hell!"

Absently, April doodled on a pad of paper on her desk. "Senator Daisy Tulane," she wrote. "Seize your power. Give 'em hell."

She rose and went to the window, which provided a panoramic vista of the city. She leaned her forehead against the cool glass. She had a sudden sense of not knowing who she was or what she was doing here. As if she couldn't quite get a grip on her true feelings, her true self.

She was here, in Rina de Sevigny's place of business, trying to begin doing Rina's job.

She was being assisted by Rina's employees, and acknowledged, with various degrees of like and dislike, by Rina's family and friends.

And she was living in the co-op apartment that had belonged to Rina. As Armand had pointed out, finding an apartment in New York was no easy matter, and besides, since the apartment was owned by Power Perspectives, it was technically hers anyway. She had moved in the day before.

Her mother was dead, but her influence was more powerful than it had been in years.

April realized that she felt a little like the second Mrs. de Winter, confronted at every turn by the esteemed memory of the paragon, Rebecca.

Isobelle waited until the end of the day to make her appearance.

She had herself announced just before five. She made a dramatic entrance, dressed in a short gray suit that somehow managed to look slinky despite its conservative cut. The blouse under the suit jacket was scarlet. Her heels were just a little too high and her black hair was scattered in wild disarray on her shoulders.

I might have dressed that way myself a few years ago, April thought. I'd have done it because I was scared, and was trying to hide that by being outrageous.

Isobelle was several years younger than she, April realized. Not much more than thirty. She couldn't have been much more than a baby when her father had married Rina. Her stepmother had been the only mother she'd known.

No wonder she was screwed up.

"I just want you to know that I have no intention of pretending to be happy about your decision to come and work here," Isobelle said without preamble. "I'm a very direct person. I don't believe in the usual office politics and hypocrisies. So I'm putting you on notice that I'm going to fight you all the way."

April nodded. "Fine."

Isobelle's eyelids flickered. "I don't believe you deserve to be sitting in that chair. If I can take it away from you, I'll do it."

"Since you claim to be a direct person, I assume that means you will use direct means, not underhanded ones?"

"I'll use whatever means come to hand," Isobelle said. "Why?" Her voice took on a mocking tone. "What are you afraid of?"

"Lots of things," April said. "Rejection, for example. Failure." She kept her voice level as she continued, "Like everybody else in the world, I would like very much to be liked and respected by the people I work with. Obviously that will be difficult here. Rina was well loved. I am an unknown quantity."

"A shopkeeper," Isobelle reminded her.

"Yes. That was something I could do, something I was confident with. This job is something else entirely. I don't know if I can do it. I don't know whether I have what it takes. But I'm certainly going to try."

"That's not good enough," Isobelle said. "While you're busy 'trying,' you could be destroying everything that we've worked so hard to build. Nobody hands over the controls of a crowded passenger jet to an untrained pilot. Power Perspectives would be far better served if you stepped aside immediately."

"Leaving the top position open to you."

"I was to be Rina's successor."

"Perhaps that is what you believed. But the instructions in her will are very clear."

"I don't think the company should suffer just because she was guilty of some sort of sentimental nostalgia as she was nearing the end of her life."

"She had no way of knowing that the end of her life was upon her," April said quietly. "She was murdered."

Tension filled the air between them. "I'm not likely to forget that," Isobelle said.

"Nor am I. You asked what I was afraid of. Well, there's another thing. My mother held this job and she was assassinated. Now I am sitting where she sat. I'd be a fool if it didn't occur to me that whatever got her killed could put me in danger, too."

"Unless you killed her."

"But I happen to know that I didn't. Therefore I know that the killer is still out there. And that he—or she—might strike again."

"If you're so afraid of that, why are you here?" Isobelle said. "Why not run back to your safe little bookstore in Boston and hide?"

"I prefer to face my fears. As for mysteries—they exist only to be solved." She paused. "My mother and I had been estranged for years. But she was my mother. Somebody killed her, and I intend to find out who. I also intend to do the job she gave me. If either of those two goals disturbs you, that is your problem, not mine. I am willing to work with you, but if you really plan to fight me all the way, you'll have to be prepared for the fact that I will not hesitate to fight back."

Isobelle nodded coolly, but April thought she caught a glimpse of surprise in her expression. "I'm glad we understand each other so well," she said. Then she turned and marched out of the room.

"She's a bitch," Isobelle said to Charlie. "The trouble is, she's a smart bitch. So it's not going to be as easy as I'd hoped to manipulate her."

Charlie shook his head. They were together at her place on the evening of April Harrington's first day at work, but Isobelle had shown no interest in sex or D&S or possible excursions to the Chateau. She was pacing the huge living room of her loft apartment, fretting about what was going to happen to Power Perspectives.

"I can't believe she took the job. I thought she was a devoted little bookseller from Boston who wouldn't have the guts to venture into a business she didn't even begin to understand. I underestimated her, dammit."

"Isobelle, calm down. You're probably overestimating her now. My impression is that she's taking this on as something of a challenge. She's not truly interested in Power Perspectives, and she doesn't appear to believe in your mother's basic precepts."

"So what? Neither do I. The point is that millions of people do believe in this self-help crap. As long as she understands that, she can capitalize on it."

Charlie was sure that in her heart Isobelle did believe in it. Otherwise she wouldn't be so passionate about making Rina's precepts work. Isobelle was flinty on the outside, yes, but he knew better than most people how vulnerable she was.

"Seize your power," was the key to getting what you wanted out of life. Isobelle knew it, and so did he. Power Perspectives was successful because Rina de Sevigny's carefully programmed system of setting goals, enforcing mental discipline, changing deep-seated negative beliefs into positive ones, and rewarding oneself lavishly for passing each milestone was a solid, psychologically sound method of effecting real life-transformation.

You truly could take your destiny in your own hands. And you could affect other people's destinies as well.

Charlie remembered how desperate his own life had

been until he'd met Rina and heard about Power Perspectives. Scion of a once-wealthy family that had lost all the power and influence of a former generation through drinking, gambling, and foolish investments, Charlie had grown up suffering from depressions so severe that he had, on several occasions, planned meticulous suicide rituals. The last one, three years ago, had been simple—involving a bottle of Chivas and the George Washington Bridge.

Rina had been driving into the city on the night when he'd nearly heaved himself into the abyss. She had been one of several motorists who'd pulled her car over and tried to stop him. The others had made no impression on him. But Rina had.

She'd come right up to him (no one else had done that—they'd hung back as if afraid that the desire to fling oneself off a bridge was a communicable disease). "You've truly come to the end of a road," she'd said to him. "Every negative thought you've ever had, every shameful act you've ever committed, every wrongheaded belief you've ever espoused have all conspired to bring you to this bridge.

"You can jump or you can take my hand. Either way, your old life is over."

She was blonde, petite, and mesmerizing. She had a strength emanating from her that he could feel right through the haze induced by seven ounces of whiskey. When she reached out her hand to him, it was as if he'd had no choice. He'd taken it and become her disciple. And he'd gotten to know this woman who had saved him, her virtues and her flaws.

Now she was gone.

But her insights—and the program she had created to

advance them—would live on. As with any philosophy, the message was far more important than the messenger.

As for April Harrington, her arrival on the scene was an unexpected complication. But Power Perspectives taught several methods for dealing with unexpected complications, and Charlie Ripley knew them all.

He went to Isobelle and took her in his arms. No erotic submissiveness tonight; tonight he was her protector. Another thing for which he could thank Power Perspectives—by seizing his own power, he had won the woman of his dreams.

"Don't worry, my love," he whispered. "April Harrington won't last long, I promise you. She feels no commitment and she has no goals. She'll be gone in a blink, and Power Perspectives will be ours."

He felt her stiffen in his arms. "Ours?"

Damn! "Yours," he said smoothly. "With myself as your loyal and humble servant, dear Mistress."

Chapter Ten

"Okay, so let's run through the likely probables," Blackthorn said. "Who killed Rina de Sevigny? And why?"

He, Carla, and his third employee, Jonas Gold, were meeting in a Mexican restaurant on the Lower East Side, munching taco chips dipped in hot salsa as they waited for their dinners to arrive.

"I vote for the husband," Carla said. "I figured I wouldn't like the guy. But I do like him. That makes me suspicious. I got lousy taste in men. All the ones I like turn out to be sleazeballs, sooner or later."

Blackthorn grinned. "Armand is certainly wealthy enough to have hired a killer—although that can be said for everybody in the de Sevigny family. We can probably make a case that he had some sort of motive. Not financial, though—he's a lot richer than his wife was."

"Sexual?" Jonas suggested. "Was the deceased fooling around with anybody?"

Blackthorn shrugged. "It's possible. So far nobody's come forward to suggest it."

Jonas was jotting down notes on a portable computer. He was young—only twenty-six—long-haired, sloppily dressed, 6 foot, 5 inches tall, and skinny but strong. He loved alternative rock music and computers, and he was one of the best karate and Tae Kwon Do experts Blackthorn had ever met. He lived for kung fu movies and information hacking, and as far as Blackthorn knew, he had no social life. But he was extremely bright.

"From the picture on the back of her books and tapes, Mrs. de Sevigny appears to have been an attractive woman," said Jonas. "Looks younger than her age. Certainly looks younger than her husband. There may be a lover tucked away somewhere."

"I'll work on that angle," Carla offered.

"I talked to Marty Clemente this morning," Blackthorn said. "He's going to cooperate with me, for old times' sake." He spoke dryly. Marty hadn't been too forthcoming until Blackthorn had called in a few debts from a long time ago.

"Okay, what the hell, I'll share," Marty had said after some heavy horse-trading. "You want to know why?"

"I can see you want to tell me," Blackthorn had said.

"Because I'm kindhearted, that's why. This is the first time you've shown a real flicker of professional interest in anything since Jessie died. I thought you were a burn-out case, Blackthorn. And that would have been a shame, because you used to be one of the best."

Blackthorn had grinned. "Well, thanks, Marty. I appreciate that, you kindhearted son of a bitch."

"One of the things Clemente told me was that the FBI got a call from some literary agent who claims to have met April Harrington at the convention just before her mother was murdered," he said. "Claimed she'd had a chat with Harrington in the ladies room and that Harrington said that her mother had once had an affair with JFK."

"Yeah, I've heard that story," Carla said. "Is it true?"

"Yup," said Blackthorn. "Rina was one of JFK's conquests. Or maybe it was the other way around. Are you ready for the latest JFK assassination theory?" He removed a small tape machine from his pocket and placed it on the table. Over the sounds of a mariachi band playing in the bar, they all listened to Christian's call to the FBI. Clemente had given Blackthorn a copy of the tape.

I've never been a conspiracy buff, personally, but what if there was some kind of plot? And what if Rina knew something about it?

I know it's far-fetched. You're probably better off investigating Rina's clients, not to mention the strange and unpleasant people who my sister hangs out with. But I'm sure you don't want to leave any stone unturned.

"I love it," said Carla. "Gee, I'll bet Rina was in Dallas on the day of the assassination. I'll bet she knows who was shooting from the grassy knoll. Now since it can't have been the sainted FBI—" she grinned at Blackthorn "—I'll bet it was the CIA and now they've killed her for it. Rina de Sevigny was the Last Living Witness to the Kennedy assassination. Wow, maybe the shooter who got her in Anaheim is the same guy who fired the second gun in counterpoint to Oswald's."

"Thank you, Carla." Blackthorn grinned at her. "Very helpful."

"I suppose we'll have to check it out," Jonas said.

Carla raised her eyebrows. "You're kidding."

Jonas sipped from the neck of a bottle of Lone Star beer. "No stone left unturned."

"You computer nerds love that conspiracy shit, don't

you?" said Carla. "Fact is, people kill each other for the simplest damn reasons. Couple of years ago when I was still on the force we had a guy who killed another guy on a commuter train cause he didn't like the newspaper the victim was reading. Wasn't that he objected to their bias or the way they covered the news, either. He didn't like the sports columnist. Thought he was trashing the Mets. Thought anybody reading a column by a man who trashes the Mets oughta die. Shot him in the throat and the guy bled to death all over the sports section. 'What's black and white and red all over?' was the joke of the day."

Blackthorn and Jonas both chuckled.

"Anyhow," Carla went on, "seems to me the real purpose of Christian's message is to get the Feebs off his own back and send 'em chasing after his sister instead. They don't like each other much, do they?"

"Nobody in that family seems to like each other much," Jonas said.

Their orders arrived. Blackthorn had the combination plate—two chicken enchiladas and a beef taco. Carla had chicken fajitas, which came sizzling, and Jonas got ready to dig into a mammoth chimichanga special.

"So does Isobelle really hang out with 'strange and unpleasant people,' whatever that means?" Carla said as she piled a tortilla with chicken, peppers, tomatoes, and onions. "Somebody needs to check that out."

Jonas pointed the neck of his beer bottle at Carla. "She's tough, isn't she?" he said to Blackthorn.

"Relentless."

"I needn't remind you that Isobelle's got the best motive," Carla said. "She's the one who lost out when Rina de Sevigny changed her will."

"We do have a report of frequent arguments between Isobelle de Sevigny and Rina de Sevigny," Blackthorn said. "Apparently they were having 'creative differences' at work during the last few weeks before the murder."

"She certainly wasn't too happy at the reading of the will," Blackthorn said.

"Just imagine how pissed you'd be if you killed some guy to get his job and found out the guy's outwitted you and handed the job to somebody else," said Carla. "Hell, it wouldn't seem fair, would it?" She took a huge bite of her fajita and heaved a sigh of pleasure.

"We'll definitely have to focus some of our energy on Isobelle," said Blackthorn. "I'm sure Marty will be doing the same thing."

"Me, I'm sticking with Christian," Jonas said. "He's too eager in his attempts to divert suspicion. Any theories on a possible motive?"

"He's always struck me as a coldhearted bastard," Blackthorn said. "I got the feeling there was some sort of tension between him and Rina. But it's possible that neither of Armand's children ever accepted her as their mother."

"What happened to their real mother?" Jonas asked.

"She died about a year before Armand de Sevigny married Rina," Blackthorn said.

"Lotta deaths in this family," Carla noted. "Christian's wife is also dead. Car accident. Now he's the single father of a twelve-year-old kid."

"Not a very good father, either, from all accounts," said Jonas. "Kate, the daughter, has been reported missing twice in the last ten months. One of the reports made it all the way to the FBI. Turned out that on both occasions she ran away from home due to conflict with her father."

Carla sat up straighter. "Did she accuse him of child abuse?"

"No. She accused him of being an asshole." Jonas

shrugged. "Hey, I'm serious. That's what she told the precinct cops. They investigated and put it down to 'my daddy doesn't understand me' teenager crap. Social Services evaluated and didn't find a problem."

Carla snorted. "Social Services, bullshit. There's a million reasons why kids won't tell the whole story about their parents. Jeez, he's probably abusing her, the sonuvabitch."

"Let's not jump to conclusions," Blackthorn said. "And let's not forget that April Harrington is the person who has gained the most from Rina de Sevigny's death."

They all chewed in silence for a few seconds while they considered this.

"So far she checks out clean," Carla said. "You've seen what I've got on her—nothing. Good citizen, exemplary businesswoman, respected expert on crime fiction, but not on crime."

"I've been checking phone records, faxes, and electronic mail," said Jonas. He grinned. "Don't even ask how. I'm looking for anything interesting, but particularly for contact between Rina and Harrington. If we can find contact, we can assume she's lying about not knowing the contents of the will. But so far I've got no communication of any kind between them."

"Dig deeper," Blackthorn said. "I think she's hiding something. I don't know why. Just a gut feeling."

Jonas nodded. "There're some other places I can try."

"Professional hits cost money," Carla said slowly. "Of all the people we've mentioned, April Harrington has the least in the way of financial resources. Any of the others could probably hide the transaction—get the cash somehow without leaving a paper trail—but not her."

"You don't think she's a killer?" Blackthorn said.

Carla shrugged. "She's lower on my list of suspects than she is on yours."

Actually, she wasn't too high on his, but Blackthorn kept that opinion to himself. He kept thinking about the way April had behaved that day in the lawyer's office. If that was acting, hell, she deserved an Academy Award.

And he kept imagining other things about her—like what it would feel like to bury his hands in that thick, wavy auburn hair. And kiss those soft lips. And caress those sleek thighs.

He hadn't thought of a woman that way since Jessie's death.

And he certainly shouldn't be thinking of a suspect that way now. Chemistry was a dangerous thing.

"There are other possibilities, too," he said. "People who weren't as close to Rina as her family, but who may have motives anyhow. Clients, for instance. The other folks who worked for Power Perspectives. Disgruntled former employees—we've got to check for those. Lovers, if there are any, of either the husband or the wife."

"And let's not forget the JFK assassins," Carla said with a grin.

"I'll be checking computer files on all the suspects," Jonas said. "If there's a paper trail of any kind, I'll find it."

"There'd better be a paper trail," Blackthorn said. "We got nothing else. No physical evidence except a bullet from a gun that we'll probably never find. Jesus. I hate professional hits."

"Hey, don't worry," Carla said, chewing hard as she bit into her second well-stuffed fajita. "Nobody's infallible. Maybe he'll kill again, leave more evidence next time."

"Now there's a comforting thought," Blackthorn said.

Chapter Eleven

"Oh, damn, not again," April muttered to herself. She was bent over her desk, in the process of adding figures on a small calculator. Apparently, she'd been making some minor mistake while entering a long column of numbers, since she kept coming out with a different sum.

She sighed, wishing she knew how to use one of those computer programs that made bookkeeping and other financial matters so easy. But so far she'd gone through life without learning the difference between a RAM and a ROM, whatever those were.

"What's the matter?" asked Charlie, who had just come into her office. He'd been very helpful over the past few days. Any questions that she had, he knew the answers.

"I'm just stumbling over some numbers. No big deal. I was checking our finances."

"Delores does the books. She's a trained accountant."

"That's great. Delores has a lot of talents." Delores, she'd discovered, was the general factotum around here.

She was a skilled secretary, an organized office manager, she was a whiz with computers, and now it seemed she knew bookkeeping as well. "I'll have to get her to take me through this stuff." She glanced at her daily calendar. "I think I have some time later this afternoon."

"If you don't mind my suggesting it, there are a lot of other things you should maybe think about doing first," Charlie said. "We've got to get moving on that new video, and if the hotel in Maui doesn't get a signed contract back from us soon, they won't hold our block of rooms."

"I understand," said April. "But I'd really like to go over the books while the subject's fresh in my mind."

"Well, I'm sure Delores'll be glad to explain everything to you." He sounded just a tiny bit patronizing, and April hid a smile. One thing she was good at was the nuts and bolts of managing money. Although she'd already discovered that Power Perspectives was infinitely more complicated than the Poison Pen Bookshop, she saw no reason why she shouldn't be able to create the same order out of chaos on a large scale as she had on a small.

Both Charlie and Delores were in for a bit of a surprise.

"Changing the subject, I've got a question for you," Charlie said.

She looked up.

"Do you happen to know anything about the book that your mother was writing at the time of her death?"

April shook her head. "What book?"

"A manuscript. I don't know the subject—something autobiographical, I believe. I had a call a little while ago from her editor inquiring about it."

"No one's mentioned it to me," April said.

"Her editor is quite anxious to get her hands on the manuscript. Under the circumstances, I guess she thinks it'll be a big best-seller."

"Well, my mother certainly led a very interesting life," April said thoughtfully. "She traveled in elegant circles, she knew a lot of famous people, and now she's been dramatically murdered. As a bookseller, I could probably sell quite a few copies myself. The self-help titles she wrote have done very well."

"Well, the manuscript seems to have disappeared. Unless it's turned up among Rina's effects."

April frowned. There was definitely a suggestive note underlying his words. "Why do I get the feeling that you think I know where it is? This is the first I've heard of an autobiography."

Charlie looked abashed. "I'm sorry—I don't mean to imply anything. It's just that I wondered if the manuscript may have been among the personal effects that were left to you by your mother. Apparently a large manila envelope was placed in the hands of her lawyer, and then turned over to you?"

"That's right. But the envelope didn't contain a manuscript."

April wasn't going to tell him that all it had contained had been a faded photograph in a cheap frame. Nor that the cheap and faded keepsake was now sitting on the table right next to her bed.

"Are you sure this manuscript exists? Lots of people who claim to be writing a book are really just fantasizing about doing so."

He nodded. "Good point. But she mentioned it to several people, and after all, she did complete several other books."

"Have you asked Armand about it?"

"I suggested to the editor that she contact him."

"Well, I'll take a look around the apartment, but I haven't seen anything resembling a manuscript. Before I moved in both the police and the FBI had been through the place. Armand, too, I believe. They didn't leave much."

"I'll call the editor back and tell her. Maybe it'll turn up."

April mused about the missing manuscript as Charlie left. An autobiography? Would there have been anything in the book, she wondered, about her?

And why, if it had indeed existed, was the manuscript missing?

"Father, what I'm telling you, dammit, is that the corporation is in trouble."

"I would appreciate it if you would not use that tone with me."

Christian raised his eyebrows in exasperation. Armand de Sevigny was such a stickler for courtesy and civility that he probably believed it would be impolite for a bank officer to call in a few overdue loans.

He and his father were meeting in the conference room on the top floor of De Sevigny Ltd. Down on a lower floor were the offices of Power Perspectives, which Christian tended to avoid. He had no desire to tangle with his bitch of a sister or her love-struck boyfriend. April Harrington was somewhat more intriguing. Attractive, too, with those long legs and that sylph-like slenderness. Of course, she was probably over her head in Rina's job, but he was secretly hoping that she found a way to blow Isobelle right out of the water.

Christian had never forgiven his sister for introducing Miranda, his wife, to her own disreputable lifestyle. If Isobelle hadn't insisted on taking Miranda to those vile clubs she frequented, seducing her into a fascination with kinky sex, the damn divorce and all the subsequent unpleasantness would never have happened.

Miranda might still be alive today.

With an effort, he refocused. "Look, Father, you have got to take this situation more seriously. We are overextended in just about every direction. I've set up a meeting for next week with our accounting firm. I'd like you to hear it directly from them, since you seem to have so much trouble believing me."

Somewhat to his surprise, Armand nodded. "Very well, let's have the meeting." He looked down at his hands. "This has always been a profitable business," he said.

"Times have changed. We've had a rough few years. There are signs that things may be picking up—certainly the economy is improving—but we must adopt some emergency belt-tightening measures if we're to ride it out until our profit margins improve. Our first priority is to solve our cash-flow problem. If we don't come up with the interest on several of our biggest loans the banks could call them in and then we'd be seriously screwed."

"Are you telling me that no subsidiary of De Sevigny Ltd. is turning a profit?"

"Well, no, not exactly—it's not that bad—we have several profitable ventures. It's just that taken together, they're falling short of those that are losing money."

"Then let's get rid of the poor performers. Cut off the limbs, if necessary, to save the body."

This was exactly what Christian was hoping to hear him say. Trim away the deadwood. Downsize. Hell, everybody was doing it.

"I think that's an excellent idea."

"We must be practical," Armand said. "Perhaps, in the aftermath of Sabrina's death I have been denying the true situation. If so, I must pull myself together, mustn't I? You are right to insist upon this."

This was a switch, Christian thought. Usually, his father

treated his opinions with skepticism, if not disdain. Was it possible that after all these years he was finally getting through to him?

"You know, it's really too bad Rina insisted on keeping Power Perspectives a separate entity," Christian mused. "I'd love to have those profits rolling into De Sevigny Ltd." He looked at his father curiously. "Why did she insist on that, by the way? When she started her company, De Sevigny Ltd. was still pretty golden. I'm sure you would have backed her. Why was it so important to her to do it on her own?"

Armand shrugged. His expression was sad, and he seemed very frail. "She was seizing her own power. I guess she no longer had any use for mine."

For the first time in his life Christian noticed that his father seemed tired . . . and old.

April jerked her head up. She had not heard the door to her office open. Armand was there on the threshold, dressed in a dapper suit and tie, but looking pale, as if he were not getting enough rest.

"Forgive me if I startled you," he said.

"No, no, it's nothing," April assured him. She rose and came around her desk to greet him. He embraced her warmly, his eyes crinkling as he gave her his Maurice Chevalier smile.

"I was upstairs in the main offices, consulting with my son. I thought it might be nice to stop by and see how you were doing."

"Thanks. I'm doing well. I'm actually enjoying myself."

"The job suits you," he told her. "There is spring in

your step and a sparkle in your eye that is delightful for a man to look upon, *cherie*."

"Well, thank you very much, sir. It's more interesting here than I expected, actually."

"That pleases me. You will take to this, I'm sure, as—how do you say it in English—as the fish takes to water."

"I don't know about that. Sit down, please. Can I get you something?"

"No, no, I'm fine." Yet he seemed slightly distressed, and he paced nervously around the room before settling on the edge of a chair. "How are you getting along with the others? My daughter, she is behaving herself?"

"There is some tension, but that is to be expected," she answered tactfully. "Charlie is easy to work with, though. And Delores is terrific. She's an excellent secretary, very organized. She seems to be doing a good job with the bookkeeping, too. I was just going over a few things with her in that area, as a matter of fact."

He raised his eyebrows. "You are familiar with accounting procedures?"

"As the proprietor of a small bookshop, I had to be. Yes, indeed. Financial management is one of my favorite aspects of business, as a matter of fact." She grinned. "I should have worked on Wall Street."

"Indeed?" He smiled. "You continue to impress me, mademoiselle."

"I see no reason why the finances of a fifty-million-dollar corporation can't be managed as successfully as the finances of one that does only one percent of that. Although Delores keeps excellent accounts, we haven't yet addressed the issue of whether our costs can be trimmed and our overall expenses reduced. I have to admit that I still don't have a very good overall picture of what all our various expenses are—" she smiled "—somewhat to Charlie's annoyance."

"I see," he said, nodding. "Well, good for you, my dear." He stood, wandered to the window, looked out, then turned. "And the apartment? Is it satisfactory? Are you enjoying it? Is there anything that you need?"

"It's a lovely apartment. I like it very much, and I'm glad to have the opportunity to live in my mother's 'room of her own.' As you suggested, it is helping me in my quest for understanding," she added with a wry smile.

"Excellent." He returned to his chair and resumed his seat.

She noticed his hands. Was it her imagination, or were they trembling? How different he seemed from the dapper, energetic Armand de Sevigny who had joined his wife on the Power Perspectives dais just minutes before her assassination. She felt a sudden and unexpected wave of sympathy for him. The loss of his wife had drained him of his own vitality.

"The only thing that continues to be difficult for me is that I still feel haunted by my mother's death," she said slowly. "It's hanging over everybody's head, I guess. I don't know whom to talk to, whom to trust."

"I don't blame you. My own trust is given only to a select few. I've been betrayed too often." His voice was not very steady, and April wanted to reach out and offer him her comfort. "My advice to you is to be extremely careful about whom you give yours to."

"Good advice. I don't want to end up the way she did."

"How sad to have to think of that. Yet you must. And trust is something you feel in your heart. It has no logical component." He paused. "If you choose to trust me, I will do my utmost to be worthy. If you don't, I will certainly understand. You are in an unenviable position, and to trust too easily could be dangerous for you."

She knew he was right. Trust never came easily for her. If she had been more able to conquer her fear that everyone whom she allowed to become important in her life would, sooner or later, betray or abandon her, her personal life would have been considerably happier.

"Perhaps, my dear, I have asked too much of you. Perhaps we all have. You are a young and vital woman. You should not be burdened by such worries."

"Strangely enough, I like the job. It's challenging. I'm not sure what I think of Rina's theories, but I am drawn to the idea that it's possible to change one's bad habits, focus upon one's strengths and talents, and turn one's life around. It's such a comfortable fantasy—the thought that one might be able to remake oneself and start over with people."

"But a fantasy nevertheless," he said gently.

She looked at him. "You're a cynic."

"No, a realist. My wife was an idealist. Her entire philosophy is set upon an overly optimistic base."

Interesting, April thought. Everybody seemed to have a different view of Rina. She was a bitch, she was an angel, she was a pragmatist, she was an idealist. No wonder she wouldn't come into focus. She had been something different to everyone.

Which reminded her . . . "Charlie asked me this morning if I knew anything about a manuscript that my mother was writing at the time of her death. Apparently her editor telephoned, asking about it."

"I thought her latest self-help book was already in production at her publisher."

"This wasn't one of the Power Perspectives series. It

was an autobiography. Was she writing such a book, as far as you know?"

Armand pressed his palms together and rested his chin upon them. "I suppose it's possible. Sabrina was always writing something—books, speeches, articles. The computer was one of her favorite toys."

"I hate computers," April confessed. "Sometimes I feel as if I'm the only one on the planet who doesn't know how to operate one."

"I am similarly ignorant. My son is scathing about my refusal to deal with electronic robotry, but I'm too old to change. Sabrina was far more modern in her thinking than I."

"So there was no autobiography among her things after her death?"

"No. Although, now that you mention it, she did occasionally mention that she would like to write her memoirs someday. I had assumed she intended to wait until her public life was somewhat less active. I don't believe she'd started work on the project, but I could be wrong."

Charlie had seemed convinced that the manuscript existed. Was this another sign of distance between husband and wife? What had their relationship really been like? How much time had her mother actually spent at the West Side apartment? Were Rina and Armand estranged?

They chatted politely for several more minutes, then Armand rose, kissed her gallantly on both cheeks, and bid her adieu.

As he left, his shoulders seemed stooped, as if he bore a great burden on his back.

April had wanted to hug him, but she'd held back, afraid of offending his dignity.

And besides, it was confusing to feel such a pull of affection and sympathy for the man who had stolen away her mother.

Chapter Twelve

Quietly, Kate replaced the receiver of the extension phone in her bedroom. She curled up on the bed. She was coming to visit. Mrs. Tulane. Daisy. She'd called to tell Daddy what flight she'd be arriving on. And there wasn't anything Kate could do to stop it because Daddy thought he knew everything and he never listened to her.

How could he be dating a woman as phony as Daisy Tulane? It was disgusting. He must be desperate. "I hate her," Kate muttered.

Maybe she could figure out a way to get rid of her somehow.

And then she'd find somebody better for him. Somebody younger. Somebody suitable. Somebody real. Somebody who would take his mind off the lady politician who was always smiling and cooing and pretending to be something she wasn't.

Kate reached under her bed and pulled out Gran's laptop computer. She turned it on and called up a file and started typing rapidly:

"I've found the perfect woman for my father. Her name is April, and some people think she might have killed Gran, but I know she didn't do it, even if Gran did abandon her when she was my age. I'm probably the only person around here who knows what it feels like to be abandoned by your mother. It makes you angry and it makes you sad, but it doesn't make you a murderer.

"She's really cool and I think she's pretty. She has dark red hair that curls and looks heavy. (Mine just hangs and it won't stay the way I comb it and even the barrettes slide out.) She's got big eyes and a pretty smile and I think Daddy would be crazy not to like her. Of course I don't know if she'd like him (personally I think he's a geek) but Gran told me that he's actually handsome and that women think he's hot.

"You wouldn't know it, though, from the way he acts. He's started seeing Daisy Tulane and she's a total loser. Worse, in fact. She's—"

Kate stopped, thought for a moment, then closed the file. She'd been planning to write more, but she had a better idea.

She went downstairs. Her father was in the library hunched over his computer. "Hey, Dad."

He jumped and she realized she'd startled him. Uh-oh. She hoped he wasn't going to yell at her. Seemed like all they'd been doing lately was yelling at each other.

He turned his head. "Hey," he said. He glanced at his watch. "Kinda late, isn't it? Tomorrow's a school day. Did you finish your homework?"

"Yes." She went over and leaned her hip against the side of his desk. His screen was full of numbers, as usual—some sort of spreadsheet. He had some neat accounting software—Kate had seen it advertised in her computing magazines.

"When's your next math test?"

"I don't know. Next week. I'll ace it, as usual."

"Don't get too confident."

"Why not?" Kate was the best student in the whole seventh grade in math, everybody knew that. She didn't even have to study—math just came naturally to her. English was harder, especially since they were doing all this stupid grammar this year. If they'd just let her write, she'd be happy, but no, they had to waste all this time figuring out whether sentences contain adjectival or adverbial clauses.

"Just because something comes easy to you doesn't mean you should neglect it."

"I don't neglect it." As usual, he didn't even know how much time she spent on math . . . or anything else. Of course, it was just as well that he didn't know how much time she spent writing. "I'm doing my homework," she'd say, then go into her room and shut the door. The homework itself she polished off in an hour or so. The rest of the time she was spinning stories, sometimes in her head, sometimes on a diskette.

"Dad?"

"Mmm?" He was looking at his screen again.

"You know April? The one they were saying murdered Gran?"

He turned his head. "That's nonsense, Kate. Who was saying that?"

"I thought everybody was saying it." Chill, Dad, she was thinking. "It's not true, I know. But people say a lot of things that aren't true."

He looked at her in silence for several seconds, then said, "Are your friends at school giving you a hard time about your grandmother's death? If so, I hope you're not letting it bother you. If there's any unpleasantness I can come in and have a talk with the principal."

Daddy to the rescue, she thought, unimpressed. It was a little late. A couple of kids had given her a hard time, yeah. So she'd given *them* a hard time, and that had been the end of that. She didn't need him. She didn't need anybody. "It's not a problem."

He looked relieved. "Good."

If it was a problem, she thought sadly, he would really hate to be bothered by it. "Actually, it's about April."

"What about her?"

"I was wondering if we could, like, invite her over to dinner this weekend? I don't think she knows anybody. And besides, she's family, sort of."

Now she had his attention. "You want me to invite April Harrington to dinner?"

He said it as if it were the stupidest idea he'd ever heard. Kate felt her face begin to turn. But she raised her chin defiantly.

"Yes," she said. "In fact, I want to invite her over on Saturday afternoon to do something with us first, and then to dinner. I want to take her to the Museum. She told me she likes art."

"Kate, you hardly know April Harrington. And I don't know her at all."

"Well, she can be my guest, not yours. But I think you'd like her, too. She's pretty, Daddy. And I guess she isn't married."

His eyes narrowed, and Kate realized she'd made a mistake. She didn't mean to blurt it out like that, but he made her nervous when he looked at her with those cold eyes that seemed to see right through her. He made her forget that she was going to be subtle and slip underneath his defenses and not let him know that she thought he and

April Harrington would be a perfect couple, and that maybe they'd fall in love and maybe even get married, and then she'd have a mother again.

"Actually, Kate, my friend Daisy is coming this weekend. I know she's looking forward to seeing you again."

"She couldn't care less about me."

"What nonsense. She always asks about you."

"Well, I don't like her. And I don't see why you have to invite her here all the time."

"I invite her here because she's the most important woman in my life right now. You're old enough, I think, to understand such things."

Kate raised her eyebrows. "You're the one who doesn't understand." She paused, looking right at him. "You're not screwing her, right? I mean, you can't be."

"You're out of line, Kate," he said in that clipped, controlled tone she hated.

"I don't care! I hate Daisy Tulane and I hate you."

Kate ran from the room, trying to reach the privacy of her bedroom before bursting into tears. She made it, but only just.

Great, just great, she thought when she was able to get control of herself again. She wasn't being smart about this at all. That was one of the reasons she hated Daisy—because Daisy was smart about how to handle Dad. She knew how to tease and jolly him into a good mood; she knew how to twist him around her fingers. Daisy was one of those females who instinctively ran circles around men. Which was pretty weird, when you stopped to think about it.

There were a couple of girls in her class like that—well not in Daisy's league of course. A smart girl— and Kate knew she was smart—ought to be able to learn something about it, though. It really made her mad that she hadn't succeeded in learning it!

Mom would have taught her, she knew.

She punched her pillow, hard.

Everything would have been so different if only Mom hadn't died.

Christian cursed and saved the file he'd been trying to work on. His concentration was shot. He was worried about how to downsize. At least his father seemed to have dropped his pigheadedness and come around to a realistic point of view. But now that he'd admitted the problem, he seemed to expect Christian to be able to solve it, which wasn't at all assured . . .

The last thing he could afford to waste his time on was how to deal with a hormonal adolescent. And yet suddenly that was the only thing on his mind.

He rose and poured himself a brandy from the crystal decanter on the sideboard in the corner. Sipping it slowly, he brooded about his daughter.

God knows he wasn't a very good father. Miranda had taken care of most of the heavy-duty parenting stuff.

It had been a helluva lot easier a few years ago when Kate had still loved toys and enjoyed playing rough-house games. He had many happy memories of rolling around on the living room floor with her, throwing her up into the air, bouncing her on his knees, listening to her delighted squeals and her laughter. Pleasing her had been easy then. She'd loved it, and so had he.

He'd noticed both with his own child and with the children of various couples that he and Miranda knew that the fathers seemed to take care of the activities—the fun stuff like toys and games and excursions to children's museums and amusement parks, while the mothers handled the serious stuff like doctor's appointments and elementary school parent-teacher conferences. His wife used to complain about having all the responsibility and none of the fun.

And it had been fun. In those days, Kate had loved him unconditionally. She was the only person ever in his life who gave him her entire heart and asked for nothing in return. And so, of course, he'd given her everything. With her he'd been able to laugh, to play, to be affectionate and emotional. She was his child, and she had complete faith and trust in him. She never judged him and she could not reject him.

That is, until the divorce. And the custody battle. And her mother's death.

He took a bigger swallow of brandy.

Kate had taken it very hard. She'd changed from a carefree, irrepressible child to a puzzling and dreamy adolescent. And all the rules had changed as well, because she was suddenly too old to roll around on the living room floor and scathingly disinterested in toys, games, and amusement parks.

She'd seemed to get along with Rina, though. And Rina, who had never struck him as the type who would be the least bit interested in budding adolescents, had turned out to be wonderful with Kate.

Now she was dead, as well.

And once again, Kate was grieving.

He took the last sip of brandy to fortify himself and went upstairs to her room.

He found her hunched over her desk, furiously typing on a laptop computer. "Hey."

She slammed the top down and rested her elbows upon it. "Don't you know?"

For an instant Christian was reminded of his former wife. Miranda closing doors, shutting him out, seeking privacy to communicate with what he later discovered was a series of lovers. And not even ordinary lovers—no, the leather-and-chain variety. Christ! What a poisonous relationship they had had.

"What are you writing? A homework assignment?"

She glared at him and didn't answer. Her diary, he thought. Did she keep a diary? What would it reveal about her, he wondered, if he confiscated it and read it?

"I've been giving some thought to your suggestion about April Harrington. If you'd like to invite her over to dinner on Saturday, you can. Daisy's not coming until Sunday."

Kate's expression brightened immediately, reminding him that it really didn't take much to please her. He would have to remember that. It wasn't as if she was a naturally difficult child.

"Can I invite her to the Met first, in the afternoon?"

"If you like. But you and she will have to do that alone. I'm planning to work on Saturday afternoon."

"Okay. You don't like being dragged around the museum anyhow."

Hiking through a crowded art museum was certainly not his favorite leisure activity. "Kate, I want to ask you something."

"What?"

"Why don't you like Daisy?"

She made a face. "I told you. She's a phony. I hate people like that."

"What exactly do you mean—a phony? Daisy's a very warm and charming lady. Most people would say she's engagingly genuine, very much herself. In fact, if she can't get elected it'll probably be because she says what-she thinks a little more often than she ought to. Politicians are supposed to say what everybody wants them to say, and Daisy doesn't do that."

"Are you in love with her?" Kate demanded.

"This isn't about my feelings, I'm asking about yours. I want to know why you persist in this irrational notion that Daisy Tulane is a phony."

"It's not irrational. You always say I'm irrational when you don't agree with me. You used to say that to Mommy, too!"

Great, he thought. This wasn't helping.

But Kate plunged on: "She's a phony because she's not what she pretends to be. She's supposedly so sweet, so nice. She even goes to church on Sunday."

"So what's wrong with that? People do go to church, you know. Most Americans do, in fact. And many of the ones who don't still believe in God anyway." He felt a little over his head. One responsibility Miranda hadn't undertaken was to provide their daughter with some sort of religious education. At twelve, Kate was old enough to be confirmed. But he wasn't even sure she'd been baptized.

"I thought if you went to church you had to be a good person, without sin."

"Daisy is a good person."

Kate gave a short laugh. "But is she without sin?"

He cleared his throat. Without sin? "Are you upset because she and I are having a relationship?"

"Oh, Daddy, please. I don't care who you go out with! And I don't want to talk about this anymore!"

This wasn't working, Christian thought. He seemed to have lost whatever good will he'd created by telling her she could invite April Harrington to dinner. He decided to revert to that subject.

"I'll speak to April and invite her for this Saturday

evening. I'll tell her about the art museum as well, and if she's interested you and she can talk to each other and set it up."

"Okay," Kate said.

"Finish your homework."

"I will."

When her father left the room, Kate opened her file to the page where she'd left off. She considered for a moment, then wrote, "I almost told my father what I know about Daisy Tulane. But I can't prove it and she'll deny it and no one will ever believe me, anyhow."

Chapter Thirteen

"I love this place," Kate said to April as they put on their colored buttons and ascended the Grand Staircase to the second floor of the Metropolitan Museum. "It's got all sorts of neat stuff. I can't believe you've never seen it before."

"Well, I've never spent very much time in New York."

"Have you ever been to, you know, all the touristy places like the Statue of Liberty and the World Trade Center and the Empire State Building and all?"

"Nope. Someday you'll have to take me to see them."

"Okay. That'll be fun."

She's so pretty and stylish, Kate was thinking, staring openly at April, who was dressed casually in white china pants and a buttercup yellow blouse with a gold and white polka dot scarf around her neck. She had on white sandals that looked comfy yet showed her small feet, the toenails painted with the same salmon polish she wore on her fingernails. Her long auburn hair was loose today on her

149

shoulders. The first time they'd met she'd worn it up in a French twist.

April had one of those perfect oval faces like the models in the fashion magazines. Her nose was straight (unlike Kate's, which curved up at the tip in what she thought was a ditzy manner) and her lips were full and juicy-looking (Kate's were thin—she hated them). She had these light, clear blue eyes with a tiny rim of dark cornflower around the outside of the irises. Kate wished she could trade her own muddy hazel eyes for April's perfect blue ones.

She's so pretty, in fact, that I ought to hate her, Kate thought. But instead she'd liked her from the start.

"So what do you want to see—pictures, sculpture, ancient ruins, Western art, Eastern art, furniture and china— what do you like best? They've got some unusual collections here, too—things you don't see in other art museums like suits of armor and neat old musical instruments. I know where everything is, so you can, you know, like, take your pick."

"I'm interested in all of it. So why don't you show me your favorite places in the museum? If I see something I particularly want to stop for, I'll let you know. You can be my tour guide, okay?"

"Okay." Kate quickly reviewed what she thought were the most important facts. She loved the museum—not only had she visited it countless times, she'd explored every corner and just about memorized every room. She'd also read a lot of books about its history, and most of the guards knew her because she was always asking them questions. She wasn't sure why she was so fond of the place—she liked it even better than the public library, which seemed odd because she loved books. Maybe she was a reincarnated curator from the turn of the century of something.

"The Met's huge—it covers four city blocks from Eightieth to Eighty-Fourth Street. Like, think about it—a building that's four whole blocks long."

"What I'm thinking is that this is a good way to get some exercise," April said with a grin.

"Nah," said Kate. "You want exercise, come rollerblading with me in Central Park." She laughed at the thought of teaching an adult to rollerblade. When she'd tried to teach Dad, he'd cursed and sworn and moved stiff-leggedly and slowly and finally fallen right on his butt. " 'Course I'll leave you in my dust, but if you're nice to me I'll come back for you."

"Listen, kid, I used to rollerblade in Boston. I've just bought a fine new pair of skates and I'm ready to take you on any time you're ready. Ten bucks says I'll leave you in *my* dust."

Wow, Kate thought, April was even cooler than she'd thought. "It's a deal!"

Kate took her first to the European paintings, especially the Impressionists, because that was usually what everybody wanted to see. Then they did the musical instruments and the Asian art, and then Kate took her to one of her favorite places, the Chinese Garden Court.

"It's so peaceful here," April said as she took in the beauty of the artfully arranged rocks and trees and curving roof of the Chinese pagoda.

"I like to sit down on the floor here and listen to the sound of the trickling water," Kate said in a whisper. "Like when stuff's really worrying me, this is a nice place to be."

"What kind of stuff bothers you, Kate?"

She shrugged. "Oh, you know. The usual."

April took her hand as they peered at the fish in the rock-ringed pool. "Is anything bothering you right now?"

Kate found herself remembering a moment just a few months ago when she had brought Gran here. She and Gran had sat in the same spot, watching the fish, listening to the tinkle of water playing on stone.

Tears sprang to her eyes. She tried to squeeze them back, but more kept coming and soon they were spilling down her cheeks. Trembling, she brought up her free arm and wiped her face on her sleeve.

April took her promptly into her arms and hugged her. This made Kate cry all the harder. Not even Gran would have done that. Gran would have pretended not to notice, or maybe patted her awkwardly. As for Daddy, he'd have gotten embarrassed and not known what to do.

April just held her, and stroked her hair, and let her cry. The last person who'd done that, Kate remembered, had been Mom. It was so unfair! At least Gran had lived to be kinda old, but Mom hadn't even . . .

Don't think of that, don't think of that, don't think of that. Kate struggled to get control of herself. Thinking about Mom was pointless. Besides, she didn't want April to think she was a crybaby, even if she was understanding and nice.

"I hate to cry," she muttered.

"Don't hate it," April said gently. "Crying is good. Crying relieves the pain in the heart, the pressure on the soul. Never be ashamed of feeling your emotions."

"I don't mind feeling them, I just don't want to show them!"

"Sometimes it's hard to tell one from the other. I believe that people who try very hard not to show them eventually lose the capacity to feel."

"I think my father's like that," Kate blurted out.

"Lots of people are like that, unfortunately."

"Gran was kinda like that," Kate said, thoughtfully now. "It was different with her, though."

"What do you mean? Different in what way?"

Gran, she reminded herself, had been April's mother. She tried to imagine what it must have been like to be abandoned by your mother. She sorta knew, because Mom had died and left her forever. But she hadn't done it deliberately.

"I think she was, like, trying to feel her emotions, you know? Like maybe she hadn't let herself do that for a while. So it was hard. But she did try."

April was staring at her as if she were saying something clever or witty or something. "You and Rina got along very well, didn't you?"

Kate nodded.

"You must miss her."

Kate clenched her fists. "I want to find the guy who killed her and watch him fry."

"What a bloodthirsty kid. That's what comes of letting you watch action movies and MTV, I suppose?"

Kate nodded vigorously. "You got it, lady."

They watched a framing exhibition in one of the lecture halls, then went downstairs to see the Egyptian art, and Kate led April with a certain amount of fanfare into the huge area dedicated to the Temple of Dendur. "Isn't this cool?" she said as they explored the inside of the massive stone structure. "It used to stand on the banks of the Nile, but it got moved here after some dam was built that would have flooded it. The museum built a whole new wing because they didn't have a place to put it."

"Usually I hate it when they move antiquities from their country of origin," April said. "But if it would otherwise have been destroyed, I guess it's okay."

After exploring the temple they sat on a stone bench opposite it and rested while watching other people go into it for a while. "I mean it, you know," Kate said.

April brushed her hair back from her face and stared into her eyes. "Mean what?"

"I want to help find Gran's murderer. I want to know who did it, and why."

She waited for April to say one of the usual grown-up things, like, "That's a matter for the police," or "Twelve-year-old girls don't solve crimes." But as usual, April didn't act like the typical sort of grown-up that Kate was used to. Instead, she nodded and said, "Who do you think may have done it?"

"I think it was one of her clients," Kate said promptly.

"Why do you think that?"

Kate hesitated. Then she said, "They used to tell her things. You know, because she helped them sort out their problems? Some people had, I guess, done things, like in the past, you know? Bad things."

"What sort of bad things?"

Kate was feeling uncomfortable. She wasn't supposed to know this stuff. Next April would want to know how she knew it. "Well some of them used to be alcoholics and drug-abusers, and their addictions were preventing them from seizing their personal power. Gran had to help them get through the blockage caused by the pressures from their pasts."

"Did she talk to you about her methods for helping people?" April asked.

"Yes, she talked to me a lot. And—well—I was around a lot, you know." She hesitated. "Sometimes I overheard stuff. You know, by accident."

Yeah, and sometimes I put a glass up against the wall and listened on purpose.

"Kate, is there anything you heard that you ought to tell the police about?"

Kate thought about Daisy Tulane. She hadn't told the police what she knew; she hadn't told anybody. Gran had said to her once, "You must remember, Kate, that there are some things that are private. They are nobody's business but your own. Do you understand?"

Besides, Daisy wasn't a killer. She just wasn't the right woman for Dad.

April was watching, and looking at her funny. So she shrugged and gave her a silly grin and said, "I wish I could think of something good to tell the police. But it was mostly just a lot of sad people who couldn't stop drinking or smoking or cheating on their wives."

"Then you don't have any real reason to think the murderer was one of your grandmother's clients?" April's face looked as still and serious as an Egyptian statue.

Kate bit her lip. "I guess the reason is—" she swallowed "—I don't want it to turn out to be somebody I know. Like, in the family, you know?"

April put her arm around her and gave her a quick hug. "No, neither do I."

April wasn't sure what to make of Christian de Sevigny.

She hadn't had much contact with him before, even though his office was at the same Fifth Avenue address as Power Perspectives. Unlike Armand, he never stopped by. In fact, when he'd called to invite her for dinner, she'd been surprised.

He was an attractive man. Strong features and hair the color of newly minted gold. His eyes were sea-green and his mouth would be sensual . . . if he ever allowed it to relax into a smile.

Although he and Kate lived in a more modern building than his father's, their two-storey apartment was similarly elegant. One thing that couldn't be denied about this family—they all had exquisite taste.

"I'm something of a collector," Christian had mentioned as he showed her around. "But I'm also a dilettante, I'm afraid. I develop an interest and pursue it with all due energy, then I abandon it. An unfortunate character trait, no doubt."

April smiled. She couldn't tell if he was sincere or simply trying to disarm her with self-deprecation.

"Porcelain is my latest passion," he went on. He stopped before a lighted china cabinet. "Sevres and Meissen—do you know the difference?"

"One's French and the other's German?"

His eyebrows went up. "Very good. You're interested in china?"

"Don't know anything about it," she said with a smile. "My European geography's pretty good, though."

Kate clapped her hands. "Don't let him give you that boring old china lecture. He does it to scare people away. If he's really boring, he says, we can be sure that they'll never come back."

April laughed. "I should try it. There are a few people at the office whom I'd like to drive away by some means or other—I didn't think of trying to bore them."

"I doubt that you'd be capable of it," said Christian.

Although he said the words expressionlessly, there could be no doubt he meant it as a compliment. April smiled and Kate, she noted, beamed.

But despite this auspicious beginning, the conversation during dinner was strained. There were too many subjects that were off limits. Asking Christian about his personal life seemed like a minefield, given what she'd been told about the custody battle he'd had with Kate's mother and her subsequent death. Talking about Power Perspectives would bore Kate, and Christian did not seem interested in April's personal life.

So the talk revolved around Kate—her interests, her dreams, her ambitions. Had she not been there, thought April, she and Christian would have probably been hard-pressed to find anything to say to each other.

April could also feel the subtle tension between father and daughter. It was a personality thing, she decided. Kate was bubbly, outgoing, and eager to please, while Christian was a controlled, emotionally reserved man whose expression revealed very little of what was going on inside. This didn't necessarily mean that he didn't feel an emotional reaction, April reminded herself, just that he himself had probably learned a long time ago to keep a tight lid on his feelings.

On the other hand, maybe he truly was a coldhearted bastard.

After dinner they sat in the living room and April decided that she was not going to allow the opportunity to pass to find out a bit more about Rina, even if it was boring to Kate. "How did you get along with my mother?" she asked.

Christian studied the brandy in the bottom of his glass. "Your mother and I really didn't have a lot to do with each other."

"You didn't like her?"

He shrugged. "We didn't always see eye to eye."

"I thought you liked Gran, Dad," Kate protested. "You even cried when you heard she was dead—I saw you."

Christian turned his Arctic glance on his daughter. "You

must have been dreaming. I haven't cried since my dog died when I was eight years old."

Kate looked stricken at the sharpness in his tone, and April hurriedly said, "Men are taught not to cry in this society, Kate. They grow up learning to control and hide their emotions. It's a shame, really. I don't think anyone—male or female—should feel obligated to hold all their emotions inside all the time. It's a difficult thing to do, anyhow."

"Like many things, it gets easier with practice," Christian said.

April met his eyes. For an instant she thought she saw something there that was worth reaching out toward—something sad, something kind. Then his lids flicked down and he raised his snifter, hiding whatever he had so briefly revealed.

Christian lay in bed that night, unable to sleep. April Harrington had left early, much to Kate's disappointment. It had occurred to him at some point during the evening that Kate had hoped to witness some sparking of interest and attraction between himself and April. She didn't like Daisy so she'd sought to matchmake for him with somebody she did like.

Actually, it wasn't a bad idea. April was a very attractive woman, and she was personable as well. She seemed easygoing and warm, and it was obvious that she'd already won his daughter's heart.

She was younger than Daisy, too.

And more sensual, he'd bet.

Maybe he should have tried a little harder to turn on the charm.

After dinner she'd questioned him—not very subtly—

about the family, his life, the business. And about Rina. He'd remembered that April owned a mystery bookstore in Boston, and that she probably fancied herself to be an expert on sifting through clues and unmasking falsehoods.

It annoyed him, frankly. He didn't like being interrogated, even gently, by an amateur.

No doubt it had showed. Indeed, by the end of the evening he'd been able to tell from the way her blue eyes had sparked and flashed that she would have loved to tell him to his face how rude and uncooperative he was. Only Kate's presence, he suspected, had prevented her from doing so.

As for Kate, she'd had nothing to say to him when April left. She'd given him a reproachful look and run upstairs to her room. When he'd looked in on her a couple of hours later, she was curled up in bed with a stuffed dog pressed to her chest, asleep.

Daisy was coming tomorrow.

Maybe she'd cheer him up, help him get his head straight, put his fucked-up life into some kind of order. Daisy believed in personal transformation. "This is the first day of the rest of your life" kind of crap.

Maybe some of it would rub off on him.

Fat chance.

But he couldn't go on like this much longer.

Chapter Fourteen

Most of the time, thought Blackthorn, tailing people was both difficult and dull. But as he followed Isobelle down a metal staircase and into the dimly lit club in the village, it struck him that this time things were proving to be real interesting.

He was following Isobelle to find out who her strange and unpleasant friends were.

It was Saturday night—the most promising, he'd figured, for meeting with non-work-related people. But although she had gone out to a restaurant for dinner, she'd eaten alone. Then home, where he'd presumed she intended to fall into bed. He'd hung around for a while, just in case she went out, hoping she did not, since his own bed had begun to hold a certain appeal.

He'd growled curses when she'd emerged just before midnight, and he'd nearly lost her as her taxi had executed an illegal turn and headed south.

Blackthorn had heard about the Chateau, although he'd

never been there. A few years ago he'd been bodyguarding a Japanese businessman who was obsessed with unusual varieties of sex. The client had insisted on visiting two of New York's other S&M clubs, the Vault and Paddles. Blackthorn had gone along in a professional capacity, and had been amazed by what he'd learned about the kinky Manhattan subculture during those few evenings.

Jessie had teased him when she'd heard his description of the Vault, which he'd given to her in loving details. "Sounds like you want to go back on your own time," she'd said. But when he'd agreed that it might be an interesting way to spend an evening, she'd quickly declined.

Sex was the only thing that hadn't been perfect in their relationship. Jessie had always been more traditional than he was, more inhibited, and less willing to experiment.

The place was crowded. A lotta kinky people in this city, he thought as he ordered a Diet Pepsi at the large square bar in the club's front room. A sign at the entrance had mentioned that alcohol was prohibited. No need to worry about that temptation, Blackthorn thought with a grim smile.

The air was smoky and the music was much too loud. Not that he minded rock music. As a matter of fact, he enjoyed it. The hard driving rhythms and sentimental lyrics had a certain primitive appeal.

He couldn't see Isobelle at the moment, so he eyed the other women in a desultory fashion. The club didn't look like much of a pick-up place. The women weren't alone. Single males abounded, but all the females seemed to be accompanied by one or more men. Some women, he noted, wore slave collars and walked deferentially beside their partners. Others were clad in spike heels and leather dominatrix gear.

Blackthorn knew from his prior, if limited, experience

that most of the folks here weren't as peculiar as they seemed. You'd think a bunch of folks who were into restraining and spanking each other must be violent, dysfunctional low-lifes, but he'd talked to a few and generally found them to be courteous, intelligent, and sane. They were dramatic, but they seemed to take joy in exploring all corners of their sensuality, even the darkest ones. There was a certain courage in that, and Blackthorn felt a grudging admiration for it.

After all, he had dark corners, too.

And besides, there wasn't much in life that shocked him.

A submissive woman dressed in a white leather bikini with leather cuffs adorning her wrists walked by with her partner. They were both heavyset—the woman might be said to be a BBW—big, beautiful woman. Blackthorn noted that a lot of the people present seemed to be overweight. Perhaps they had a larger-than-usual hunger for all the pleasures of life.

Then he noticed a slender, striking, leather-corsetted domme. There she was. Isobelle.

She hadn't seen him. She and her partner—whose back was to him—had brushed by no more than three feet away, but she'd been oblivious. There was a glazed look on her face that Blackthorn recognized from his observations at the Vault. Some folks were so excited simply by being here, on view for all to see, that they entered their erotic "space" spontaneously, as if they were drugged.

Isobelle de Sevigny was into kinky sex. Blackthorn took another sip of his Pepsi as he pondered what, if anything, this might have to do with Power Perspectives and Rina's death.

Did a fascination with fantasy power games correlate in any way with a propensity for real-life violence? There was no evidence that it did, yet how could one know for sure? From where did such impulses spring? Was there something in Isobelle's past that had given rise to her kink, and, if so, what else had it engendered?

Blackthorn set down his nearly empty glass on the bar and followed her into the back room.

On a platform in the middle of the room was a paddling horse upon which a scantily clad male submissive was lying. His partner, an attractive blonde dressed in a leather skirt and vest, black stockings, and impossibly high heels, was spanking him rhythmically with the flat of her hand. A crowd stood around, watching, some of them caressing their partners. When the domme picked up a leather paddle to continue the scene, the group energy seemed to heighten.

Isobelle, however, covered her mouth with her hand and yawned.

Blackthorn stepped up behind her. "Now how could you be bored in a place like this?" he said, close to her ear.

She whirled. "Blackthorn!"

Her partner turned also, and Blackthorn's eyes narrowed in recognition. Christ. It was Charlie Ripley, from Power Perspectives. An intriguing complication . . .

"Hello, there, Ripley. Small world."

Ripley looked embarrassed. No wonder. Jeez, thought Blackthorn, I'd be embarrassed too if somebody was leading me around on a chain.

"Look, this is hardly the time or the place," Ripley said. "We're off the job at the moment."

"I'm on the job, myself. I work odd hours."

Isobelle slipped between them. "Let me talk to him, Charlie. I imagine this has to do with my stepmother's murder. Just give us a few minutes."

"I really don't think—"

"It's okay," she said impatiently.

Like the good slave he was, Charlie Ripley subsided.

Isobelle drew Blackthorn back from the action to a corner that was quieter and less crowded. "This is too much. What the hell are you doing here?"

"Maybe I come here often," he said.

She flashed him her brilliant smile. "Funny. I haven't seen you here before."

"Or maybe I prefer to act out my fantasies at home."

"Gee, Blackthorn. Do you have fantasies? I would have thought you far too single-minded. No, wait, I've got it. You're the implacable cop. I'm the miserable offender. You track me down, snap the handcuffs on me, and toss me into a cell to be interrogated, using all sorts of dastardly methods." She smiled again. "Only trouble is, I don't play the submissive role."

Blackthorn shrugged. "Now that's a shame. So much for my fantasy."

"On the other hand—" Isobelle looked him over and her smile became more expansive. "For you, darling, I might consider switching."

"Likewise," he said, grinning back.

She laughed shaking her mane of hair. "Seriously. You seem pretty comfortable here. Are you in the scene?"

"You mean, do I come here when I'm not on the job? Nope." He took a pointed look around, his eyes following an attractive dark-haired woman as she knelt gracefully at the feet of her "master." She was wearing a crimson merry-widow corset and, except for wrist cuffs and a collar, very little else. Her long, slender legs were encased in black patterned stockings, attached to the bottom of the corset with black lace straps. Her dom, whose hands gently caressed her breasts, was tall, slender, good-looking, and perhaps a few years younger than she. His face was vaguely familiar and Blackthorn thought he might have seen him somewhere—Wall Street, perhaps.

"I'll admit, the place does have a certain kinky appeal," he said.

"I could introduce you around if you'd like."

"Thanks, but I don't socialize much."

"Because of Jessie's death? You're still mourning her?"

He nodded. Sometimes it seemed as if he'd be mourning Jessie forever.

"Did you and Jessie ever get into this stuff?"

Good old Isobelle—always saying exactly what came into her head. Enough of this, he thought. "Look, I didn't come here to talk about me. I've got a few questions for you. Will you come outside for a few minutes?"

"Why should I?"

"Look, we can do this now, while you're relaxed, or tomorrow in your office, when you'll presumably be stressed out and overwhelmed with work. Your choice."

"I'm here to enjoy myself, Rob. I don't want to clutter up my mind with a lot of unpleasant thoughts. This is my escape. My refuge from the real world. If you want to talk, we can talk here, but let's make it fast, okay?"

He nodded toward Charlie, who was watching them as they moved into a more secluded corner. "He appears a little green at the thought of being found out. You can tell him afterwards that I don't give a damn about his erotic proclivities. Solving a murder is all I'm interested in."

"Don't worry about Charlie. I'll deal with him."

"You sound pretty confident about that," he noted.

"He's in love with me. I've been warning him not to get too attached, but I'm beginning to think he's one of those obsessive personalities. It's difficult to find good submissives. Especially good male submissives. You guys are too used to being naturally dominant in the real world."

"Did Rina know about your interest in kinky sex?"

"I wouldn't be surprised," she said calmly. "Rina knew a lot of things. She kept close tabs on people. She used to tell me how it is important to get to know one's friends and relations—really know them, stressing the 'really.' It was part of her personal power philosophy. Know yourself, and know everyone around you."

This was new information. "You say she kept tabs on people. What exactly do you mean?"

Isobelle shrugged. "Everybody confided in Rina. She knew a lot of secrets. She used to say she was helping people by providing a sympathetic ear, but I always thought there was more to it than that. I think she relished knowing people's most private and personal secrets. And I don't think she'd have hesitated to use them, if it ever became necessary."

Blackmail, in other words, he thought. A motive for murder? "Maybe someone wants to silence me," Rina had told him when she'd hired him for the job. She'd admitted to knowing "too many secrets about too many people."

"If you want to understand Rina," Isobelle went on, "you have to understand her deep interest in power. She called it personal power, as if it were something new and different, but just plain power-seeking is all it really was." She waved her hand at the shadowy figures in the smoky basement. "Power exchange. That's what it's all about. Discipline. Control. These were issues Rina understood, even if she didn't choose to act them out in a forum like this one."

She patted the palm of her hand with her crop. "You have to place Rina in the right context. Few people do. They think she represented empathy, altruism, and love, but that's bullshit. She, at least, was honest enough to call her foundation Power Perspectives, because that's what it's all about."

"Did you and she discuss these issues?" Blackthorn asked.

"Frequently. I was straightforward with her and she was straightforward with me. Power Perspectives changed her life. She moved from being Papa's powerless wife to the mistress of her own fate."

"Not entirely," Blackthorn reminded her. "In the end somebody else dictated her fate."

Isobelle made a face. "Yeah, and she would have hated that."

"So how well did you and Rina get along?" he asked after a short pause.

Isobelle put her hands on her hips and stared at him through half-closed eyes. "Here it comes. Do you think I'm the one who hired her killer?"

"Did you?"

"For the record, no. But I know I can't expect you—or the cops, for that matter—to believe me. I certainly haven't gained anything by her death, though—you might keep that in mind."

"You expected to benefit from her death. You believed yourself to be slated to inherit Power Perspectives. The existence of April Harrington must have been a nasty surprise."

"Yeah, maybe I should have her killed as well."

Charlie chose this moment to return to her side. He nodded to Blackthorn as he took Isobelle's arm nondeferentially. "They're about to start the slave auction in the other room," he said.

Isobelle tossed Blackthorn a jaunty smile. "Ah, the

highlight of the evening! We don't want to miss that, do we?"

"You've been very helpful," Blackthorn said.

"Anytime." Her tone was dry. "Actually, I'm having a party next weekend. Friday, if you'd like to come. It's my birthday, and I'm going to celebrate rather extravagantly." She grinned. "Bring a date, if you like. Or come alone. There'll be some singles present; maybe you'll get lucky."

"An appealing possibility," he said, grinning.

Blackthorn decided to skip the slave auction. Isobelle had given him plenty of other things to think about.

When he got outside to his car, the cellular phone was ringing. "You're working late," he said to Carla when he heard her voice. "Whatcha got?"

"Heard from Jonas," she said. "You're gonna love what he coaxed out of some confidential data base about April Harrington."

"I'm gonna love it, huh?"

"Trust me," Carla said.

Chapter Fifteen

The sun was setting as April entered Central Park. She'd been walking to and from work every day, partly to get some exercise, and partly to drink in the excitement of the city.

She loved New York. She'd always been a city lover— Washington and Boston were two of her favorites. But New York had everything from gaudy hustle and bustle to true grace and beauty. She loved its vitality and diversity. She loved the street vendors with their easily folded-up suitcases full of watches and jewelry of questionable provenance, the hot dog carts, the skyscrapers, the mad traffic, the graceful old architecture, the general air of doggedness and individual freedom.

The city had always been the center of immigration and that was still the case—when you dreamed of coming to America, you dreamed of coming to New York. There were always newcomers, learning their way around the city. She felt as if she were part of a long tradition.

Power Perspectives was in an office building near the corner of Madison Avenue and Sixty-third Street, and April's apartment was on West Sixty-second Street between Broadway and Columbus. So her typical route home was to walk west one block to Fifth and enter the park near the zoo, cross on various pathways to the exit on Central Park West, which put her a short two blocks from the co-op that had formerly belonged to Rina.

She'd never realized Central Park was as large as it was—three long blocks wide and approximately fifty short blocks long. At first she'd been a little wary of walking there alone, but Kate had pooh-poohed her concerns. "It's a lot safer than anybody admits. Nothing's ever happened to me in Central Park. Just don't hang out there in the middle of the night, and you'll be fine."

And it was true that the park was always filled with people engaged in various activities. There were walkers and joggers and hikers and bikers, yuppies on rollerblades and showmen on regular roller skates who performed intricate feats of skating to the loud music of their boom boxes. There were street musicians and amateur actors who would choose a spot and perform, whether anybody was watching or not. There were lovers, some more discreet than others. Not to mention horse-drawn carts filled with tourists and mounted police on patrol.

This evening, though, a Sunday, seemed quieter than usual. She'd slept until nearly eleven—a rare luxury—then gone into the office. There was so much to learn about her mother's business that working at least one day per weekend seemed like a sensible idea. And it had been great to have the entire suite of offices all to herself for a change.

Without the usual hustle and bustle of a regular weekday, she had lost track of the time. So it was not until fairly late that evening that she began her progress along one of her favorite paths in the southern end of the park.

It was too cloudy to observe the setting sun, but the gathering darkness confirmed that night was coming on. By the time she came out on the other side, she figured, the sky would be completely black.

She quickened her footsteps. The footpath that was usually crowded with people out for a bit of fresh air was almost deserted now. Thunder growled in the distance, and April wondered if the threat of an impending summer electrical storm had kept some of the usual evening joggers inside.

She envisioned the way ahead of her. It was well lighted, and as long as she kept to the roads through the park, she ought to be safe.

She hoped.

She rounded a curve. Coming toward her at a distance of about fifty yards were three youths who looked about eighteen or nineteen years old. They were wearing baggy clothing that looked too hot for this weather. Did that mean that they were carrying concealed weapons? They were laughing and joking with each other, and they seemed harmless enough, but everything she'd ever read about the Central Park Jogger flashed into her mind, and she wished she'd taken a cab.

Don't be such a wimp! Goodness heavens, she reminded herself, if anyone knew how to survive in the streets, she did. She'd done her best to suppress all memory of that portion of her life, but every now and then it rose up to haunt her . . . more and more often now, since Rina's death.

Just last night she'd had a nightmare. Someone was following her. She knew he wanted to kill her but she didn't know why. She ran, trying to escape, but he was faster.

She felt his breath on the back of her neck and then his hands closing around her throat.

She'd woken up, trembling and drenched with sweat. She'd turned on the lights and sat there in bed with her arms clasped around her knees, trying to banish the images of the dream. She hadn't dared to lie back down and go to sleep.

So far no one had questioned her about the summer of '69. She'd been told at the time that her records were sealed; this must have been the truth.

The young men were nearly upon her. April held her breath as they passed each other without incident. Get a grip, she ordered herself.

She entered an area where the trees were thick alongside the path. Up ahead on her left was the Wollman Rink—the roller-skating area, although Kate had told her it was used for ice skating in the winter—and the minigolf and basket-shooting backboards. The lights were brighter there and she was sure there would be some people lingering over a late game of miniature golf.

She walked faster, caught her foot on an uneven outcropping of pavement, and stumbled. For an instant she thought she was going to fall, perhaps sprain an ankle or something—but she managed to keep her balance. She breathed a sigh of relief, then started as she felt a light touch on her arm.

April whirled. A tall man was just behind her. She hadn't heard him coming. His face was in the shadow of the big tree to their right, but she had no interest in his face or for that matter in anything else about him. Her instinctive response was to run.

She jerked away from him and sprinted down the pathway. She could see the lights of the roller rink—it wasn't very far . . . surely he wouldn't do anything, not so close to civilization . . .

She heard him curse and then she heard the sound of footsteps chasing after her.

Just like in her dream.

"Hey!" he shouted. "Dammit, April, take it easy."

He knew her name. The rational part of her brain was ordering her to reevaluate the situation, but the part of her that dreamed dreams and knew panic was still in control. He was gaining on her. She could hear his footsteps pounding the pavement.

"April!" he called again. His voice was familiar, but she was brimming with adrenaline; her muscles were full of it.

She sensed him reaching out for her and she ran sideways, stumbling towards the trees. Her breath was tearing out of her lungs and she was panting. Off the path the ground was uneven. She couldn't run faster here, this was stupid, why had she—

"Jesus," he huffed, coming alongside her and then swerving, herding her towards a thick grove of trees. "Slow down. You are not about to be raped and murdered."

"Blackthorn," she gasped.

"Yeah, it's me, and I haven't mugged anyone in years."

She slowed to a trot, then stopped abruptly, taking refuge in the shadow of a large oak. He overran her and came back, breathing hard, too, she noted, although he was not as winded as she.

She grabbed her side and bent over. Swallowing huge quantities of air.

"You okay?"

She nodded, gasping.

"What d'you run for?"

"You came out of nowhere. You frightened me!"

"You deserved it, strolling through Central Park at night. What the hell did you think you were doing?"

"I'm going home. I always walk home this way." She was breathing easier now. She stretched and then ran her fingers through her hair, which was wildly strewn on her shoulders.

"It's nine o'clock at night. You can't be that ignorant about New York."

"Okay, then what are you doing here?"

"I'm following you, obviously. And it's a good thing, too, if you're going to be so cavalier about your safety. Although I certainly didn't set out with the intention of playing bodyguard."

April leaned back against the trunk of the oak tree. Her blouse had pulled out of her waistband and was creeping up her midriff. She tried, unobtrusively, to pull it down.

He looked at the spot and grinned. "Nice."

Damn him, she thought. I will not let him humiliate me. "What do you want?"

"I think it's time you and I had a little talk."

She looked around, wondering why he'd picked Central Park for a talk. "So talk. You've got five minutes."

"Why, thank you, but it's going to take somewhat longer than that. You want to go find a place to get a cup of coffee?"

Did he expect her to suggest a change of venue? Her apartment perhaps? "Right here is fine."

He shrugged. "Okay." He looked her over and she had the feeling he was mentally undressing her. But all he said was, "You are, I take it, finding your job interesting?"

"Yes. Both interesting and challenging. More so than I expected it to be."

"Rumor has it that you handled yourself very well during your first week. People are pleasantly surprised."

She quickly decided not to take offense. "I'm pleasantly surprised myself."

"Of course, the real question has not yet been addressed—even if you succeed in terms of your administrative skills, what happens when it's time for new books, new tapes, new inspirational seminars? Are you the guru your mother was, April? Are you grooming yourself to go out there and make more converts, lead more suckers into the Promised Land?"

She shrugged. "I have considerable difficulty imagining myself in that role."

"So do I," he said. He moved closer. He leaned one hip against her oak tree. He was casually dressed in black chino trousers and a short-sleeved white shirt. The jeans were tight, and emphasized the rather appealing curve of his buttocks and the long muscles in his thighs.

He looked good for a man who must surely be approaching middle age. He had to be at least forty, perhaps a couple of years older. His eyes, she noticed, were very blue, with thick dark lashes.

"It would be a fascinating case study of the blind leading the blind. Or rather—" he smiled unpleasantly "—the blind leading the dumb."

"Oh, really?" She inched sideways. He was too close, and something about the tightly coiled energy in his body made her feel vulnerable. "In what sense am I blind?"

"In the moral sense. At least by my definition. But who knows, it might not stop you. Most of the gurus of our time or any other have been skilled at schemes and deceptions, so maybe you'll just ease on in."

"What the hell are you talking about? Come on. Spit it out, Blackthorn. It's too late in the day for word games."

"Ah, you're very direct, aren't you? I like that in a woman."

She glared at him.

"Honest, direct, and straightforward. Except when you lie. Have you ever noticed that it's the honest and direct folks who have the greatest success at lying? Nobody expects them to lie."

"In what manner have I lied to you?" she asked softly.

He moved closer. "In neglecting to tell me—or anybody—about your criminal record."

She held his gaze for several seconds, then looked away. She felt the stress build in the pit of her belly. I was afraid of this, she thought.

"I don't have a criminal record."

"Look, April." His voice was low and confident. "I'm not bluffing and I'm not on a fishing expedition. I have copies of your files. Would you like to see them?"

"Yes," she said tightly.

He took several sheets of paper, folded lengthwise, from the back pocket of his jeans. April glanced through them quickly, feeling sick.

"Well?" He raised his eyebrows expectantly. "Nothing to say, for once?"

"I was a juvenile. The records were sealed."

"Yeah, well, this is the nineties. There are no secrets on the information highway. Nowhere to run, nowhere to hide." He took the sheets away from her and returned them to his pocket. "You were tried in the juvenile system in Washington, D.C., in 1969 for second-degree murder. Seems you stabbed a guy to death."

So, she thought. It was going to come out, after all.

Chapter Sixteen

"I was acquitted," April said. "Innocent until proven guilty, Mr. Blackthorn."

"Yeah, I know. You got off. Is that why you weren't worried about paperwork? Did you think acquittals simply vanish without a trace?"

April turned away from him. There was a grassy slope just a few feet away. Unceremoniously, she sat down.

Blackthorn joined her. "Spare me the state-of-shock act, okay? You must have known there was a good chance I'd find out about this. I can't believe Anaheim or the feds didn't turn it up at the beginning of their investigation. It was buried pretty deep, I must admit. But my computer guy is terrific." He paused. "You want to tell me about it?"

She raised her head. "Do I have a choice?"

"No."

She wasn't afraid, she realized. She was relieved, in a way. She was sick of worrying about this. She met his eyes steadily. "I stabbed him, yes, with a letter opener." She paused. "Do you want to know why?"

"I think I can guess why," Blackthorn said slowly.

"No, I don't think you can." Her hands were clenched in her lap. "My attorney—who was very good—defended me by claiming that the man—his name was Miquel— was trying to rape me. That was his interpretation, not mine. Mine was that Miquel was trying to kill me. I believed it then and I still believe it now."

He looked at her. His blue eyes seemed to bore into hers. "Talk to me," he said.

Her memory of the top-floor apartment with the view of the Washington Monument was still vivid. She'd loved to sit in the open window with the humid evening breezes ruffling through her long, unruly hair, imagining herself at the top of the Monument with the world stretching out in all directions. On several occasions she had climbed to the top, so she knew how broad the world looked from up there. It was a world in which she could do anything, be anything. Nothing was impossible to dream.

"When I was sixteen, I ran away from the boarding school in Connecticut where my mother had left me," she told Blackthorn. "The mother superior was a bitter woman who believed that God had assigned her a mission to beat all willful young girls into shape. I hated her.

"I kept waiting for my mother to come and take me away from there. But a year went by, and then another. Rina didn't come.

"I think I'd have gone crazy if it hadn't been for the books I found in the school library. I read voraciously, everything I could get my hands on. There were a lot of nineteenth-century romances and adventures in the library, along with the complete work of Alexandre Dumas, Charlotte Brontë, and Charles Dickens."

It was Dickens, she remembered, who'd started her thinking about running away. His characters seemed to lead lives that were even crueler and more appalling than her own, yet they were clever, and they survived. If David Copperfield could do it, she'd told herself, so can I.

"I waited until the spring of my fourth year. I was tall for my age. I sneaked out of the convent school early one morning, bought myself some hair coloring in a drugstore and dyed my red hair black, a trick I remembered from Rina's instructions about evading bill collectors. Then I got out of town.

"It was 1969, and there were live-ins and street people and potheads everywhere. I hitchhiked south to Washington, D.C.—I don't know why—maybe because it was the home of the president of the United States, and JFK had briefly been my mother's lover.

"I hung out with a variety of college dropouts, war protesters, and flower children. I made posters, held up picket signs, cooked beans and rice for the long-haired males who were the self-appointed leaders of the movement, and marched my feet off on behalf of the cause. It wasn't the cause I really cared about, though. What the peace movement gave me, I think, was something I'd yearned for all my life—the feeling that I belonged."

Gently, Blackthorn touched her hand. April glanced up at him. He was listening intently, his expression serious, his eyes compassionate.

"Life wasn't easy, though," she went on. "I shared a small apartment with four other girls. My clothes were old and ragged. Sometimes it was a problem getting enough to eat. But none of that mattered towards the end of the summer of 1969 because I was in love—" she smiled wryly "—and love makes everything okay.

"It was a hot, sticky August day, and I was the only one

of the five roommates who was home. I was waiting for my boyfriend. I'd met him two weeks ago at an antiwar demonstration. He was twenty-one, and I'd told him I was eighteen.

"His name was Miquel. I loved the way the syllables seemed to roll off the tongue. He was from Mexico and spoke bad English, but of course that didn't matter at all.

"He had the sexiest eyes. Dark brown and very soulful. Sometimes they looked a little hard, which made me wonder what his past life had been like. He hadn't told me much, except that he was poor, but proud.

"We were planning to visit the Smithsonian together that day. He'd never been, and he wanted to see the aviation display. He had a dream of someday learning to fly . . ."

April shifted uneasily on the grass. Telling the story had already brought some very vivid images into her head. She wished she didn't have to continue . . . and yet she knew she did. Not just because of Rob Blackthorn, but because this was a piece of her past that she had been avoiding.

"Miquel came by the apartment to pick me up. I invited him in and offered him a Coke. He was wearing jeans and a ragged T-shirt. His skin was tan, and his hair was long and dark and curly. His body was incredible.

"I showed him around, I remember feeling shy about it, and very conscious that we were alone. We weren't lovers. I was a virgin, in fact. He'd kissed me a couple of times, but that was all.

"I didn't take him into my bedroom—I just pointed it out from the threshold. He gazed at the two narrow beds in the tiny room and sipped his Coke.

"I had to go to the bathroom, so I left him alone in the hallway. When I came out, Miquel was waiting for me.

He grabbed me in the hallway and turned me to him and began kissing me passionately.

"Next thing I knew, he'd lifted me in his arms and was carrying me into the bedroom. I knew I ought to protest, but it was all so exciting, and, I foolishly thought, so very romantic."

Blackthorn pressed her hand, but April hardly noticed. "He carried me to the bed, choosing my roommate Julie's instead of mine, but I didn't bother to correct him. He laid me down and fell on top and continued kissing me. He was heavy and strong, and when I tried to shift to a more comfortable position, I couldn't.

"I was never entirely sure, afterwards, when my arousal turned to fear. It was something to do with the way he didn't *say* anything. He unbuttoned my blouse and pushed it aside to caress my breasts, but his hands were cold and impersonal. He was kissing me, but it didn't feel right. It felt more as if he was trying to distract me and keep me occupied.

"And then suddenly he put his hands around my throat and started to squeeze. At first I thought he was just fooling around, but his grip turned painful and I couldn't breathe." April's heart fluttered as she remembered how it had felt to gasp for breath. "I struggled, but he was on his knees now, straddling my chest, and I looked up into his eyes and saw something there that chilled my soul. I didn't know this man. He wasn't cute, sweet, mysterious Miquel. He was a killer.

"I tried to thrust him away. I tore at his fingers around my throat, at his face, at his hair. I could feel the rapid pulse pounding in my ears, and my lungs were screaming for air. But the pain around my throat got worse and worse, and I was so dizzy that I couldn't think or breathe. I knew I was going to die . . ."

"Jesus, April," Blackthorn said. He pulled her into his arms, and she held on to him as if he were anchoring her to the earth. She didn't resist, but she didn't really look at him, either. She was looking into the past.

One of her wildly thrashing hands swiped at the bedside table that Julie had littered with paperback books, her water glass, some letters from her boyfriend in New York, and . . . something sharp. April dimly remembered that Julie always used a silver letter opener. Her grandmother had given it to her, saying that "ladies never tear open their mail."

With her last surge of consciousness, April groped for the handle, found it, gripped it, then lunged upwards and slashed her arm down at the same moment, sinking the point of the letter opener into the middle of Miquel's back.

He groaned and his grip on her throat loosened. April smashed him in the face with her other hand. He rolled off her and fell onto the floor.

She stumbled from the bed, sobbing. Without looking to see what condition he was in, she ran from the apartment.

"I remember banging on the building superintendent's door, and shivering in the hallway while the woman went upstairs to investigate. And all I could imagine was the police coming and interrogating me and finding out who I was and where I'd come from. They would send me back to that horrible boarding school in Connecticut. Worse, they would notify my mother and tell her the story of how I'd let a man into my bedroom and how he'd tried to rape me and kill me.

"It was too much for a sixteen-year-old to contemplate. I lost my nerve entirely, and I fled the superintendent's apartment, leaving behind the few possessions I owned, seeking the safety and anonymity of the streets.

"For three weeks I wandered from one ramshackle

shelter to another, earning a few coins by begging on street corners. I was in a constant state of terror—torn between nightmares about Miquel, my mother, Armand, and the police. I didn't understand what had happened, or more importantly why; and I didn't know if Miquel was alive or dead. The thought that I might have killed him was horrifying, but even worse was the thought that he might still be stalking me.

"Finally one night, hungry, exhausted, and emotionally wrung out, I sought refuge with a kindly priest whose mission was to help the 'flower children.' I told him my story, he comforted me, and together we contacted the police.

"That was when I learned that Miquel had died in the hospital. It wasn't directly because of the stab wound, but because of an infection that had set in afterwards, but apparently that doesn't matter to the courts. I'd caused the wound and therefore I was responsible.

"Also, before dying he'd given a false statement to the authorities insisting that he'd done nothing criminal, and that I'd stabbed him in a jealous rage because he'd expressed an interest in my roommate.

"Meanwhile, the bruises on my throat that would have helped to establish my side of the story had, by this time, vanished. So the police arrested me for second degree murder."

April folded her arms tightly around her middle and shivered.

"You need a break?" Blackthorn said. "I can see this is hard for you to talk about."

She looked at him. Although he had not said anything particularly comforting, the expression in his blue eyes was sympathetic, and she could feel the emotion coming off him in waves.

She sighed. "I'm okay, I think. After all, I guess this is what I'm supposed to be doing—confronting my past. It's why I approached my mother at the ABA, and it's why I decided to accept her job. It's just—" Her voice trailed off. She looked at Rob Blackthorn. "Have you ever killed anyone?"

"Yes," he said.

"It doesn't go away. Even when it's self-defense. It never goes away."

"No," he agreed. "It's not supposed to. If it did—that would be an indication that something was seriously wrong."

She nodded. "I've never understood what happened. It came out in the trial that Miquel was an illegal alien. No one knew exactly where he'd come from. They did trace him back to his village in Mexico, but apparently he'd left there six years before, and nobody knew where he'd been or what he'd been doing in the meantime. I suppose he must have been some sort of wandering sociopath. Did he kill anyone before his attack on me? If so he got away with it because he'd never been arrested."

"He may have been a serial killer," Blackthorn said. "We know now that they sometimes move from state to state, making it a lot harder for police to put the evidence together."

"Running from the crime scene was the worst mistake I could have made. It would have been easier to convince the judge if they'd had the physical evidence of the bruises on my throat. And, as it turned out, I'd run away for nothing. During the entire process of being arrested and tried, I kept expecting my mother to show up. But she never did, even though she and Armand were back in New York by that time, for at least part of every year."

"No wonder you were angry with her," Blackthorn said.

April nodded. "After it was over and I was free, I came to my senses about a lot of things. I understood and accepted that Rina had truly abandoned me and that I would probably never see her again. Which was fine with me. I no longer *wanted* to see her again. I also realized that the life I'd been leading was pointless and wasteful. It was a turning point for me. I guess you could say that I grew up."

Blackthorn made an affirmative sound.

"Father Jacobs—the priest I'd turned myself in to—arranged for shelter for me in a community center for troubled teenagers. I got a part-time job in a donut shop and I went back and finished high school. When I got out, I found a clerical job and went to college in the evening. It took six years, but I got my degree."

Blackthorn nodded, and she realized that he probably already knew this, thanks to the miracles of modern data processing.

"I put the past behind me. All of it—my mother, the nuns, the counterculture, Miquel. It seemed a good way to live. Forgetting the past was the only way to make the present tolerable and the future worth looking forward to."

"Some of us live entirely too much in the past."

She shot him a curious look. He knew all about her now, she thought. But she knew nothing about him.

"Why'd you change your mind about that?" he asked.

She shrugged. "I made a lot of progress over the years. But at some point I got stuck. I realized I wasn't happy. I was married—I suppose you know that too?"

He nodded. "To the guy who gave you your current last name."

"Jonathan Harrington, yes. He was a good man. But it didn't last. I could never—I don't know—I couldn't completely relax. I expected him to leave me. Finally, I left him."

"If you initiated the split, he couldn't?"

She nodded. "Something like that, I guess. It was the same with other relationships. Finally it became evident that I probably wouldn't ever allow myself to be happy until I understood why my mother had abandoned me."

"So you decided to confront her."

"And when I confronted her, she died." Unexpectedly, her voice broke. Once again, Blackthorn reached out a hand. She took it and felt the warm pressure of his fingers. It felt good, very good. He was gentle, and there was something amazingly comforting about him.

"That's one helluva story, April."

"Do you believe me?"

He shrugged. His thumb drew lazy circles on the back of her hand.

"I've told you the truth."

"Why didn't you tell it to me sooner?"

"I was acquitted. I didn't know whether they kept records on people who turn out not to be guilty of a crime. And if they did, well it was juvenile court, and I was hoping that whatever paperwork they had on me was sealed. I didn't want to play back those memories. I didn't think I'd have to."

He did not reply.

"I'll admit I've been afraid somebody would find out, though," she said. She paused. "I don't suppose there's any point in my asking you to keep what you've learned confidential?"

"Depends on the incentive," he said slowly, as she watched a smile take shape on his lips.

Her body received his message even before her mind could analyze it. She shook her head, surprised. Yet he was still holding her hand, and the contact was creating a pleasant little buzz.

He was coming on, and amazingly, she felt receptive.

"I don't believe this." She kept her tone light. "I tell you a bitter story about sexual violence and you respond with sexual innuendo?"

"Men are scum," he observed.

In spite of herself, she laughed. He was sitting very close to her, but there was no longer any sense of threat emanating from him, except of the sensual variety.

She liked him, she thought suddenly.

She definitely liked the warmth and sensuality in his palm . . .

"At the will reading, I was surprised to hear that Rina left something to you, in memory of your late wife. When did she die?" she asked.

He seemed surprised at her change of subject. For a moment she thought he wasn't going to answer. Then he nodded once and said, "Nearly two years ago. She had cancer."

"I'm sorry," April said gently.

"So am I," he said with more fervor than she had ever heard in his voice.

"It must be very hard," she said tentatively. "I mean, there are so many ways that relationships end, but death— being widowed at a relatively young age—that's unusual."

He nodded. "It's not like divorce. And you're right, there aren't too many people who understand. Even the widowed persons support groups are usually made up of older people, people who've spent a whole lifetime together . . ." His voice turned off and he appeared slightly embarrassed.

"A good friend of mine lost her husband in a car accident a couple of years ago," April said. "Maggie, actually, the romance bookseller who was with me at the convention in Anaheim. It's been a tough adjustment for her. She has two young children whom she has to raise entirely on her own."

"Jessie and I didn't have children. I've often regretted that. But you're right. It would have been hard for me to manage if we had had children. It's been hard enough to take care of myself during the past few months." He looked into space for several seconds, then turned back to her. She saw the way the muscles moved in his jaw and felt a strong desire to stroke his body and smooth away some of that pain.

"You seem to have lured me neatly off the subject," he said in a much colder tone.

Retrenchment time. Men, she'd found, could only handle a limited amount of vulnerability.

"The question is," he went on, "how much, if anything, of what you've told me tonight is relevant to the current investigation?"

"Do you honestly believe it has anything to do with what happened to Rina?"

"No," he said after a moment. "I guess not."

"Well then, my suggestion is that you let it go."

"And let you off the hook."

"Yes."

He seemed to have moved closer to her. Certainly his face was closer. His blue eyes glittered just above hers, and she realized that if he brought his face down but a few inches, he could touch her lips with his.

"But sexual harassment," he said slowly, "is not to enter into these discussions at any point."

"No," she whispered.

"May I ask you something?" he said.

"Go ahead."

"Did your experience with Miquel—who got what was coming to him, in my opinion—sour you on men?"

"Yes," she said. "For a long while it did. But not for always." She paused. "And has your wife's illness and death soured you on women?"

"Yes. I haven't looked at a woman since Jessie died."

She swallowed. "You're looking at me."

He moved closer still. "Not as a woman. I'm looking at you as a suspect."

"I don't believe you."

"I advise you to believe me," he said even as he slid his hand into her hair and anchored her head. "I have no interest in you as a woman. And I wouldn't dream of sexually harassing you."

"Then why—"

"Open your mouth."

"I—"

"Good," he said and kissed her.

Chapter Seventeen

The kiss lasted a long time, and Blackthorn was thrilled to feel April's initial resistance fade as he increased the pressure on her soft, warm lips. The feel of her tongue moving tentatively in response to his ignited a fire deep in the pit of his belly, and he gathered her close in his arms and caressed her neck and shoulders until he heard a soft moan coming from the back of her throat.

God, it felt good. He drank her in. She tasted and smelled delicious. To touch her was to realize the depth of his hunger. And hers. He could tell from the way her defenses uncurled and fell away that she was a woman for whom passion and sensuality were very, very important.

Blackthorn allowed one hand to slip around in front. Body to body was the only reality that existed. It had been so long. Too long.

She was wearing a silk blouse inside her suit jacket. It buttoned up the front. If he could just get those buttons undone so he could get at her. Her breasts, he knew instinctively, were lovely . . .

It was she who broke the embrace as soon as he touched her breasts through her blouse, pulling away from him unexpectedly, leaving him high and dry. She sat with her knees raised and her arms folded across them in a gesture that was nervously self-protective. Under his stroking hands, her auburn hair was tumbling haphazardly over her shoulders.

"April?"

She didn't look at him.

"Don't phase out on me," he said, trying to make it light, but having difficulty controlling his breathing. "I didn't intend that to happen."

She still didn't say anything. But she got to her feet, and started to pace back and forth under the oak tree.

"Okay, okay, I admit it, I did intend it to happen," he said. "In fact, I've had a thing for you from the first time I saw you and have been fantasizing about getting my hands on you all week. So there. Stop that pacing. You're making me nervous."

She stopped in front of him and propped her hands on her hips. She looked belligerent. Her lips were pouty (well-kissed, he thought smugly) and her eyes were flashing fire at him. Amazon woman, he thought, and had a swift image of how she would look dressed in a black leather corset and fondling a whip at a club like the Dungeon. Or—better still—on her knees before him clad in a nineteenth-century ball gown with one of those low-cut bodices that was just begging to be ripped.

"I wish I'd never gotten involved with any of you," April said.

"Any of—"

"Anyone associated with the de Sevigny family!"

"What does that mean?"

"It's just that I feel, I feel—" she hesitated "—I feel as if I'm being seduced on all sorts of levels here. You're all so masculine, so smooth. You're each charismatic in your own way, and you're used to walking all over people."

"Wait a moment here. Don't include me in the de Sevigny family. I'm just the hired help."

"Dammit, there's something going on. I can feel it. It's beginning to give me the willies. There's something—" again she hesitated "—something evil going on."

"Murder is evil, I agree."

"People aren't what they seem. Somebody is playing a complicated game of cat and mouse, but I can't seem to figure out who. I can't trust my own impressions of people. And it seems as if it's been going on for years. I trusted my mother and she abandoned me. I trusted Miquel and he tried to murder me. The people I like are not necessarily trustworthy, and as for the people I don't like—" Her voice trailed off.

"You don't like me, yet you liked kissing me—is that what you're hinting at?"

She raised her palms in an apologetic gesture. "I'm getting to like you better," she confessed.

"Well, then—"

"But still, these, uh, these hormones, they only add to the confusion. I don't need any more confusion, Rob."

It was the first time she'd ever called him Rob.

He liked it.

"If it makes you feel any better, I'm having some of the same misgivings. Feeling hormonal towards a suspect is not recommended in the Homicide Investigator's Guide."

"Look, it's late. I'm going home."

"Not alone, you're not. It's well after dark now. I'll walk you."

She looked at him, her eyes level. "I can't invite you in."

"I know," he said. Damn, he thought.

"Not that I wouldn't like to," she said, this time with a smile.

Gently, he stroked her cheek. "Sometimes it's the wisest course to go ahead and act upon your feelings. Take a few risks. Live a little dangerously."

She gave an uneasy laugh. "I already am living dangerously."

Back off, he ordered himself. Too much eagerness was never the best course. And besides . . . he knew he'd regret this when he was out of here, away from her, in control of himself again. Allowing himself to be tempted by her would be harmful to both of them. It couldn't possibly go anywhere.

He didn't want to be hurt by April Harrington.

Nor did he wish to hurt her.

The rest of their walk through the shadows in Central Park was uneventful, but April was glad to have Blackthorn at her side. In the darkness it was far too easy to imagine villains behind every rock and tree.

They emerged on Central Park West and walked the two blocks to her building on West Sixty-second Street. When they reached the glass doors that led into the lobby he made no attempt to follow her inside. But he surprised her by saying, "I've been invited to a party Friday night. I was wondering if you might like to come."

She blinked at him. "You mean, like a date?"

"Not exactly," he hedged. "Actually I figure it's a good opportunity for us to do a little digging."

Us? Was he regarding her now as an ally rather than an adversary? "In the investigative sense, you mean?"

"The party's being given by Isobelle and her boyfriend. Apparently it's her birthday next weekend."

"Who's her boyfriend?"

"You know him, April. Charlie Ripley."

She shook her head. "Isobelle and Charlie? They're seeing each other?"

"You sound surprised."

"They seem so different. Charlie's so—so nice, so co-operative and helpful, but Isobelle—"

"Yeah, I know, she's been giving you a hard time."

That was an understatement. "She and I don't get along, Rob. I don't think she'd like to have me at her birthday party."

"Nevertheless, she invited me and suggested I bring a date," he said with a grin. "I'm sure she'll be a courteous hostess." He hesitated. "I'm not worried about that, actually."

"Then what are you worried about?"

"I suppose you might term it an unusual sort of party," he said slowly. "People are likely to be dressed in some rather odd get-ups. Tell me, are you easily shocked?"

She tilted her head to one side as she considered him. "What do you think?"

"I'd say not, on the whole. Tell me this, then: Have you ever felt the urge to act out an erotic fantasy?"

April felt her cheeks growing warm. Sure, with you, was what she was tempted to reply. Her lips still felt tender where he'd kissed them. And there was still that restless feeling deep inside. It had been a long time since anyone had made her feel anything similar. "Murder shocks me a whole lot more than sex," she managed.

He nodded. "Me, too. Okay, let's go to the party, then.

If it makes you feel uncomfortable, we can leave. I'll pick you up around eight."

"Wait. What should I wear to this mysterious party?"

A mischievous light came into those big blue eyes of his. "Black leather would be appropriate, if you get my drift."

Silence while she digested this. Then, "You're kidding."

"Nope."

"Isobelle?"

"Charles?" he said with a similar intonation.

April laughed. "You're right. Isobelle's a little strange anyway, but Charlie seems so clean-cut. Isn't he a born-again Christian or something?"

"You gotta watch out for the clean-cut ones."

"Blackthorn? What are you going to wear to this kinky party?"

His only answer was a devilish laugh.

Daisy Tulane enjoyed the hard pattering of water on her naked back as she stood in Christian's shower, freshening up after her flight from Dallas. As she stood there, she allowed all the random thoughts of meetings and appointments, press conferences and campaign planning strategy sessions to wash off her and twirl away down the drain. She was here, with her handsome young lover, to relax. All those burdens would be waiting for her when she flew back to Texas, but for now, she was going to forget they existed.

Seize your power, change your life. The pouring-troubles-down-the-drain routine was one of dozens of imaging tricks promoted by Power Perspectives that she still used on a daily basis. She had meant every word she'd said in that famous infomercial she had made for Rina's company. Rina's methods worked.

But you had to be dedicated and disciplined to make them work, and Rina had been better at that, Daisy thought with a sigh. Rina had been better at so many things.

She finished showering and dried herself with one of Christian's huge, fuzzy towels. She went to work on her hair with a silver-backed brush and her blow-dryer. When that was done she stood naked in front of the mirror and considered her body. She was pleased to see that the fat was staying off. It had better, considering all those grueling hours spent in the exercise room. Dieting was not a problem—her old distaste for food still persisted after all these years. It's not much of a problem staying slender if you have no appetite.

Well, no appetite for food. Daisy pulled on the pink and ivory teddy she'd bought at Victoria's Secret during her last retail therapy outing. It was exactly the sort of thing she hoped Christian would adore. It made her look feminine, sensual and . . . eager. Eagerness was a feeling she was trying to cultivate.

After a light redo of her makeup, she padded out into the bedroom, looking for him. He must still be downstairs. She took one more glance in the mirror, fluffed up her hair, smiled the candidate's smile, then stepped out into the hall.

As she passed Kate's room, the door opened. The girl stood there on the threshold, dressed in pajamas and clutching a cute stuffed puppy.

Daisy wished she'd thrown a robe over the sheer teddy. It was after midnight. Didn't she ever go to sleep?

"I had a nightmare," Kate said. Her voice quavered and she looked as if she were about to cry.

Instinctively, Daisy put her arms around her. But Kate jerked away. "Don't touch me!"

"It was just a bad dream, honey," Daisy said soothingly. "Some of 'em are awful, though, I know. How about a nice warm cup of cocoa? That always makes me feel better."

"I hate cocoa," Kate said.

And you hate me, too, don't you? Daisy thought. Poor kid. It wasn't surprising, considering all the losses she'd sustained. Her mother's death had been bad enough. And now Rina's . . .

"You won't be able to fool my father forever," Kate said. "He may be blind, but he's not dumb."

"I'm not trying to fool your father, Kate," Daisy said patiently. "One thing your father and I both believe is how important it is to be honest about everything."

The girl blinked at her, then burst out laughing. Daisy felt a tightness rush along her nerves. It was silly, of course, but she didn't like to be laughed at. Attacks, she could deal with, even personal attacks. People with thin skins shouldn't get into politics, and Daisy had worked hard on making her hide as tough as a Texas armadillo. But mocking laughter could still penetrate it, she realized to her chagrin.

Even the mocking laughter of a twelve-year-old.

Why was she laughing? she wondered. *What did she know?*

She forced a smile. "You go on back to bed, now, hon, okay? Think happy thoughts and the dream'll pass and morning'll be here before you know it."

"Goodnight," Kate said, politely this time.

"Goodnight, Katey, hon. See you in the morning."

Kate closed the door. Daisy started down the hall again, a little confused by her behavior. Anything was possible if

the child was bleary with sleep, but she'd looked completely wide awake.

"Daisy?"

She turned. The door was once again open and Kate's
smile was malicious now. "Um-hmm?"

"You're gonna lose the election," Kate said.

Laughing again, she slammed her door.

Daisy flushed with anger. My daddy would have taken
a brat like her out behind the woodpile and whaled the living daylights out of her, she thought.

Christian better darn-well do something about that
child.

Chapter Eighteen

Something was wrong, April realized.

As she unlocked the door to her apartment after leaving Rob Blackthorn downstairs in the lobby, she felt an instinctive wariness. Everything looked just the same as usual—the doors and windows appeared to be closed, and all the lights were off, just as she had left them. But something didn't feel right.

Don't be so jumpy, she told herself as she stood still in the front hall. The living room and dining area were to her left. The small kitchen was straight ahead, and the bedrooms were down a long corridor to the right.

All was silent except for her own rapid breathing.

It didn't smell right, she realized. There was a faint odor of—of something. Disinfectant, perhaps. It smelled as if a cleaning lady had been in to scrub the floors. But April didn't have a cleaning lady.

Maybe there had been a maintenance problem in the

building while she'd been gone? She'd left for work around noontime and she hadn't been back since.

Slowly, she walked over to the kitchen, flipping on the lights as she entered the small room. It didn't look as if anything had been disturbed—all cabinets and drawers were closed, just as she had left them. From there she walked through into the dining area and back into the living room. Again, it was neat, as usual, but . . . had that chair been pulled so far away from the wall? It didn't look quite right. And that pile of magazines and newspapers—they'd been messy, but had they been that messy?

Stop imagining things! she shouted at herself.

She walked slowly down the hall that led to the bedrooms. Her palms were slick. If someone were hiding, it would be up there, in one of the closets, perhaps, or in the bathroom.

The bathroom on the right side of the hallway was empty. Her bedroom opened on the left. She hit the light switch and bright light flooded the room, filling the corners. No one leapt out at her. She took a quick look in the bathroom, the closet. Her clothes were hanging there, undisturbed.

Nothing. No one.

April leaned back against the wall, drawing a deep breath. She must have been mistaken. Maybe she'd just imagined the smell of disinfectant. She couldn't smell it now.

Maybe she was working too hard and worrying too much.

Blackthorn had rattled her, too. She'd been truly terrified when he'd chased her through Central Park. And then that kiss—so sensual, so seductive . . .

The last room to check was the spare bedroom, immediately at the end of the hallway. She was using it as an office. Frequently, she would come home at the end of a long day at the Power Perspectives office only to sit for hours in here reading and trying to absorb as much as she could about the company. She listened to Rina's audiotapes and watched her inspirational videos. She reviewed the notes of her mother's planning sessions for the various new directions of the company, as well as her personal notes.

The door to the office was closed. She couldn't recall whether she'd left it that way.

As she pushed open the door, the scent that she'd thought she'd imagined burst out at her. It was as if she'd just entered a medical clinic or a hospital—the smell of iodine-based disinfectant was powerful.

Poised and ready to run, she hit the light switch. There was no sound or movement in the room. But the room was a wreck—drawers open and papers spilled all over the place, books turned out of the bookshelves, utter chaos on the surface of her desk.

Painted in high mustard-colored letters on the white wall over her desk were the words, "Power Corrupts. You're Next, Bitch."

"I'm sorry to drag you back here tonight," April said to Rob Blackthorn when he knocked on her door a little later that evening.

He shrugged in that loose-shouldered manner of his. "Hey, I'm glad to be here, whatever the reason."

As he entered she felt a jolt of emotion. Those pesky hormones again. He wasn't a drop-dead handsome man, but he was the physical type she liked—tall and hard and lean.

After discovering the mess in the office, April had

phoned the police. A pair of cops—a man and a woman named Cirillo and Flack—had come quickly, but they had not stayed long. Cirillo rather rudely made it clear that they had far more important cases to deal with in New York City on a hot June night than breaking and entering. Flack, the woman and "good cop" of the pair, had been more sympathetic, but even she had little consolation to offer.

If they knew—or cared—about Rina de Sevigny's murder in California, they gave no indication of it.

A crime-scene team headed by a couple of young techies had quickly dusted, taken measurements and a few photographs. Lieutenant Flack, meanwhile, had offered April the usual advice about investing in better security locks, maybe an alarm. Then she and Cirillo had packed up and left.

"I discovered the break-in as soon as I got inside," she told Rob. "It doesn't look like anything was stolen. The intention, it seems, was to frighten me."

"Did it work?"

April was about to declare that she was more angry than frightened, but the words stuck in her throat. She folded her fingers together. Her hands felt cold.

"I think maybe it did," he said. He touched her upper arm in a light, comforting manner. Something in her body surged, throwing up sensual images from earlier in the evening.

"I've read about how it feels when someone breaks into your home," she said. "How helpless and vulnerable you feel. I hate admitting it, but it's true."

He nodded. "Psychological terrorism."

"It looks as if somebody is trying to scare me, drive me away." She clenched her fists. "But I'm not going anywhere, dammit."

"That's the spirit."

He glanced around the living room. "Nice place."

"Haven't you ever been here before? When Rina was using the place, I mean?"

"My company was hired to guard Rina during her trip to the West Coast, not before." His eyes came back to hers. "So where's the damage?"

"Back there." She pointed down the hall. "I'll wait for you here. I don't want to look at it again."

"Why don't you make a pot of coffee—that'll give you something to do," he said, smiling. "And me something to drink."

"Okay."

"Betadyne," he told her a few minutes later. "That's what they used to write the words. You must have had a bottle of it in your medicine cabinet."

"Actually the bottle was sitting right there on my desk. I cut myself last night and used it as an antiseptic."

"Where's the stuff now?"

"The police bagged the bottle and took it as evidence."

"That's what you smelled when you entered the place. You took an unnecessary risk. Whoever broke in could have still been present. You should have backed out your door and called the cops from somewhere else. Or come back down to see if I was still hanging around."

She glanced up at him. "Were you?"

He grinned. "Hey, it was hard to leave. I thought you might change your mind and I might get lucky."

"You're full of shit, Blackthorn," she said, but she kept her tone light.

He sipped the coffee she had made for him. "So did the cops believe you about the break-in?"

"What do you mean? How could there be any doubt?"

"You could have faked it."

She blinked at him. "If you're here to make more accusations, I'm in no mood, I'm warning you."

"Bear with me for just a moment on this."

"Blackthorn—"

"You called me Rob earlier this evening."

"There was a point earlier this evening when you actually seemed rather likable!"

He grinned again. It was almost impossible not to like him, she thought. Despite the seriousness of the situation, that mischievous light kept coming into his eyes. "Look," he said, "I'm just trying to see this from the point of view of the New York City police. Just how seriously did they take this crime, by the way?"

"Not very."

"If the perpetrator's intention when he broke in was to mess up your office and write a threat on your office wall, why didn't he bring his own writing materials? The use of something that was right there in your office suggests a certain spontaneity about the action. Or else, possibly, that you did it yourself."

She tried to keep her patience. "I did not do it myself. Nor did I hire a killer to shoot my mother. I'm sure this is very disappointing to you, but you're going to have to come up with a better solution if you truly want to nail Rina's killer."

He nodded. "That sad possibility has occurred to me." Again he reached out and touched her arm. Then his hand slipped down until his palm slid into hers. "You okay?" he asked. His voice was gentle.

She shrugged.

"I'm sorry if I seem to be continually hassling you. I'm thinking like a cop, you see. Well, maybe more like an FBI agent."

She shook her head, saying nothing.

"And you hate all law enforcement types, right, after what you went through as a teenager?"

"They're not my favorite people in the world, no."

"I don't blame you. Don't like 'em much myself. Still, cop instincts can be useful, and I've got a feeling about this. Seems to me there was more to this break-in than just the determination to frighten you."

"But nothing was stolen."

"Maybe not. But still—well, let me show you. Come on back with me to the office."

As they walked down the corridor together, April was glad, after all, to have him here. There was something very reassuring about his tall, strong build. If they came back . . . the thought no sooner crossed her mind than she suppressed it. It wouldn't do to worry about things that would probably never happen.

"The police told you this was reckless destruction?" he said as they entered the carnage that remained of her office. "I disagree. Things have been tossed about, yes, but look at the way the papers and folders from your drawers are tossed individually around. That means somebody went through them all, one at a time. The drawers were not simply overturned and emptied. They were searched."

"But if they were searching for something, why just in this room? Why wouldn't they search the rest of the house as well?"

"Maybe they found it."

"Found what?"

"I don't know. I was hoping you could tell me."

She thought for a moment. "I don't own anything particularly valuable, and although I'm sure Rina did, there were no personal items of any sort here when I moved in."

"There's no computer here," Blackthorn remarked. "I

see a typewriter, but no computer and no printer. That's a bit unusual in an office nowadays. Was there a computer when Rina was living here?"

"No. The furnishings are all hers, and I've left things pretty much the way I found them. I don't like computers and I've never learned to use one, so I have no need of one."

He poked around some more, then said, "You know, the other possibility is that the rest of the apartment *was* searched." Blackthorn tugged on her hand and led her into her bedroom. His fingers seemed to tighten briefly as they were confronted by the king-sized bed, and she wondered what it would be like to be entering this room with him with a pleasanter goal in mind.

"It's possible to toss a place without leaving anything to show for it. Perhaps the idea was to get in here and quietly remove whatever it was the perps were looking for, leaving no calling card at all. But when they failed to find it— whatever it is—the plan changed. They decided to scare you into submission." He opened the top bureau drawer where she kept her underthings. "Very neat," he noted. "Hate to say it, but it's easier to search a neat drawer than a messy one."

She peered in and felt a little *frisson* of fear. "Wait a second. That black bra shouldn't be on top."

He turned to her with a slight grin on his lips. "No?" He plucked the black bra out of her drawer and turned the fragile confection over and over in his big hands, as if he expected it to reveal a vital clue.

"No. I keep the white ones on top. They're the ones I'm more likely to wear to work."

"A shame." He glanced at the front of her blouse as if trying to see through it and determine whether or not she was telling the truth. "I like black, myself."

She smiled. "You and all men."

He handed her the bra and returned to rummage around in the drawer. "How about the panties? White ones on top there, I see. No, here's a silky little scarlet pair, close to the top. Should they be farther down in the pile, or do you sometimes wear red panties to the office?"

She ignored the comment, opening another drawer to check her hose and stockings. "You're right. Somebody has been in here."

"You sure?"

"It's subtle. I didn't notice before. I was looking for the same kind of disarray we found in the other bedroom." She abruptly remembered thinking that there was something wrong with the pile of magazines and newspapers in the living room. "But, yes, nothing is exactly the way I left it."

"So they were looking for something. Question is, what?"

"The manuscript," April said suddenly.

"What?"

"Maybe they were looking for Rina's manuscript. Apparently she was writing an autobiography. It didn't turn up among her things after her death."

His eyes had narrowed. "How do you know this?"

"Charlie Ripley told me. Actually, he wanted to know if I had it. He'd gotten a call from Rina's editor inquiring about it."

"Why did he think you had it?"

"I'd received a large manila envelope from Rina via her attorney. Apparently Charlie and Isobelle were speculating that it might have contained the manuscript."

"But it didn't?"

"No. It was just an old photograph of my mother and me that last summer we spent together on Cape Cod. I guess she thought it would mean something special to me."

"An autobiography," Blackthorn said, musing. "I wonder if, in the course of telling her own story, Rina revealed anything she knew about others. Isobelle told me that Rina enjoyed the power of knowing people's secrets. She was intimate with a dizzying array of powerful figures—in politics, the arts, business, and even professional sports. If she was thinking of publishing any of these secrets, it could be the motive for her murder."

"So whoever killed her would naturally want to suppress the autobiography."

"Exactly. Had Charlie or Isobelle ever actually seen this manuscript?"

"I don't think so. Nor has Armand. I asked him about it the same day."

"But her editor at Crestwood-Locke-Mars knew of its existence?"

"That's what Charlie said. But I know a few authors as a result of my business, and they often bounce ideas off their agents and editors long before they've got anything down on paper. In other words, Rina may have intended to write her autobiography, but not yet actually done so."

"The phantom manuscript," Blackthorn said. "Did it exist or not? And if it did, was there something in it that was secret enough—and dangerous enough—to get her killed?"

He stayed for half an hour longer. April refreshed his coffee, which they sat down to drink in the living room. She deliberately chose a seat on the chair opposite the sofa where he was sitting.

From the coffee table he picked up the photograph of

her standing with Rina in front of the cottage. She usually kept it in her bedroom, but after the break-in she had removed it from her bedside table and brought it with her into the living room. She wasn't sure why. Silly, really, the way she kept studying the old photograph as if she expected it to reveal some vital piece of information.

Blackthorn, too, peered closely at it. "Is this the picture she left you?"

"Yes. The keepsake, as her lawyer referred to it. It's so strange. She leaves me the business she's built with her bare hands, but it's not personal, and despite all the propaganda, it's hard to find her there—Rina the real woman, Rina, my mother. That photograph is the only clue, the only link to the woman I once knew."

"You must have had other mementos of your life together."

"I left them behind when I ran away from school. I was furious with her. I didn't want anything that would remind me."

"Maybe this picture was her only link to the past, too."

April shrugged. "Maybe."

"She was a beautiful woman."

"Yeah."

"You look like her."

"Thanks. I guess."

He smiled. "I meant it as a compliment. I like the red hair better than the blonde, though."

"It's not red," she objected, smiling. "It's auburn."

"That's what all red-headed women say." He glanced down at the photograph again. "Where was this taken?"

"On the Cape. We had one of those 'housekeeping cottages' in Brewster for the summer that year. 1963. She met Kennedy there. He came into the restaurant where she was waitressing. My mother was never one to miss an opportunity."

"Well, there's something to be said for that quality." He beckoned to her, then patted the spot beside him on the sofa. "Come here."

April felt the spark run through her again. He looked very tempting, lounging there, his long legs stretched out to the side of the coffee table, his lean body giving off an air of lazy masculine assurance. She felt very vulnerable. He seemed to penetrate her defenses without even trying.

And yet . . . she liked the way he made her feel. It was as if the conflict between them that she'd felt ever since the day of Rina's murder had built earlier this evening to a crescendo when he'd chased her through Central Park and confronted her about her past. Since then, with empathy and understanding, it had begun to resolve itself. Besides, they both wanted to solve the mystery of who had murdered her mother.

And now, because of the way he had kissed her, touched her . . . they both wanted something else as well.

But it was happening too fast. She was not ready for any further complications.

"I'd better not," she said.

He gave her a long look, then nodded slowly. "You're right, of course. You'd better not. I'd better not. We'll both be sensible, and I'll go."

She bit her lip.

He paused, then said, "And if he returns?"

This was intimidation, pure and simple! "If I require your services as a bodyguard, I'll be sure to call you."

A glimmer of a smile appeared. "Touché." He rose with obvious reluctance. "Actually, I don't think you have anything to worry about. They'll look elsewhere for the missing manuscript, and so will we. As for the 'You're Next,

Bitch,' my gut feeling on that is that it was a gratuitous threat, designed to mislead us."

"I hope you're right," she said as she showed him to the door.

"I'll see you Friday night, okay? Eight o'clock. Lock up securely after I leave, okay?"

"Okay. Yes."

She wondered if he would kiss her as he left, but he did not.

Sensible.

How sensible would they be on Friday night?

Chapter Nineteen

The large-screen video in the conference room came alive with an early morning panorama of the Brooklyn Bridge (shot at huge expense from a helicopter) and the sound of Power Perspectives' energizing theme music. The camera angle narrowed as the shot closed on a figure standing in the middle of the bridge's span, her arms stretched out as if to embrace the entire city of New York. The woman was smiling, her long auburn hair was blowing in the wind.

"The world at your feet?" the woman said, her lilting voice blending in nicely with the upbeat music. "Anything is possible when you focus on what you want and go for it!"

The shot then angled toward the city and zoomed in slowly on several landmarks—the World Trade Center towers and Wall Street, Rockefeller Center, Fifth Avenue, Park Avenue, the United Nations building, and the Plaza Hotel.

All the while the woman's voice-over was saying, "At our Power Perspectives Lifechange seminars, we teach you to find that magical quality within yourselves that will make your dreams come true. The future is what you make of it. Your life is yours to shape. The power is within you—all you need to do is unlock it. Power Perspectives will give you the key!"

The video then segued into a familiar series of affirmations from celebrities, beginning with Daisy Tulane, newly declared candidate for the Senate from the state of Texas, who proceeded to tell the camera everything that Power Perspectives had done for her.

Charlie Ripley pressed the remote control to stop the tape. "We've all heard Ms. Tulane's spiel before. Let's have some comments on the intro. It's rough, essentially unedited, but you ought to get the idea."

"Wow—id was great!" Delores said, raising the shades and giving April a big grin. "Ya look jist like a movie star."

April grinned. It had been a curious rush of excitement and embarrassment to see herself on screen. This was the sort of thing she associated with Rina—this high-profile video advertising. Making a spectacle of herself on television had never been one of her dreams, but . . . it had been fun!

The speed with which the video had been produced also amazed her. This was Thursday, the end of her second week at Power Perspectives. Charlie had set up the shoot and dragged her out to the site early in the morning on Tuesday. Two days later he had something that he called "rough" but that looked, to April, amazingly professional.

"I liked it too," said Charlie. "I was concerned about not having Rina to do the shoot, but I think we can call April an unqualified success."

"I'm not so sure about that," said Isobelle, rising from her chair in the back of the conference room. "In my opinion, she lacks the charisma that was so palpable with Rina. She was better than I expected—I'll give her that—but let's not get carried away."

"Hey, I agree with Isobelle," April spoke up quickly to say. "Not only is this something I have no experience with, but I don't believe in it, either. Rina did."

"What don't you believe in?" Isobelle asked.

"Power Perspectives. The whole thing. Seizing your power and changing your life. I'm not convinced it works." She shrugged. "Filming it on the Brooklyn Bridge was very appropriate."

"For someone who doesn't believe in what she's saying, you did it fairly convincingly," Isobelle said.

"Next you'll be saying you liked my performance."

"I didn't like it. But that video had to be filmed before the end of this week so it will have to do."

It was grudging progress, April thought, but progress nevertheless. Maybe Isobelle would eventually come to accept her, after all.

"Well, I liked it very much," said Charlie. "I think we should go ahead and print it. Get it out there as quickly as possible. There's been too much negative publicity. We don't want any of our clients or our potential clients to begin to worry about the future of Power Perspectives now that its founder is gone."

"I agree," Armand said from the doorway. They all turned around, surprised. April hadn't realized he was in the building, much less in the conference room. "Congratulations, my dear," he said to April. He was shaking his head as if he didn't quite believe it. "Even more than I'd expected, you are proving to be a worthy successor to my dear wife."

Isobelle rose abruptly and left the room.

"Are you angry?" Charlie asked.

"No, as a matter of fact I'm not," said Isobelle.

"It's business. Nothing to do with us personally. She did a good job on the video. She comes across as very sympathetic. Different from Rina, but convincing nevertheless. It wouldn't have been fair not to give credit where credit is due."

"Credit is due to the director and the cameramen," Isobelle said coldly. "We both know that April went kicking and screaming to the shoot. Let's not exaggerate her talent, okay?"

"Look, I don't want you to think—"

"Oh, please, Charlie. Stop coddling me. This is the goddamn reason why nobody in their right mind beds down with a co-worker. In the long run, it just doesn't work out."

"What do you mean, it doesn't work out? It's working out fine. Please don't start imagining trouble where none exists."

She rolled her eyes at the ceiling. She was going to have to find a way out of this relationship. The pressure from him was subtle, but she could feel it constantly. He wanted more than she wanted, and it was beginning to affect both their performances at work.

Even the sex wasn't as good as it had been. There was something missing. She didn't get the pleasure from him that she had found in the beginning—he wanted too much—too much stimulation, too much humiliation, too much pleasure. At the end of a lovemaking session, she felt exhausted, and not in a pleasant way. She felt as if he were slowly sucking her dry.

He claimed to be dedicated to her, and she knew he was. Yet it was always his fantasies they were acting out, his needs that were being catered to and met. Sometimes she wondered whether he ever saw her as a real person, with needs of her own.

He stroked the back of her neck. She wanted to shake him off. She resented his proprietary manner of touching her whenever they were alone. "I love you, my lady," he murmured.

Good form required that she respond, "I love you, too," but she didn't feel it at the moment. So she didn't say it, despite the expectant expression on his face.

"I know you've been under an unusual strain these past few weeks," he said slowly. "I'm worried about you. I want you to know that I'll do anything I can to help you reduce that stress."

"Thanks," she said. Lighten up, she ordered herself. He's a nice guy. Most men wouldn't bother to be so solicitous.

So why did it annoy her?

Get your act together, woman!

Charlie was sweet, thoughtful, and considerate. She was lucky to have him. Compared to some of her former lovers, he was a prince.

All too well, she remembered how lonely and miserable she'd been before he'd come into her life. So why couldn't she just relax? Stop feeling so damn restless? She'd chased too many men out of her life. This was one she'd better make some attempt to hang on to.

She looked up at him and forced a smile. "Are you doing anything after work today?"

"Nothing that I wouldn't gladly give up on your account."

"Good. Come at eight, then. I'll try to be home early. Perhaps I'll even cook dinner."

He smiled and agreed.

Charlie Ripley rejected one after another of the gemmed necklaces that the clerk in Tiffany's presented for his perusal during his lunch hour. They were elegant, but he wanted something special.

Saturday was Isobelle's birthday and he wanted to surprise her. He would have preferred to present her with an engagement ring, but he knew she wasn't ready for that yet. Isobelle was independent; it was one of the many things that had drawn him to her. It was going to take patience and care to overcome her need for autonomy.

Sometimes he wished he understood a little better what was going on in that mind of hers. Not that she wasn't a frank and open woman. But even so, there was a part of her that remained elusive. All too often she would get that distant look in her eyes and he would feel her slipping away from him, going into a landscape where he could not follow.

It had been happening more and more lately. And this morning, after the screening of the videotape, she had been positively nasty. He hadn't thought that she would take offense over his compliments to April. In the past, Isobelle had always been fair, even if people weren't fair to her.

He knew that Isobelle wasn't anywhere near as hard and brittle and sure of herself as she sometimes made out to be. He'd seen her vulnerabilities. He had heard her cry. He had listened to her talking, haltingly, about her innermost feelings, her most precious dreams. Oh, yes, she was dominant during sex, and he liked it that way, but afterwards when they were lying quietly in each other's arms, she turned to him for protection and reassurance. He took pride in being able to provide her with both.

But lately, it seemed, they weren't enough.

It was April, he thought. Her presence at Power Perspectives was very disruptive.

"Here's something in an old-fashioned setting," the clerk said, opening another box. "If you want something ornate, this might have appeal."

"It's lovely," he said, excited by the flash of red. Rubies. Yes. The deep crimson fire would suit Isobelle very well.

It was expensive, but nothing was too good for the woman he loved.

Chapter Twenty

April selected a black cocktail dress to wear to the mysterious party. It had a halter-type front and the back was bare from the waist to the shoulders. She pulled on a pair of black Swiss dot pantyhose with the lacy black underwear that Blackthorn had seen in her drawer. She finished the outfit off with two-inch black heels.

She decided to leave her hair long and loose for a change. It fell nearly to the middle of her back. Jonathan, the man to whom she had been married for a few brief years, had always loved her hair. Every time she'd threatened to cut it, he'd pleaded with her not to. She'd almost cut it after the divorce, in defiance, but something had prevented her from doing so, and now she was glad. With the cocktail dress, her thick auburn tresses looked especially rich and full.

"Whew—a good hair day," she said aloud, grinning at her reflection in the mirror.

Blackthorn arrived as promised at eight. He was more

casually dressed in a dark sports shirt and trousers, but when she asked if she was too formal, he grinned and answered, "You look terrific. I'm impressed." Reaching out, he touched a lock of her hair. She went still as he ran it through his fingers. "I didn't realize it was so long. You usually pin it up in that prim knot. You should leave it loose more often."

Men, she had noticed, just loved to give advice!

"I was hoping you'd have solved the murder by now," she said jauntily as they stepped into a cab.

He groaned. "You and me both."

"It's gospel in police departments—well maybe only in fictional police departments—that if the killer isn't found within the first three days, the chances drop considerably that the case will ever be cleared."

"We won't find the killer. He's a professional. But I hope we'll discover who hired him. The motive will probably turn out to be as simple and as venal as motives for murder usually are. Sex, money, revenge, or fear. Those are the only reasons folks kill each other."

"I don't think my mother cared very much about sex, despite her many lovers. Money was a different story. Money gave her security. I think she needed that. I've often wondered whether she loved Armand, or just married him because he was rich and could take care of her for the rest of her life."

"He took care of her all right."

April shot him a look. His lips were pursed tightly together. "Don't you like Armand?"

He shrugged. "No reason not to, I guess."

"I think he's charming." Indeed, Armand had taken her out to lunch the day before, after the showing of the new video. They had spent a pleasant hour together, and April was amazed at how easy it was becoming to overlook the fact that this was the man who had separated her from her mother.

Blackthorn shook his head slightly. "Clearly he has that effect on women. Always has, I'll bet."

"Do you think he could have killed his wife?"

"Could he have done it—sure. But did he? Hard to figure why. We've searched high and low for any evidence of either of them being involved in an extramarital affair. All we have is that Rina spent many of her nights in the apartment. There are doormen there, as you know, and we've questioned them. No reports of a lover. Same in his building. No strange women dropping by to visit.

"No, the worst we've heard about him so far is that he's a control freak. As long as he has everybody and everything under his thumb, he's, as you say, charming. When things go a little wrong for him, though, he apparently shows a different side. We've come across a number of people who have had bad experiences with what they describe as his hot temper. But Rina was murdered in cold blood, not hot."

"Sounds as if your investigation has been very thorough so far," she said. She was glad to hear that she hadn't been the only person into whose past he had probed.

"Thorough, yes. Successful, no," he said morosely.

Isobelle lived in the Chelsea section of the city, in the West Twenties, an area that looked rather dark and foreboding as the taxi approached what appeared to be several old sprawling warehouses. "Do people actually live in those?" April asked.

"Some very rich and clever people live here. They bought up the warehouses cheap and converted them into loft-type apartments. Some of them are incredibly spacious. Their value has gone through the roof now, even though it's not exactly the Upper East Side."

The taxi dropped them off at one of the more uninviting-looking buildings. But there was an impressive security system inside, complete with cameras and a rather sleepy looking doorman.

They took an old-fashioned cage-style elevator up to the third floor. They got off in a dark hallway, and Blackthorn knocked at the first door on the right.

A stranger opened it. He was six feet tall, handsome, and proudly clad in a crisply starched maid's uniform—black satin with white lace trim. He had nice legs, April noticed as they walked past him into the cavernous apartment.

"Good heavens," she whispered to Blackthorn. "This isn't the usual Saturday night cocktail party, is it?"

"Nope," he drawled.

"His figure is better than mine."

Blackthorn's sexy blue eyes gave her a thorough once-over. "No way."

The place was hot, dark, and crowded with people wearing fetishy costumes. April saw a policeman's uniform complete with a Sam Browne belt and shiny knee-high boots, a cowboy with spurs on the backs of his boots, and a lasso in his hand, numerous males in black leather vests and/or trousers, and several women in tight corsets, black stockings, high heels, and very little else.

Sensuous classical music was playing from several speakers. It covered, but didn't entirely blot out, some strange rhythmic sounds that were coming from some other room.

April looked around in astonishment. She felt herself blush as a man clad in nothing but boots and a vampire cloak brushed by her, leering.

"You okay?" Blackthorn said.

"Just a little wide-eyed. This is amazing."

"It's a D&S party," Blackthorn told her. "Isobelle and Charlie are in the scene."

"Uh, what scene?"

"That's the lingo for folks whose lifestyle includes the erotic aspects of dominance and submission. You know—bondage, spanking, that sort of thing. I mentioned black leather, you will recall."

Mentioned it, yes, but April hadn't entirely expected to see so *much* black leather. I'm from Boston, she was thinking. I'm not used to this sophisticated New Yorker stuff!

"So it's a sort of sexual fantasy party?" She inched a little closer to him. Some of these folks were scary-looking.

He noticed and slipped an arm around her shoulders. "Yes. People act out their fantasies in a controlled environment. It's all completely consensual, and they're dedicated to safe and sane play. It seems kinky, but you'd be surprised how ordinary most of these people are in their ordinary everyday lives. They keep business hours on Wall Street in conservative suits and narrow ties, then they let loose after dark."

She turned to look at him. "How do you know so much about it?"

He shrugged. "It's amazing what you pick up in my line of work. One of my clients was into this stuff. I had to bodyguard him during his visits to some of the local sex clubs." He squeezed her shoulder. "If you're too uncomfortable, we can leave."

In fact, she *was* uncomfortable, but she suspected it had as much to do with the general atmosphere of excited eroticism as with any feeling of shock. It was rubbing off on her, she thought wryly. All these bodies, all this feeling of something in the air, and Blackthorn beside her, looking considerably sexier than most of the other males in the place, and obviously enjoying himself.

"Where's Isobelle?" she asked.

"She's probably busy disciplining some eager submissive," he said with a smile.

She raised her eyebrows. "Disciplining?"

He nodded. "Isobelle is a top or a dominant. Our friend Charles is a bottom or a submissive. Most people seem to prefer one or the other role."

April watched a couple on the other side of the room. The man was wearing a collar to which was attached a chain-link leash. He was being led around by a woman in a red leather miniskirt and a cone-bra that looked like something out of a Madonna concert.

"This is wild," she murmured. "Aren't they embarrassed? I mean, what people do in the privacy of their bedrooms is one thing, but this . . ."

"I suspect it's comforting to find that other people are into it too. If you're a woman, for instance, who enjoys being mastered in the bedroom—hey, that's the sort of thing that is pretty hard to admit. It's not politically correct, after all. You might feel guilty about having such feelings. But if you could share them with others, you might not feel so bad."

April knew she was blushing more than ever. She had a secret passion for sexy romance novels—the kind Maggie sold in her romance bookshop in Somerville, Mass.—the ones with the pirates, cowboys, and Mexican bandits on the covers. Maggie indulged her passion by providing her with the latest hot novels in exchange for the latest mysteries. It was a good exchange.

She cast a quick glance at Blackthorn. Had he guessed her interest in such fantasies? Perhaps he'd noticed the books in her shelves when he'd been in her bedroom that night after the break-in.

And he? Was his interest in all this purely academic? She thought not. She sensed that he was as titillated by the atmosphere as she was.

He caught her looking at him and smiled. He leaned his face toward her and for an instant she thought he was going to kiss her—here—in public, the way so many other couples were doing. But all he did was whisper, "April? You sure you're okay with this?"

She nodded.

"We can leave anytime."

She took a deep breath and squared her shoulders. "I'm fine. Let's find Isobelle."

Isobelle, who was chatting with Justin, a dominant friend of hers who owned a leather shop in the Village, saw Blackthorn coming. She smiled. So he'd come after all.

Then she saw April.

Well, shit. This was an unexpected development.

April was walking close beside him, clutching his arm. But her head was high, and she was looking around with what appeared to be more curiosity than apprehension or distaste. As for Rob Blackthorn, he moved with the same masculine authority and grace that was natural to him, and Isobelle observed that his tall, well-made body was not going unnoticed by the other women present. If he were to declare himself to be the erotic dominant that Isobelle sensed he could very easily be, at least a dozen women right here in this room would be down on their knees in a second.

They made a good couple, she thought. Both were tall,

slender, and striking. Her thick auburn hair and fair skin made a lovely contrast to his swarthy good looks, her fragile beauty to his rugged attractiveness. Were they lovers? she wondered. Not yet, perhaps. But it was obvious to her, if not to them, that it was inevitable.

Everything is so easy for her!

She stepped toward them, tapping her riding crop lightly against the palm of her hand. "Welcome to the dungeon," she said, giving them both a slight bow.

"Hello, Isobelle."

In your face, April. "Glad you could come," she said, addressing Blackthorn. She reached out and brushed her red fingernails along the inside of his arm. "I didn't realize you'd be bringing a date."

"I'm glad he did," April said. "Looks like quite a party."

"And it's hardly even begun. I hope you'll stick around for some of the special events. The Kinky Theatre Company is going to be putting on a performance a little later, and Lady Althea is going to be displaying her new slave Carlos, who has presented her with a new Argentinean leather cat direct from the gauchos."

Blackthorn grinned. "Now that sounds irresistible. Since we don't want to miss it, we'd better find a quiet room and get on with our less pleasant business right away."

"A quiet room—that might prove to be a challenge." Isobelle flicked her crop through the air just a couple of inches from April's face. She flinched, and Isobelle smiled. "I'll see what I can do."

She would have liked to see April a lot more nervous and intimidated. What would it take, she wondered? Separate her from Blackthorn and send Burt and Randy over to harass her a bit. Either one of them was big, broad, and sinister enough, and if she convinced them that April was into a little verbal humiliation from strangers, they were creative enough to carry it off.

But Blackthorn's arm was around April's waist, and he didn't look as if anything was going to pry it loose.

Isobelle led them first into one bedroom, then backed out when they all saw that it was being used. "Sorry," she said. "The fun's starting early."

"I didn't know people had parties like this anymore," April said. "I thought this sort of thing went out in the early eighties, with the advent of AIDS."

"It's not casual sex," Isobelle said sharply. "Most of my friends are committed couples. Safe sex is the rule. And D&S scenes don't necessarily require sexual contact in the usual sense, anyhow."

Blackthorn and April exchanged a quick, skeptical look. Isobelle gave a short laugh and added, "We may be kinky, but we're not stupid."

She found an empty room—a small guest bedroom—and ushered them inside. She shut the door and latched it behind her. There was no place to sit except on the double bed that took up most of the room. The bedspread was rumpled, as if someone else had been using it not long before.

Isobelle sat down on the side of the bed and crossed her legs. As Blackthorn copped a quick look at the creamy expanse of her lower thigh, she grinned at him. "Eat your heart out, Rob."

"What heart?" he said, grinning. He remained standing. The better to intimidate the witness, Isobelle supposed.

"Somebody broke into April's place and trashed it a few days ago," he said without preliminary.

Isobelle shrugged. "I heard. It happens. New York is not a very friendly city."

" 'You're Next, Bitch' was written on the wall."

"Sounds as if someone wants you to get out of town, April. Am I going to be handcuffed and read my rights if I confess that I, too, would be glad to see you go?"

"Whoever did it deliberately made it look as if intimidation was the motive," Blackthorn continued, "but we believe he—or she—actually had something else in mind. The place was searched. Subtly but thoroughly. The perp was looking for something."

"I think that's my cue to ask what he was looking for," Isobelle said. She yawned elaborately. "Consider it asked."

"We think they may have been searching for Rina's manuscript," April said.

"Really," Isobelle said. She waited a moment then forced herself to say, "What manuscript?"

"Did you know she was writing an autobiography?" Blackthorn asked.

They made a nice tag team, Isobelle thought. But how did they know about the manuscript? "She may have said something about it."

"May have?"

"All right, I knew. She asked me for information about some things that had happened before she and my father got married."

"What sort of things?"

"Nothing much. Details about our lives as children, stuff she didn't know. It was all background, I think. That's what she said, anyhow. I thought the project was a bit silly, to tell you the truth. Who cared, really? It's not as if she were a politician or a movie star. What people really wanted to hear from Rina was the secret of sex, success, and happiness. How-to books are much more profitable than reminiscences."

"Did she show you any of the manuscript?" April asked.

Isobelle shook her head, affecting boredom.

"Was it entirely about Rina's life or did she plan to expose secrets about some of her clients who were movie stars and politicians?"

So that was what they were wondering about. Isobelle considered. Rina had gathered information, she was sure of that. "Why reveal her secrets? Seems to me they were worth a lot more to her if she kept her mouth shut."

"Are you suggesting that your stepmother was blackmailing her clients?" Blackthorn asked.

"And that she was killed as a result?" Isobelle finished for him. "It's occurred to me, yes." She waved her hand at the room behind them. "She knew about this. I don't know how she knew, but she did. She confronted me about it one day. Gave me to understand that my erotic lifestyle was bad for the image Power Perspectives was trying to project. She ran through quite a vivid scenario of how I would be likely to feel if a story about my activities made the gossip rags and became the talk of the town."

"My God—did she ask you for money or something?" April asked.

"No, no, of course not, but she made it clear that she was holding it over my head. An incentive, perhaps, to keep me on my toes at work. It backfired on her, though. I was already working my tail off and she knew it. And the idea of exposure didn't worry me as much as she expected it would. I told her it might even be good PR. There's no such thing as bad publicity—that sort of thing.

"So she backed off and never mentioned it again. But I've often wondered how somebody else might have responded to the same tactics. Rina liked these little power games. Who knows to what extreme she may have carried them?" She paused and smiled. "I wouldn't be a bit surprised if Rina had something on everybody."

"Who else knows about her autobiography?" Rob asked.

Isobelle swiftly considered and rejected several replies before saying, "That's impossible for me to say. My impression was that she did not discuss it with very many people."

"Armand?"

Isobelle shrugged. "I suppose so, although I've often wondered how close they actually were during recent years. She spent a lot of time, apparently, in that other apartment."

"Charlie told April that Rina's editor had called inquiring about the book, so Charlie, obviously, knows."

"So what?" Isobelle said, still affecting a casualness she did not feel. What the hell was Charlie up to, anyway? Sometimes he was a bloody stupid fool.

Blackthorn continued, in that patient, dogged tone, "And what about Christian, did he know about the manuscript?"

"I've no idea. Christian and I rarely talk. But if she asked me things about the past, it's reasonable that she asked him also."

"What exactly is the problem between you and Christian?" Blackthorn asked.

"Oh, please. Problems between him and me go back far too many years. Our values are different. We don't like each other. It would be dishonest to pretend otherwise."

"Are you aware that your brother told the FBI to focus their investigation of Rina's death on you?"

Isobelle could feel her cheeks grow hot. "No, but I'm not surprised. He'd love to have me out of the way. He and my father both. A woman is not supposed to be interested in business. Apparently it indicates a sad lack of feminine decorum. I've been the bane of their existence ever since I announced that I intended to have a career in the family business at the age of fifteen."

She paused, then added, "My brother resented Rina and, even more so, me. We were a slap in the face to his antiquated ideals of male domination. And as long as you're investigating the family, you might want to ask him where he was the night his wife so conveniently ran her car off the road and died."

Isobelle watched with some satisfaction as Blackthorn and April exchanged a glance. "I expect Rina knew all the details," she added. "As I said, she had something on everybody. Now, if you'll excuse me, I've really got to get back to my party."

As she left them, she hoped that they were as startled about her final revelation as she had been about several of theirs.

"What was that all about?" Charlie asked. He didn't like the tight, weary expression on Isobelle's face.

"More questions, more theories. Mr. Blackthorn is exploring every possible angle. I just gave him another one to think about."

"And what was that?"

She frowned. "They're looking for a manuscript of Rina's that appears to be missing. Apparently they believe it contains something important."

"The autobiography," he said, his face expressionless.

"They say you told April that Rina's editor had called to ask about the manuscript." She paused. "You didn't mention that to me."

"I didn't think it was important."

"Rina had led me to believe that no one knew about her

autobiography. Certainly no outsiders in the publishing industry. She was highly secretive about it."

Charlie shrugged.

"What was this editor's name?" she asked.

"I don't remember. Actually, when I went to call her back, I couldn't find where I had written her number."

"Was she with CLM or some other company?"

Charlie shook his head. "I didn't ask."

"Did you know about the autobiography? Before her death, I mean?"

Charlie tried to gauge exactly what she was getting at. She seemed unusually anxious. "Your stepmother and I got along pretty well, but she didn't confide in me. The only writing projects of hers that I was interested in were those that directly had to do with the marketing of the Power Perspectives program and seminars." He waited a moment then added, "What are you worried about? What does this missing manuscript have to do with us?"

Isobelle waved a hand impatiently. "Never mind. Let's get back to the party."

Whenever she was evasive, he felt uneasy. "Look, I'm sorry if I—"

"Just drop it, Charlie. I really don't want to talk about this anymore."

He reached out and touched her throat. "The necklace looks lovely on you."

"Indeed it does. And I thank you for it."

She was under a lot of stress, he knew. It was necessary to make allowances. So many obstacles constantly springing up between her and her own view of success—first her father and his chauvinistic view of the world, then Rina, who had encouraged her at the same time that she'd held her back. And now April, who was not only proving to be far more effective at her job than anybody had anticipated, but who had also, it appeared, been appointed by Blackthorn to be his junior detective.

"I wish there were something I could do to bring a genuine smile to your face," he said.

"Don't worry about me," Isobelle said tightly. "I'll be fine."

Chapter Twenty-one

Outside it was thundering and the air was thick with that edgy feeling generated by a summer storm. A fine drizzle was beginning to fall. To April it felt refreshing, after the heat and the tension in Isobelle's loft.

"I don't see any cabs," she said.

"Saturday night, and raining—they're hard to come by. Let's walk down to the avenue—we'll pick one up there. D'you mind walking?"

"No, not at all. The drizzle feels good, actually."

He reached out and took her hand. April was acutely aware of the pressure of his fingers on hers as they walked west, towards Seventh Avenue. For several moments the silence between them was unbroken, but for the click of her heels on the sidewalk. There was a cool breeze and a bit of a haze, and the light from the streetlights was hazy and dim.

"Do you believe what Isobelle said about her brother?" she asked.

"I'm not sure what to believe. I'm having a lot of trouble sorting out the truth from the lies."

"She and Christian obviously don't get along. She might be trying to throw suspicion on him."

"Yeah, I know. She strikes me as a woman who's become bitter over the years. Probably from working so hard and never getting much credit for her accomplishments. It's her father's fault. Everybody I've interviewed agrees that he's always put his son first, even though he and Christian have never had a particularly warm or cordial relationship. Male chauvinism at its worst."

"I don't mean to sound harsh, but that doesn't excuse her behavior."

"No, you're right. But her brother's just as bad. He's been making every effort to cast suspicion on her. You can be damn sure that I'll be checking out every detail of his wife's fatal accident."

They walked in silence for several moments. April's mind was awhirl. She didn't like Isobelle, but it was hard to imagine her planning a murder, hiring a contract killer, giving the go-ahead. Christian, collector of beautiful art objects, seemed more the type. She could well imagine him weighing the options, calculating the risks, laying out the plans. "I don't care what happens to Christian, but I'm worried about Kate. She's a terrific kid. But her mother's dead, her father's difficult, and if there's any chance he had something to do with that accident—"

"I know. It's a nasty thought. Sorry, kid, but your daddy's a killer. He's going to prison and you're going into a foster home."

"Oh, Rob, no!"

"What else are they going to do with her? Send her to live with Isobelle? Can you see her inviting her teenage friends over for pizza parties in the dungeon?"

"Oh, God, what a family."

The rain came down a bit harder.

"I live near here," Rob said. "Well, in the Village." He gave her a wry smile and said, "Maybe not that near, actually. A few blocks south, a couple more west. But I could offer you a cup of coffee or something. Unless—"

April hesitated, but only for a moment. Why not, dammit? There was so much to talk about, and, well, did she really want to be sensible?

"Okay. That would be fine."

The pressure from his fingers grew slightly stronger. "Good. Wait, there's a cab coming. Got his light on as well." He stepped into the street to flag the taxi down and they climbed inside. Rob gave an address on Christopher Street and they were both silent, as if wondering what—if anything—they had just agreed to.

His apartment was on the top floor of one of the old, narrow townhouses in Greenwich Village. It was small, but cozy. The living room had a fireplace, and he lit a fire there to warm them from the effects of the drizzle.

April sat on one end of the brown leather sofa facing the hearth and watched the flames engulf the kindling and lick at the logs. She couldn't get out of her head the image of a lovely blonde-headed woman kneeling at the feet of her tall partner in the tight leather pants. Her wrists had been secured behind her back in leather cuffs, but in spite the restraints, there was an expression on her face that seemed to proclaim her freedom.

April envied that woman. In order to do something like that—to allow herself to be so helpless and vulnerable— she would have to trust her partner completely. How could she be so open? How could she have such faith in a partner's essential goodwill? For her it would be a mini-drama filled with emotional peril.

On the other hand, she reminded herself that she was here in a strange apartment, alone with a man she didn't know very well, a man who had hounded and harassed her, wrestled her to the floor in Anaheim, and chased her through Central Park.

Did she trust Rob Blackthorn? No, why should she?

So why had she accepted his invitation?

She glanced over at him. He was sitting on the sofa, also, but he'd left a space between them. He was lounging back, his hands folded behind his head, his long legs out-stretched. Through his tight trousers, she could see the smooth contours of the muscles in his thighs.

Oh, God, she thought. She was here because she wanted him. It was as simple as that.

He caught her eye and smiled sideways at her. "What are you thinking?" he asked.

She laughed and shook her head.

He took one arm out from behind his head and ex-tended it towards her. She sighed as his hand slipped un-derneath her hair and lightly caressed the back of her neck.

"Can I ask you something?" she said.

"Sure."

"You knew my mother before you were hired as her bodyguard, right? How did you know her?"

He seemed to hesitate. She noted that the movement of his fingers against her nape briefly stopped. At last he said, "I met her a couple of years ago, after Jessie, my wife, got sick."

She moved a little closer to him on the sofa. Talk to me, she wanted to say, but she didn't dare say it aloud. She trusted her eyes to do the encouraging for her.

"Jessie knew of Rina's work—she'd been kinda into that New Agey sort of stuff. She was diagnosed with ovarian cancer. By the time they found it, it had already spread." He was keeping his voice rock-steady; she could sense the effort it took. "She started with the traditional treatment—chemo and all—but she had a horrible time with it. She reacted badly to the drugs—much worse than most people, apparently. Going to the hospital for treatment became something that terrified her. I felt like a jailer dragging a helpless victim to the torture chamber.

"Someone she knew gave her a copy of one of Rina's books—the one on health and alternative medicine. Jessie was strongly affected by the idea of healing through positive thinking, laughter, music, optimism, meditation, all that stuff. She told me she needed to focus, to marshal her energy, to control and direct her thoughts. All this was more important, she decided, than chemotherapy."

Slowly, he shook his head. "I didn't agree. I thought she should save all her energy for the medical treatments and not waste her time—or her hopes—on magical cures. But when I saw that she was determined—well, it wasn't the time to fight her. And I realized that it made her feel good just to think there was something over which she could still exercise a little control.

"Rina's book on cancer also had a powerful effect on her. She found it 'emotionally healing,' or so she said. She used to keep the paperback version under her pillow, read a bit from it every night before she went to bed. She wrote to Rina, and they began a correspondence." He paused, and April could see the tension in his neck and shoulders. "When Rina found out we were living on Long Island, she came to visit. She urged Jessie to contact several 'healers' who specialized in cancer. Gradually, Jessie got so caught up in it all that she refused all traditional medical treatment. I objected to this, but I guess by then I was looking for miracles as well.

"Anyway," he said tightly, "she got worse, not better. But Jessie never gave up hope. Power Perspectives did not save her, but it cheered her and calmed her, and I guess it made her feel she had some control.

"When she died, not only did Rina come to the funeral, but she also stuck around for a few days and made sure that I stayed off the bottle. I'd promised Jessie, but, hell, she was gone and all I wanted was to be with her again."

"You used to drink?" April asked.

"I was in Nam," he said, as if that explained it. "It was worse afterwards. That adjustment to coming back to a 'normal' life—I'm sure you've heard how many vets explain how difficult that was, after living in hell. Anyway, I was lucky—I shook it young. I've never been a drinker since, although I've been badly tempted a couple of times. The months after Jessie's death were the hardest. Rina kept in touch. She knew I didn't believe the Power Perspectives bullshit—in fact I was angry because I felt that Jessie had gotten so caught up in it that she'd refused the conventional treatments that might have helped her. But she continued to call and check up on me anyhow. There's no way to account for her kindness, except to say that it *was* kindness."

April shook her head. This was incredible. Her mother had done all this?

"That's why this case has been such a puzzle to me from the first," he went on. "The things we're learning about Rina—or the things we think we're learning—it's all so contradictory. How could the same woman who befriended Jessie and looked after me be the person whom Isobelle just described to us? How could she be the same woman who abandoned you and never looked back? God knows people are complex and often behave unpredictably, but I can't seem to get a fix on Rina. Nothing is coming together, nothing makes any sense."

"Yes, I know," April said. "It's confusing to me as well. Kate adored Rina, and Kate is no fool."

Somehow they had both inched closer to each other during his recital, and now they were in the middle of the sofa, the sides of their thighs brushing. His fingers were still busy on the back of her neck.

"Listen. There's something you'd better understand," he said.

She looked up at him.

"When Jessie got sick, it changed something in me. I used to be a fairly even-tempered guy. Optimistic. Sure life had its ups and downs, but I went with the flow. I never got so far down that I couldn't pop back up again within a few hours. You see?"

She shook her head. "Uh, not really."

"Her getting cancer so young and dying of it was something that made no sense to me. I guess I had the world logically organized before then. Hell, maybe that's why I originally went into law enforcement. I believed in some sort of abstraction I thought of as Justice. Even though, working for the government, I saw the deals that were being cut, there was still—I don't know—there's a certain idealism about law enforcement on the federal level that isn't shared by the usual local police force. We were the ones in the white hats. We didn't take bribes—hell, the honor and glory of our country was at stake. We fucked up often enough, sure, but we were stand-up guys. When innocent people suffered, we rode out to right the wrongs, and now and then we actually succeeded."

April caressed the palm of his hand. She could see now where this was leading, but she didn't interrupt.

"But when Jessie—" he stopped for a moment to clear

his throat. "She was an innocent victim, but there wasn't any bad guy. I looked for someone. Anyone." He looked at her. "But I came away feeling there was no justice, and no hope of justice. I realized that everything that happens in this life is random. Nothing makes any sense. And suddenly I had nothing to hang on to anymore. When she died it was like I'd lost my mooring and was floating in space."

She'd felt something similar, April realized, when her mother had left her on the pier in New York Harbor.

"I don't believe in God," he said. "I don't think I ever did except maybe for a while as a kid. I don't believe we survive in any form after death, and I don't believe I'm ever going to be reunited with my wife's spirit or any such nonsense like that. But even so, it's been hard for me to—to let her go. She still exists in—in my heart and mind and I even talk to her sometimes. It's an illusion. An emotional crutch, maybe, or maybe an avoidance mechanism." He paused. His face was very close to hers and his blue eyes were glittering. "Anyway, I'm telling you this because I like you. I'd like to sleep with you—I guess you know that. In fact, you're the first woman I've felt that way towards since Jessie died." He shook his head. "But, the thing is, I'm dead inside. I've nothing to offer you but physical pleasure. I don't want any complications in my life."

She nodded. "I understand. I think." She sighed. "Would you like me to leave?"

"No," he said quickly. "God knows, I want you to stay. But if you feel you have to leave, I'll understand."

April closed her eyes. She could hear the ticking of a clock and the rain pattering on the frame of the open window behind them. Every few moments, the fire crackled and hissed. She believed what he was telling her. He was in her life to investigate a murder; when the murder was solved, he would disappear. They had no future.

But they were here, together, tonight.

And she liked him. Very much. She found him sensitive and emotional, as well as rough-tough sexy.

She tilted back her head and looked up at him. "And if I want to stay, despite the warning?"

He held her stare. Slowly, a hint of a grin took shape on his lips. "You don't pay much heed to anybody's warnings, do you?" His hands moved into her hair, which he caressed gently. "If you stay I'll think you're a reckless and adventuresome woman."

"Who, me?"

He leaned over and kissed her mouth. She parted her lips and felt the tip of his tongue touch hers—a sharp sweet jolt of pleasure.

"Yeah, you," he murmured. Then his kiss turned passionate, almost rough.

The leather sofa creaked as they moved into each other's arms. April felt one of his thighs slip neatly between hers as he pulled her closer to him, one strong arm wrapping firmly around her shoulders, the other hand moving to explore her breasts through the fabric of her dress. She arched as his fingertips found her nipple and brushed it lightly. The maddeningly gentle touch continued as he explored her mouth in a leisurely manner with his tongue.

It felt right. She needed the intimacy of a simple human touch. She needed to move with him, feel one with him, for however long it lasted. If it was only tonight—well then she'd do whatever she could to make tonight a night she would always treasure.

Their embrace became feverish as they both seemed to melt into each other. Her hands pulled at his shirt, which was an impediment. She yearned to feel his warm, smooth flesh beneath her fingertips and palms.

He raised his head. She reached up and touched the corner of his mouth, and his tongue darted out and licked her finger. "Will you come into the bedroom with me?"

"Yes," she whispered.

They rose together, and he took her hand in his as he led her down a short hall past a closet and bathroom to a large, airy bedroom. "Excuse the mess," he said, indicating the clutter and the unmade bed. "Wasn't expecting company."

"I don't mind."

"The sheets are clean, at least," he said as he pulled her down beside him on the bed. "Changed 'em yesterday."

She was laughing. "That's more recently than I've changed mine."

"I've never been the neat type," he said ruefully.

"It's okay."

He kissed her again and the slight feeling of awkwardness vanished. Rob Blackthorn might not be a flawless housekeeper, but he could certainly kiss.

April stopped thinking and simply let herself feel—his tongue artfully touching hers, his warm breath on her lips, his fingers cruising lightly over her body. He reached around behind her back and found the zipper of her dress, which he slowly lowered. He pulled the now-loose bodice of the dress away from her breasts and murmured appreciatively.

She, meanwhile, went to work on the buttons of his shirt, parting the fabric a little more as she pried open each button and lowered her head to kiss each new spot of bare skin. He growled low in his throat when she uncovered one of his nipples and stimulated it with the tip of her tongue.

He wrestled her out of the dress, his movements swift and sure. They were both breathing quickly now as need and desire were beginning to push the boundaries of control. He tore at his belt and then at the zipper on his trousers. She wrestled with her pantyhose. They both tossed clothes haphazardly around them, then turned to each other, naked. His body was strong and beautiful, she thought, blushing slightly as she felt him examine hers.

"You're lovely," he whispered.

"So are you!"

He opened a drawer in the small table beside the bed. He removed several small square packets and tossed them on the bed. "I hope we need them all," he said, grinning.

"I was about to ask—"

"No reason to worry, but it's wisest to be careful."

April lay down in the middle of the bed and reached out her arms to him. He joined her, pulling her slightly until they were both lying on their sides, facing each other. He reached out and caressed her breasts. Looking directly into her eyes, he gently pinched one nipple between his thumb and forefinger. Carefully, he increased the pressure, and the tiny jolt of pain caused her to moan and squirm against him.

"That wasn't meant to hurt but to remind you that I could be your master," he murmured.

Her eyes widened. "I *thought* you seemed awfully interested in what those people were up to at that party."

"Yup. I keep remembering some of the things we saw."

"So do I!"

She felt his knee nudging at her legs. His blue eyes were overbrimming with sensual heat as they looked down at her.

"I was afraid you'd be shocked, but you weren't."

"No, in fact, I envied those women."

"You envied them? Which ones? The submissives or the dommes?"

She could feel herself blushing. "The submissives. I envied their trust in their partners."

"What would it take for you to trust a man that much?"

She shook her head. "I don't know."

His head came down and he kissed her. She clutched his shoulders and held on tightly as the kiss—and the passion—built. Vaguely she remembered her mother's last speech there in the room at the ABA where, a few minutes later, she would lie dead. "The truth is, we trust dozens of people with our very lives each day," she said. In retrospect, it seemed ironic.

And yet . . . April realized that she must feel at least the beginning of trust in Rob Blackthorn. Otherwise she wouldn't be here, like this, completely open and vulnerable to him.

"You okay?" he whispered.

"Yes," she said. "Oh, yes."

His hand slipped between her thighs, gently but insistently strumming, and the fire between them built, and there were no more words. Whatever they had to say to each other was better expressed in touches, caresses, sighs, moans, and all the other sounds of love.

He explored every inch of her body with his hands and his mouth, then lay panting while she returned the favor. They teased each other, built it, drew it out. April was beside herself by the time he finally pressed her down and forced her legs apart, but he was as frantic as she. She could feel the thin sheen of sweat on his skin, hear his tortured breathing as he strained to hold back his release a little longer . . . just a little longer. But it wasn't necessary because as soon as she felt him inside her, she exploded with a series of keening cries. And then he was with her, tumbling over the same exquisite edge.

"Wow," she whispered, when she could speak.

"Wow, indeed." They lay sprawled in exhaustion for several minutes, then he turned her so she was cuddled to him, her bottom pressed into his belly, his arms around her from behind. "You comfy, pretty lady?"

"Mmm-hmm."

He yawned loudly. "Will you be insulted if I doze off a bit?"

"No, since I'm about to do the same!"

He chuckled. "You are remarkably easy to please. I like a woman who's easy to please."

"And I like a man who's so very good at pleasing."

He wound her long hair around his arm and tenderly kissed the back of her neck. "You make me very happy," he murmured.

She smiled in the darkness and slipped her fingers into his.

Chapter Twenty-two

"I've got the police and press reports on the accident that killed Christian's wife," Carla said. She was chewing on the last few bites of a submarine sandwich while making a bunch of Saturday morning phone calls.

"And?" said Blackthorn. He had to force himself to concentrate. His mind kept flashing back to images of last night—April's fevered eyes, her throaty little moans, the way her fingers trailed so lightly over his flesh . . .

"And it was ruled an accidental death. The victim had a blood-alcohol level of 1.2. That's over the limit for legally drunk. It seems that she and the boyfriend were celebrating and they missed a curve and drove right over the edge of a New Hampshire road. The car rolled and bounced several hundred yards down a steep slope, crushing the front section where the lovers were seated. They both died at the scene of multiple trauma."

"Any sign that they might have been deliberately forced off the road?"

"No, but there's no sign that the police looked for any evidence of foul play, either. It's a bad stretch of road, and apparently there have been accidents there before. The state has been criticized for not installing a secure guardrail in the area. The one that was there was too flimsy, and gave way under the impact. However, Jonas did turn up something interesting on Christian on the background check."

Blackthorn waited.

"He once had a brief fling in France as a race car driver whose chief interest was long distance, all-terrain rallies."

"So we can probably assume that he possesses both the skill and the nerve to stalk another driver and force him off the road."

"Sounds like a good bet to me, Boss."

"Do we know his whereabouts on the night of his ex-wife's death?"

"There's nothing in the police report about that."

"I think we'd better have a chat with Christian de Sevigny."

"Right. Meanwhile, there's something else kinda interesting here. Ms. Harrington told you that Ripley had told her that Rina's editor from CLM had called asking her about an unfinished manuscript, right?"

"Yeah."

"I just had the editor on the phone. She's away for a few days—took awhile to track her down, and she was none too pleased, this being a weekend, and all. Anyhow, she denies making any such call."

"Hmm. Are you sure it's the right editor?"

"Rina had the same editor for all her books. The woman's been with the outfit for years. She laughed about it, said it was unusual in publishing."

"She doesn't know anything about an autobiography?"

"Says Rina never discussed the project with her. No reason for her not to be telling the truth, is there?"

"None that I can think of."

"So Ripley's lying. Or Harrington."

Blackthorn thought about it. He was sure April hadn't been lying. Charlie? Maybe. If Charlie himself had wanted to locate the manuscript, it might be a smart idea to cover his own interest by claiming to be asking on somebody else's behalf. On the other hand—

"CLM did her self-help stuff, right? She might have taken her autobiography to another publisher, one that specializes in that sort of thing. The editor in question might be a different editor altogether."

"Yeah," said Carla, sounding skeptical. "I suppose."

"Call her agent. He'd probably know if Rina was considering another publisher. In the meantime, I'll question Charlie."

"That Charlie gives me the creeps," Carla said.

"How come?"

She shrugged. "I dunno. It's a subtle thing. Everybody I've interviewed says he's terrific—kind, sweet, industrious, a real gentleman. Still, I get these bad vibes. Hey, maybe I just can't relate to decent men."

"Must be why you and I get along as well as we do," Blackthorn said.

"I don't believe this," Christian said. "You actually have the gall to stand there and suggest that not only have I hired a killer to murder Rina, but I also hired one to bump off my former wife?"

It was Saturday afternoon, and Christian had been trying to get a little more work done before Daisy arrived. She had a fund-raiser in Washington during the day today, and was going to take the shuttle up for the night. He was actually going to see her twice in one week.

Blackthorn had shown up unexpectedly, saying that he had a few unanswered questions about Rina's death. Christian had been strongly tempted to tell him to go fuck himself, but he'd thought better of it. There was a murder investigation going on, and even though Blackthorn had no official part in it, he had worked for the FBI, and no doubt he was still in touch with his former colleagues. These guys seemed to be suspicious of everybody, and there was no point in making them even more suspicious.

But if he'd had any idea in advance what Blackthorn was really going to question him about, he'd never have let the bastard in.

"Actually," said Blackthorn, "you could have bumped her off yourself. I understand you've done some rally driving. You could have headed up there that night after you lost in court, followed her, seen a sudden opportunity, and seized the moment."

"I see. Then, when it came time to murder Rina, I wouldn't hesitate. Having gotten away with one murder, I'd be confident about my chances to successfully pull off another."

"Exactly. Success is a drug."

"Let me get this straight." Christian had to use all his considerable willpower to keep his temper. "First I killed Miranda. Then I arranged to have Rina killed—why? Because she'd figured out that I killed my ex-wife? The second murder was planned to cover up the first?"

"That's about it, yeah."

Christian shook his head. "Christ. You guys must be desperate. How long have you and the cops and the FBI and God knows who else been working on this case? It's almost three weeks since Rina died and this is the best you can come up with?"

Blackthorn was unmoved. "Where were you on the night of your former wife's death?"

"Now look. Against my better judgment I've let you in and I've listened. All I've heard so far is shit. I'm not talking to you. I want you out of here."

"If you've got nothing to hide, there's no reason not to talk. Nothing you say to me's official, anyhow."

"Well, unofficially," he said sarcastically, "I was with a woman that night. So I've got a goddamn alibi, and your brilliant theory is bullshit."

Blackthorn took this calmly. "Her name?"

Good question, thought Christian. His memory of that night was not good. He'd been drinking and feeling sorry for himself because the court case had gone against him and he'd lost Kate. But he'd picked up the courtroom clerk—good-looking woman, odd name. Never seen her again, of course, but maybe she'd remember him. He'd spent the night with her, well, part of the night, anyway . . .

Alexa? Audrey? Some out of the ordinary name like that. But he had no idea what her surname was, if, indeed, he'd ever known it.

"Her name is none of your damn business. I'm not some street punk you're shaking down. If there's ever any official testimony to be given, I'll do it in the presence of my lawyer." He paused. "You might consider retaining an attorney yourself. Because if you persist in this, I'm going to have to give some serious thought to a slander suit, and maybe one for professional misconduct as well. They got malpractice insurance for bodyguards?"

The geniality in Blackthorn's face faded and he took another couple of steps into the office. He picked up a six-inch-high porcelain shepherdess—eighteenth-century French—from a marble-topped table and examined her. "This is nice. You collect this stuff, don't you?"

Christian frowned at the casual way he was holding the piece. It was insured, but irreplaceable. "Put that down."

Blackthorn fumbled it and Christian leapt to his feet as the shepherdess fell toward the floor. Blackthorn expertly snagged it at the last moment and held it up triumphantly. "Oops," he said.

Christian drew a slow, careful breath. "Get the hell out of here."

"The cop'll also be talking to you about your kid. Seems we have several reports of her running away. Sounds like trouble at home—maybe some kind of abuse. We're gonna have to check all this stuff out."

"Get this straight, you bastard." Christian's voice was measured and cold, but he was enraged. "There's no trouble and there's certainly no goddamn abuse. You'd better hire a lawyer, Blackthorn. You're going to need one."

Blackthorn did not appear to be overly impressed with this threat as he left.

Christian grabbed the telephone. Who was this son of a bitch, anyhow? What, exactly, did any of them know about him? Rina had hired him, and he'd blown that assignment. Had his father ever checked him out to find out exactly how reliable this Blackthorn character was?

It seemed that Robert Blackthorn was determined to uncover every little thing in everybody's past that looked the slightest bit suspicious. But how well would he stand up to the same scrutiny?

"Father," he said, when Armand picked up the phone. "I think we've got a problem."

"What's the matter, hon?" Daisy said. "You got something on your mind?"

They were in his king-size bed that evening. He was naked. Daisy was dressed in one of those teddy-things she liked so much—this one was violet with ivory trim. She thought they were sexy. Christian would have preferred to have her naked and not to have to figure out whether the crotch snapped or was closed with the nasty little hooks and eyes. The damn underwear was a lot more trouble than it was worth.

Daisy was kneeling about waist level beside him, her hair a mess and her cheeks flushed with exertion. She'd been sucking him off, or trying to, for about fifteen minutes without success.

"How do you think it would feel to be sucking the cock of a murderer?" he said casually.

Daisy started. She didn't use expressions like "sucking cock," so he imagined it'd take her a few seconds to get past that to the good part.

"What're you talking about, hon?" She slid up, with obvious relief. She didn't like oral sex. She forced herself to do it. Sometimes it seemed like she forced herself with everything to do with sex . . . for all her personal warmth, Daisy was a cool customer in the bedroom.

"I got accused of murder today, that's what I'm talking about. Not just one murder, either, but two."

Her eyes narrowed. "You mean the police are trying to develop a case against you for Rina's death?"

Develop a case? He wondered how often she'd actually dated that police commissioner down in Houston.

"I'm not sure about the police, but that idiot security agent—Blackthorn—the one who let Rina get shot right under his fucking nose—he's after me."

"Well, why would you murder Rina? You didn't have anything against her."

"Blackthorn figures I killed Miranda first—ran her off the road and caused her accident in some sort of fit of rage after losing custody of Kate. Rina found out about it, he says, and threatened to blackmail me. So, naturally, I murdered her as well."

Daisy laughed. Usually Christian liked her laugh, which had that sweet Southern charm. But tonight it sounded a little wild.

"They're desperate, hon," she said after a moment. "That must be it. They're looking for anything they can find on anybody."

"Probably."

"When your wife died—"

"Ex-wife," he said sharply.

"Yes, of course, I'm sorry. Anyhow, when she died, did anybody suspect you then of having anything to do with her accident?"

"No, of course not. Or, if they did, they didn't inform me about it. I was questioned, sure. I mean, the timing was a little awkward. She died the same day as the custody verdict—well, early the next morning, actually. It was one of those weird twists of fate."

"I don't believe in weird twists of fate," she said. "We make our own destiny."

"Yeah, well, you're into the Power Perspectives bullshit and I'm not. Some people's destinies are made for them. Like Rina's, for example. You're not going to sit there and tell me she chose to be assassinated?"

"No, of course not. But it must have been her own actions that led her to that moment. She must have done something—hurt someone, betrayed someone, made someone hate her. That's how it works, hon. Somehow—maybe even without realizing it—Rina wove the noose that tightened around her own throat."

"If there's a fucking noose around my throat, it's Robert Blackthorn who's putting it there. Goddamn the bastard to hell."

Chapter Twenty-three

April was working in her office Saturday night when the buzzer rang. She glanced at her watch. Nearly eleven.

Blackthorn? she thought. He hadn't called. She didn't think he would just show up, but he'd surprised her before . . .

She fluffed up her hair on the way down the hall to the intercom. "Yes?" she called down to the doorman in the lobby.

"Kate's here, Ms. Harrington," he told her. He knew Kate of course—all the various doormen who worked down there did. "She was about to let herself in with her own key, but I thought you oughta be informed first."

"Okay, thanks, send her up," she said. Much as she liked Kate, she couldn't help feeling a bit disappointed that it wasn't Rob. He'd brought her home early this morning, kissed her passionately, and mentioned that he'd be working on the case all day. He'd said nothing about when they'd be getting together again, but she knew she'd hear from him, sooner or later.

She'd been in a pleasant daze all day, thinking about him. He was a wonderful lover—giving, caring, and sensitive. But he wasn't afraid to take control and make demands, either, and that had been very exciting.

Hearing footsteps in the hall, April unbolted and pulled open the apartment door, and her young friend scurried inside, looking bedraggled and damp. She had a backpack over her shoulder, which made a loud thump as she set it on the floor.

"Kate? It's almost eleven o'clock. You shouldn't be running about the streets of New York at this hour."

"I had to come. I'm sorry, but he's got that horrible woman there again this weekend, and I couldn't stand it any longer. I decided to leave. Can I spend the night?"

"What horrible woman?" April asked as she caught the soaking raincoat that Kate was peeling off before it struck the oriental carpet.

The girl made a face and gushed, "Hi, y'all, Ah'm Daisy and Ah'm running for the United States Senate, and believe me, sugah, I need yoh vote."

April grinned. "You don't like Daisy? I'm surprised. I got the impression at my mother's funeral that everybody liked Daisy."

"She's such a phony. Besides, he's, like, seeing her. It's disgusting. She's old enough to be his mother, and they're, like, sleeping in the same bed."

"She's not that old. And men have relationships with younger women all the time. No reason why it shouldn't happen the other way around."

"Well, why's it have to happen with my father?"

April shrugged. She wondered what Blackthorn had found out about Kate's mother's death. When Daisy Tulane heard that her handsome young lover might have had something to do with two violent deaths, she would no doubt find it politically expedient to end the relationship.

"Daisy and your grandmother were good friends, weren't they?" April remarked.

"Friends? Yeah, they were friends all right," Kate snorted. She headed for the kitchen. "You got any pizza?"

"No, but I can make you a sandwich. Does your father know you're here?"

"Nah, I sneaked out. They were busy in the bedroom with the door closed." She looked over her shoulder and made a face. "Really disgusting."

A few minutes later Kate was seated at the kitchen table gobbling a peanut butter sandwich and washing it down with a tall glass of milk. April made herself a cup of tea and sat down opposite her. "What did you mean just now, speaking so sarcastically about Rina and Daisy?"

Kate shrugged and looked uncomfortable. "I told you, Daisy's a phony."

"Haven't you seen your grandmother's infomercials?" April persisted.

Kate looked at her as if April had just revealed a streak of incredible naiveté. "Those are scripted. They aren't real. Gran explained it to me once. They're like a television play. It's all lines."

"I know that, Kate, but the testimony of the people interviewed is presented in such a manner that viewers are asked to accept it as relatively sincere."

Kate raised her eyebrows.

"Kate, I want to ask you something." She'd never thought of questioning Kate about Rina's relationships, but she was the obvious person, since she'd spent so much time with her stepgrandmother.

"Yeah," Kate said, reaching for the milk carton to refill her glass.

"Did Rina ever say anything to you about a book she was working on?"

"What book?"

"We believe she was writing a book about her life."

"You mean her autobiography?"

"You know about it?"

"Sure. She even read to me from it a couple times. It was cool."

April felt her excitement grow. This was the first independent confirmation that the manuscript had even existed. "Kate, do you know where she kept the manuscript?"

"Why?"

"Well, because it seems to have disappeared. That is, nobody's been able to find it since she died."

Kate stopped eating. "Wow. Is that a clue?"

"I don't know. But I'd certainly like to have a look at the manuscript. So would Mr. Blackthorn. He's interested in it, too."

"Oh, him. I don't like him." She bit into her sandwich. "Maybe he killed her."

"Don't be silly. He was her bodyguard."

"I saw a movie once where the bodyguard was the killer. He was perfect because he knew all her routines, you know? He had, like, access to her. No one guessed he was bad to the bone. Well, except the woman—she guessed it at the end, when it was almost too late."

"Yes, well, in this case Blackthorn is trying to solve the murder. And that manuscript might be important. Did you actually see her working on it?"

Kate nodded. "But I never saw an actual manuscript or a book or papers or anything. I mean, I never saw a print-out or anything. She read to me directly from her computer screen."

April opened her mouth and closed it again. She felt like an idiot. No wonder they hadn't found the book. They were looking for a large, bulky manuscript instead of a file or a bunch of files on a computer.

"What?" said Kate, munching again.

"Nothing." Once again her computer illiteracy was coming back to haunt her. One of these days she was going to have to learn to use one of the bloody things. "I've been stupid, that's all."

Kate nodded, as if adults being stupid was far too common an event to bother commenting on.

However, not all adults were stupid, April reminded herself. The police must have thought about the possibilities connected with the computer age. She'd been told that the police had examined all the computers at the office, and she remembered that Blackthorn had commented on Rina's not having a computer here at the apartment.

"Which computer screen are you talking about? The one in her office at Power Perspectives?"

"Her laptop," said Kate. "Mostly, when I saw Gran working, she worked on that."

"I didn't know she had a laptop. It's not here or at work. Do you suppose Armand's got it?"

Kate's face had gone red. "I liked the laptop a lot," she said slowly. "She used to let me use it whenever I wanted to." Her eyes darted away and she began to gnaw on her bottom lip. "I figured she'd have wanted me to have it. I mean, she knew how much I wanted to be a writer. So I— I didn't think there'd be any harm if I just kinda borrowed it."

Oh, wow, thought April. Rina had owned a laptop computer. And Kate, who'd had the run of this apartment both before and after her murder, had taken it.

The missing manuscript was in the hands of a child.

"It was wrong, wasn't it?" Kate said a few minutes later. She looked and sounded stricken. "I should have asked before taking the laptop. It's like, stealing, isn't it?"

"I'm sure you're right that your grandmother would have wanted you to have it," April said quickly. "But you should have told somebody, yes. It might be important, depending on what files are on it. Where is the computer?"

"Oh, well that part's easy." Kate vanished into the hallway and returned with her backpack. "It's right here. I take it with me everywhere, in case I need to write something down that I don't want to forget."

She opened the heavy backpack and pulled out a slim boxlike machine. "This is it."

April laughed, partly with delight and partly with relief. Was the mystery about to be solved?

"I haven't erased anything from the hard disk. Want me to find the files for you? I'm a whizz with computers."

April wasn't sure if they should be doing this at all— she should probably phone the police, or certainly Rob, but—

"The battery's low," Kate said as she tried to boot up the laptop. "You gotta recharge it pretty often. Never mind, we'll use the AC." She rooted around again in the backpack and pulled out a cord with a power pack attached to it. While she attached it to the computer, April plugged the other end into the wall outlet.

The little machine began to whirr. "Okay, now we're cooking," said Kate.

As April watched, the machine beeped once then flashed a series of paragraphs and graphics across its silvery screen. Kate's fingers flew over the keyboard, producing colorful new screens and cute little pictographs.

"Well, I don't see it," she said after a couple of minutes. "There's not much stuff here in Gran's files. No games or anything. Well, except Solitaire—that comes automatically with Windows. Nothing really fun or challenging, though. I've got some great games on the big 486 at home."

"Anything to do with computers is challenging to me," April said wryly.

Kate was concentrating on the screen. "It's a nice machine, though. Not as fast as a desktop of course, but it's got a color monitor, which is cool. Most laptops don't."

April nodded. She was leaning over Kate's shoulder, trying to figure out what she was doing.

"See, I'm in the file manager. I'm looking for the files to her book, but they aren't in here."

"How do you know?"

"I remember the filename. She was calling it Memories. You know, like Memories One, Memories Two, and so on. Probably had a new file for every chapter. There ought to be lots of files here, but there aren't any. At least none with that name."

"Maybe she changed the name to something else."

"Sure. Maybe. Let's pull up a few and see. We gotta go into her word processor, like this, see? Or we could just view it from DOS, but the text won't be formatted that way."

"If you say so," April said.

"You really don't know how to use a computer? That's awesome. I thought everybody could use Windows, at least. It's easy. Want me to teach you?"

"Yes, but not right now. The most important thing at the moment is to find her autobiography."

"This all looks like correspondence. Letters and stuff. See the things that say 'ltr' as the filename extension? People often use that for letters. Or 'let' or maybe the date."

She pressed some keys and the text of a short letter showed up on the screen. April could see from the inside address that it was to a woman in Arkansas whose name she did not recognize. It seemed to be in reply to a fan letter or something—just the usual "seize your power" sort of stuff.

"Bor-ing," said Kate. She called up several other letters, but none looked particularly interesting. Still, thought April, she would have to learn to use the machine well enough to read through them all individually, in case there was anything in Rina's private correspondence that might prove helpful.

"Let me try some of the other directories," Kate said. "But she doesn't have much on here. There's a personal subdirectory—shall I go into that? It sounds familiar—this may have been where the book was stored."

"Yes, let's see what's in it."

"Hmm. This is weird," said Kate a moment later. "The directory's empty. Except for the two base files that always get created when you make a directory."

"Can you make a directory and not use it?" April asked.

"Sure. You can also use it, then delete the files. I'm gonna try something, okay?"

"You know what you're doing here, Kate. I don't."

"There should be a utility here that will undelete a file if it hasn't already been written over. That's just in case you erase something by mistake. Okay, so I'm going to try and undelete files with the names Memories One, Memories Two, and so on. Maybe they're still here."

The computer whirred again. Kate tried several combinations then shook her head. "Nope. That's too bad. Acourse it still doesn't prove that they weren't ever here. She could have written over them herself and then deleted those files, which would have been an extra security precaution."

"But wouldn't that erase all her work?"

"She would have backed it up, though. You know, on floppies? Portable computer diskettes, that is. You know the kind I mean."

"Those flexible thin things," April said.

"Yeah, well in a laptop we use the three-and-a-half-inch square ones. That reminds me, I forgot to check the A-drive. It would be funny, wouldn't it, if the backup diskette was here all the time. I never use the A-drive. That's stupid, by the way—everyone should back up their work on a floppy."

She pressed a button on the side of the computer and probed around with her fingers. "Nope. No floppy." She looked up at April. "But that's where the book is, I'll bet. If it's not on here and it's not printed out in a hard copy form, then it's probably stored on a backup diskette."

"Why would somebody write a book on a computer then erase it and store it on a floppy?"

"So somebody couldn't do exactly what we're doing now. It's a lot easier to hide a diskette than a computer. I know it was on here. That I'm sure of. I'll bet if you find the diskette you'll find the missing manuscript. And maybe Gran's murderer as well."

April hugged her. "You may be right."

"I'll bet it's here someplace, hidden. Or if not here, maybe in Gran's office. Can I help you look for it?" The girl clenched her fingers into fists. "I want to get the guy who did it—I really do."

"I understand how you feel. But I'd feel a lot better if I knew you were out of it. Safe, I mean."

She looked up at April with huge round eyes. "You think they'll try to kill us?"

"Not you, of course not. Not me, either, I hope."

Kate tightened her grip. "Be careful, okay?"

"I intend to be. Now let's call your father, okay? He must be worried about you."

"Let him worry," Kate growled.

Chapter Twenty-four

"April thinks she knows why Gran was murdered," Kate announced to her father and Daisy Tulane the next morning at breakfast.

Her father made a face as he buttered his toast. "So does everybody."

"It's important to discover the motive," Kate went on. "You have to analyze the mind of the killer and unlock his—or her—heart."

"Aren't you a little young to be thinking about murder, Katey, honey?" Daisy said.

"She's obsessed with the subject," her father said apologetically to Daisy. "My daughter, the new Sherlock Holmes."

Kate scowled at him. He thought she was fooling around. He didn't believe that she actually *knew* anything.

"I love a good mystery myself," Daisy said. "Didn't April Harrington used to own one of those murder mystery bookstores? I'll bet she's the budding detective."

"She just doesn't want to be murdered like her mother was," Kate said impatiently. "That's, like, a pretty good reason for wanting to solve a crime."

"Lord alive, why should anybody murder April?" asked Daisy. As usual, she wasn't eating. No matter what kind of food was offered her, it had too many calories. But she didn't look anorexic, Kate had decided. Her boobs were too big.

"Because she knows too much," said Kate. She put a big forkful of blueberry pancakes generously covered with maple syrup into her mouth. She noticed that Daisy watched every move. Eat your heart out, lady, she thought. "The main motives for murder are greed, lust, and keeping somebody from talking to the police. April's smart. She's finding out a lot of stuff about her mother. Even more than the police, she wants to nail the killer."

"You're being overly dramatic, as usual, Katherine," her father said.

And you're being insulting as usual, Dad, she wanted to say, but bit it back. It had been so exciting to help April look for Gran's manuscript last night! For the first time, she'd felt as if she really might be able to help unmask the murderer.

"Gran was working on this book about her life. But before she could finish it, she was shot. Now the book has, like, disappeared. We think somebody killed her to prevent that book from ever being published."

Daisy and her father exchanged a quick glance. Kate dug into her pancakes again and waited. They were both paying attention. She loved it when they stopped cooing to each other and listened to her.

"She wrote a lot of books," said Daisy. She fiddled with her spoon. "What was so special about this one?"

"This was an autobiography, not one of those self-help

things. It was about her. Her life, her past, all that stuff. And it told stuff about her clients—maybe some stuff that nobody wanted told." She looked at her father and added defiantly, "Nobody knew what had happened to the manuscript. But April and I have pretty much figured it out."

"You have this manuscript?" her father demanded.

"Well, no, not yet," she said quickly. "But I think April does. Or at least, she will have it soon if she doesn't already. I gave her this idea, you see, and—" She broke off, wondering if she'd said too much. April had told her not to tell anybody about the missing computer diskette. Especially since they didn't even know for sure that there *was* a missing diskette.

At first, Kate had been convinced that Gran had hidden it somewhere in her apartment. That must have been why the place had been burgled and searched. The killer, too, must know about the diskette—or at least about the manuscript.

But she and April had gone through the place one more time last night, without success. The Sixty-second Street apartment was all straight-edged and contemporary and there simply weren't too many good hiding places.

This morning, though, Kate had had a new idea. She was trying to think up an excuse to search Grandfather's place as well. Gran had spent some time with her husband, after all, and in that huge, fancy townhouse she might have had more nooks and crannies to hide something in. Especially something as small and thin as a 3-1/2-inch diskette.

"I haven't seen Granddad for a while," she said now, changing the subject, to her father's obvious relief. "D'you think he'd mind if I dropped over to visit him this afternoon?"

"What a nice thought, Katey," Daisy said. "He must be

lonely with Rina gone. Why don't you call your father?" she suggested to Christian. "Maybe you could invite him to dinner."

"Actually, I'd rather go to his place," Kate said. Then she thought that sounded rude, so she added, "It's a neat old apartment, built in the Roaring Twenties, or sometime when people were really rich. I could go over there and you two could, like, be alone."

That got their attention.

Adults were really disgusting, Kate thought.

When Daisy Tulane returned to Dallas the following evening, she was exhausted and demoralized. Her campaign director had faxed her the latest opinion polls. Instead of gaining in the standings against the two middle-aged white males who were running against her in the primary election, she was losing ground. Voters were always suspicious of a woman candidate, especially in the South.

Maybe seizing her own power wasn't going to work, after all. Maybe none of the masquerades would work, not even the one she was indulging in with Christian.

Ah, Rina, she thought. *I was never as good at this as you.*

Had she done the right thing? It was so impossible to know. Rina was gone, and she had to move on. She could be a good senator, she was certain. She had so many wonderful ideas and plans, and there was so much to be done . . .

You must take control of your own life.

That was all she had tried to do. But now they were looking for Rina's manuscript. And if they found it . . .

She found the letter atop a neat pile of newspapers on

the marble-topped table in the foyer of her home. Because it was marked "confidential" her secretary had left it unopened. It had come in a regular business envelope. Her name and address were neatly printed in ink. There was no return address, but the letter had been postmarked in New York City.

The envelope contained a single sheet of 8 1/2 by 11 typing paper. *"It's not over yet,"* were the words that were neatly printed in what looked like the same handwriting as was on the envelope. *"Others know what you are trying to hide. Soon everybody will know."*

That was all.

But it was enough.

Calmly, Daisy folded the letter and slipped it back into its envelope. She walked across the foyer to the ornate mirror that hung over a large Chinese porcelain vase (chosen on the recommendation of Christian) in which were blooming a riot of summer flowers. She examined her reflection in the mirror, something she had had difficulty doing for years.

There was no one else there, she assured herself. Nothing lurking around the edges, nothing hiding behind her image, no one whispering her name. All there was was Daisy, cool and collected, in control.

Part Three

Chapter Twenty-five

Gerald Morrow checked into the Plaza Hotel without incident. He was pleased to see that the client had reserved him a suite. Old-World-style—elegant. The sort of place he'd have killed to get into back in the days when he was a young punk lifting cars from the streets of Brooklyn. He smiled. The sort of place he killed to get into now, he thought, smiling.

Morrow—not his real name, of course, and not the name he'd used on the register downstairs, either, but he'd been thinking of himself as Gerald Morrow for this job, since it was the name he'd used last month in Anaheim— went over to the tall window with the heavy brocade curtains and gazed out over the city of New York. There it was, all those noisy thoroughfares, those graceful buildings, those patches of parkland, and all those people spread out below him. Busy little bees, all hurrying about their daily activities. Self important. Believing that they and their petty little concerns mattered.

Fools.

He raised his arm and sighted along it to his out-stretched index finger. "Pow," he whispered, imitating the recoil of a gun. A skyscraper exploded. "Zap," he said, and a city transit bus burst into flame. "Bang," he said once more as people everywhere fell to their bellies, writhing and moaning in terror.

"I've got the power." He listened to himself and added, "Maybe I'm a little crazy, but what the fuck."

Morrow turned away from the window and seated himself on the sofa at one end of the elegant room. He laid his briefcase on the mahogany coffee table and opened it. Removing a slim manila envelope, he opened it and slid out the photograph, which he propped up against a slender vase that contained a single rose.

The client had hired him for another job. He'd been pleased, apparently, with the outcome of the last one.

Another woman. Some shooters didn't like doing women, but Morrow specialized in women. Unfortunately, there was little demand in this profession for his special talents regarding females, so, like everybody else, he accepted routine contracts on men. But when someone wanted a woman taken out of circulation, they knew who to call. No one did it as thoroughly—or as lovingly—as Gerald Morrow aka Too Many Other Aliases to Name.

This one was going to be a special challenge, though. The client didn't want the usual clean shooting, fast get-away. "It's got to look like an accident," he'd been told. "Even the police have got to believe it's an accident. We can't risk anything that looks like a professional hit."

It cost a lot more to set up an "accident." But this was the best kind of murder. No detailed investigation, no trouble with the police. Morrow had arranged several "accidents" and a number of "suicides" as well. He liked them. They were more personal, somehow. They often involved more personal contact with the target, which might be good or bad, depending upon the individual.

He was looking forward to having personal contact with this target.

She was beautiful. But the photograph didn't do her justice. It didn't reveal how lustrous her auburn hair was, nor did it show the lively sparkle in her eyes. Those features he remembered, having already seen her once in person.

The eyes were important. He always noticed their eyes. He found it particularly intriguing to watch their eyes as the bullets shattered their bodies. There was the essential mystery of life, death, and eternity—there in that split second when the eyes changed from expressive to empty, living to dead.

If he could understand the eyes, he would understand the soul. More and more he had faith in the soul, and in the afterlife. Something vital vanished at the moment of death—vanished and went . . . somewhere.

Deep down in his lower consciousness, Morrow knew a spurt of fear. If there was an afterlife, what would it hold for him? Briefly, he remembered images of fire and torment retained from the rantings of a crazy parish priest. He'd been a good Catholic boy. He'd believed in heaven and hell.

Now he believed religion was for fools. If there was anything afterwards it was much more complex and much more exciting than fires for the evil and harps for the good. And hell was bound to be ever so much more exciting than heaven. If there was a hell, he looked forward to it. He yearned to be eternally consumed.

He focused on the photograph. April Harrington—his angel. They would visit hell together. She would be there, of course, despite the look of purity and innocence. All women were bound for hell. Like Eve, their mother, they were filthy with sin.

He smiled. "Go directly to Hell, Ms. Harrington. Do not pass GO. Do not collect $200. Wait for me there. One of these days, I'll get bored and join you. Save me a seat in the Eternal Sauna. Tie me to the same stake with you in the flames."

Leaning back, he admired the juxtaposition of the single red rose and the 6-by-9 photograph. Hmm. He reached for the phone and dialed the concierge. He asked for the number of a reputable florist.

Not entirely wise, he reminded himself a few minutes later as he placed his order.

He smiled at the Target's lovely face.

But worth the risk.

"You have another admirer?" Blackthorn asked, lightly fingering the soft petals of the opening rose. It graced the center of the coffee table in her living room, its loveliness accented by a delicate silver bud vase.

April blinked at him. "You didn't send it?"

"No." He was surprised to feel a twinge of jealousy.

"It came without a card. I assumed it was from you."

Damn, thought Rob. He wished it had been.

They had come to the end of another week, and made no further progress. Both he and the authorities had questioned Kate de Sevigny. The FBI techs had gone over Rina's computer with the most sophisticated of high-tech gear, trying to recover the files that Kate had insisted she'd seen. But either Rina—or somebody else—had been very careful. The files had not been recovered.

And the floppy backup diskette, if indeed it existed, had not been found.

Meanwhile, he'd been unable to develop anything on Kate's father. His ex-wife's accident had never been treated as a possible homicide, and without some kind of physical evidence there was no reason to reopen the case. Besides, Christian, it turned out, claimed to have an alibi for that night. Some woman named Augusta whom he'd met at the courthouse where the custody case had been decided. Marty and his people were checking it out, but they weren't enthusiastic about this particular line of thinking.

"It's almost as far-fetched as the JFK conspiracy theory," Marty had said.

The case was cold.

Blackthorn was beginning to wonder if it would ever be cleared.

"Supper's ready," April called from the kitchen. She had invited him over for dinner. He'd told himself he ought to refuse the invitation and distance himself from his involvement in one of the principals in a murder case. But his rational and sensible thoughts on the subject kept getting undermined by flashbacks to the pleasures of his first night in her arms.

She'd resisted him in so many ways—his impression of her right from the first time they'd met had been of his own pursuit and her resistance. The fact that he hadn't been pursuing her romantically at that point didn't make any difference. From the moment he'd tackled her in Anaheim to the chase through Central Park, to the moment at Isobelle's party when she'd come willingly into the shelter of his arms, he'd been after her. And when she'd finally surrendered, there had been a wholeheartedness about it that had taken his breath away.

Yet, at the same time, on some level at least, it had alarmed him. His feelings for her were too strong. He liked her, first of all—liked her spirit, her energy, her warmth. He liked the fact that she'd overcome an emotionally wrenching past and had made a success of her life professionally, and he admired the way she was so determined to confront and resolve her various emotional demons.

And, in addition to the liking, he felt a powerful desire for her. Her joyful sensuality had completely bewitched him. It had been so long since he'd known anyone like her. Jessie, much though he'd loved her, had never been passionate and uninhibited about sex.

Still, he had to keep reminding himself that she was a woman who'd been abandoned by the most important figure in her life. Later, she had been betrayed and attacked by the lover she had turned to for affection, barely escaping with her life, and then by a system of justice that had seen her as the archetypal bad girl—villainess, not victim. On some level, he knew she'd been haunted by these events.

He did not want to cause her further pain.

He did not want to be the next person in her life who got close to her and then walked out of her life.

He certainly shouldn't be here tonight, knowing that each night they spent together would get them in deeper. He wouldn't be here, except . . . except . . .

For the past few days he'd begun to feel free, for the first time, of his obsession with Jessie. It was scary to see the glimmerings of freedom, and even scarier to realize that it felt good. But these were emotions that he simply couldn't resist exploring.

He wandered into the small kitchen. She was tossing the ingredients of a salad—he could see various kinds of baby lettuce, scallions, cucumber, goat cheese, tomatoes. She was broiling swordfish shish kebabs with mushrooms, onions, and fresh basil. "Smells wonderful," he said, lifting her hair and kissing the back of her neck.

"Mmmm. Stop that or I won't get the salad finished."

He slipped his arms around her from behind and toyed with her breasts through the silky summer blouse she was wearing. "We could skip dinner," he suggested as she arched backwards against him, making a soft sound in her throat.

"Oh, no," she said, tossing a grin over her shoulder. "I don't cook very often, but when I do I expect my efforts to be savored!"

"Okay, we'll savor the feast first—" his hands slipped down over her belly and brushed across her thighs "—then turn our attention to a different hunger."

She turned in his arms so they were chest to chest, thigh to thigh. "Are you hungry for me?" she murmured.

"Ravenous," he said.

She laughed joyfully. "Let's eat later," she said.

Chapter Twenty-six

"Justin, I need your help," Isobelle said to the leather-crafter who ran the Bleecker Street specialty shop Scenic Pleasures.

Justin took her hand and kissed it. "For you, lady, anything.

"I've got to talk to you." She glanced around at the customers—only two at the moment, a gay couple who were examining leather and chain harnesses. The shop sold a wide selection of leather garments, including skirts and trousers, corsets, vests, bras and bikinis. They also sold D&S toys—whips, paddles, collars, and various kinds of restraints. "Can we go downstairs?"

He nodded and left the shop in the hands of his assistant, a petite red-haired woman whom she vaguely remembered seeing at a party with her female lover.

The shop opened onto the four-story townhouse that Justin had owned in the Village for over twenty years.

"Downstairs is the dungeon," he reminded her as they went into the residential part of the house.

Isobelle nodded. "I know."

He looked at her closely for a moment, but said nothing. Together they descended to a dimly lit basement that had been reappointed as a D&S dungeon. Isobelle had been to several scene parties there. It contained the usual wall-mounted shackles, a set of wooden stocks, a paddling bench, a bondage swing, and various rings hanging from the ceiling.

There was a worn sofa against one wall where people could sit to cuddle or rest. She went to it and sat down, held out a hand to Justin, who joined her.

He was about medium height—not much taller than she was—and stocky. His hair was salt and pepper, as was his mustache. He had large dark eyes that were very seductive. Isobelle had no doubt that much of his power with women came from simply gazing silently at them with those expressive eyes.

"What's the matter?" he asked her.

Isobelle bit her lip and considered her answer. She and Justin had never been lovers, since they were both exclusively tops, but they'd supported each other through various heartaches and relationship bust-ups. She'd known him for several years, and they liked and respected each other.

"Hey," he said. "I can see that something's wrong."

"Look, you're one of my closest friends in the scene." She gave a brittle laugh. "And people in the scene are just about my only friends these days."

"They're good people," Justin said.

"I know. Why do all the vanilla people think we're so goddamn weird?"

"Not to mention sick, sadistic, and dangerous," he said dryly.

"It enrages me sometimes. I've always thought it was a lot healthier to acknowledge one's dark places and to find harmless ways to play with these sides of ourselves than it is to hide, repress, and deny all that stuff."

"That's for sure."

"People are hurting each other daily in all sorts of underhanded ways—and denying it. Yet they see a dominant carefully and lovingly disciplining a submissive and they say it's perverted."

Justin said nothing. She knew he'd heard it before— everybody in the scene shared similar opinions. She wasn't saying anything new . . . just putting off what she'd really come here to say. And to ask.

"Justin, we've been friends for a long time. I've seen you play. I know your partners trust you. I know you've earned and deserve the faith they have in you."

He looked at her, obviously curious about where this was leading.

Spit it out, for chrissake. "I want to submit to someone. No. I need to submit. Not as any kind of permanent thing. Just once. You're the only person I can think of whom I trust enough to dom me."

"You honor me," he said quietly.

"Will you do it?"

He took her hands in his. She thought he looked a little bemused, yet, at the same time, pleased. "If you're sure it's what you really want."

"It's—it's necessary." She glanced around the dungeon, noting the bondage frame, the shackles. Funny how different it looked knowing that she would be yielding—instead of taking—control. She could see where it could be a scary place, after all.

Rina, she thought.

"Isobelle?"

"I'm all right." She managed a smile. "I'd like to do it now, today, if that's all right with you."

"Look, let's take it slowly, okay? Let's just sit here for a while and relax." He leaned back and put one arm around her shoulders. "I'm trying to get used to the idea that one of the dearest and most beautiful dominas I know is asking me to top her," he said wryly. "Would you like to tell me why?"

She shook her head. "I can't."

He looked at her with those brown eyes and considered. "Am I correct in assuming that there's some kind of emotional conflict going on?"

Isobelle laughed shortly. "You could say that, yes."

He nodded. "In that case, we'll plan for an emotional safeword as well as a physical one. If things get too heavy for you, use it and I'll stop instantly."

"Of course. But—" she hesitated "—I don't want a novice submissive's scene. I want it severe. As intense as you can give, without causing harm."

"So what you're asking for is a punishment. There's something you're feeling guilty about, and you'd like me to give you a means of expiation."

She laughed nervously. "You're very wise, old friend, but let's not psychoanalyze this too much."

"Fair enough. Tell me one more thing, though. You couldn't just switch with Charlie?"

"No. I don't trust him to know what he's doing as a dominant. Besides," she paused, "I'm not sure how much longer I'm going to be seeing Charlie."

His eyes grew speculative. "It's not working?"

She clenched her fists. "No."

"I'm sorry."

She shrugged.

He caught her hand in his. "Now, huh?"

"If you have the time and the energy."

"Now is fine. I should tell you, though—it might change things between us."

"Meaning what?"

Justin's dark eyes twinkled at her. "Meaning if Charlie's on the way out, and there's any chance that you can play the submissive role, I'm not sure I want to agree to 'just once.'"

He was telling her that he could be more than just her friend. She shook her head slowly, touched. But he didn't know her, not really. He didn't know what he was asking. "I can't think about that now," she said.

"No problem." He switched to a more businesslike tone. "I have to ask you a few practical questions."

"Yeah, I know the drill. Okay, I'm healthy, I have no heart problems, no asthma, no back or other skeletal problems, no HIV or other STDs, no phobias that I know of. My safeword is simply 'safeword,' which is easiest to remember and unmistakable. Nylon rope is fine, so are leather cuffs. I know you won't use metal handcuffs or anything else that could cause nerve damage in the wrists. Any kind of whips, canes, and paddles are okay. Oh, and that reminds me—"

"Whoa." He put one hand over her mouth. "Easy. I can see it's not going to be easy for you to give up control."

He released her, and she smiled sheepishly. "I'm sorry. I do trust you."

"Keep repeating that and you'll begin to believe it deep down, where it counts."

She drew a deep breath. "Justin, I don't want you to think that I—"

"Shh. Intellectual trust is different from physical trust. The second I *will* have to earn."

She liked him very much, she thought. Too bad she hadn't chosen a man like Justin in the first place.

"When I was a kid, I had fantasies of submission," she admitted. "I still have them, sometimes. But I've always been afraid of it. Afraid to give up that control." She laughed shortly. "The men I've trusted have almost always betrayed me."

"Well, you'll find no betrayal here." He rose and walked to a wooden chest on the far side of the room. He rummaged inside it then lifted something out. When he returned Isobelle could see that it was a slave collar made of soft black leather. "This will help with the transition into power exchange," he said, showing her the locking mechanism and the small padlock that would fit through the rings. "It should fit you." He held it out. "Put it on."

Isobelle could feel her heartbeat quicken. She'd put collars on many male submissives, but she'd never worn one herself. "Help me," she said as she struggled to secure the end flaps of the collar.

He shook his head. "I want you to do it yourself. Donning that collar means you're surrendering your power, your control. It symbolizes your submission. Do you understand?"

She nodded. Beneath her apprehension she was beginning to feel aroused. Maybe it would be okay, after all. Justin was very experienced. He knew exactly what to do, what to say.

She got the collar fastened and, with trembling fingers, she slipped the padlock through the metal loops and clicked it closed. There was a tiny brass key in the bottom of the lock. She removed it and put it solemnly into the palm of his outstretched hand.

From the chest Justin removed a pair of leather wrist cuffs and a matching pair of ankle cuffs. She saw him checking the cuffs, and she knew he would gauge each item he used for its safety and be meticulously careful in every way. Within reach was a medical pack that was undoubtedly well-stocked with first-aid supplies.

He also extracted several paddles, cats, a riding crop, and a cane from the wooden chest. He saw her looking at them and raised an eyebrow. "One would think you'd never seen toys like these before."

"Let's just say I've never seen them in precisely the way I'm seeing them now!"

Grinning, Justin took her hand and pulled her to her feet. He led her over to the standing bondage frame that dominated the center of the room. It was constructed of sturdy two-by-fours that appeared to have been sunk into the concrete floor about six feet apart. There was a crossbar overhead, higher than a tall man could reach. Metal rings were set into the wood at several intervals on the uprights and the crossbar. Thick nylon rope hung from several of the rings.

He took her face between his palms and gently kissed her lips. It felt nice, she thought. *Very* nice.

Then he stepped away from her and picked up the cuffs. "Wrists first."

She suddenly felt vulnerable, helpless, and although she trusted him, scared.

But she was glad she felt these things . . . that she *could* feel them . . . that she was not—as she had feared—dead inside.

Rina, she thought again, as Justin came toward her.

Chapter Twenty-seven

Her lover was with her again.

He'd been there every night this week.

But he left early in the morning. Invariably.

He was going to do it here, Morrow decided. In her apartment. Not during the night, of course, for obvious reasons. His instructions were very clear on that.

He would wait until he was sure she was alone. Tomorrow morning would work just fine.

Gerald Morrow's hunt for his new prey had brought him to the laundry room in the basement of her co-op apartment building. Getting past security had been ludicrously easy, especially on a Friday night. He'd simply waited outside across the street until he saw a large bunch of yuppie joggers headed inside, then quickly joined them. He'd dressed in nylon athletic shorts, a T-shirt, and running shoes, so he melded right in. The security guard had barely given him a glance as he piled into the elevator with his "friends."

He'd then had the leisure to check various floors to get the layout of the place, the fire doors, and all the exits. The laundry room had provided him with a change of clothing—jeans and a shirt taken from separate dryers.

He had also gotten the key to her apartment, which was an unexpected bonus. He had planned to lock-pick his way in—a particular specialty of his. But in the course of checking the security desk in the lobby from the stairwell, he'd seen the guard leave his post about an hour ago, probably to go to the can. The guard had taken the precaution of locking the lobby door and posting a note to inform any resident who wanted to get in that he'd be back in five minutes. Morrow had quickly ducked in, pulled open a few drawers, and found a supply of extra keys to most of the apartments. He'd located April Harrington's and slipped it into the pocket of his new jeans.

The guard oughta be fired.

The necessity to make it look like a convincing accident was what had made Morrow decide on her building. The trouble with real accidents was that other people were frequently involved. In car accidents, for instance, either someone else besides the Target was in the car, or you took the risk of injuring someone in another car (or a pedestrian, of course). Also, car accidents were unpredictable. All too frequently the Target didn't die. Especially with all these new cars equipped with air bags—modern technology was putting a crimp in the car accident business for professional assassins.

In certain parts of the country you could force the Target off the road and over a cliff, which virtually assured the desired outcome, but that didn't work in New York City.

What the city did have in abundance were high buildings. Still, tossing somebody out of one without making it obvious that they'd been pushed wasn't the easiest thing in the world to accomplish.

Household accidents were Morrow's particular favorite. They were common and believable. And since they happened indoors, when the Target was alone, they were less risky and unlikely to go wrong.

They also allowed for personal contact. And for this case especially, personal contact was an intriguing possibility. The Target was a lovely woman. The more he stalked her, the more attached to her he had grown.

April Harrington was going to die in a household accident. In her kitchen perhaps. Or her bathroom. People were oh-so-vulnerable when they bathed.

Her bathroom. Yes. She would leave the world as naked as she had entered it.

As he gave a quick check to his equipment—gun, surgical gloves, nylon rope, and a few other items, Gerald Morrow savored the thought.

"What are you doing?"

The voice was like the crack of a whip, and Kate leapt away from her grandfather's bookshelves.

He snapped on the overhead lights, illuminating her in her nightgown, her feet bare, holding a volume that she'd just removed from a high shelf in the library. It was one of Rina's books, and she'd been checking it, and others, in hopes of finding a computer diskette tucked between the pages.

Kate was spending the night at her grandfather's. Her plan to search his penthouse apartment for the diskette last weekend hadn't worked out; he'd been indisposed and unable to see her. But tonight she'd come for dinner and together she and Granddad had played Scrabble (she'd beaten him, as usual), and then she'd yawned and said she was *so* tired and could she please sleep here instead of going home?

"I thought you were an intruder," her grandfather snapped. "I was just about to summon the police."

"I'm really sorry," she said, closing the book. "I was trying to be extra quiet. I didn't think you'd wake up."

"Why are you in here? What are you looking for? Don't you have better manners than to go poking around in people's personal things?"

He sounded really angry. Looked it, too. He got angry sometimes, she knew. But she didn't think he'd ever been angry at her before.

"I was just—" She hesitated, yelling inwardly at herself for not planning for this eventuality. "I couldn't sleep. I needed something to read."

"I thought you were extremely tired, which was why you asked to stay here in the first place."

"I was. I fell asleep and all, but then I, like, had a bad dream and woke up and couldn't get back to sleep. It was a really nasty dream. A nightmare. I was scared and I kept tossing and turning and finally I got up and came downstairs." Kate could hear herself speaking too fast and she wondered if he was buying it. Granddad was usually so— so nice. He always smiled, gave her hugs, listened to her, encouraged her. But now—

He came across the room toward her, and Kate tried her best to look innocent. Maybe she should just tell him what she was really looking for? But April had ordered her not to tell anybody. For that matter, April had ordered her not to look, but to leave that to the proper authorities.

Granddad reached out and took the book away from her. Quickly, he flipped through it. "This is one of your grandmother's books. Its subject is the treatment of cancer." He looked up, his blue eyes nailed her like lasers. "I doubt that this would have made pleasant bedtime reading for you. Why were you examining it?"

Oh, Jeez, she thought. He wasn't buying it. "I wanted to read something of hers. Something that she wrote, even if it wasn't very interesting. I—I miss her." She tried to make her bottom lip tremble and realized that it was trembling already. His unexpected arrival had startled her, and she was beginning to wish she'd never left her bed.

"Kate, I expect you always to tell me the truth. It would wound me deeply to think you were lying."

"I am telling you the truth!" she cried. "I loved Gran! Somebody murdered her and I want to know who. So does April. Somebody killed her mother and my grandmother and we both want to solve the crime!"

Granddad sighed deeply. His expression changed and his anger seemed to dissipate. He shook his head once, back and forth, then he drew her into his arms and hugged her. "We all want to solve the crime," he said gently. "But you are only twelve years old, little one. Solving murders is something you must be content to trust to the police."

"That's what April says, too," Kate admitted.

"That is very sensible of her," he said. "Now come. I will take you upstairs and read you a real bedtime story. A French fairy tale, just like the ones my mother used to read to me when I was a child."

But I'm not a child, Kate thought rebelliously. She didn't say it aloud, though. She figured she was in enough trouble already for one evening.

"Thanks, Grandfather," she said.

April slipped off her robe and stepped into her bath. She was looking forward to luxuriating in a tub of warm fragrant bubbles. Closing her eyes, she sank into the hot water, feeling her body slowly relax.

She thought, fondly, about Rob. He'd left about an hour ago. Too early, as always. She would have loved to sleep in with him some morning. But he was a slave to his work . . . to his frustrating murder investigation.

Things were getting better between them all the while. At first she had thought that he was the sort of man who withdrew emotionally after lovemaking. The first night they'd been together he had fallen asleep afterwards, and made only a halfhearted protest when she'd risen early the next morning to leave. And subsequently, for several nights, despite their easy camaraderie and the passionate abandon of the sex, he had remained a little tentative with her.

But last night something had changed. He had loosened up . . . well, perhaps they both had. At one point, she had looked up into his face as he'd leaned over her, playing idly with her hair, and whispered, "I could get used to this," she'd said.

"You're not the only one," he'd returned with a smile.

The whole thing had been awkward for him, she was sure. It was against his personal rules to get mixed up with one of the suspects in a murder investigation—if indeed she still was a suspect from his point of view.

Besides, he obviously still had a lot of unresolved feelings about the death of his wife. But last night, neither of these considerations had seemed the least bit important.

As for her own feelings, she liked him more each time she saw him. She respected his thoroughness and his intelligence. And she loved his body. The sexy things he whispered in her ear when they made love aroused her to a fever of excitement that was stronger than anything she could ever remember. She could almost imagine falling in love . . .

Whoa, she thought. Better not get carried away.

She reminded herself that Rob had made it very clear on their first night together that for him this was an adventure, not a serious involvement.

She had better slow down a little. And she had better guard her heart.

He would give her five more minutes, Morrow decided. By then she would be totally relaxed. The water would still be warm and she would be most comfortable. After a few more minutes it would be cooling off. She would notice that and no longer feel quite so much at ease.

He wanted her at ease. Death should be a time of serenity and peace. For so many people the last few moments of life were harsh and painful, but she deserved better. She deserved to slide as effortlessly out of life as she had slid out of her clothes.

In some ways, he would have preferred to simply put a bullet in the back of her neck. She wouldn't know it was coming, wouldn't be afraid, wouldn't feel a thing. Sadly, though, because of the client's demands, her death would not be that peaceful—for either of them.

Getting into her place had been ridiculously easy. In fact, this whole thing had been rather dull so far. No challenge to it at all.

Her lover had left on schedule. Morrow had lurked in the utility room, which gave him both a clear view of her apartment entrance and quick access to the stairs. The new rosebud he'd ordered delivered had come at precisely 9:00 A.M., and he'd watched as April had gone downstairs in response to the call from the mail room. As soon as she was in the elevator, he'd let himself into the apartment and concealed himself in the closet in her spare room/office, usually the door least likely to be opened.

He'd been prepared to wait as long as necessary. Or to seize any unexpected opportunity that might arise. Sooner or later she would either use the kitchen or take a bath or a shower, and he'd preferred to wait for one or the other. If she'd tried instead to leave, he would have resorted to a quicker—if riskier—method.

One way or another, April Harrington was going to die.

She had chosen the bath.

He waited, watching her through a crack in the bathroom door. Her eyes were closed. She looked peaceful. Slowly, he pushed open the bathroom door.

He had the nylon rope in his hands.

"April," he said.

Chapter Twenty-eight

"Hmm?" She almost seemed to be dreaming. Lazily she opened her eyes. Morrow watched the confusion, then the fear come into them. Those blue eyes widened as she jerked herself upright, and he thought, oh, yes, she is exquisite.

She cried out something like "who are you?" so he showed her the gun. Then he watched her face as she realized who he must be, and why he had come.

In the personal cases, this was always the moment of truth: knowing they were going to die, how did they confront it? He had seen every possible reaction from fear to denial to crazy resistance to devil-may-care courage. One man had flipped him the bird just before having his brains blown out. Another had smiled and thanked him. "You're doing me a favor, friend," he'd said.

April Harrington clenched her fingers into fists and raised her chin. "Who hired you?" she demanded.

He shook his head. It was never a good idea to engage in unnecessary conversation with the Target.

"You killed my mother, didn't you?"

She sounded more angry than afraid. "Stand up," he said.

She shook her head. "No."

He cocked the gun and moved two steps closer to the bathtub. "Stand up, please," he amended, giving her a genial, if slightly mocking, smile.

"Just shoot me and get it over with!"

"I'm not going to shoot you." Since this was the truth, he felt comfortable saying it, even though it might give her momentary false hope. He didn't like to lie to them. It was dishonest. But when finishing the job meant getting some cooperation from the Target, a little fudging on the truth was sometimes necessary.

Besides, people needed to have some hope. It made them much more willing to please.

"You're not going to shoot me?" Her voice was quavering a little now.

"No. Stand up."

"I'm naked."

They worried about the oddest things. "It doesn't matter. Open the drain first. Let some of the water flow out."

She stared at him a moment, then leaned forward, and flipped the metal drain release.

"Good," he said soothingly. He would close the drain again before he left, but the tub was too full at the moment. Nobody took a shower in a tub full of water.

"Is there a bathmat? Are you sitting on one?"

She nodded. There was a hint of a tremor in her jaw.

"I want it out of there. Slide it out from under you and give it to me."

Her eyes never leaving his face, she lifted herself and

reached underneath her body. The mat was suctioned to the bottom of the tub, so she had to wrestle with it. He was growing impatient when she surprised him. Her hands came slapping out of the water, splashing water directly at him and sending the bathmat of soap flying at his face. He cursed and ducked. The Target screamed. If he hadn't checked the soundproofing on this place he might have been worried.

With his gloved hand he seized a hunk of her hair and jerked it taut. She screamed again, in pain this time. He leaned over her, his face close to hers. He could smell her fragrance—it was quite seductive. "Shut up. I don't want to hurt you. But I will."

In fact he didn't care about hurting her, but he didn't want to leave any marks on her body. The cops would be looking closely for any signs of a struggle. Homicide victims who came into contact with their killers almost always had defensive wounding—it was one of the primary ways of establishing the difference between murder and accidental death.

For the same reason, he had dressed in his light nylon running shorts and a sleeveless T-shirt. The running shoes now had rubbers fitted over the soles. Surgical gloves, of course.

"Stick your right foot up on the side of the tub," he ordered in the same calm voice.

She made no move to obey. Clearly, she was the stubborn type. He dropped a two-foot-square piece of clear plastic to the floor beside the tub and quickly knelt there, one hand still fastened in her hair. Then he shoved her face forward into the several inches of water that were left in the tub.

Her entire body stiffened as she fought to get free, but with one hand in her hair and the other firmly planted between her shoulder blades, he had purchase, strength, and leverage. Her hands grabbed at the sides of the tub, but these were porcelain, further slickened with bubble bath, soap, and water. There was nothing for her to hold on to, and nothing to do any damage to her flailing hands either.

He counted slowly to thirty. It didn't matter if she got water in her lungs—the official cause of death would be drowning anyway.

He jerked her face out of the water. She gasped for breath, coughed, choked, cried. Tears were streaming out of her eyes. He reminded himself to be sure to wash any dried tears off her face before he left. Tears—body fluids—would be deemed physical evidence.

The proper manipulation of the physical evidence was the secret of making a murder look like an accident. The crime lab people had made such huge advances in the past decade or so that it was getting increasingly difficult to put anything over on them. Close personal contact between two people—such as between two lovers or between a killer and his Target—almost always resulted in the transfer of physical evidence—the most minute sort only detectable with the latest high-tech methods and instruments.

Like all true professionals, Morrow had studied the latest techniques in crime scene analysis. The slightest mistake, he knew, could give him away. This case had already had too much contact for his liking.

"Put your right ankle up on the side of the tub," he repeated. This time, coughing and sputtering, the Target obeyed.

With quick economical movements he looped a hobble around her ankle and pulled it taut. It was thick cotton that he had carefully encased in plastic to avoid the transfer of fibers. The nylon rope went over that, and the padding prevented it from coming in contact with her body.

It would leave no marks, transfer no evidence.

"What—what are you doing?" she whispered.

The rope was secure. "Stand up."

"If you're going to kill me, just—"

He shut her up by grabbing her head again and slamming her face back down into the water. This time he only held her there for ten seconds and she was screaming, "No, no! All right, all right!" when he let her up.

She rose clumsily to her feet. The water level was down to no more than three inches now—good enough. "Close the drain and turn on the shower."

Her hands were trembling as she moved to obey.

Holding the rope loosely in his right hand, Morrow moved around behind her. She was fumbling with the shower controls. He tried not to be distracted by her slender body, which was even more lovely nude than dressed. Perfect breasts, nice ass. He'd have loved to run his hands over that ass—without the gloves so he could feel her warm supple flesh—but it was impossible. Forensics would find his sweat, his hairs, tiny flakes of his skin, and enough DNA to send him up for the rest of his life.

Her body jerked as the shower came on full force.

Morrow tightened the rope, but not enough yet to pull her off balance. She was still confused—she hadn't figured it out. He was going to jerk hard on the rope, pulling her right foot out from under her. She would go down hard, striking the front of her head against the wall, the tub, or the metal taps. If the blow didn't knock her right out, it would daze her, giving him the opportunity to take her head in his hands and smash it down harder against whatever part of the tub she had naturally landed on.

Once she was unconscious, the three inches of water

left in the tub would enter her lungs and do the rest. He would wait until he was sure it was over, of course. He would slip the rope and the cotton batting from her ankle and take everything with him when he left.

He reminded himself that he'd better draw the shower curtain before he left. Nobody took a shower without drawing the curtain. . . .

The cops would find a dead woman who had regrettably slipped as she was turning on the shower, knocked herself out, and drowned. Maybe if she'd kept the rubber bathmat in the tub when she'd bathed it wouldn't have happened. People were so careless.

Unexpectedly, the Target turned toward him. "I want to know who hired you. Was it Christian? Did you also murder his wife by forcing her car off the road?"

He ignored her questions. There were too many details to consider. "Turn back toward the shower and put your hands on top of your head." He was obsessing over the logistics. Getting the hands out of the way was a problem. Hands were all too useful at breaking a fall. He'd have tied them behind her back if there hadn't been too much of a risk of leaving marks.

"Dammit, I want to know! Is it Isobelle? She's the only one I can imagine who stands to gain by my death. Is this how badly she wants Power Perspectives?"

"Shut up."

"Go to hell—I've got nothing to lose!"

"Yeah, you do. You can die easy or you can die hard. Doesn't matter to me. We got all the time in the world, you and me. You think I'd do this work if I didn't enjoy it? I kill women and I like it."

She had a *really* nice ass, he was thinking. She was brave, too. Breathing fast, trembling, but no more tears. Funny how often women were actually braver than men.

Lotsa guys would have been whimpering and babbling before this.

"What do you want from me?" she said.

He smiled. "Just the satisfaction of a job well done."

"You get that by killing people?" Her tone was scathing.

"It's not personal," he said. But he was lying. It was personal. And he really would have loved to take his time with her, forget all about this accident crap.

In the front of the apartment, a door slammed.

Morrow went rigid.

"April?" a voice called out. "Hey, April, are you home?"

Shit!

As April screamed, "Kate, *no!*" Morrow understood. It was that damn kid! She must have a key.

He was on her before she could scream again, his arm around her neck, his hand jammed over her mouth. He lifted her out of the bathtub—she wasn't light, but his muscles were highly trained—and dragged her to the bathroom door while he engaged the lock. She was struggling so he doubled up his fist and hit her just under her left cheekbone. She went limp but he didn't think she was totally out.

So much for not leaving marks.

He laid her down on the floor, where she moaned and drew her legs up into a fetal position. Only two choices now—abort the job or kill them both.

"If there's any problem, cut your losses and get out," the client had said. "This has got to be convincing as an accident. One murder investigation is bad enough."

Damnation. This would have been a beautiful murder, too. He'd been about to take her. He wanted to take her.

Even now the temptation to take her was almost impossible to resist.

Her eyes flicked and came open. She was dazed, but conscious. And she was lovely. Slender and naked, with that thick mane of hair, those clear blue eyes. He wanted to watch the life ebb from those eyes. He wanted to look into them, and understand the mystery lurking there on the edge of eternity.

The rope was still around her ankle. One economical move and it could be around her neck.

Chapter Twenty-nine

It was the sound of Kate's voice that brought April back. Absolutely sure she was going to die and hoping only that it would be over fast and wouldn't hurt too much, she had felt trapped. It was like being trapped under a thin layer of ice on a frozen pond. She could still dimly see the world she loved, but she was too paralyzed with cold and with fear to break through.

But letting go of her own life was one thing. Allowing a twelve-year-old to join her in death was something else entirely.

And so she'd screamed. He, the killer, had hit her, hard. She was amazed that she was still alive.

Where was Kate? Had she heard? Had she run from the apartment? Was she even now notifying security, calling the police?

"April?" the girl's voice called out tentatively, from the hall.

The rough hand clamped over her mouth again and

April felt tears come into her eyes. Her head was hurting, especially the left side of her face. Her body was weak; she wasn't sure she could move or make a sound.

She looked up into the killer's face—really saw it this time so she'd never forget it—and saw him looking at her naked, vulnerable body, and she read something in his expression that she couldn't put a name to—something unspeakable.

And she knew she couldn't allow Kate to be exposed to the evil that was lurking here.

She managed to get a hand free, and somehow she curled her fingers around his arm. She tried to indicate with her eyes that she wanted to speak. That she understood the need for quiet. That she would not scream.

He understood. It was odd—it was as if there was a bond between them. She could face that evil. She could address it. Maybe she could bargain with it.

He lifted his hand a fraction of an inch from her mouth. "I'll get rid of her," she whispered. "She hasn't seen you. She doesn't know you're here. She's just a child. Don't hurt her, please."

Utter silence between them. Then, slowly, the killer nodded.

April rolled over clumsily and got to her knees. He stayed with her, holding onto her shoulders, her hair. Like a lover, she thought. Like Blackthorn . . .

"I'll make an excuse," she said, low. "I'll tell her to leave."

"Do it," he said, sounding indifferent. "But be careful. Screw up and the kid's gone."

She believed him. She had looked into his eyes. If he had ever had a conscience, it was gone.

April reached for the knob of the bathroom door.

* * *

Kate thought she'd heard April yell something at her, but she hadn't been able to make out what she'd said. She hesitated on the threshold of the doorway that led back down the hall to the bedrooms. What if she had a boyfriend in there?

The idea that April might have a lover stopped her cold. She was pretty enough, but having a lover would mean she wasn't interested in Daddy. And since April was Daddy's last hope to become a decent human being, Kate didn't like this idea.

She wondered if her breakup tactics would work better on April and her boyfriend than they seemed to be working on Daddy and Daisy Tulane.

What could she do? She really wanted to talk to April. She wanted to tell her that she'd searched at least part of Granddad's place last night before being caught, and that she hadn't seen any sign of the missing diskette.

She heard low sounds coming from the bathroom. She shook her head. What were they doing in there? Taking a shower together or something? It was kinda odd. April's voice had sounded funny, too.

What if something was wrong? Kate's imagination started working overtime. What if it was the killer? What if he was here, in the apartment? What if he had April?

Don't be silly, she told herself. The last time she'd thought such a thing, it hadn't been the killer at all.

Still, hadn't it been "No!" that April had shouted?

And how come she hadn't said anything else?

Kate looked at the entryway and then at the archway leading into the kitchen. She hesitated for a moment, then dived into the kitchen. Something was wrong. She could feel it.

The phone was there and she could call 911. She grabbed the receiver, looking around the small kitchen for a place to hide. There was none. She punched in the numbers and heard the call go through and the ringing sounds but no one answered. She'd read articles about it—there were so many 911 calls in the city that nobody could answer them all. Sometimes it took twenty minutes to get through . . .

"Kate, is that you?" April called out from somewhere down the hall.

Kate's heart stopped pounding quite so hard. "April, are you okay?"

"I'm fine, Kate. Just busy at the moment, that's all. I've got a friend here. You'll have to come back later, okay?"

She did have a lover, Kate thought. God, adults were all the same. It was really disgusting.

"Police emergency," came a voice on the telephone.

"Oh, sorry," Kate mumbled. "Never mind."

"You see, she's leaving," the Target said. She and Morrow were listening at the door to the bathroom. His gun was at her throat.

He heard the kid call out, "Sorry to have disturbed you. I'll come back tomorrow." She sounded both sarcastic and disgruntled. Christ, teenagers were rude these days. Oughta be taught a lesson, all of them.

They heard the front door to the apartment slam.

"She's gone," his victim said.

"Maybe, maybe not."

She was looking at him in some alarm. "Didn't you hear her leave?"

"Shut up." He stood and jerked her roughly to her feet. "She better be gone. We're gonna go check."

He pulled her out, still naked and dripping wet, into the hallway. Staying behind her, one arm around her throat, he forced her to walk down the corridor toward the living room. Physical evidence all over the damn place now. He couldn't believe this had turned into such a fucking mess.

Stay flexible, he ordered himself. There still might be a way to pull it off.

"How'd the kid get in, anyhow? Did you give her a key?"

The Target shook her head. "She must have gotten it from Rina."

"She just pops over anytime she feels like it?"

"Pretty much, yes."

"Almost got herself killed."

The Target shivered. No way she could hide it, pressed against his body the way she was. Naked, vulnerable, and about to die.

Morrow felt the power, savored it, held it close. He could see, feel, taste, breathe her fear, and it thrilled him. Better than sex. Killing had always been better than sex.

This was fucked up, but he was enjoying it anyway.

He knew a guy who'd once told him that his days as a professional assassin were numbered because he loved the killing too much. He was probably right. You had to be crazy to enjoy this. Morrow worried, sometimes, about being crazy. And about going to hell.

On the other hand, at moments like these, both madness and hell seemed a small price to pay for his pleasure.

He forced her into the living room. They could see that the door to the apartment was securely closed. At least the kid hadn't left it standing open, for any fool to wander in . . .

Now what? The kitchen was a good place. Lots of lethal objects in a kitchen. He was thinking fast, being creative—

Out of the corner of his eye, he thought he detected a slight motion. It was coming from the kitchen. As he swung around, bringing the muzzle of his gun with him, reacting faster than thought, he saw—Jesus—he saw a head—

April screamed as his finger squeezed the trigger. The recoil jerked them both. The silencer deadened the sound to a pop, but it felt wrong—he'd aimed too high—he'd aimed for an adult. Goddamn it, this must be the kid—the brat hadn't left, after all . . .

Then Harrington had pulled herself free somehow and now she was digging her fucking teeth into his arm, his shooting arm, and she was screaming and the kid was screaming and he got off another shot. The kid's voice was cut off in mid-shriek and the Target started shouting "No-No-No!" and everything was chaos. He was swinging the gun toward her when she suddenly jabbed her fingers into his eyes. Then he was screaming in pain and rage and the bitch cracked his kneecap with her foot and he felt his fingers losing their grip on the gun. He heard it fall and the fire in his eyes was unspeakable and he slapped out viciously at her and knocked her off her feet. But he couldn't see the gun and she was probably going for it and he thought, the bitch'll kill me for sure if she finds it. She was yelling, "Kate-Kate-Kate!" but there was no answer from the kid. Shit, it had all gone wrong.

Morrow remembered where the door was and backed towards it. The pain in his head was so bad he wanted to vomit but even more he wanted to get out of there before she shot him, before she did hotly what he so coldly had done for years . . .

He found the door with his hands and pulled it open. The Target was on the phone, sobbing into the receiver. "She's been shot, she's unconscious, please come quickly!"

He stumbled out into the corridor. He couldn't believe it. The kid hadn't left after all, and the bitch had blinded him.

Chapter Thirty

"She's going to be okay," Blackthorn said. He hung up the phone and gave April the latest news from the hospital. "The charge nurse says she's got normal EEG activity, no significant brain swelling, and that her vital signs are good. She'll have a headache, she'll have to take it easy for a while, but she'll be fine."

"Thank God," April whispered.

They were downtown in the precinct police station, taking a brief break from the whirl of official questioning that had begun the moment the cops had shown up at April's apartment. One of the two officers who had responded to the initial call, Janice Flack, was the same cop who'd come with a different partner to April's apartment when it had been broken into two weeks before. On Rob's insistence, she'd called in a couple of detectives from the city homicide department. Marty Clemente, meanwhile, was on his way down.

Blackthorn hugged April, but he could feel the numbness in her body. He dragged his hands through her hair, smoothing it back from her stricken face. She shook her head slightly, and he knew she didn't want him to touch her too much. He sighed and backed away.

O'Brian, one of the homicide dicks, called them back into the interview room.

"Look, the kid's gonna live, and that's great," he said. "But we're from homicide. She ain't dead, she ain't my concern." O'Brian, a big paunchy man, was snapping his gum. His partner, Murphy, was a thin quiet man who seemed content to remain in the background while O'Brian did his "bad cop" routine. "You give us a body, someone actually offed here in the great city of New York, and we'll look for a killer."

"You don't believe this asshole is a killer then you've got a problem," Blackthorn said.

"Yeah, well, we'll let your fed friends help you out on that one. The Feebs are good at that. The Fuckin Feebs—that's what we call 'em, Blackthorn. Aren't you glad to be outta the Fuckin Feebs? 'Course we don't like to work with you private assholes, either. Everybody thinks they've got a better way to do our job."

"Let's just take down all the information," Lieutenant Flack interrupted. She was trying to make peace. "We can all insult each other later, okay?" She looked at April. "You say you got a good look at his face? You'll be able to identify him from a mug shot, you think?"

"I think so, yes."

"We'll get out the books. I know you're tired, but I'd prefer you do it now, while the image is fresh in your mind."

"All right," April said wearily.

"You're probably not going to have this guy in your

rogue's gallery." Blackthorn said. "God knows how many people he's killed, but he's probably never been arrested."

"You never know," Janice Flack said evenly. "This was not your typical professional hit. This guy was in close enough to get his hands dirty."

"Why didn't he shoot me?" April asked. "He had the gun."

"It was supposed to look like an accident," Blackthorn said. "Once Kate showed up, that became impossible. If he shot you, there was no way. He was probably under orders not to proceed in the event that something went wrong."

"But everyone would have known it wasn't an accident!"

Blackthorn glanced sourly at O'Brian and his partner, Murphy. "If it's not provable as homicide, these folks don't get too interested."

"Hey, look, buddy, we got more cases than we can handle already, so don't give me that crap," O'Brian said. "You got one little problem to solve and you devote your whole day to it. Me, I gotta load of stiffs, with more coming in every couple hours, and the boys upstairs with the bean counters are keeping track of how many of those cases I clear, and how fast. I don't have time for this shit."

"If the guy was smart he'd have killed you anyhow, in spite of his orders from whoever hired him," Flack said. The homicide guy's ranting seemed to have no effect on her whatsoever—she remained focused on the matter at hand. "If he'd thought it through more carefully he would have realized this. We can presume that whatever reason existed for wanting you dead still exists. It's going to be a lot harder for them now, though. You'll be on your guard. The perp should have acted while he had the chance, accident or no accident."

"You're right," said Blackthorn. "I'll be protecting her now."

"Hope you do a better job than you did with the lady in Anaheim," O'Brian said.

Christian de Sevigny paced the small hospital room where Kate lay unconscious. A fractured skull, the doctor had said. A concussion, of course. But she should come out of it okay, they'd assured him. It didn't look too bad; she should wake up.

What if she didn't? Oh, God, what if . . . ?

Her head was swathed in bandages and her face looked so pinched, so small. It seemed as if the blow had caused her to lose several years of her age and she was eight again, or nine. So small, so delicate. Lying there so still.

Over her bed, the monitors beeped away. The video screen showed the waves of the electrical activity in her heart. Jumping numbers registered her pulse rate—the vital sound of her child's heart.

The bullet had cut a shallow furrow through hair, skin, and the surface of her skull. It had not penetrated her brain. If it had been an inch lower she'd be dead.

As he watched the monitor the years were swept away and he remembered standing beside Miranda in her gynecologist's office all those years ago, listening in astonishment as the doctor used an ultrasound monitor with a microphone to transmit the static racing that was the unborn baby's tiny heart. He remembered thinking that that beating would be going on uninterrupted for another eighty years or so—that's how strong it had sounded, how indestructible.

The body that had sheltered and nurtured that tiny beating heart was lying still beneath the ground. And today—

the sound that had seemed invulnerable—the sound that he'd always figured would go on in the world long after he was in the ground, too—had nearly been silenced forever.

It's all my fault.

It was as if a curtain had been torn away and he was able to see clearly for the first time in years. This was what it had taken. He looked at his daughter and felt the tears gathering in his eyes. This.

No more. No more.

Enough is enough.

It ends here.

"It's over, Charlie," Isobelle said.

He blinked noncomprehendingly. "What?"

"I don't want to see you anymore. We'll work something out at the office. It will be hard for a while, I'm sure, but it will get easier as time passes. I'm sorry, but this is the way it has to be."

She had invited him over. She would have preferred to break off with him by phone, but that seemed too cowardly. He'd accepted the invitation eagerly, clearly anticipating many kinds of pleasures, although considering what had just happened to April and Kate, she couldn't believe he was so insensitive.

He shook his head as if what she was saying to him was making no sense. "Isobelle, I don't understand. What do you mean, it's over? I'm in love with you!"

"I'm sorry. I warned you not to fall in love with me. I never promised you anything, Charlie. I told you not to get too dependent on me."

"You're the one who's dependent on me!"

Jesus—is that what he thought? No wonder she'd been

getting so many alarming vibrations. "That's your fantasy. That's what you want me to be. You want to take care of me, I know. You want to protect me." She was trying to sound gentle but firm. She didn't want to give him even the slightest hint of hope. "But I don't need that from you—or from anyone—and it's vital that you understand it." She poured all her convictions into her voice. "I run my own life and I take care of my own problems. I always have and I always will. I don't want anyone meddling in my affairs. I'm sorry if that sounds harsh, but I've warned you before."

"Look, I know you're upset about your niece getting shot and all that," he said. "The killer's on the loose again, and that's scary. And that's why you need me. You need me to protect you. My God, Isobelle, next he could come for you."

"This has nothing to do with that." She could hear her voice shaking.

"Of course it does, Isobelle. It has everything to do with that."

She turned her back on him. Her stomach was churning. How had her life turned so crazy? When Rina had been alive it had been hard, yes—the fights, the misunderstandings, the competition, the struggle for power. Working with Rina had never been easy, either for her or for Charlie, despite his seeming good nature. But it had been easier than this.

"Please leave, Charlie."

There was a long silence. Then, "There's someone else," he said heavily. "You've got another lover, don't you?"

She didn't think of Justin that way. Justin was a good friend. He'd given her something that she'd desperately needed, and in the process he'd helped her make up her mind. But Justin—his dungeon, his toys, his body—had been the instrument, not the cause.

"This has nothing to do with anyone else except you and me. I can't see you anymore. Our relationship isn't working. It's you and I who are alone responsible for that, so please don't go looking for outside causes."

"But why?" His voice had turned plaintive, perhaps even a little scared. "I love you, I'd do anything for you, please, Isobelle, don't do this to me!"

"My God, I don't want a man who would do anything for me," she said, impatient now. "I want a man who respects himself more than that. I don't want an obsessive man, a man who tries to mind-read, who thinks he knows what I need and desire, and acts accordingly. Don't you understand? You're suffocating me."

She regretted the words as soon as they were out. Dammit, she thought, would she ever learn to think before she blurted things out?

He was shaking his head. He looked as if he were about to cry. "I can't believe what I'm hearing. I just can't believe you could think such things about me. I love you. Damn you, doesn't that count for anything?"

"It counts for a lot. It makes me very sad and regretful. But it doesn't change my mind. You'd better leave."

He reached out for her, trying to embrace her. Isobelle retreated, but he followed her, seized her around the waist, wrapped one arm around her shoulders. She made an involuntary sound—she was a little sore back there. Charlie looked into her face, his brow furrowed, then without warning, ripped at her blouse.

"No!" she cried, enraged that he would attempt such a thing. But he persisted, pulling the light summery fabric down over her shoulders to reveal the thin faint marks that lingered there. She should have waited to confront him. In a few more days all traces of her session with Justin would have been gone.

"I can't believe it!" he shouted. "You let somebody do that? You let somebody dom you? Who is he? Who is he, dammit, I'll kill him!"

"Get out," she said. "Get out now, Charlie, or I'll call the police."

He slapped her. Right across the side of her face. She staggered and nearly fell.

"Get out," she said, her voice icy with her effort to control it. "Get out of here and don't ever come back. We're through, you son of a bitch."

He left, cursing and slamming his fist into the wall. Isobelle locked the door behind him and went into the living room. Shaking, she dug out a cigarette from a pack she hadn't opened in days and lit it. As she inhaled deeply nightmare images filled her head. He had hit her. Her ears were still ringing with the force of his blow. Until recently, she would never have dreamed that Charlie Ripley could be capable of violence, no matter how upset he was.

What had Charlie said a couple of weeks ago: *April Harrington won't last long, I promise you. She'll be gone in a blink, and Power Perspectives will be ours.*

What would the police say, she wondered, if she told them *that*?

"The worst of it is, I did what he ordered me to do," April said. "It was like a dream. I couldn't believe it was happening. I knew he'd come to kill me but I didn't believe I would die."

"I know," Blackthorn said.

The crime scene techs were still working on her apartment so he'd taken her back to his place after several hours with the police, then Marty over at FBI headquarters. She was exhausted, and more rattled than he'd ever seen her.

"And now that it's over, it's all getting fuzzy. As if I can't quite remember, somehow." She looked at him, her blue eyes alarmed. "I remembered when I talked to the police. Why can't I now? Is this some kind of stress reaction?"

He nodded. "Don't worry about it. Our bodies are wiser than our brains at times like these."

"I remember his face," she said and shuddered.

"You're probably one of the few people who has seen it and lived."

She looked puzzled again. "I have images, but it's as if my linear memory is shot. You know? I know some of the things that happened, but I can't seem to clarify the exact order. It's all confused."

He said nothing. He'd dealt with enough trauma victims to know that what she was feeling was entirely normal. There was no way to stop her from trying to sort it out. He'd urged her to take the tranquilizer that the doctor had prescribed to calm her, but she had refused.

"I think I resisted at one point, and so he forced my head down into the bath water. I couldn't breathe, and it was just like people say—I felt total panic because all I wanted to do was breathe, but I knew that if I opened my mouth all that dirty bath water would rush into my lungs and I'd be dead. And then it didn't matter and I didn't care and I was just about to do it anyway because my body was screaming at me to breathe, to breathe . . . and he let me up. After that I think I did whatever he told me to do."

"Anybody would have."

She looked at him. "Not you."

"Yes, me."

"No. You're strong. You would have resisted all the way."

Blackthorn pictured himself drunk with a bottle and laughed shortly. "There's a lot you don't know about me. I'm not so strong. Sounds to me as if you showed a couple minutes of weakness, that's all. Then you kicked his ass, you and Kate."

"Kate," she whispered. Tears popped into her eyes.

He held her. "She's going to be all right, hon. She'll be fine."

"I thought she'd left. I was sure of it. I still don't understand what she was doing, pretending to leave, then hiding out in the kitchen."

"Spying on you, probably. You know how kids are. Or maybe she knew something was wrong."

"He shot her. She's just a child. He—"

"Ssh. Stop replaying it. You both survived. In fact, the two of you were really something. He had a gun, but you drove the asshole off with your bare hands."

"He got away."

"We'll get him," he assured her. "He fucked up. He's dead meat."

She looked at him. "You sound so hard."

"I'm harder than you know."

She nodded, then her eyes slid away again.

"I need a shower," she said a few minutes later. Then as if hearing her words for the first time, she shuddered. "No," she whispered. "No, no, I can't."

"You're cold. Come, I'll carry you to bed."

"I feel dirty. I want to wash—but how, after that happened . . . I never want to get into a bathtub again."

He lifted her unresisting body and carried her into his own small bathroon, the one with the stall shower. He set her down and reached into the stall and turned on the taps.

The crime techs had worked her over earlier, taking scrapings from underneath her nails and going over her entire body with a laser, looking for evidence. He wasn't sure how much of it she remembered. Maybe she had blotted it out just as she had the details of the attack itself.

"No, please," she said as he urged her toward the shower. "I can't, I can't."

He slid his arms around her and kissed the side of her throat. "I'm here. I'm not leaving you. You don't have to do a thing. Trust me, my darling, trust me."

She pressed her face against his neck. Slowly, she nodded.

With slow careful movements, he stripped off the bathrobe he'd given her and let it pool beneath their feet. He caressed her and told her she was beautiful. The steam from the shower was already beginning to warm up the bathroom. He pulled off his T-shirt and shucked his jeans.

"Rob, I don't know—"

"You're okay," he said, and, supporting her tightly around the waist, helped her step into the shower. She shivered as the warm water struck her naked body; he held her close. He gathered up a bar of soap and gently began massaging her back with it. She pressed herself against him and shuddered, and then she began to cry.

"I've got you," he murmured. "It's okay, baby, it's okay."

Her body convulsed against his into loud, wracking sobs. He held her close, continuing the gentle massaging of his soapy hands over her neck, her scalp, and the supple muscles of her back.

When she'd cried herself out and seemed more relaxed, he soaped up a washcloth and smoothed it over her body from head to toe. He tried to prevent himself from becoming aroused, but this was impossible. He wondered if the killer had become aroused at the thought of killing her, and the idea that he might have made Rob feel dirty, too. He scrubbed his own body as well; as if it could wash away the evil that had enveloped them all.

"Daddy?"

The voice was low and groggy, a little plaintive, a little uncertain, but Christian leapt to his feet. He leaned over her. One of her hands was moving, and her eyelids, barely visible in the swath of head bandages, were fluttering.

"It's okay, baby, I'm here, I'm here."

"Daddy, where am I?" She sounded scared. Her eyes came open, then shut again against the bright ICU lighting. "My head hurts."

"You're in the hospital. But you're going to be okay, Kate." Christian sat on the edge of her bed and took her small hand in his. Her fingers clutched convulsively.

"What am I doing in the hospital?" She sounded astonished by the idea.

"Never mind, sweetie, just rest. We can talk about it later."

"I want to know now," she insisted, and Christian found himself smiling with relief. She was, thank God, her normal contrary and impatient self. She sounded alert and clearheaded.

"You got shot, Kate," he told her. "Probably by the same guy who murdered your grandmother. Fortunately, in your case, his aim was off. The bullet grazed your skull, which is why your head hurts. But it didn't cause any significant damage."

"Someone tried to murder me?" She thought about it for a moment. "Wow."

"Do you remember anything, Kate?"

Her expression changed from wonder to fear. "April. What happened to April? Is she all right?"

"Yes, she's okay. Your going to her apartment when you did put you in danger, but it probably saved her life."

"She's not dead? You're not lying to me, Daddy, are you?"

"No, I swear to you. April's fine."

"And I saved her life?"

He smiled and kissed her gently on the cheek. "You did indeed. You're quite a heroine, as a matter of fact."

"You think so?"

Oh, God! Did she think he wasn't proud of her? Hearing the uncertainty in her voice, he remembered the ways he'd failed her, the ways he simply hadn't been there for her. Things were going to be different from now on. "I'm very proud of you, sweetheart," he said.

She broke into a smile. "I love you, Daddy."

He hugged her as tightly as all the tubing and monitors would allow.

Chapter Thirty-one

April stood at the window in her office looking out over the city. In the background one of Rina's audiotapes was playing. In an earnest, upbeat tone Rina was saying:

What a mistake we make when we believe ourselves to be buffeted by fate! The truth is, our destiny is in our own hands. We become who and what we are because of the choices we make. Not big, momentous choices, but the little unconscious habitual decisions that we make over and over every day.

We make these decisions because of our beliefs about ourselves and each other. If, for example, I believe for whatever reason that I am lazy, disorganized, and incompetent, I will act in a manner that is lazy, disorganized, and incompetent. What you are to be, you are in the process of becoming. The role you act is the role you own.

The place where you have arrived in your life is entirely logical. You placed yourself upon the road that led there a very long time ago. There is no mystery about the condi-

tion of your finances. There is no mystery about your professional success or your personal relationships. Where you are now is where you ordained yourself to be.

And if you are not satisfied—as most of us aren't, at some point in our lives—there is only one person who can do something about that. That person is you. You can change your life. You can reshape your destiny. You can take control of your own power and recognize the joy and the vitality of your own existence. You can change all your negative beliefs about yourself. You are not trapped, you are not helpless! As long as there is breath in your body and determination in your heart, you can still have everything you've ever dreamed of and be whatever it is you really want to be!

She sounded so positive, April thought. She believed what she was preaching. She spoke as if she had been there, done that. As if she had intimate knowledge of exactly what it felt like to be powerless.

How could this be?

April reached out a finger and pressed the button to stop the tape. Then she rested her chin in her hands and stared at the faded photograph in the tin frame that her mother had left to her. She had been ridiculously attached to the picture. She carried it to work with her in the morning and home at night, setting it carefully on the table beside her bed. She studied it often, as if it were the key to the mystery of Rina de Sevigny.

Mother and daughter. Waitress and brat leaning against their dilapidated summer cottage. Had Rina felt powerless then, during the summer when she'd successfully seduced the president of the United States?

Had she felt powerless when she'd convinced Armand

de Sevigny, scion of a wealthy, snobbish family to take her as his wife?

When had Rina ever felt powerless?

Why had she started Power Perspectives in the first place? Why had she needed it?

Dammit, I need to think!

April got up, went to the closet, and grabbed a nylon athletic bag. She removed a T-shirt and a pair of running shorts and changed into them. Then she pinned up her hair and covered it with a Boston Red Sox cap.

She left her office. Blackthorn's orders were that she should stay in. Ever since the attack in her apartment five days ago, he and his staff had hovered over her constantly.

But it was a beautiful summer day, and she was so tired of looking over her shoulder and being afraid.

Carla's gaze followed her as April passed her post and headed for the elevator. She did a double take and jumped up. "Hey! Almost didn't recognize you in that get-up. Where're you going? You didn't tell me you were going out today."

"I didn't know," April replied as she stepped into the elevator car.

Carla followed her. She patted her pocket—probably checking her gun. "So where are we headed?"

"Central Park. I need some exercise."

"No way," Carla said. "Too dangerous."

"Look, I can't stay cooped up forever. It's been nearly a week and there's been no sign of the guy."

"He's out there," Carla said grimly. "I can feel it."

"Well, you didn't recognize me for a minute there. Let's hope he doesn't, either."

"You need exercise, we'll secure a gym for you, for chrissake."

"I'm going to Central Park."

Muttering, Carla followed.

The park was crowded as usual during the warm bright days of summer. April walked fast, got well out in front of Carla, then quickly put on the rollerblades that she'd hidden in her athletic bag. Then she folded up the nylon bag and stuffed it into her back pocket.

As she was getting ready to move, she caught sight of Carla entering the park behind her from Fifth Avenue. Giving her a jaunty wave, she pushed off. Carla yelled something at her and began to run.

"Gotcha!" April called over her shoulder and pushed off.

It felt terrific as she skated by a crowd of teenage bladers who were performing for each other. She cruised along a drive with bikers and other rollerbladers toward the center of the park. On the broad expanses of Sheep Meadow, college-age kids were playing Frisbee. Others were lying about, absorbing the summer sun.

She doubled back past the band shell where a single would-be actor was reciting Shakespeare to an indifferent crowd, past the fountain and the boathouse on the pond, and pumped up the slope that led toward the Ramble. The park there was sheltered and wild. Almost forestlike, with trees thick with their summer leaves. If someone wanted to attack her, this would be an ideal spot. But she was moving very fast, and unless he was on skates himself, he wouldn't be able to keep up with her. Carla had long ago vanished into the distance.

To hell with him! I won't live the rest of my life afraid!

The rhythmic feeling of her own muscles alive and at work was very calming. She got into the rhythm and let it carry her. The rhythm helped her to center herself and bring the world back into focus.

Seize your own power! Let go of fear!

Had Rina believed what she had preached? There was every indication that she had. Everybody who'd come in contact with her since the beginning of Power Perspectives insisted that she had been sincere. It must be true. Why else had she cared about people like Kate and Jessie Blackthorn? How had the same woman who had abandoned her daughter inspired so much loyalty and love?

There is no mystery about your professional success or your personal relationships. You can reshape your destiny.

If what she said was right, then there was no mystery about the people who loved Rina . . . nor about the one who had killed her. No mystery at all.

The place where you have arrived in your life is a logical one because you placed yourself upon the road that led there a very long time ago.

Why had Rina been successful? Why had she been killed? Were the answers to the two questions related somehow?

There was sense to be made of this, surely, if only she looked at it the right way.

No one attacked April in the Ramble. She continued to move fast, but she did not look over her shoulder. But when she emerged safely on the east side of the park, near the Metropolitan Museum of Art, she looked back at her imaginary pursuers and laughed out loud with the joy of taking a risk and winning.

Winded from the hilly run, April sat down on a bench and took off her rollerblades. She unfolded the nylon athletic bag and dropped the rollerblades in it. She exited the park and walked down Fifth Avenue at a leisurely pace. What had happened to Carla? She felt a twinge of guilt at the thought of Blackthorn's assistant struggling to keep up with a wildwoman on skates.

As she passed the museum she noticed that one of the side doors was open and a truck was pulled up there. Crates were being carried into the place—a traveling exhibition, probably. One crate, made of simple wooden slats, contained nothing but empty, although ornate, picture frames. She was reminded of the framing demonstration she and Kate had witnessed at the museum on the afternoon they'd visited together. Kate, thank God, was home from the hospital and doing fine. "Why did you stay in my kitchen after I'd told you to leave?" she'd asked her.

"I figured you had a lover," Kate said calmly. "I was investigating to find out who he was."

As far as she knew, the identity of her lover was one mystery that Kate had not yet solved.

"Dammit, woman, how could you take such a risk?"

"Don't yell at me, please."

"You deserve to be yelled at," Blackthorn said that night when he arrived at the office to take over from the still-very-angry Carla. "You deliberately ran out on Carla, making it impossible for her to do her job."

"I needed to get some exercise. Can I help it if Carla couldn't keep up?"

"You're acting like an idiot!"

"No, I'm not, Rob. Even if he knows how to rollerblade, which I doubt, I'm sure the killer wasn't conveniently carrying a pair along with him. I'm sick of huddling indoors and I'm tired of having a panic attack every time I venture into the fresh air! I can't live like that. I won't. It's time we brought this whole thing to a head. It's time to confront them and see who cracks."

"If they haven't cracked so far, there's no reason to think—"

"I don't believe that. I don't believe this isn't just as stressful for the murderer as it is for me. More so, maybe. Besides, I'm beginning to think my mother was right about some of the things she preached. Seizing your power. Taking control of your own destiny. Dammit, Rob, if I'm going to continue in this job, I've got to find out once and for all whether I believe in her principles."

"Believing in her own principles brought Rina de Sevigny to an early grave."

"Maybe so. But if we're to believe what she says about her own personal transformation, she would have died a lot sooner if she hadn't found something to believe in. She was going to kill herself, remember? And it occurs to me now that we know that, but we don't know why. She supposedly had everything. But she wasn't happy. She had to transform her life, for godsake. Why?"

Blackthorn shrugged. "Good point. You're right. We don't know the answer to that. I'll bet her autobiography would have told us why."

"Exactly. And maybe the killer knows that. Maybe the manuscript is important not for what it reveals about Rina's clients, but for what it reveals about Rina herself."

"Maybe. But there are too many damn maybe's in this case. Too many theories and not enough facts." He glanced at his watch. "I hope you're through here for the day because it's getting late. I'm hungry and I want to go home."

He was definitely in a pissy mood tonight. But April

was determined not to be cowed. She was still in a good mood as a result of "seizing her power" this afternoon.

She gave him a mischievous smile. "I'm ready. Your place or mine?"

"This is for you," said Rob.

They had settled on her place, and he had insisted on stopping at a small grocery store on the way home and picking up a couple of steaks and the makings of a salad. "You always cook for me," he said. "Tonight I want to do something for you."

He had made her a lovely meal, and now, as they sat over coffee, he handed her a flat square box. "Open it. Sorry it's not wrapped."

"Gee, it's not my birthday or anything."

"I want you to have it."

In the box, nestled on cotton, was a necklace made of beaten silver. It was solid, like a choker, and set into the handcrafted silver were several black and white stones.

She looked up at him, smiling with surprise and pleasure. "Rob, it's beautiful. I don't know what to say." It must have been fairly expensive, she was thinking.

"Do you like it?"

"It's gorgeous!" She fingered the silver, admiring the crafting. This relationship was still in its beginning stages, and she wasn't entirely certain how to interpret such a gift.

"May I?" He took it from her. "Lift your hair."

She gathered her thick hair in one hand and pulled it up out of the way while he fastened the silver necklace around her neck. When he secured it in the back, it was snug, but comfortable.

"I was a little worried it might not fit," he said. "It looked so small . . ."

"I have a little neck," she said, smiling. "It fits fine."

He touched the silver in front, just above her pulse point, and gave her a wicked grin. "It looks a bit like a slave collar."

"Ah hah! So that's your motive!"

He raised his eyebrows. "Someday," he said.

"Threats, threats!"

He took her head between his palms and pulled her close. "Kiss me," he ordered.

She obeyed.

But later that night it was Rob, not April, who had an anxiety attack. He was lying with her in his arms, half asleep, dreaming or fantasizing—he wasn't sure which. He saw her melting in his arms. Shrinking, turning transparent, slipping away from him. He jerked up, his heart hammering, uncertain for a moment whether he was holding April's loving body, or Jessie's corpse.

What if he lost her? He'd been making one mistake after another. She had almost died.

It took him a long time to fall back to sleep again.

In the morning, he told her. "Listen, April," he said slowly. "I think maybe it's time for me to back off this case a bit."

"What d'you mean, back off?"

"I think somebody else should be guarding you. I'm thinking of Jonas, actually. He's younger than I am, probably stronger and certainly quicker. Plus he'll have the objectivity that I lack."

"I don't get it, Rob. What are you saying?"

"I'm saying that I don't think we should see each other for a while."

She touched his face uncertainly. "Why not?"

"Because you're not safe with me." He shook his head, once again seeing fragments of the dream. "I can't keep you safe."

"Of course I'm safe with you!"

"Look, it's not up for discussion. Rina died in my care. You almost died last week because I wasn't alert enough to the possibilities. Obviously I'm losing it, and I'm not going to take any more chances with your life. You need protection and I'm going to see that you get it."

"That's the most ridiculous thing I've ever heard."

"Look, I don't interfere in your business and I don't want you interfering in mine. Nobody who's emotionally involved with a client has any business to be protecting their life. I'm too vulnerable. Too liable to make mistakes. It can't continue."

She sat up in bed. She was still wearing his lovely necklace—it had remained on her throat ever since he had given it to her and placed it there. "This is an excuse, isn't it?"

"What do you—"

"You're feeling vulnerable because you're feeling something that you don't want to feel. It's the old approach-avoid thing. The man begins to feel close . . . he expresses affection, he makes gestures, the woman responds, and suddenly it's too much for him. He's allowed himself to get too emotionally involved. So he backs off to a safer distance. Is that what's happening here?"

He shrugged. "I don't know."

"I don't think it has anything to do with how well you can protect me. I think what it's really about is how well you can protect yourself."

He regarded her steadily. "You may be right. But the fact remains that for whatever reason, I don't feel that I can do a good job. We have to find this killer and stop him. We have to unravel the heart of the mystery of who hired him in the first place. Worse, we have to contend with the possibility that there has been some sort of professional parting of the ways here—that it has become personal. That the killer may now be working for himself."

"You mean he'll come after me even if nobody orders him to do it?"

"I'm afraid of that, yes. Why does someone become a professional killer? The money's good, but it's a high-risk vocation. He's violating the most ancient laws of how one human being behaves toward another. It takes some sort of pathology to do it, and this guy has apparently gone over the edge. The rose was a warning sign. Cold professional killers don't send roses to their victims."

"We don't know for certain that the killer sent that rose."

He looked startled for a moment. "I think we can assume it."

"Are you saying that even if we find out who hired him and throw him—or her—into prison, I still won't be safe?"

"Yes. You're at risk, and so, I suspect, is Kate, who also saw his face. Our job is tougher now. On the other hand, we have a few more clues. We'll get him, eventually. But it's going to require a complete commitment of time and energy, and I think, frankly, that I'm better used as an investigator than as a bodyguard. Jonas has done more bodyguarding recently than I have, anyway. I trust him completely, and so can you."

"I don't like this, Rob. It doesn't feel right to me."

"Trust me, April. Please."

"I trust you," she said. But deep in her heart she wondered if it was true. Did she really trust anybody? Had she ever, since Rina had left?

Chapter Thirty-two

When the door to her office opened unexpectedly and a man walked in, April's heart turned over.

She must be more nervous than she'd realized.

"You okay?" said Christian de Sevigny. "I didn't mean to startle you. Didn't you hear me knock?"

"Uh, no," she said. She'd been daydreaming. But he must have knocked pretty damn softly. "Usually my secretary buzzes me and warns me when someone's about to come in. A nice perk—having a secretary." She managed a smile. "That's a first for me, I'll admit. I did my own clerical work in the bookstore."

Christian glanced at the paper-thin gold watch that graced his angular wrist. "It's twelve-thirty. She's probably gone to lunch."

April nodded. Where was Carla? she wondered.

Christian, after all, was one of the suspects.

Right on cue, Carla's head popped in the door, checking. April nodded to her. For now, it was okay.

"How's Kate?" she asked.

"She's much better. Pretty much back to her normal self, in fact." He shook his head. "Now that it's over, she seems to be taking inordinate pride in the fact that she got shot and lived to tell about it. She's on the phone constantly with her friends, telling them all the gory details."

"But it's not over," April said.

"No," he agreed. "It's not."

Almost a week had passed and nothing much had happened, except that Isobelle and Charlie suddenly seemed to be at each other's throats. The rumor was that the romance had ended, but neither had confirmed it, and April didn't feel close enough to either of them to ask.

As for her own romance, that seemed to have fizzled also. Blackthorn had indeed backed off. Jonas guarded her now at night, and Carla during the day. She had hardly seen Rob at all.

She was trying not to focus on how much she missed him. If she thought about it too much, she felt those old feelings rising in her—that sense of being abandoned. She told herself over and over that this was a silly, irrational reaction. That Rob was a professional, and this was how he felt he had to do his job. That he'd given her the necklace—and that it must mean something. That men always bounced back and forth in this manner, and that if she just waited it out, he would return, and move closer to her than before.

Anyhow, she reminded herself, she had more serious problems to worry about.

"Listen, there's something I want to speak to you about," Christian said. "It's about the investigation."

"Okay. Go ahead."

"Actually, it's about Robert Blackthorn." His glacial

blue eyes were looking straight into hers. "After he came to my home and started making a lot of wild accusations, my father and I did some checking into his background. We found something. It might not seem like much, but, well, it's strange. I thought you should know about it, since he and his people are watching out for you."

"What are you getting at?"

"It's easier, actually, to show you." He handed her an unsealed envelope. It contained an enclosure that looked like a Xerox of a newspaper article.

"I don't know how well you know Blackthorn," Christian said as she removed the article and unfolded it. His tone seemed to indicate that he *did* know how well she knew him. "But this seems to me to be a fairly important piece of information. After all, as we've agreed, there are many reasons to want someone dead. Revenge is one of the oldest motives."

The enclosure was a clipping from a local newspaper in the small town on Long Island where Blackthorn had lived with his wife until her death. It was a letter to the editor, apparently in response to an article on alternative healing. Its tone was scathing, and it read, in part:

"To promote hope and optimism in seriously ill patients is fine as long as these so-called 'alternative healers' don't interfere with traditional therapies that actually have some chance of working.

"But to brainwash cancer patients with stories about the horrors of chemotherapy and radiation therapy in order to lure them away from the medical establishment and thereby get their business and collect their money is unconscionable.

"Someone very dear to me is dead because she paid far greater attention to the comforting—but medically use-less—banalities of the 'self-help' organization Power Per-

spectives. If she had spent less time trying to 'find her own power,' and more subjecting herself to the proven powers of modern medicine, she might still be alive today.

"Power Perspectives, and organizations like it that make phenomenal amounts of money offering useless panaceas for all of life's pains, are collectively responsible for killing thousands of credulous clients every year.

"They must be stopped, by any means possible."

The letter to the editor was signed "Robert Blackthorn."

April shook her head and read it again. The clipping was dated a little more than a year and a half ago, which must have been shortly after his wife had died.

She looked up at Christian. She could feel her heart racing. "What are you trying to suggest with this?"

"Merely that if I were you, I'd want to know as much as possible about the man to whom I was entrusting my life."

After Christian left, April sat still and silent at her desk. She was alarmed at how quickly her imagination spun out a wild tale of suspicion and treachery. Halfheartedly, she told herself that she'd spent too many years working in a shop that specialized in murder mysteries.

Her imaginings went like this: Blackthorn was secretly an enemy of Rina's. He had pretended to be her friend, got himself hired to guard her, and then himself engaged the killer of the Anaheim convention center. He had allowed him into the seminar room and, knowing full well the identity of the real shooter, he had tackled April and thereby created the diversion that had assured the assassin's escape.

His reasons for all this? Revenge. He blamed Rina de

Sevigny—and Power Perspectives—for his beloved wife's death.

"They must be stopped, by any means possible."

He had believed that Rina's death would cripple the organization. Mission accomplished.

But then April had come along. And although she didn't share her mother's fervor for these methods, she was a good manager, both of people and of finances, and so far she'd done a creditable job of keeping the company together. Power Perspectives was still in business, and seizing your own power was still all the rage, despite its founder's death.

So he'd decided to kill her as well.

After all, she was a danger to him. She'd persisted in digging into the mystery of her mother's death. She'd even suggested that an examination of Rina's relationships with her clients held the key, and one of Rina's clients had been Jessie Blackthorn.

Stop it, April.

She hugged herself, trying to interrupt the wild spiraling of her thoughts. Don't do this to yourself. Don't suspect everybody you come in contact with!

No, she told herself, if she was going to suspect anyone in this, let it be Christian. He'd probably shown this material to her purely to sow more confusion, wreak more havoc, and direct suspicion away from himself.

She took a deep breath. The thing to do, of course, was turn the material directly over to Rob, and let him handle it.

Irresistibly, her eyes were drawn back to the words he had written to the small-town newspaper. "Someone very dear to me is dead . . . collectively responsible for killing thousands of credulous clients every year . . . any means possible . . . they must be stopped."

In a state of grief, a man might be capable of making some pretty wild accusations.

But these sentiments were very strongly expressed.

Rob, Rob. She flashed back to the way he had loved her, the way he had held her in his arms. The silver necklace he'd given her, which she frequently wore against her skin. He was a wonderful lover. But—how well did she know him, really?

What are the prerequisites for trust?

"May I ask you something, Kate?" she said a little later on the telephone. She had called Christian's home to speak to Kate. Armand had picked up the phone. He'd explained that he was staying there for a few days with his son and his granddaughter. "After everything that's happened, I need to be close to them," he'd said.

"Sure," said Kate.

"You once told me that you didn't like Rob Blackthorn and that you thought he might be the murderer. I want to know why you said that. What made you think it? Do you know anything particular about Mr. Blackthorn that you haven't told the police?"

"Not really," Kate said.

"But—"

"Once he came to the apartment when I was there. To see Gran. He didn't know I was there, spending the night. They had a fight. I heard him yelling at her. It was awful."

"When was this, Kate?"

"I don't remember exactly. A while ago."

"Did you hear what they were arguing about?"

"I didn't pay much attention. Grown-ups are always arguing about something. I just remember it because it was loud and angry and I was afraid somebody was going to get hurt."

"And it was at the apartment? My current apartment, you mean? Are you sure about that?"

"Positive."

Nice place.

Haven't you ever been here before?

No. My company was hired to guard Rina during her trip to the West Coast, not before.

Why had he lied?

"Mr. Clemente, this is April Harrington. I believe you know who I am."

"Yes, indeed I do, Ms. Harrington," the FBI chief said over the telephone.

"I need to ask you a question. It's about the investigation. Actually, it's about Mr. Blackthorn."

"Blackthorn is no longer associated with this department," Clemente said.

"But he was associated with you at one time? He was an FBI agent?"

"Why do you ask?" Clemente said in the tone of a true civil servant—distant and unhelpful.

Because I'm sleeping with him and I need to know if he's a murderer!

"He has led me to believe that he was formerly an employee of the FBI."

"That is true. He was. He resigned a couple of years ago."

"Why?"

"Why don't you ask him yourself, Ms. Harrington." There was something in his tone that suggested to her that he knew about her relationship with Rob.

"I understand that it had something to do with his wife's illness and death?"

"He took it hard, yes. This made him a less than effective agent."

"Did he actually resign or was he asked to leave?"

There was a pause on the other end. Then once again, Clemente said, "I think that's something you'd better ask him yourself."

The hesitation and reluctance told it all, she thought. She hung up the phone wondering if Rob had been forced out of the FBI.

April couldn't eat any supper that night. Her stomach was queasy. She told himself over and over that she was being silly . . . that because of all the stress she'd been under, she'd lost faith in her own judgment.

How could she trust a man whom she couldn't see, couldn't hear, couldn't touch?

Rob shouldn't have left her alone!

Gerald Morrow had not given up, even though his orders had been to back off. Despite the danger from possible police surveillance, he was still staking out the Target's apartment.

The client, however, had not been pleased over the fuck-up. The client, in fact, had gone ballistic.

No surprise. He'd expected it. He'd blown it, lost his weapon, nearly lost his eyes, for chrissake. He'd spent a week bathing them several times a day and had been terrified that his vision was permanently affected. Couldn't even go to a doctor. The cops would be on the lookout for anybody with an eye injury.

Fortunately, in the last couple of days, his vision had cleared.

The bitch hadn't been strong enough to do any lasting damage. She was good, but not good enough.

Everything was different now. The client had ceased to be important—this was between the Target and himself. He was paying his own way now. He didn't give a shit if he never heard from the client again. He was working for himself.

He had given himself a contract to kill.

And it wouldn't be over until April Harrington's lovely body was nothing but a lifeless husk.

Chapter Thirty-three

Jonas usually arrived at around 8 P.M. to take over for Carla, and April was determined to question him, as gingerly as possible. Both Jonas and Carla had known Rob longer than she had, and she was sure they wouldn't be working for him if they didn't trust and believe in him. She'd been reluctant to speak directly about her doubts to Carla, since she and Rob seemed to be so close, but Jonas was young, and maybe she could glean something from him about Rob without making him too suspicious as to why she was asking.

When Jonas knocked, she opened the door eagerly, hoping that a conversation with him would set her mind at rest.

When she saw who was standing on the threshold, she took an automatic step backward. "Rob!"

"Hey, how many times have I told you not to open the door before checking to see who's out there?"

"It's you!"

"Yes, and it could just as easily have been the killer, back for another try." He pushed past her into the apartment, carefully closing and locking the door behind him.

"Where's Jonas?"

"I gave him the night off."

They looked at each other. April swallowed hard. She felt as if she were choking on her own heart.

"I thought you'd be pleased," he said after a moment.

She smiled tentatively. "I am. I'm just surprised. You told me—"

He moved closer and took her into his arms. "I know what I told you. I've been trying to stay away, but it's been hard."

As soon as he touched her, April felt her body respond to his. His mouth brushed her gently, then with more insistence. The tension inside her seemed to melt.

This is ridiculous, she thought. It's all been ridiculous, all this suspicion. I would know, surely, if there were any danger from this man. Wouldn't I know?

Had Rina known? Someone had arranged to have her murdered. Someone she knew. She'd taken what precautions she could, but they had not been enough.

He touched her throat. "You're wearing the necklace," he said. His voice was husky. "It looks good."

"I love it," she said, but she couldn't make her gaze hold his.

"Have you learned anything new?" she asked as he followed her into the kitchen, where she started a pot of coffee.

"A couple things, yeah. We found the woman whom Christian claimed to be with on the night of his wife's accident. Augusta—the first name—is pretty unusual, and he said he'd met her in the courthouse. As it turned out, she wasn't that hard to find."

"She's real, then?"

"She's real all right. She works as a legal clerk in the same courthouse where the divorce and custody case was decided. She remembered Christian de Sevigny and was able to confirm the assignation. He was with her all night, she says. Had too much to drink, in fact, and passed out, but not before impressing her well enough with his erotic abilities for her to remember him instantly. Did I have his phone number? she wondered. She'd love to see him again."

"So Christian's in the clear?"

"Regarding his former wife's death, yeah, I guess so. Augusta's got no reason to lie—she says she never heard from Christian again. And the idea that it might not have been an accident was just speculation, anyhow."

April shook her head. For Kate's sake she didn't want Christian to be a killer. But at the moment, she wanted anybody other than Blackthorn . . .

"Charlie Ripley, on the other hand, has moved up on the list," he said. "I had a long talk with Isobelle. Seems she ended it with Ripley because she'd become suspicious after the attack on you and Kate. He kept saying he'd do anything for her, and seemed to be taking a rather proprietary view of Power Perspectives. His obsession started to spook her. She began to wonder what if there were matters that he'd already taken into his own hands."

"Killed Rina, you mean, for Isobelle's sake? Then, when Isobelle didn't inherit the company, he'd decided to get me out of the way as well?"

"That's about it. She has no proof, and I think she's feeling a little guilty about being so suspicious of her former lover." He shrugged. "Charlie did lie, though, it seems about receiving a call from Rina's editor about the missing manuscript. He denies it, but I've talked to Rina's editors and her agent and none of them had ever heard of the project. If no one called, this would suggest that Charlie has some interest of his own in the location of the manuscript."

"I presume you've looked into the possibility that *Charlie* was at any time my mother's lover?"

He nodded. "We've come up with zilch on that. But sure, it's possible. It's also possible that Isobelle is the killer and that she's trying to direct our attention elsewhere. There's been a lot of that going on."

This seemed like the perfect moment to bring up the matter of her own suspicions, and to show him the note and clipping she had received. But she hesitated, and Rob plunged on:

"The FBI has concluded a thorough analysis of the general financial picture of the entire De Sevigny operation. Clemente filled me in, then Armand and I had a talk about it. Things are not rosy, financially. The corporation has lost a lot of money over the past few years. He and his son are wrestling with various proposals for downsizing. Power Perspectives, on the other hand, has been an enormous money-maker. But it's separately organized and there's no way to funnel profits from Rina's company into De Sevigny Enterprises as a whole."

"So there was no reason for Armand to kill his wife and take her money?"

"No. We've been looking for that from the start, of course. When rich folks die mysteriously, it's amazing how often the motive turns out to hang somehow upon their wealth. Clemente has been high on the husband as the doer all along, but he's pretty much given up on that now. Rina's company was carefully organized to be separate from the rest of the family's resources, and there's simply no way that Armand could have benefited financially from her death."

"Isn't that, in itself, a little odd? I mean, usually when a husband or wife dies, the surviving partner is financially impacted."

"Rina was an independent woman," he said slowly.

"My point exactly. They ran their own separate businesses, they lived in separate apartments. Why did they stay married at all?"

"Why does anybody stay married? They just get used to each other, or they're too lazy or too scared to make a change. I don't know. As I say, we've run down the adultery thing. Nothing that we can find on either side."

"I can't see him killing her," she said.

"That's the trouble. We can't seem to see anybody killing her."

I must be too imaginative, April thought. At one time or another, she'd managed to see everyone killing her, even Rob himself.

She served him a cup of coffee. "Are you staying?" she asked.

He smiled. "The killer's still out there." He brushed his fingers lightly over her breasts. "I'd say your body still requires some serious guarding."

"I can see why you like your job so much—the benefits aren't bad, are they?"

"The benefits are terrific."

Making love that night was, for the first time, a little scary. He seemed to be in a strange mood, and April herself was jumpy. At one point, she asked him, trying to sound as casual as possible, why he had lied to her about having been in her apartment before. Looking embarrassed, he answered that as he recalled the conversation, her place had just been broken into, invaded. He'd been conscious of how that must feel to her, and he hadn't wanted her to feel as if everyone in the world had already trooped through her apartment.

April wasn't sure she bought this explanation. But lying open and vulnerable in his arms, she dared contemplate no other.

April and Rob were both asleep when the phone rang at 5:30 in the morning. April reached out wildly toward the bedside table, grabbing for the phone. Her hands knocked something off the table—she heard it clatter on the floor as she flailed around trying to find the phone. Her heart was beating unevenly. She hated being awakened by the phone.

She found it and put it groggily to her ear. "Hello?"

"I'm sorry to call at such an hour," said a familiar voice with a French accent. "Were you sleeping?"

"Armand?"

"Oui, c'est moi. I need to talk to you."

She didn't think Armand had ever called her before. Certainly not at this time of night. "Is it Kate? Is something wrong?"

"No, no, Kate's fine. Actually it's about Robert Blackthorn. Christian showed me those newspaper clippings. Is he still bodyguarding you?"

"Um, yes."

"Is he there right now?"

"That's right," she said in as neutral a voice as she could manage. Rob was stirring. Well, maybe half-asleep. He had opened his eyes briefly when she'd made all the racket reaching for the phone, and now he looked as if he was trying to rouse himself.

"Can you go in another room? Make some excuse? It's important."

She put her palm over the receiver. "It's my friend Maggie, from Boston. She's depressed. I've got to talk to her for a few minutes, okay?"

Blackthorn made a grumpy sound and rolled over.

"Don't worry, I'll take the phone in the other room."

Thank God for portable telephones, she thought as she exited the bedroom. Rob wasn't moving. She hoped he was back out.

"Okay," she said to Armand. "I've got a couple of minutes of relative privacy. Go ahead."

"I'm sorry to bother you, but I'm worried. He was in charge of Rina's security at Anaheim. It never occurred to me to think that perhaps he engineered things so that the killer could get to my wife."

"I don't believe he did," April said quietly.

"Of course you don't. He is your lover. You cannot believe evil of him." Armand's voice was gentle, philosophical. "It is very difficult to imagine that someone we love could be capable of deceiving and betraying us. But it happens. All too often, we are hurt by those we love."

She said nothing. She could still feel the imprint of Rob's warm and knowing hands on her body.

"April, I found something. That's why I'm calling. I found a computer diskette that my wife must have been using shortly before her death."

The blood rushed to her ears. He'd found it? The diskette existed, after all?

"Kate and I had a little chat," he continued. "After her accident she confessed to me that the night before she encountered the killer, while she was staying overnight at my home, she searched among my things for this diskette. She did not find it. But I thought of some hiding places that she would not have known about. And just over an hour ago, I found the diskette and examined it on the computer downstairs in my library."

"Rina's missing autobiography?" April tried to keep her voice even. Did he know the murderer? Is that what he was trying to tell her? Was there something on the diskette that implicated Rob?

"Perhaps. There are a number of long files. All I've had time to examine is some of the correspondence. I found some letters that had passed between my wife and Robert Blackthorn. They are angry and confrontational, on his side, especially. And I also discovered a memo, written just before the trip to Anaheim, in which Sabrina makes a note to dismiss Blackthorn and his firm as soon as she returns to New York. 'I just don't feel safe with him,' she writes."

April touched the silver necklace that was clasped around her throat.

"Are you there?" Armand said, after a moment.

"Yes."

"For your own safety, I think you should leave. Is he asleep?"

"I think so."

"*Cherie,* I beg of you, get away from him. Now."

She tiptoed back into the bedroom. Rob was turned on his side away from her, and he was snoring. As quietly as possible, she grabbed her clothes from the floor where he had thrown them as he'd undressed her. Images of what they'd done together threatened to overwhelm her. She banished them. She'd think about that later. She'd think about all of it later. Right now she just had to get out of here so she could decide what to do.

She carefully put the portable phone back on its holder. What she had knocked down when she'd reached for the phone turned out to be Rina's keepsake—the photograph of both of them in the scratched tin frame. As she picked it up she saw that the glass in front of the picture had cracked in the fall. There was now a jagged line running down through the center of the photo, right between herself and her mother.

For some reason this seemed like the last straw. April felt tears spring into her eyes. Everything was going wrong. Her mother was dead, her lover might be the murderer, and now the damn picture was ruined as well . . .

Clutching it to her, she fled the room.

She took the stairs. She checked to see that there was no one but a sleepy security guard in the lobby. She got out past him, quickly, looking up and down Sixty-second Street as she stepped outside. Nobody leapt back away from her into the shadows.

It was just before six in the morning, and the city was slowly awakening. There wasn't much traffic yet, but in a couple of hours, it would be gridlock.

She walked quickly to the corner, holding the large pocketbook into which she had dumped a change of clothes and—she wasn't sure why—Rina's now-broken photograph. It was early, but this was New York. As soon as the light changed up at the next block, she saw a couple of taxis approaching. She flagged one down, he pulled up, and she climbed in.

"Come here, to me," Armand had said. "Together we will notify the police." It was tempting. But the way she felt now, she didn't trust anybody. If she couldn't trust Blackthorn, whom she'd held in her arms and loved, then she certainly wasn't going to trust Armand, Christian, or anybody else in the de Sevigny family.

She would have to trust herself.

"Take me to the Port Authority Bus Station," she said to the cabbie.

Morrow was across the street parked illegally in front of the Lincoln Center garage complex when he saw his prey come out of her building and catch a cab. So. It was happening. She was on the run.

He pulled the car onto Columbus Avenue. Not too many cars. Following her would be easy if she did what she was supposed to do. But in his experience, you couldn't count on that.

Sure enough, she got out of the cab at the bus station. *Shit.* The only predictable thing about the Target was that she was quick, and always did the unexpected.

Looked like she was leaving town.

He ditched the car at the curb and followed her into the station. He caught sight of her immediately, her red hair was a dead giveaway. She was in line at one of the windows behind a fat woman who looked like a bag lady.

He hung back. He didn't think she'd recognize him even if she looked him full in the face. He was wearing a scruffy beard now and he'd had his hair cut punk-short and bleached it blond.

When it was the Target's turn at the window, she suddenly shook her head and changed her mind. Then she strode away, heading for an exit on the opposite side of the building.

He followed, cursing. Now what?

She looked behind her nervously as she exited the bus terminal, but Morrow was still behind the glass door and knew she couldn't see him. He ambled out when she was about fifty yards ahead, and followed her as she walked south. He waited for her to flag down another cab, but she walked quickly and purposefully, as if she knew exactly where she was going. He hoped she wasn't about to take refuge with a friend. He assessed the situation on the street. Dark, seedy section of town, but, as always, traffic in the street and pedestrians. He could take her now, but there'd be witnesses. He'd really prefer to get her alone.

She walked fast towards Madison Square Garden. And Penn Station.

Where did you go when you were frightened and unsure whom to trust?

You ran toward the place where you felt the most secure. And for April, that would not be New York City, but Boston, MA.

That must be it. At Penn Station, she could get an Amtrak train to Boston. More comfortable than the bus. He vaguely remembered that there was one that left sometime around now. He'd checked it out earlier during his research—where the Target might go if she decided to run.

Sure enough, she looked behind her once again, then ducked into the Eighth Avenue entrance to Penn Station, near the departure point for the Amtrak trains.

He'd guessed correctly. April Harrington was headed home.

"Hey, Boss, what's going on?"

"Carla?" Blackthorn had a headache. He rubbed the back of his neck with one hand while he tried to focus on the phone. "What the hell time is it?"

"It's six A.M. Where's April?"

"I don't—"

"Shit, are you all right? You're not hurt or anything, are you?"

"Just asleep."

"Well, while you're lying there sleeping, the body you're supposed to be guarding has apparently done another one of her disappearing tricks."

Blackthorn grabbed the phone and checked the apartment as she spoke. But he knew without checking that he'd fucked up again. He was alone.

"Are you tracking her?" he barked into the phone.

"Is she wearing the necklace?"

"She was when we went to bed."

"Gee, what'd you do to her, Boss? Spooked her somehow? I've got her at Eighth and Thirty-first Street at the moment—that's Penn Station. Looks to me like Ms. Harrington is on the run."

"Goddammit!" he barked into the phone.

Chapter Thirty-four

The Poison Pen Bookshop was dark and silent when April let herself in at around noon. It was a Sunday, and the place was closed.

She felt a sense of immediate relief. Surrounded by books that were shelved as high as the ceiling in the relatively small space, she felt safe and protected. Strange, dangerous, and fantastic things happened between the covers of these books. There were a thousand stories whirling around her. She and other fans of the genre could read them, identify with the characters, share the excitement and their fears and their glories. Always they were safe in the knowledge that good would prevail over evil and that justice would triumph in the end.

She would have liked to stay. But the bookstore was too obvious a place to look for her.

In the books, disappearing always seemed so easy. But in real life April had found her options sharply limited. She hadn't been able to rent a car in New York, because there wasn't any way to do it without giving her real name to the car company. She couldn't fly anywhere for the same reason. Buses and trains didn't require your name—not if you paid for your seat in cash. Fortunately there had been a bank machine in Penn Station.

Here, though, she could get a car. Or, at least, borrow one.

There was a phone booth down the street at a gas station. She glanced at her watch as she dialed. Maggie lived in Somerville, just a few blocks away. April could walk it easily.

She hoped she was home.

Maggie answered, sounding bright and chirpy. "Maggie, thank God," April said.

"April? What's the matter? You sound awful. Are you in trouble again?"

"Maggie, I need your help."

"Of course. What can I do?"

Two hours later, April was on the road again, this time in the driver's seat. She knew she didn't have much time—she'd been too predictable—Blackthorn would find her. But all she needed were a couple of days to reflect, to think things through, and, most importantly, to decide whom, if anybody, she could trust.

She was crossing the Cape Cod Canal on the Sagamore Bridge, headed for Brewster, Mass., where she and Rina had spent the summer in 1963.

April had never been back to the Cape. This was a little odd for a woman who'd spent most of her adult life in Boston. Although the Cape was a natural vacation spot, she'd taken her vacations instead in Maine, New Hampshire, or Vermont.

Cape Cod drew her now, though. Here lay the beginning of the strange and twisted path that had led Rina away from her job as a waitress and put her on track for interacting with rich and famous men. It all went back to that summer when she'd met and loved the president.

It seemed hard to believe, but Sea Breeze Housekeeping Villas were still there, right where she remembered them, just off a pitted dirt road leading down toward the sea from Route 6A in Brewster. They were old and badly in need of fresh paint. A faded, lopsided sign at the entrance to the driveway proclaimed a Vacancy, and from the looks of the place, quiet, with hardly any cars on a lovely June day, April suspected there were a lot of vacancies.

An elderly man answered her knock on the end cottage, the one with a small sign that said Office and was missing one of the f's. He looked her over and seemed incredulous when she declared that she'd like to rent one of the cottages for the night.

"You ain't one of them state inspectors, are you?" he said, looking her over through narrowed eyes. "I had the exterminators out here just over a week ago, just like I said I would."

Great, she thought, hoping they'd been after roaches rather than rats. "Just a tourist."

"We don't get too many," he declared. "Least, not this early in the summer. July, August, maybe, when all the other places are crammed full, then we take the overflow. There's a real motel, just up the road."

"I like cottages," she said. "Besides I stayed here once, many years ago, 1963. Were you the owner then, by any chance?"

He shook his head. "I'm not the owner now. My son is, but he don't lift a finger around here. Put me to work, fig-

Keepsake * 357

uring it was better than sticking me in a nursing home.
Seems an odd place to want to reminisce. The cabins are
musty and the furnishing's old. Wouldn't catch me staying
in one of 'em."

"Is number seven free?"

He glanced at an old wooden key rack where several
rows of rusty keys were hanging from faded ribbons.
"Yup, it sure is," he said, taking down the key.

"I'll pay cash," she said, taking out her wallet.

"Fine, sign the register," he said, handing her a pen and
pushing a moth-eaten volume toward her. She glanced in
the front of it, wondering . . . but it only went back to
1978.

She scrawled "Judith Exner," smiled, and handed him
back the pen.

Morrow had nearly lost her in Cambridge.

As he had expected, she had gone to the bookstore. He
hadn't been able to watch both exits at once, and she must
have gone out the back, since only luck enabled him to
catch sight of her hurrying into a gas station on the corner
to make a phone call.

Obviously she was afraid of being tracked. But she
didn't seem to realize that she'd been carrying a tail ever
since she'd left her apartment in New York.

She left the gas station on the opposite side from where
she entered it, but instead of doubling back to the bookstore, as he'd expected, she disappeared somewhere behind it. He gave her a couple minutes, in case she was
simply being cautious about returning to the bookstore,
then set off in pursuit. When he got around to the back of
the gas station, she was nowhere to be seen.

It was part instinct, part luck that sent him back to the

car he'd rented. There were only two possibilities for streets, and he could cover them much faster by car than on foot.

It took him several blocks to acquire her again, just in time before she entered a three-decker house over the line in Somerville.

Of course. Her friend Maggie. The woman who had accompanied her to the ABA convention. He'd forgotten she lived so close by.

He'd cruised by the house and found a rare parking slot a block away. He waited nearly an hour, hoping she hadn't once again slipped out a back way.

Turned out to be a very good thing he'd rented the car. When she left, she drove away in a green Toyota, and she wasn't wasting any time in getting out of the area.

Keeping well behind, he followed her.

All the way to the Cape.

The cottage looked much smaller than she remembered it. She'd noticed that before about things from childhood—to a child everything seems larger than life.

Even allowing for the changes that thirty years of wear and tear and little care had wrought, the place was pretty sad. There was a narrow living room area—no TV, she noted—as you stepped inside, with a sink, an ancient two-burner stove, and a half-size refrigerator toward the rear. The bedroom was separated from the main part of the cottage by a ragged curtain. Within it was a sagging double bed that April could have sworn was the same one that had been there thirty years before. It had a knotty pine headboard at one end that she remembered. Had the mattress ever been changed? She sat down on it and sighed. Probably not!

There was dust everywhere, and dirt ingrained in the cracks between the floorboards. This, at least, was different. When she and Rina had spent those summer weeks here, the place had been spotless.

And the new curtains had fluttered over what were now small, grimy windowpanes . . .

Why am I here?

She sat down in a battered chair in the living room, suddenly depressed. And tired. She'd been on the run since early in the morning, and she'd had very little sleep last night. She didn't know exactly what she was running from, and it seemed totally futile to have come to this place. Her memories were not going to help her understand her mother. Everything that had happened to change Rina had happened *after* those weeks they'd spent here, in this tiny cottage.

She picked up the photograph with its now-cracked frame. She stared at it, seeing the cottage in the background, the number seven painted in a big white numeral by the front door. The number was still there, but the paint had faded. Everything had faded, even her memories.

She'd have to replace the glass. Maybe have the thing reframed while she was at it. Get a decent frame. This one was loose, from the fall this morning, probably. It had always bothered her that a photograph that her mother had left her as her only personal memento had come in a cheap tin frame.

She stared at the loose frame and thought, for some reason, about the day she'd gone rollerblading in Central Park. Going past the museum, seeing a crate full of picture frames being unloaded, being in the museum with Kate, listening to a lecture on framing. *The importance of the frame to a work of art cannot be overestimated . . .*

Ohmigod.

She turned the photograph over and began to pry the heavy cardboard back off the picture. It ought to slide down through the metal rims of the frame, but it was very stiff. The cracked glass protested, and cracked a little more as she pulled the thing apart, impatient now . . .

The cardboard backing came away. Out came the glass and the photograph, and tucked between the picture and the backing was a 3 1/2-inch computer diskette.

Inscribed on the label were the words, "Rina de Sevigny: Autobiography."

"I don't believe it," she whispered.

She'd had the missing diskette all along.

And now here she was in the middle of nowhere, far from Kate, without a computer. She had the missing document in her hands, but without the laptop, it was useless to her.

Oh, Kate, Kate. Where are you when I need you?

She thought briefly of getting back in the car and driving back to Boston. She could use Maggie's computer, or even take the shuttle back to New York.

But she was here, and she was tired. Tomorrow morning, she decided. Her curiosity, powerful though it was, could wait one more night.

It was earlier than her usual bedtime, but she might as well sleep. Get up early. The sooner she fell alseep, the sooner morning would come and this mystery would be, at last, resolved.

She pulled out her nightgown and got ready for bed.

The place was perfect.

Small. Isolated. Hardly any people around, except one old guy in the office. So much for the Target's brainpower. Picking this dump had been a stupid move.

She was alone, and soon he'd fix it so she had nowhere to run.

She was history.

He'd wait until full dark. When she was deeply asleep he'd slip in there and take her.

She had hurt him—hurt his eyes. Humiliated him as well. Made him abort his job, and damaged his reputation. For that she was going to pay. She was going to die slow. No need to bother about the client's stupid instructions. No need to do anything . . . except enjoy.

So many times over the past few days he'd imagined what he was going to do to that slim female body. He'd played it out in every detail. No need to worry this time about making it look like an accident. It would be artful, elegant. Yeah, and slow.

He'd brought the necessary items, including rope, duct tape, and several appropriate tools of the trade.

Her arms and legs tightly bound.

Another piece of rope—a relatively short piece—would be tied in a slip-knot around her neck and secured to the headboard. When he began to torture her, the pain would make her struggle. It was a response she would have no control over. And as she struggled, the ligature around her neck would be pulled taut. Eventually she would strangle herself.

She would know what was happening. She would understand. She would see that surviving depended on not reacting to the torture, and for a while he would allow her to think that she could control her reactions . . . . could, perhaps, survive. Then slowly, inexorably, he would demonstrate that pain was her master. He would watch her hope change to panic, her panic to despair. And in the end, she would welcome death.

The thought of her alone and vulnerable in the dark was

unbearably exciting. He wanted to go in now, get started. Savor it. Make it last.

Patience, he told himself.

Killing time until killing time.

Chapter Thirty-five

Despite her weariness, April had difficulty falling asleep. She lay awake in the darkness for more than an hour, tossing and turning on the sagging, lumpy mattress. She heard little scratching sounds outside that might have either been branches brushing the walls of the cottage or perhaps the vermin which had inspired the call to the exterminators.

She fell into a troubled sleep.

And came awake sharply as a hand smoothly covered her mouth to prevent her from screaming and a powerful arm held her down on the bed.

"Shh. It's me," said a familiar voice.

Blackthorn!

She felt a moment of pure panic.

Somehow he had followed her. He had come to kill her, and this time she would not escape.

"April, I know something spooked you, but you're going to have to trust me." His voice was clipped and she could hear no softness or sympathy there. He was on her bed, holding her down. His legs were straddling her thighs with only a musty sheet between them. "You have no choice. The killer's outside."

She stared up at him in the darkness. She could only see a dim outline of his face and she couldn't read his expression. He kept his hand over her mouth, taking no chances that she might scream.

"I crawled in through one of the back windows. I'm reasonably certain he didn't see me, but it was pure luck. Until I got here, I didn't realize anybody else was following you."

She shook her head. I don't believe you, she tried to convey. There was nobody outside. It wasn't possible. His being here wasn't possible. How had he found her?

"You were wearing a wire," he said as if he read her thought. "You didn't know it, but ever since the day you took off rollerblading in Central Park, we've been monitoring you electronically. So far it's worked pretty well." He touched the silver necklace at her throat. "There's a remote tracking device in your necklace. Another one is hidden in the briefcase that you take to the office every day. It was the first one that led me here. Thank God you kept it on when you decided to flee me."

Yes, she thought, she'd kept it on. That meant something, didn't it?

"When you got on the Amtrak train, I went to the airport. Was in Boston before you. Rented a car and simply followed, staying fifteen minutes behind you. Unless he also planted electronics on you—which I doubt—the killer was a lot tighter on your tail."

Again she shook her head. She writhed against his hands, not violently, but trying to let him know that she hated being restrained.

"April, why did you leave like that? What frightened you? You were acting skittish all evening. Are you suspicious of me?"

She nodded.

"You think I'm in some way responsible? That I had something to do with Rina's death?" He sounded completely baffled at the thought.

If I had only been able to read the diskette, she thought. Then I'd know. There wouldn't be this nagging doubt.

"Well, whatever you believe, you're going to have to trust me now, at least for a little while. He looked like he was getting ready to move . . . we don't have much time."

Her eyes had adjusted to the darkness and she could see him better now. Why would he lie at this point in the game? She was completely at his mercy. He could do whatever he wanted, and get away with it.

Tentatively, he lifted his hand from her mouth. "Just keep quiet, okay?"

"Give me a reason to trust you, Rob," she whispered.

He considered. "Because you love me?"

"That's a lousy reason!"

"How about because I love you."

She swallowed. Something in the pit of her stomach seemed to fall away. She closed her eyes. "If you're going to kill me now, just do it and get it over with."

"What I'd like to do is slap some sense into you," he said savagely. "You'd better have a damn good reason for this . . . that's all I can say. Otherwise, when we get back to New York, I'm going to take you over to Isobelle's place and borrow one of her whips. I can't believe that you—" He cut himself off. There was a low sound at the door.

Blackthorn abruptly pulled her off the bed and down to the floor. She saw him fumbling at his belt as he found and drew his weapon—a large snub-nose handgun. "Roll under the bed. Lie flat and cover your head with your arms."

She obeyed, lying on her belly and pulling her arms up so they were mostly covering her head. It didn't prevent her from looking, however. The foot of the bed was turned toward the front of the cottage, and from underneath with the dust (and, doubtless, the cockroaches) she could see the bottom of the door.

Blackthorn rearranged the pillows and blankets, then moved silently away from her into the kitchen area six feet away. She could see his legs, taking cover to the side of the refrigerator. His gun was directed at the cottage door. It had a flimsy lock.

They heard the faintest squeak, then the door swung silently inward. It was difficult to see because of the darkness in the cottage and the stealth of the invader. April imagined herself asleep in bed, hearing nothing, seeing nothing, waking to the same horror that had nearly overtaken her in her bathroom less than two weeks ago.

As she watched his shadow slink into the cottage, she was damp with sweat and her heart was slamming into the floor. All she could see were his legs as he moved towards them. He was wearing jeans and sneakers or running shoes similar to the ones he'd worn the first time he'd tried to kill her.

He was closer now. Could he see the bed in the darkness? Could he see that although the covers were tousled, there was no one there?

She wished Blackthorn weren't so far away! She hoped—oh, God!—she hoped he would be quick, and if he had to shoot, accurate . . .

"That's far enough," she heard Rob say. The place was

flooded with light as he hit the switch in the kitchen wall. "Drop the knife and hit the floor."

Morrow whirled toward the sound, raising the knife, tightening his arm and shoulder for the throw. He was quick and fast with a knife, but the bullet was faster. He heard the crack before he felt the pain. In fact, there was no pain, simply an impact in his chest knocking him backwards, against the bed, grabbing and reaching, feeling things slip from his hands and the floor heaving upwards at his face.

As he rolled onto his side, doubled up, he saw her face. There beside him on the floor. Her eyes staring into his, but not in agony or in supplication. Not acknowledging his power and surrendering to his will. No fear, even, nor anger. No, she was looking at him in worry . . . or concern.

As his eyes closed he heard her voice. "Don't die, dammit!" she cried.

Why not? he wondered. Why should she, of all people, care if he died? She should be triumphant. She had defeated him for the second and final time.

"Who hired you?" she demanded. Vaguely he felt her shaking his stiffening body. "Who paid you to kill my mother? Who sent you so persistently after me?"

He was ready to tell her. Why not? He felt no loyalty. She'd proved to be a worthy adversary. Let her have her revenge.

He would have told her, if he could have spoken before the darkness closed . . .

"You killed him," April said.

Blackthorn rolled the killer over, studied the wound, felt the throat for a pulse. "He's alive. High chest, right side—he's got a chance. Breathing's steady. There's no phone here, right? Run to the office and wake that old geezer. Smash the window if he doesn't answer and dial 911."

"If he dies we won't have a witness against the person who hired him."

"The bastard deserves to die," he growled. "But, yeah, you're right. Hurry. I know some first aid."

He felt her drop a quick kiss on the top of his head. "I don't mean to criticize. He was going to throw that knife. You saved our lives."

Yeah, but at what price? "It's never easy to shoot someone," he said.

She left, and he applied pressure to stop the bleeding in the creep's chest. Didn't look too bad, actually. The guy was probably out from the shock. He might come round at any time.

He pulled the blanket off the bed and covered him, but not before a quick go-through of his pockets. Once the cops arrived, the place would be sealed as a crime scene and they'd all be hauled in to spend the rest of the night answering questions.

He couldn't find a gun. But the guy was carrying a fanny pack containing several lengths of rope—narrow and nasty. A cigarette lighter, but no cigarettes. A second knife, three industrial strength sewing needles, an awl, a pair of blunt-nose pliers, a roll of duct tape, a tightly folded clear-plastic raincoat, and a pair of surgical gloves.

Blackthorn's usually strong stomach rose as he considered what the killer had intended to do with these items. The raincoat and gloves, no doubt, were to protect him from the blood.

He thought of April as he'd found her—peacefully

stretched out in the bed. Jessie had died easily compared to what this asshole had had planned for April.

He stumbled to the entrance to the cottage and threw up into the bushes just outside the door.

He tried to think of Jessie, and how she had died . . . what she had said . . . how she had looked, but his mind was filled with April, her red hair, her laughing eyes, her smiling face. He could have lost her. Dammit, he wasn't going to lose her.

"I love you, April," he said.

Chapter Thirty-six

"It might be withholding evidence," April said, "but after all this trouble I was not going to turn this diskette over to the police without seeing what was on it myself!"

"I don't blame you," Blackthorn said.

"Now if we can just get to a computer."

"No problem. I have a laptop in my car."

She threw her arms around him and hugged him.

But a few minutes later, sitting in the hotel room to which they'd retreated after a long session with the local police, he turned on the computer and hesitated before inserting the diskette into the disk drive. "Are you sure you want me to read it with you?"

She nodded.

"Think," he told her. "You still don't know who hired Morrow. Suppose it turns out to be me, after all. Maybe I shot him so he couldn't expose me."

She made a face. "Look, I'm sorry. I just—I didn't know whom to trust." She had told him about the newspaper clipping that Christian had shown her, and how it had shaken her faith. He'd tried to explain to her how angry and bitter he'd been after Jessie's death. He'd written the letter to the editor, yes, he'd said. That had been a particularly bad time, and he'd needed to find somebody—anybody—to blame. But later he and Rina had become friends.

"And trusting's hard for you," he said.

"It has been, yes." She paused. "But sometimes you have to make a leap of faith." She reached out and took his hand. "I trust you, Rob."

He kissed her gently on the mouth. "Since I've been with you, I've been alive again. And Jessie—well—I think I can finally accept her death and begin to let her go. I love you."

She could feel her heart open. "I love you, too."

The files were there. They were organized into chapters—"mylife.1, mylife.2," etc. But the first file on the diskette was simply named "April.let."

With Rob's help, she called it up on the screen and together they began reading:

To my daughter:

April, I am writing this more as an exercise, I think, than as an actual letter. I hope that we will see each other again and that I will be able to talk to you in person. I hope it will never be necessary for you to read this letter, or that if you do, you will already have understood . . . and forgiven me for the great wrong I have done you.

It is so difficult to know what to say to you after so

many years. Ironically, the more time passes, the more dif-
ficult it becomes. I have wanted so many times over the
years to reach out to you. Yet at the same time I dread
doing so because I am afraid you will respond to me in
the only manner that I deserve.

I know that there can be no excuse for the way I have
treated you. Nevertheless, I feel compelled to explain.

Perhaps this explanation is more for myself than for
you; perhaps I will never even share it with you. Perhaps I
am the one who must somehow learn to understand.

And to forgive.

Forgiving oneself is always the highest hurdle.

I have come to believe that we make our own destiny.
We are free human spirits who make the choices that lead
us either to success or disaster. Or, in my case, both.

One thing I have learned is to be rigorously honest with
myself. I confess that I was never a good mother. Worse,
to my mind—and it is difficult to write these words—that I
never loved you enough. This is not your fault. I can't
imagine a more lovable child than you were during the
years we were together. But I had not been brought up
with love, and I certainly had no love or respect in those
days for myself. Where there is fear, there can be no room
for love, and my heart and mind have been darkened by
fear for much of my life.

April, I never told you about our background—my orig-
inal family, that is. It was not a past that I ever wanted to
remember—a brutal drunken father who used to beat me
on the slightest excuse, a sad-eyed mother who never
came to my defense. I ran away from home—a ramshackle
farm in Kansas—when I was seventeen. I guess I was fol-
lowing my mother's advice. She'd attempted to run off
with another man when I was fifteen. I still remember her
saying to me, "It's a man's world, hon, and all a woman

can ever do is find herself a good man. If the one you got ain't no good, use your wiles and get one better."

She found herself a better man, but when she eloped with him, my father swore to track her down. This he did. There was a fight between the two men, and in what they later claimed was an accident, my mother was killed.

All the brunt of my father's anger and grief at her loss fell on my shoulders. The beatings and the verbal abuse escalated, and my existence had become unbearable. I often used to fantasize about hanging myself from a rafter in the barn.

I'm not telling you this in order to try to extenuate my own behavior, but rather to emphasize something that I don't think you ever understood. You wanted a family— longed for one, in fact. And I knew no way of explaining to you that sometimes a family represents the most vicious kind of intimacy. There is nothing sacred about the blood ties of a family. Our real families are the ones that we put together ourselves, with love and caring for one another.

I know, also, that I never told you very much about your father. Let me tell you now that he was a gentle man, as different from my own father as anybody could imagine, and that I loved him. He was, however, married. He and his wife had taken me in when I arrived friendless in St. Louis after leaving home. She was an invalid, and I'm not proud of myself for trying to steal him away from her. But I was bitter when he told me that he had vowed to stay with her for better or for worse.

I ran away again, and he never knew about you, April. If he'd known I'm sure he would have wanted to see you, espcially since he and his wife had no children of their own. I was afraid, in fact, that if he saw you, he might try to take you away from me, and that was a thought I couldn't bear.

I was, of course, too young to be a mother.

I didn't know what to do, or how.

When you cried—which was all you seemed to do the first three months—it frightened me. Like all teenage mothers, I thought having a baby was like having a perfect, beautiful doll. I was unprepared for nursing, colic, fevers, sleepless nights.

And I was always afraid those first few years that my father would somehow find me. In my dreams, he never ceased to pursue me, so I was always on the run.

I was afraid that if he found me, I, too, would die.

April looked up from the computer screen. As she reached for the glass of water on the bedside table, she realized that her hands were shaking. Whatever she had expected, it was not this stark recital of unpleasant facts.

"You okay?" Rob said gently.

"I never knew any of this."

He squeezed her hand. "It's pretty intense."

She nodded. "Rina never told me anything of her personal history. My earliest memories were simply of moving from town to town while my mother indulged in new love affairs, often with some sort of authority figure in the community—the chief of police, the minister, the mayor. I never understood why this was happening; I took it as a matter of course. New curtains in the house . . . a new lover in Rina's bed."

As she spoke she picked up the photograph of herself and Rina leaning against the trailer. She tried to look at her mother objectively—the natural blonde hair, the perfect, classic features, the tiny waist, the full breasts. Rina's physical assets were the sort that were bound to attract the attention of red-blooded males everywhere, and she had exploited them relentlessly.

As to why she had done this, it was clearer now. She'd been brought up by a violent domineering father, and her mother had contributed to the idea that a woman could not survive without a man. But if he wasn't good enough—"Get one better." If he proved to be difficult or violent—run.

She looked back at the screen.

As for what happened the next few years, I'm sure you remember. We kept moving. I was afraid to settle down, and besides, I kept thinking about how badly we'd been living all our lives. I wanted something better—for me, for both of us. It seems I was always afraid of something—of not having enough money, of not being able to take care of you, of my father—or even your father—tracking us down.

You remember the Kennedy thing, I know you do. For me that was the most marvelous thing that ever happened. He was everything I'd ever dreamed of in a man. I couldn't believe it when he responded to my flirting. I thought I must be imagining things until he made it clear that he actually wanted me in his bed.

I played it cool, of course. Always, always, always. I'd learned that young. Never let a man know what you're really thinking, really feeling.

Jack was the first man I'd ever met who knew more about the battle of the sexes than I did. And of course when he left the Cape that summer, he never had the slightest intention of seeing me again. I moved us to Washington because I wasn't about to let some guy walk out on me, even if he was the President of the United States.

It didn't do me much good as far as he was con-

cerned—he'd already lost interest by the time of that day in Dallas. But what it did was lift my imagination and my ambition to new heights. I'd had a taste of what was possible if you really did mate with the top dog. And I wanted more.

Having been the president's mistress, even for so short a time, increased my chances with other men. God, they were fascinated. And he was good-natured enough to help the situation along by introducing me to some likelies. That was how I met my husband, of course. Armand knew the Kennedys—you'll remember how cozy Jacqueline was with anybody of French blood or ancestry.

Armand seemed like the answer to all my prayers. He was handsome, charming, and sophisticated. He was attentive and kind. He was outrageously romantic. He made me feel like a princess born in a beautiful chateau in the Loire valley.

Of course I fell in love with him.

Of course I believed in him.

Of course I agreed to do anything he asked of me.

It took a long time before I saw through his facade.

In reality, April, my husband Armand is the most controlling man I have ever met. He is a master at assessing people's weaknesses and exploiting them. He always knows exactly which buttons to push.

I never would have expected that I, of all women, would ever be dominated and manipulated by a man. After all, I had vowed, after running away from my father's house, that no man would ever again possess that kind of power over me.

But I have also learned that we are ourselves controlled by the deep beliefs that we hold about ourselves, our limits and our capabilities. And there must have been a part of me that believed that once you find the top dog and mate with *him, you must try to keep him happy, at least until he proves himself weak and worthless and you see it's time to move on to someone else. That, after all, is what my mother did.*

Again April stopped reading. One phrase in particular was reverberating through her brain. "He is a master at assessing people's weaknesses and exploiting them."

She looked up at Blackthorn. He was looking at her.

"Armand," he said.

"It was he who called and frightened me out of your arms. He told me he'd found a computer diskette with a memo from Rina, saying that she was going to fire you because she didn't feel safe with you. He wanted me to leave you, come to his place instead. My God, do you suppose . . . ?"

He was nodding grimly. "Thank God you didn't go."

"You really think Armand's behind this entire thing?"

"It fits. Your mother had her own apartment. She created her own business. In her lectures she stressed personal determination and independence. She must have been trying to break free."

"And he couldn't let her go?"

"Something like that, I'll bet."

They read on, and April learned that her mother's marriage had not been the idyllic match that she had been led to believe. Armand had been charming for the first few months, but gradually he had changed. Or, not so much changed as revealed his true colors.

He had always promised me that we would send for you and have you with us. I believed him. The boarding school he arranged for you to attend was one of the nation's finest, and he never hesitated to pay the expenses, which I couldn't have afforded by myself.

But every time I tried to pin him down about removing you from the school and bringing you to live with us, he made some excuse. And at last I came to realize that what he really wanted was for me to devote myself to his children and be a mother to them. He was very proud of his two children, although he was always hopeless at getting along with them. They came from an illustrious family, and I gradually began to understand that he did not want to tarnish them or their family by exposing them to the illegitimate daughter of a common waitress.

My husband is a complex man. His congeniality and his generosity are quite real. He has many friends because he knows how to treat people, how to earn their admiration and respect. But his goal is power. Mastery. He operates expertly as a benevolent dictator, but the benevolence vanishes the moment his mastery is challenged. And in the long term, his closest relationships sour because deep inside he is a weak man who is severely threatened by the slightest challenge to his authority.

In terms of how this affected our relationship—it's simple—I am not a woman who can submit for long to another personality, and my efforts to resist the way of life he sought to press upon me quickly brought us to each other's throats.

For all intents and purposes, our marriage has been over for nearly twenty years. Then why, you wonder, have we remained married all these years?

Because I made a bargain with the Devil.

My soul was not at stake, but you, my daughter, were.

April, this is the hardest part of all to tell, in part because for years I could not bring myself to accept that it was really true.

That you are alive today is truly a miracle.

My husband—the man I married and believed I loved— conceived and carried out a plan to have you killed. But he failed, because you yourself struck at and dispatched the assassin. For which they tried to put you in prison.

"Oh, God," April moaned.
Rob held her closer.

I now believe that the man—the illegal Mexican alien— who tried to strangle you when you were a girl of sixteen was hired by my husband to kill you. His motive was selfish and single-minded—he wanted nothing more to interfere with my concentration on his family, and particularly, on his son. He wanted me free from all ties, with no excuse left.

When it failed, somehow I knew. I confronted him, and to my surprise, he acknowledged the truth. I threatened to go to the authorities. He pointed out that I had no proof, and that no one would believe me. I packed my things and told him I was leaving him. He made it clear that if I left, he would have both of us killed.

It was then that we struck our miserable bargain. I would remain with him and masquerade as his happy wife. In return, you would be safe. But I was not allowed ever to communicate with you again.

April, perhaps you will wonder as you read whether I am telling you the truth. You will marvel that a woman as strong, independent, and self-reliant as you must recall me to be could be so much at the mercy of her husband. Why did I not simply go to the police? How did I ever get so enmeshed that it was impossible to extricate myself?

Why, now that I am successful in my own right, have I not revealed Armand for the monster he is?

In answer, all I can say is that unless you have been a woman controlled and oppressed by a man, you cannot imagine how devastating it is. You feel as if you have no choices. You are terrified, helpless, confused. You lose your will and the confidence that shape the events of your own life. You become a person whom you no longer recognize.

If you have heard anything about Power Perspectives, you know what happened to me (although no one ever knew why). I became severely depressed. I gained a large amount of weight. I lost all interest in my appearance, sometimes going for days without washing my face or my hair. I abused tranquilizers and alcohol, and I yearned each day for death.

It ended with my conceiving a complex plan of suicide, every detail of which I lovingly planned and nearly carried out. Indeed, I was about to go through with it when a voice inside reminded me that if I died, Armand would have won. He would have reduced me to such utter submission that no spark of life remained in me—very literally.

My life was my life. It was all I had, all that was my own. And I somehow managed to convince myself that some small part of it remained within my own control.

Thus was Power Perspectives born, and with it, my own rebirth.

Now Power Perspectives is strong. And so I am. Now, at last, I am ready to confront my husband and unmask his evil. I'm ready, at last, to end this marriage and be who— and what—I truly am.

I'm ready also to proclaim my love for the person who has seen me through so much heartache in recent years.

When I begin my life anew, it will be, I hope, with the true partner of my heart.

And I hope too, when this is done, that you and I, my long-missed and yearned for daughter, will be reunited at last.

The letter ended there—signed with a flourish—not Rina de Sevigny, but Rina Flaherty.

Blackthorn skipped back to the beginning of the document and noted the date. "She wrote it a couple weeks before she contacted me for protection. She probably did confront him. And realized that he still held the higher cards."

"So he had her killed to prevent her from 'unmasking' him?"

"I'd say so, yeah. She had slipped his control. She'd been getting away from him for a long time, clearly, but now it was really over. The marriage, his reputation, everything."

"So she did have a lover," April mused, staring at the last few sentences. *The true partner of my heart.* "I wonder who?"

He shrugged, then had to stifle an enormous yawn. "I'm not reading the rest of those files tonight. The sun'll be up soon. Let's get some sleep. You must be even more exhausted than I am."

She nodded with some reluctance. "Will the killer— what's his name—Morrow? Will he name Armand when they question him, do you suppose?"

"He'll name him, all right," Blackthorn said. "He's got no choice. Either he names him or I cut out his heart."

April shivered. He sounded like he meant it, and she was glad! She pushed the computer aside and lay down.

"There's one thing I don't understand. I can see why Armand decided to kill Rina. But why me? Why send that horrible killer after me?" She shook her head. "Armand and I got along well. I mean, I really thought he liked me. How was I a threat to him?"

"I don't think the assassin's actions today had anything to do with Armand. It was personal. You somehow changed from being a professional hit to the object of an obsession. The guy had slipped over the line."

She snuggled closer, needing his warmth for reassurance.

"As for the original motive for your murder, I suspect Armand wanted to accomplish two things—scuttle Power Perspectives once and for all and throw any suspicion more firmly onto somebody else. Isobelle, for example. Or Charlie, her lover. She appeared to have the strongest motive for Rina's death, and with you out of the way, things would look even worse for her."

"So what you're saying is that his plan to have me killed was completely cold and analytical. I wasn't real to him, wasn't a person. I was just a pawn in a deadly game."

"Something to be moved around and controlled, yes. That's how he treats people. I suspect the only person who is real to Armand is himself."

"I'm remembering that day on the docks as he and my mother sailed out of my life. I was just a kid—bewildered and scared. And I felt nothing from him. He didn't care what happened to me. I was completely insignificant. I hated him for that."

"Smart kid. You saw the real Armand."

She shuddered. "I feel sick."

He wrapped her in his arms.

"Now what?" she whispered.

"Now we get him," Blackthorn said.

Chapter Thirty-seven

When the doorbell rang, Kate was working on her newest mystery story, "The Bathroom Murders," which featured a teenage girl as the amateur detective who foiled the killer and solved the crime. She opened up to find April and Mr. Blackthorn and that FBI guy who'd questioned her in the hospital. They came in, and they were followed by two New York City cops. They all looked pretty grim, and she felt a wave of fear. Had they come to arrest Daddy?

April drew her aside. "It's okay, Kate," she said gently. "Is your grandfather here?"

"Yeah, he's been staying here for a couple days. Are you okay? They said you were missing!"

"I'm fine. Where's your father?"

"He's in his study, I think." Actually, he was in there with Daisy, who had shown up unexpectedly. But it didn't sound like anything too disgusting was going on. In fact—she'd listened a little at the door—Daisy had been crying. Maybe they were breaking up. If that was true . . . well, Kate felt a little guilty. Maybe she shouldn't have sent Daisy that anonymous letter . . .

"Grandfather's upstairs." She glanced uneasily at Blackthorn and the cops. "What are they doing here?"

"They need to talk to your grandfather."

"Why?"

Blackthorn joined April. He was right on top of her, she thought. Like they were close. She'd thought it before and now . . . Jeez, just as she'd maybe gotten Daisy out of the way, Blackthorn was all over April.

"The guy who shot you?" he said. "We got him last night."

She shook her head. *Got him?* "What d'you mean? Is he dead?"

"Nah. Hospitalized, though. Surrounded by guards. He killed a lot of people. The FBI searched his apartment and found a scrapbook full of evidence. He'll be going to prison for the rest of his life."

"Wow," she said. "I'm glad. You mean the case is, like, solved?"

Blackthorn nodded. "He told us who hired him, yes."

Kate squeezed herself with her arms. "Not my father?"

April hugged her hard. "No, Kate. It was Armand."

Grandfather? She felt a coldness touch her. Yeah, she thought. She remembered the night she'd slept at his place and gotten caught searching through the books in his library. Sometimes, Grandfather, like, wasn't all there.

"What's going on here?" a voice behind her demanded. Daddy. She turned around as Blackthorn's attention shifted.

The FBI guy was already starting up the stairs. Didn't they need a warrant or something? Or were they like vampires—if you let them in, they could do anything they wanted?

Daisy was at his side, but they weren't touching. Her makeup was all streaked from her tears.

God, thought Kate, it was like everybody had gone crazy.

April left Kate to her father and the policemen who were explaining it to him. She and Blackthorn went to the foot of the stairs to meet Armand.

He descended, dapperly dressed, as usual, his face pale but composed. His eyes focused on April and his pupils dilated as if he were surprised to see her here, healthy and alive.

She knew for certain, then, that it was true.

But when he reached the bottom of the staircase Armand looked right at her as he said, "These accusations hurt me very much. How could you believe such a thing of me, April?" He sounded sincerely wounded. "These men are accusing me of planning my dear wife's death."

"And mine," April said.

"There is no basis whatsoever for these accusations," Armand said. He sounded convincing enough to make her understand why he'd been able to fool so many people for so long. He was either a superb actor, or he believed his own lies.

"Your hit man confessed," Blackthorn said in a clipped, angry voice.

"And you would take the word of some thug—some professional contract killer—over mine?"

"I would take my mother's word," April said quietly. She held up the computer diskette that she'd found behind the photograph. "You didn't have it, after all, I did. She left it to me, along with an explanation of the first time you tried to have me killed, when I was sixteen years old."

Armand blanched. For the first time, he looked uncertain, old. He turned to his son. "Have you nothing to say?" he demanded. "This is your home. How could you allow these people to enter on such a fool's errand?"

Christian shook his head. Daisy was beside him; he took her hand. "You're my father, and I would stand by you if I could. But I'm sorry to tell you that I believe the accusations." He glanced at Daisy. "They make sense, now that Daisy has told me the truth about her relationship with Rina."

As April looked at Daisy Tulane, whose tear-streaked face testified to some profound personal trauma, the last piece clicked in her mind.

I'm ready also to proclaim my love for the person who has seen me through so much heartache in recent years. When I begin my life anew, it will be, I hope, with the true partner of my heart.

Daisy stepped forward. Her hands were trembling but her voice was proud as she said, "I can't hide it any longer. I've decided to withdraw as a candidate for the Senate. I don't think the state of Texas is ready for a bisexual politician who once had a serious love affair with another woman." She paused, turning to Armand. "Rina was my lover. She was going to leave you, as you know. What you didn't know—what we desperately tried to conceal for a thousand different reasons—was that she was leaving you for me."

"That is impossible!" Armand said. He made a sudden move toward Daisy, and one of the cops grabbed him. *"C'est incroyable!* You tell a lie! Sabrina was never unfaithful. She would never have dared!"

"It is possible, and she did dare," Daisy said. "I am the one who has been the coward . . . I am the one who could not face up to the truth about my own nature." She looked toward Blackthorn. "I knew about Rina's autobiography, of course. I thought that if it was found, it might help to reveal the truth about their marriage. I didn't know that he had killed her, but I did know that she was going to leave him."

"Why didn't you come forward sooner?" April asked.

"I was afraid. I knew that if it came out, it would destroy my candidacy. I preferred to deny what I knew in my heart to be true—about that, about a lot of things." She cast a quick glance at Christian. "I tried to make myself believe that Rina had been murdered by one of her clients. Or by anybody else *except* Armand. I tried to convince myself that I was not involved in any way. But I did attempt to help the investigation. I called her office and pretended I was her editor. I inquired about her autobiography. I hoped this would be enough to start a search, and to find it if it hadn't already been destroyed."

"Oh, wow," April said. "The mysterious editor—it was you. Charlie didn't make it up, after all."

Daisy looked puzzled. It obviously hadn't occurred to her that anyone would have thought that Charlie had made it up. "That was me. It wasn't much, I know. But it was all I was capable of at the time."

"This is nonsense," said Armand. "I do not understand what *any* of you are talking about." He muttered something in French that April didn't catch, then added, with dignity, "I have nothing more to say. I wish to speak to my lawyer."

"You can speak to him from the slammer," Blackthorn said, as one of the cops read Armand de Sevigny his rights.

Chapter Thirty-eight

April called the meeting in her office at Power Perspectives exactly two weeks after the arrest of Armand de Sevigny for the murder of his wife.

Isobelle was there, of course, and Charlie. Christian came down from upstairs, where he was struggling to revamp the company that his father had brought to the brink of ruin. And Rob Blackthorn was lurking at the back of the room, and Kate had come also, at April's special invitation.

"I've been doing a lot of thinking lately," April told them all. "In particular, I've been thinking about seizing my own power, and what that means to me."

She paused, looking at each of them in turn. "It's been wonderful for me, working here. I've discovered new talents and abilities that I didn't realize I had. But, ultimately, Power Perspectives is not for me. It was my mother's life . . . but her life is not mine.

"I've decided to resign my position here. I hope Isobelle will replace me. I sincerely believe that she is much better suited to run Power Perspectives than I."

Isobelle grinned. She looked outrageous as ever, clad in a short leather skirt and a demure white blouse, and there was an easiness and warmth about her that April hadn't seen until recently. She'd heard rumors that she had a new lover, a dominant this time. Apparently the shift in roles agreed with her.

"Charlie assures me that he would like to stay on," April continued, "but that will be up to Isobelle as chief executive officer. Since you both have so much experience with the company, I hope you'll find a way to work things out."

"I don't expect that to be a problem," Isobelle said.

April glanced at Charlie, who was seated in a chair that was pulled quite close to that of Delores, the secretary. Charlie seemed to catch Delores's eye for a significant look before nodding and saying, "No problem at all."

Charlie and Delores? April thought. The man was incorrigible.

"As for me," she added, "I'm going to return to doing what I love most—selling books. But since I've come to feel so at home in New York—" she paused and flashed a smile towards Rob "—I've decided to stay and sell them here. There's a shop for rent in Greenwich Village that looks as if it would be perfect for a mystery bookstore. I'll be signing a lease next week and starting a Poison Pen Two right here in New York." She smiled. "After that, who knows? Maybe I'll take my mother's advice and dream big dreams. I can imagine a chain of mystery bookstores, spreading all over the Northeast." She smiled. "We own our own lives," she added softly. "By believing in ourselves, we can make our fantasies come true."

"Well, I'm going to be a famous writer someday," Kate

chimed in. "And you're going to sell my books in your stores!"

"Hey, can I be the famous detective whose adventures you write about?" Rob asked with a grin.

"Nah," said Kate. "She's going to be a woman. Nobody wants to read about male detectives anymore." She raised her fist in the air. "Women rule the world!"

"You've got the right idea, kid," Isobelle said.

"Right on!" April agreed.

"Right on?" Blackthorn whispered. They were together in his apartment at the end of the day. "You were reliving your days as a flower child?"

"Mmm, maybe." They were in bed. She was naked, except for his silver necklace clasped tightly around her throat.

"Women rule the world, huh?" He touched her in a way that suggested that at the moment, at least, he was very much in control.

"Well, maybe not all the time," she conceded.

"I'm thinking of taking you to one of Isobelle's parties, now that you and she are suddenly such good friends."

"That would be . . . interesting," she said, laughing.

"Liven up our sex life a little."

"As if it needs livening up!"

He grinned and kissed her gently. "I love you," he whispered.

"I love you, too, Rob. And I trust you completely. With my life."

"So you don't mind having a full-time, live-in body-guard?"

She smiled archly. "My body requires a lot of heavy-duty guarding."

"I've noticed!"

Again they kissed. She held him close, enjoying his warmth, his heartbeat, the regularity of his breathing. "And Jessie?" she asked, carefully.

"I dreamed about her last night. In the dream she was standing down at the bottom of our bed."

"Um, I'm not sure I—"

"No, listen. She was smiling and she looked as if she— I don't know—approved. She blew me a kiss, and then she turned her back and walked away." He paused. "I used to dream about her a lot. But somehow it felt as if that was her farewell . . . as if she was releasing me."

"And you were releasing her."

"Exactly. Before she died she made me promise that I wouldn't grieve forever. That I'd find someone to love and get on with my life. It's just that I wasn't interested in doing that, until I met you."

She nodded. "I understand. It's the same for me, with Rina. Now that I know about her life—about her struggles and her dreams and so many of her feelings—it's as if I can finally let go of that driving need to know why it all happened the way it did. Now, at last, I can see her as a real person. And I've come to understand that she was a human being, with flaws and weaknesses, just like the rest of us. She was in an impossible situation. But she did her best. And that's the most we can expect of anybody."

"So you've forgiven her, haven't you?"

"Yes," she said slowly. "I guess I have."

And that night she had a dream. Rina, young and blonde and beautiful, climbing into a helicopter to fly off with a famous man. As the aircraft rose, she looked out a small window, and there was panic in her eyes, a fear that April, at ten, had been too young to see.

Then, in the dream, April looked in a mirror and saw

that her own eyes were free of fear, of anger, of confusion, of mistrust and self-doubt.

Nestling closer to her lover, she slipped into a peaceful sleep.